PUSHKIN AND THE QUEEN OF SPADES

Books by Alice Randall

THE WIND DONE GONE

PUSHKIN AND THE QUEEN OF SPADES

PUSHKIN
and the
QUEEN *of* SPADES

Alice Randall

HOUGHTON MIFFLIN COMPANY

BOSTON • NEW YORK

2004

For information about permission to reproduce selections
from this book, write to Permissions, Houghton Mifflin Company,
215 Park Avenue South, New York, New York 10003.

Visit our Web site: www.houghtonmifflinbooks.com.

ISBN-13: 978-0-618-43360-5
ISBN-10: 0-618-43360-0

Library of Congress Cataloging-in-Publication Data
Randall, Alice.
Pushkin and the Queen of Spades / Alice Randall.
p. cm.
ISBN 0-618-43360-0
1. African American women college teachers—Fiction.
2. Pushkin, Aleksandr Sergeevich, 1799–1837—Appreciation—
Fiction. 3. African American families—Fiction. 4. Parent
and adult child—Fiction. 5. Interracial dating—Fiction.
6. Football players—Fiction. 7. Mothers and sons—Fiction.
8. Russian teachers—Fiction. I. Title.

PS3568.A486P87 2004
813'.6—dc22   2003067566

Book design by Melissa Lotfy

Printed in the United States of America

QUM 10 9 8 7 6 5 4 3 2 1

"To a Brown Boy" is reprinted by permission of GRM Associates, Inc.,
agents for the Estate of Ida M. Cullen, from the book *Color*
by Countée Cullen, copyright © 1925 by Harper & Brothers;
copyright renewed 1953 by Ida M. Cullen.

To Daddy and Detroit

Hope is the thing with feathers.

— EMILY DICKINSON

ONE

LOOK WHAT THEY DONE TO MY BOY!

I want to say it, too. Pushkin strides across the screen of the television. There is a television in my corner bar, one of the 219 million in America, and he's up there on its screen. He's a football player. He's a freak of nature. His hands are immense. His heartbeats are few. Fifty million people have watched him on a single Monday night. He has given a Russian girl a diamond ring. He means to get married. My son is a football player engaged to a Russian-born lap dancer, a girl named Tanya who danced at a club called Mons Venus. There is a God and he's punishing me. This much bad luck cannot happen by accident.

I have walked down to the corner to drink and disappear. It should be easy. A black woman in a hillbilly bar vanishes into the shadows of irrelevancy, especially when she wears preppy clothes.

It's third and long. I've got to make something happen. I've seen too many wins and too many losses not to know.

I bought the beige dress; I will bite my tongue. Got me three fingers of Cutty Sark and half a Valium. My sweet son, my only-born one, is to be wed. I've got everything in the world but an invitation.

So here I am in Babylon on the Cumberland, trying to wish I'd never borne him. Professors of Russian literature do not spawn football players. Their sons do not marry lap dancers. And when they do . . . the professor is invited. It belongs to the professor, it belongs to me, to decline. I am a professor of Russian literature; she is a lap dancer. If I had stayed invited, I would not have gone. But I am no longer invited—the invitation has been rescinded. Pushkin's enormous sable hand reached across a table and snatched it back.

After all I have done, I should have slapped his face. How many other women would have carried their pregnant eighteen-year-old selves all around Harvard? Every other woman I know would have aborted his unborn ass. Other mothers have only to say, "I changed your dirty, dirty drawers," or "I sent you to the best schools in this country," and their sons do what they want them to do. I can make both of those claims in both those languages. Why won't he do right? Why doesn't he comply? I could kill him.

I sound just like my daddy when I say that. I want to go very Marvin Gaye's father on Pushkin. I'm crazy like my mother when I feel that, but I'd kill myself before I would hurt him. That's a promise I made before he was born, a promise I have every intention of keeping. He can't imagine that. If he could, he would stop telling me how much I am hurting him. I can't listen anymore. I'm the mama and I know what is best. I know he doesn't need to know who his daddy is and he probably shouldn't be marrying a white girl. That's what I know. When did he stop listening to me?

My grandmother could throw a book across a room at her six-foot-tall sons, my father and his brothers, and they didn't dare move. They would let the book fly right toward their faces just because their mama had said, "Don't make me go upside your head." They respected her. They trusted her aim. They did what she wanted them to do till the day she died. Pushkin's little white girl has provoked me to remember that black mother and what she was due and how sweet a black family can be, just in time for me to lose mine—again. I can't stand to lose it twice.

Tanya's very existence is cruelty. Thin—you see the daylight between her thighs when she stands; tall—enough to look him straight in the face; and pale—there is a preternatural whiteness to her hair, a queer mixture of yellow and silver and white. Tanya is striking. Even at twenty-two, she is not a girl. She's one of those big-breasted, narrow-hipped waifish Amazons seldom found in nature. Gabriel teases me about Tanya's breasts. He says if I had breast-fed his stepson, I would not be in this predicament. It's hard not to laugh, but I manage.

That Pushkin would, or could, love Tanya, I experience as untenable, if unintended, sadism. That I could, or would, feel this way about his beloved, Pushkin experiences as unimaginable, if unassailable, proof of my insanity, or as a vestige of archaic, banal racism.

No: he feels something blunter, that I'm a racist bitch. I had imagined many brides for Pushkin. Not one of them resembled this creature, which, adding insult to oft-counted injury, is called Tanya. She cannot be named Tanya. She will not be called Tanya. It is too unfortunate.

Once upon a time a long time ago, broken straight through the center of my heart, soft violet tattooing tender parts, I let my brain be me. When I took my seat in a white-painted chair, flaking and cracking, to rock infant Pushkin, slung over my shoulder like a sack of sugar, reciting equations—six plus six is twelve, fourteen minus two is twelve, three times four is twelve, two plus two plus eight is twelve, twenty-four divided by two is twelve—did I know as I rocked and spoke on the beat that he was sucking in the patter of crazy truth? There are many expressions of the same quantity, many identities for the very same number. Struggling to achieve some simple understanding of the nature of number kept me afloat, simple computations of small sums, a way to say, "Brain, don't fail me, now." A way to say, "The number man can." A way for the brain to gratify equals reassurance. And now, so many years later, when I am mama to a boy any other mama would be proud of, my brain has failed me.

I love Pushkin like the moon loves the tide. Everybody heard me say, I love Pushkin. I said it over and over. I say, "I love Pushkin more than the moon loves the stars above."

I speak that way, in superlatives ending in prepositions. These are not the flaws that matter. I would like to write that I used to say, "I loved Pushkin like the tide loved the moon." But what I said was something with competition in it. Pushkin's got competition in him. Maybe that's a good thing. For the most part, I can't help but think it's petty use Pushkin has put to my ambition.

I love Pushkin. He doesn't believe that anymore. He has equated my rejection of Tanya with a rejection of him, equated my telling him who his father is with love. I won't accept and I can't tell. These are the flaws that matter.

The last time I said, "I love Pushkin like the moon loves the stars above," Pushkin made a joke of it. He said, "But we don't know if that's Pushkin your son or Pushkin the poet. Maybe it's just Pushkin the town, where, quiet as it's kept, you kissed some white lips of your own, that you love."

• • •

3

My meal arrives. It is the plate of food I always order when I eat in this place—grilled cheese sandwich, French fries, a cup of black coffee, and a Cutty Sark. There are twenty-seven fries.

Sometimes I need to eat a strip of potato fried in grease. It's the oldest ritual known to me to which I still hold. Sitting in Nashville, slowly inserting the hot snack into my mouth, I can be in all my towns—Motown, D.C., Petersburg, Cambridge, and Music City—at the same time.

Everybody always leaves me very much alone. Which leaves me time to think.

There is a question I've got to ask myself. I don't know what the question is, but I know there's a question. After the second shot of Cutty Sark, I know what it's got to be. I need to say, "Self, what the fuck is wrong with me?"

I hear Pushkin saying, "Moms, you all right."

They say in the South all the mother of the groom has to do is wear beige and bite her tongue. That is not true for this mother. I am not right. But I am trying to be. I am trying to be right in time for you. It is a week before your wedding. I am trying to get myself ready. Trying both ways I know. I'm going to write my way in or shoot my way out.

I've got a present for you. A manuscript. If you come to see me before your wedding, you'll get it. If you don't, I'm going to set a match to all my pages wrapped up in leather and ribbons.

I'm trying to figure out if there's something I want to accuse you of, confess to, or apologize for. I know this: I don't want to injure you and I don't want to lose you. I would rather injure or lose myself.

Last week I purchased a gun, something very much like the gun the poet Pushkin used in the duel that ended his life. The man who sold it to me was pleased it was going to a significant Pushkin scholar. I am not a significant Pushkin scholar. I am a scholar of the significance of the shadow of Pushkin on his darker brothers and sisters in the United States. Pushkin is the great Afro-Russian, and I am the scholar of Afro-Russianness.

How does a black mother tell a black child the facts of life, when they are so often so poisonous? How did the poet Pushkin's dusky mother do it? Can anecdote be some kind of antidote? Is intellectualism some kind of balm? Or do we all just lie till the day we die?

"Truth," says my mother-in-law, "is a peculiarly risky proposition for a black mother." She states my case exactly. But then she

adds something: "A boy requires protection. A man requires tru؟
Maybe that's why so many black mothers seek to keep their sons as
babies. Yet again I am guilty of a stereotypical sin.

I'm eating a lot of French fries these days. Precisely 204 in the
last week. I'm going to get too fat to get into my size-eight beige
dress. Rose will have to let it out.

A hundred years ago, in 1903, W.E.B. Du Bois published *The Souls of
Black Folk*. Du Bois was the first African American to graduate from
Harvard with a Ph.D. and the first person, white or black, to have his
book published in the Harvard historical series. Before Pushkin had
his first real date, I purchased a first edition to give him as a wedding
present. I bought my *Souls* at auction in New York. Nestling the eb-
ony-covered tome with gold lettering away in one of my cupboards,
I felt comforted, knowing we would never starve. If robbers came,
they wouldn't recognize the value of the volume. They would snatch
up whatever little cash, electronics, and jewelry they found, leaving
our treasure untouched and invisible to avaricious eyes. If flames
came, I could catch Pushkin by the hand, tuck Pushkin's patrimony
under my arm, and get away clean. Spending that particular four
thousand dollars made me feel safe. I had acquired what I understood to be a kind of permanent portable shelter, an umbrella of brilliant blackness for us to rest under.

I didn't wait for your wedding. Or maybe I did. Maybe you married the NFL. I gave you the book just after your draft day.

That was a mistake.

Earlier this year, around Christmas, when I was still in and out of
Pushkin's house, I found that first edition of *Souls* on a shelf in his library. It was stamped all over with pale faded rings from where it had
been used as a coaster.

What I held up as a roof above us, the dignity of negritude,
Pushkin understands as a barricade between us, the vainer trappings
of the niggerati. Up to now I have craved the shelter more than I
have feared the barricade.

If my head, if Pushkin's mama's head, is bloody and muddled
now, maybe it's because I've been bashing it up against the stony
monument I have raised in my mind to Du Bois.

Du Bois received his A.B. from Harvard in 1890; I received mine
from Harvard in 1981. Pushkin was admitted to Harvard, but he
didn't enroll. He went to Michigan. He played Michigan college

means something. I don't know what it means. I just
doesn't share my memories. Pushkin hates Harvard;
hates me.
. What is naming him for the best black brain and the
heart about?

Superlatives ending in prepositions again. I used to tell Pushkin
the joke about the Negro student from way down South who made
his way to Harvard. Push used to like to hear me tell it. First day of
school, this student be looking for a li-bear-ee! Wide-ner Lie-bear-
ee. It's the first time in Cambridge for this dark boy. He notices
a blue-eyed, smart-looking chap. Our dark boy thinks "chap." Walking across the campus paths spins thoughts of *This Side of Paradise*
and Scott Fitzgerald into his mind. Our Negro student observes to
himself, "That chap looks like he know where he be going. He look
like he could be a friend." Our night-bright son from way down
South thinks this thought because he comes from a place so broken,
the best friends he has are Nick and Jay from *Gatsby*. So he thinks
"chap," says "chap." Says it right out loud because he stands six feet
and five inches. Says it even if Jay was a gangster, or because Jay was a
gangster, and especially because he was a gorgeous and doomed
gangster.

At this point in the story, about the time Push was eight, I would
always say, "Folks from way down South love the gorgeous and the
doomed." Then Push would embellish: "Particularly folks from our
family, who were ever so beautiful and refuse to be damned." Then
my boy would wait for me to recommence with the telling, and I
would start back to talking, looking right into Pushkin's night-dark
eyes. "So the brilliant Negro boy asked, 'Where's the li-bear-ee at?'
by way of introducing himself. And the golden blond boy, who had
not read his Fitzgerald—this being nineteen sixty-three or four and
Fitzgerald having fallen out of fashion with, and having yet to be re-
discovered by, the academy—this sky-eyed Exonian who had been
far too busy to be bored and thus had had no need to read every book
in the local public Carnegie Li-bear-ee shelves, this new true-blue-
blooded Cambridge denizen, responded with patronizing grace, "At
Harvard we do not end sentences in prepositions." And the colored
boy said, "I fix that right quick. Where's the li-bear-ee at, asshole?"

After these words we would both laugh, my boy and I. And my
boy, who I thought would never end his sentences in prepositions,
learned to tell this story when his voice was still pitched high. His

6

voice would run over and above mine and we would laugh. I loved him then. Or did I love my ambition in him? Or did I love knowing he would never make my mistakes?

So now he makes his own. Pushkin 'n' Tanya. She says she comes from Pushkin the village. I don't believe it. But life plots elegantly. Maybe it's true.

And maybe Sven Andersson was killed by a hit-and-run driver who didn't know his name. And maybe somebody nailed forty dollars to a dope-house door.

Once I was the Negro student at Harvard. I lived there in the shelter of the shadow of W.E.B. Du Bois. I have loved Du Bois a good long while. Loved him like I love a man in whose arms I have frolicked. Loved him almost like I love Gabriel Michael, my atheist husband named for two angels. Du Bois would have understood this. In his essay "Of the Training of Black Men," he concludes, if I remember correctly, "I sit with Shakespeare and he winces not. Across the color line I move arm in arm with Balzac and Dumas, where smiling men and welcoming women glide in gilded halls."

Observe one of the little-recognized habits of the oft-unrecognized African American intellectual—the making of friendships across the chasm of death, particularly the friendship of authors, especially white authors. Somehow friendships with dead white poets and novelists and theologians feel less disloyal than friendships with living ones. I shared with Pushkin my passion for Emily Dickinson. Have I disclosed that once upon a time I considered Emily to be one of my very best friends? Did my love of Emily somehow prepare Pushkin to love Tanya?

Clearly, this subject is deranging me.

Pushkin, Harvard was the world I wanted for you, because it was the safest world my mind could imagine. Carrying you inside me, I had time to contemplate the reality: the world wasn't very safe. I limped into Harvard and across the Yard as into my own particular Bethlehem, out of my own peculiar Egypt. Harvard was my haven-home. How soon I would lay the baby in the manger! I read, and read again, the course catalogue. It became for me a sacred text. Knowledge not included in the curriculum of Harvard University would not exist. I was careful not to taste any of the offerings of the psychology department.

So much to learn, so much to forget. So much of what I knew no longer existed. So little of who I was found reflection in the books and lawns of this new place—and that was a good thing.

And if I lost something to be valued in all that shedding, as I moved from D.C. to Cambridge, then it was nothing I valued. I was all about amputation and amnesia. Every loss was an unburdening that transformed survival from a possibility into a probability. Nothing not taught at Harvard was real.

I would be black and I would be brilliant and I would be safe. You would be black and you would be brilliant and you would be safe. We could live in an ebony tower. Harvard would help and we would do the rest. Facts not taught at Harvard did not exist. That is the lie that sustained me.

My bar and my house are both in South Nashville, near Vanderbilt. Fisk is across town, in North Nashville. More and more these days, I find myself lost on the Fisk campus. I walk across the lawn in the afternoon light and stand in front of the statue of W.E.B. Du Bois erected opposite Jubilee Hall. It's a sturdy work of art brought into being by a man who once upon a time cut my husband's hair. Contemplating this likeness of Du Bois (created by an artisan who trained himself to harness volume by shaping the kink on the heads of future lawyers and doctors, Fisk and Meharry men, the curls on the heads of plumbers and electricians, and the lamby-wool crowning the heads of valets and chauffeurs), I am in awe of the artist who groomed and celebrated every head presented to him. I look at the sculpture of Du Bois and I feel joy. I remember the stocky presence of genius undeterred. Du Bois stands alone in his jacket with his books, striding, presiding over the campus in death as in life.

He is engaged with me.

I have also stood in front of the statue of John Harvard. I have a picture of my sister, Diana, and me standing there below John Harvard's feet. We are smiling, wearing graduation gowns and mortarboards. John Harvard is above us in a chair. The base of the statue is tall, taller than the statue itself. The base is of some light stone. It is rectangularly cut. The word *Harvard* is simply carved across the front. Atop this base is a bronze figure of a man in stockings and breeches, in some kind of waistcoat with some kind of gown, perhaps his academic gown, open and flowing. On his right knee is an open book. His left hand looks as if it were about to reach into his pocket, if he had such a thing. There are marvelous pompoms or bows, large and frilly, atop each of his shoes. Amid the busyness of the Yard, this is a statue of John Harvard at rest. His resolute, regular features with their refined, masculine bone structure are in repose as he looks up from his book. I have stood at John Harvard's feet. I have eaten at his table, slept beneath his roof, and I am grateful for the privilege.

He is distant from me.

I wanted you to go to Harvard, but I wanted you to understand all this as well. It is as simple and complex as that. When Tupac screeches "Being black hurts," I know it is true. And I lean toward those who know it too.

Where it hurts worst is in my mommyness.

This all started twenty-five years ago. I was eighteen, but I would not abort my son. My mother, Lena, ordered me to get an abortion. She deposited funds in my checking account. I spent the money on baby clothes.

I couldn't do it. I could hear Pushkin calling for my love. My cells could hear his cells sounding out to me, pounding out to me. And my soul could hear my body. My mind couldn't hear one quick measure of that music. Knew for sure it couldn't stand this baby. Feared its genes, feared birthing it, feared carrying it. Feared being disgusted by it. Feared disgusting myself. Thought for sure I'd gone to crazy. But that I left till now. Then, his self was calling to my self and I would not, could not, deny him. It was the first thing I knew about us. There was a hierarchy of needs, and his came first. I felt my soul expand.

Don't hostages fall in love with their kidnappers? Wasn't I held hostage by this baby? What a strange back door I walked into love through. Stockholm syndrome. Whether I was his kidnapper and he was my hostage, or I was his hostage and he had kidnapped me, or none of it applied at all, I have yet to get straight. But right after thinking I couldn't do it, I decided to have my baby.

I started loving Pushkin, I loved him more than the moon loves the sun. Why has he betrayed me? Because I play Cordelia to his Lear, returning silence for question, while he plays Othello to my rival's Desdemona, the only way you play Othello, tragically? Who is it I will not betray? What is it I meant to say?

Nothing. I meant to say nothing. Maybe, baby, silence don't get it. Who said that? Somebody from Detroit.

Let me begin again. I live in Nashville, Tennessee. I am a professor of Afro-Russian literature. I got my doctorate from the University of London. I am forty-three years old. I have tenure at Vanderbilt and a son who is twenty-five. Everybody worships my son except me. He's a football phenom. They call him "the Phenom." He played in a Super Bowl before he was twenty-two years old. What can that mean to me? I wasn't there. I couldn't let myself be there. My undergraduate degree is from Harvard. He and I went to Harvard together. No, we didn't. That's a lie. I so want it to be true, I say it as if trying out the possibility. But there are no new possibilities in the past—there's just a robber-woman named Perkins in Detroit who took care of my boy when I went to school. Just a place called Motown where we, each in very different times, once both lived.

Standing where I stand now, I should have kept him with me. I could have put Pushkin in some kind of backpack or baby carrier, some Snugli, some sling, some thing, some fucking piece of cloth. Pay me now or pay me later. How heavy could the baby have been? Can you keep a three-year-old bound to your back? I don't know.

I just know that I didn't. I left him in Detroit. I went back to Cambridge. Is he punishing me now for abandoning him then? I don't know what he did all day. I remember what I did: learn Russian, read Russian, speak Russian. Articulate a future for us. Seek an alternative to the English language. Abandon my mother tongue. Find a new unspoken word for every important thing I wanted to say. Find a new alphabet for love. Show myself every day I can do something difficult. Love Pushkin; learn Russian. Twinned improbabilities. Success at one became my proof of the possibility of success at the other.

I wish I had kept Pushkin with me. I wish I could have thought of Harvard as a welfare office. If I had asked this of it, if I had asked, I might have received. Daddy-Harvard is abundantly treasured. I did not ask.

And now Pushkin is marrying a white Russian lap dancer and insists on knowing who his daddy is.

I cannot even tell what upsets me more, the white girl part of this mess or the daddy part of this mess. If he knew the truth then, maybe he wouldn't be making this mistake. After everything white folks have done to my family, Pushkin wants to give one a ring. If he knew, he would not do this. Maybe there is time to let him know. Then again, if he knew all our truths, maybe he would just be a different dark stereotype—black man behind bars. The first omission was but a cornerstone to a larger edifice. A mother's work is never done. He needs protection.

Why won't he simply accept the obvious? I was his daddy and his mama. Why won't he let it be like that? And if he can't let his daddy be me, why can't he let his daddy be W.E.B. or Pushkin or Malcolm? If I swallowed his daddy's sin, why won't he swallow my lie? Part of the answer has to be he doesn't know how much sin and sorrow I had to swallow to bring him to life. That's nobody's fault but my own.

This is not the reprieve I desired. This is not the compensation I required. I shock myself with my desire for emotional reparations, but I acknowledge the desire—it is real. I want the man who was my boy to sustain within his heart the judgment that I am the most beautiful woman in the world. I want my son to desire a woman who looks like me. Or, at the very least, looks like the girl I used to be.

He wants Tanya.

"Look what they done to my son," sobs the Mafia don to the undertaker. And I keep thinking about it. Pushkin is confounded by the fact that *The Godfather* is my favorite movie. He expects me to prefer *Dr. Zhivago* or *Reds*. High-tech hoodlums with assault weapons, not literature professors, watch *The Godfather* over and over, quoting the lines like a Bible. It's part of the way they understand themselves. "What in the fuck has that got to do with you, Moms?"

I smile and tell him the truth that makes sense to him. I say, "*Anna Karenina* is my second favorite movie." He lets that be enough.

If I answer Pushkin's question, who will it hurt? If I answer his question, who will he hurt?

I have never been so glad and never been so sorry that Pushkin knows so little about Detroit, about Motown, about the outlaw hoodlums who were and are my people. If he walked around with a pistol in his waistband, if he walked around like Daddy and the uncles, I could not begin to think of telling him the truth.

Don Corleone wanted transformation. He wanted things not to be as they were. You can only want that desperately; it is an audacious desire.

I want that. I have the audacious desire. I want Push to be Pushkin again. I want to harvest the seeds I planted. I want my son to be who he is not and want who he does not. I know this is wrong, but it is true. And it is nothing I have willed myself to do. It just is.

You just want your daddy.

A hard thing about hearing you call for your daddy is that it makes me remember calling for mine. The harder thing is knowing you feel about me the way I felt about my mother when she silenced my call and cut me off from my daddy. Rage. Rage at the mother for removing the father. I can't do anything about that. The only way I can prove I am right and you are wrong is to answer your question, tell you who your daddy is and watch the news do its damage. I won't do that. I won't hurt you. That was my only rule. I would get to hear you say, "Moms, you were right." I feel sure you would say, "I wish I didn't know." I would hear that. But I would see my tall man get shorter, my strong man get weaker. I have seen that happen in my family before, a big man get chopped down by a small piercing moment, or a big man who didn't because a woman kept her mouth shut. I will feel your rage before any part of me makes any part of you small.

I turned on my own daddy for you. I cast him out of my mind, because I knew if he knew it all, he would never accept you. You make me glad my daddy is dead. If he was alive and he turned his back on you, I would turn my back on him. If he was alive, he would turn his back on you. You are making me remember things I don't want to remember. Tanya has provoked me into remembering people—not people that I don't want to remember, people I am afraid to remember. I don't know how to remember who my daddy and his people are at the same time that I remember who your daddy is without putting a bullet in my brain. And I won't have the strength to remember who your daddy is, and how to love you, if I don't remember who my daddy is and who his people were. How is it you don't fucking understand that?

I want to shake you and say, "Remember who you are! Remember who I am!" But you can't remember what you have never known.

If you insist on the truth of your beginning, how do we get to any kind of happy ending? I never knew the answer to that, never figured any answer but to cheat, to lie about the beginning. Now you won't let me cheat. You take away the win we have almost achieved and say, Play the game again with a clean whole deck. I say, There are no clean whole decks.

I will do what I have always done for you. Take the next step, ignoring the likelihood of failure. We are deep in the shit of truth. Maybe the thing for me to do is to try to keep on walking. Like every other mother who ever lived in the world before me, I am prepared for the shit of truth by all my baby's dirty, dirty diapers.

Then again, as we both know, I am not so well prepared. I wasn't the one who changed most of your diapers. I made such a good life for you that that wasn't supposed to matter. Your father wasn't supposed to matter either.

It would not have been better for you, but it would have been better for me if I had let them wash you down a drain. They say Russian girls do it all the time. I wonder if she's done it. I wonder if she's done yours, done mine? I wonder if she's done my grands? Done to me what I wouldn't do to you. Not even when I was eighteen years old.

I was bold then, bold and cold. That first week I rocked you in my arms, crooning, "Baby, baby, don't get hooked on me." That's the kind of crazy baby bitch I was then. But how did you know? How do you know? How is it that I, who was once bold and cold, am now only and vaguely old? How is it that I was betrayed, after I turned you every which way but loose?

TWO

TITTIE TASSELS?

One of Pushkin's teammates claims that Tanya can make the tassels on her right tittie spin clockwise while the tassel on the left one spins counterclockwise. This white boy swears he had a snake's-eye view of the occurrence.

We are at a birthday party for one of the receivers' wives, a sealskin beauty celebrating her twenty-seventh in the home provided by her peculiarly strong black man. I am invited. Tanya isn't. This is the very beginning and things are almost as they should be.

Three of us—Pushkin, the defensive tackle with the claims, and I—are shooting pool (in the only billiard gazebo I have ever seen) when this statement is made. Not loudly. Not cruelly, just a soft, sudden joke. I expect Pushkin to respond decisively. His trash talk is legendary. I'm told by players too awed by my position as an adored mother to quote my son verbatim that Pushkin is a poet of the cussing insult. Pushkin says nothing. He just smiles, then hangs his smiling head. He shakes the dangling, hanging, smiling head back and forth for seconds upon seconds.

This is not my son. My son does not hang his head. My son does not smile. The defensive tackle takes the shot that ends the game. He scratches on the eight ball; black and white pop into the same pocket, one after the other.

"You have no understanding of physics," Pushkin taunts.

Before turning on his heel and walking toward the lawn, the tackle puts one of his hands on each of Pushkin's shoulders. Nobody is smiling now. He looks Pushkin directly in the eye as he speaks. "You gonna kill Moms!"

It is possible I am going to kill myself.

I rack. The strangest thing is that Pushkin is not offended by the leering language directed at his woman. Pushkin breaks. We both eye the geometries of the table. "They were a lot of folk in the club the night I met her. She did what she did. She is who she is." He explains this while studying my body to determine which way I'm going to break. "Look. She doesn't wear tassels on any part of her anatomy or person. Not even her loafers."

I laugh. I've made my point. She's fit to be the subject of a joke. This little lap dancer won't last long. Pushkin will not stay interested in a piece of fluff. We are back in our game.

A waiter appears, carrying the cake on a silver tray. Multicolored tapers sparkle and pop as the dessert moves across the narrow field of new-mown hay that makes a fine tax deduction and separates the Italianate garden from the California contemporary house. The garden overlooks a manmade lake where chubby swans swim as little girls, beige and white and brown, throw brioche crumbs. Most of the guests are gathered on a circular stone terrace at the center of the planting. From this vantage, green extends in all directions until it touches blue. All the young daddies are rich. All the young wives are beautiful. It is summertime after a winning season.

A chorus of "Happy birthday to you, happy birthday to you" rises from the crowd. The wish is old and broad. It is as wide as the places and circumstances we have separately sung are far-flung. The celebration is real.

I forget Tanya. I am yearning for nothing. I see my Gabriel Michael across the lawn talking to a lovely brown lady, and I know I will be with him when he takes off his clothes. If I were to hear Tanya's name again, I would be surprised. I would not be surprised if I never hear her name again.

Gabriel and I leave for home just as the sun begins to set. I shower and start brushing, fluffing, and swallowing. We are just settling in between our gray sheets when the phone rings. I have no intention of answering. We are about to get really busy. The caller ID spells out *Pushkin X.* I grab the phone.

"Hey, sweetie."

"Windsor? This is Tanya. Pushkin's friend."

"That's—" I stop myself. I was about to say "an interesting word for it," but I remember it's Pushkin's name on the caller ID. He is probably right beside her. "This is a nice surprise," I say.

I can't believe this lap dancer has the unmitigated gall to punch in my professorial seven digits. I am surprised that Pushkin would give them to her.

She's inviting me to lunch. She wants to talk to me about American poetry. She says she's thinking of doing some writing of her own. I choke on, or back, my guffaw. She says she's developing a performance art piece that might interest me. Performance art. Instead of an interesting word, now we're getting an interesting phrase. Tanya says that Pushkin says I might be able to help her. I don't want this girl telling me what my boy thinks.

"I'm not sure I can help. I don't teach poetry."

"You write about poetry."

"That's a thing altogether different."

"You have published poetry."

"A long time ago."

"And you wrote some songs, yes?"

"He's told you a great deal."

"He's proud."

"That's nice to hear."

"He talks about Moms a lot."

"That could be nice or not so nice."

"It's nice."

I concede round one. Lunch with Tanya will amuse me, and I'll get the ammunition I need to beat her decisively in round two. When she's gone, I will regale Pushkin's wife, the mother of my as-yet-unborn grandchildren, with stories about the Russian stripper. White or black, Pushkin's wife won't be a stripper. It's going to be fine. I can afford to be nice.

I ask her what kind of food she prefers. She wants to know what I like; she wants to play host. I assert the privilege of my age and position — mother ranks above girlfriend. She says she eats everything. I just bet she does.

Where's racism when you need it? Why couldn't this Cyrillic slut have been offended by having my ebony prince ogle her — whatever point or curve on her person he was ogling the night they met?

Tanya offers to pick me up. Pushkin told her I don't like to drive. This is a bad sign.

She arrives dressed in black and earnestly eager for our few hours together. This is a very bad sign. In the pictures Pushkin showed me she was wearing brightly colored clothing. Eagerness to please the mother usually indicates strong interest in marrying the son. Imitating the mother's dress is pathological. Of course, my black is expensive, silk, and well tailored. Older bodies need more help.

We eat our very first lunch alone at a place called Martha's. A purpose-built gray box of a building houses a gift shop, lavatories, and the restaurant. Separated by the big barn, where generations of black and white men worked together to make horse history, from Belle Meade Mansion, the structure that houses Martha's was built to fade away into its environment. It's not quite as interesting as Gabriel Michael's designs, but it's a very pleasing space.

Inside Martha's, the walls are hung with colorful, primitively rendered pictures of vegetables painted by the chef's husband. It's a comfortable country place. We are seated at a sunny two-top. I am neither comfortable nor pleased.

Our table looks out onto a little greenhouse. I almost expect to see my salad growing. Instead there are four potted evergreen trees and two small raised beds of out-of-season flowers. I wonder if they are edible. There are no paintings of flowers on the walls.

The world and I are one beat off; Tanya and I seem strangely synchronized.

We both order fried green tomato salads with hot coffee, both pass on the savory chive biscuits. By the time I realize that she is trying so hard to be polite that she isn't consulting her own taste, it is dessert. I refuse to place my order until she states her desire. She chooses peppermint ice cream over chocolate cake. I stay with the black coffee.

Up to dessert, conversation over the meal is surprisingly boring. The South is a place of ironic alliances, straightforward collaborations, and brutal betrayals between blacks and whites. Some of the most vicious and some of the most gracious take place in the southern kitchen, some in the southern bed. As my son has already introduced her to the southern bed, it seems a delicious irony for me to introduce her to the table. Unlike Martha's fried green tomatoes with roasted whole kernels of corn drizzled over, Tanya is fizzling, not sizzling.

Then the dessert arrives.

She does want to talk about American poetry. Visions of Emily Dickinson collide in my head with visions of strippers and poles. I hold Martha's heavy white pottery cup, marked with the pink half-moon of my lipstick lingerings, up to my face as a kind of veil between us, as Tanya prattles on. I feel safe enough.

The waitress, Annie, an aspiring singer with bright red hair, comes by often and silently. They like me here. Annie knows I will go through half a pot and leave a big tip. Tanya recites fragments of some of her favorite poems. I am completely unfamiliar with these works. My mind is flipping through recent publications, my recent readings. I don't recognize these voices at all. I give up.

"What's that in? I'm not familiar with that author."

She states a name. Something is vaguely rattling around my brain. She repeats the name again. Robert Diggs. I read a lot. I'm reaching deep. I think I've got it. But the answer doesn't feel right. Yet and still, my little soldiers rarely fail me.

"Masta Killa from the Wu-Tang Clan?"

She shakes her head. "RZA."

"I was close."

"RZA. He's a genius."

"First he was Prince Rakeem." My backup forces are arriving.

"I thought you would know the Wu-Tang Clan."

"I've read a little about them."

What is there to say? Thank you, Spady, for teaching me to read and remember that all facts might be useful one day? But what is she really talking about? What does she want with my boy? What does she want with me?

I am trying to form an equation, trying to figure this out. I keep getting distracted by the four businessmen eating at the table across from us, who are obviously distracted by us. They take turns allowing their gaze to dart and linger in our direction. They are obviously intrigued and attracted. I am embarrassed. Tanya is amused.

"Pushkin didn't tell me his mother was so beautiful."

"Perhaps he doesn't think so?"

"You look great."

"For my age?"

"No, really!"

"When I was your age, he was four years old."

"That's when you lived in Petersburg?"

"You know a lot about us."

"I'm learning."

I am past ready to change the subject.

"What are the names of the other Wu-Tang Clan members?" I

speak this sentence as archly as possible. I forget that tone is hard to translate.

"Gza, Method Man, Ghostface Killah, Inspecta Deck, RZA, U-God. And Raekwon and Masta Killa."

"You seem to know them very well."

"It's classic old school. I would like to meet them."

"Maybe Pushkin can arrange it."

There are benefits to having tone not translate. I'm making full use of those advantages and planning to make full use of them in the future, as long as this unbearable blond future hangs over my head.

"I dance to rap records."

"Dance."

"I'm a stripper."

"Really."

"Well, I was a lap dancer. Since Pushkin and I hooked up, I don't leave the stage."

"Stripping is better than lap dancing?"

"It depends."

"On?"

"Lap dancers make more money. Stripping is an art form."

"Really?"

"I don't have the necessity of making money now."

Silent as she comes and goes, Annie is taking some of this in. I put my hand over the top of my cup to indicate I don't want any more coffee. I want the coffee, but I don't want her to hear any more of this mess. I have to eat in this restaurant again. I will want to eat in this restaurant again. Pushkin needs to drop the Cyrillic slut before her name appears with his in the tabloids.

"I've heard about a club in New York. It is run by women and the customers are women. Everything is natural. If you've had any cutting on your tits, you can't perform there."

"Really?"

"The Blue Angel. It is where I want to debut my new act. It's the best club there has ever been."

"Really?"

"Most girls want to dance at Scores or Manhattan Dolls."

"Really?"

"Really. Pushkin says he'll buy me a club if I want to keep dancing."

"Really?"

"Really. He says I should call it Nekkid."

"Do you know the difference between naked and nekkid?"

"A bad accent?"

"It's a joke I taught Pushkin."

"Really?" She's mirroring my language back to me. She beams proudly as she does it. I get that arch tone thing going again.

"Naked," I explain to her, as I once upon a time a long time ago explained to Pushkin, "is being without your clothes on. Nekkid is being without your clothes doing something you're not supposed to be doing."

"Who decides?"

"Excuse me?"

"When the clothes are off, I think a person should decide for themselves what they should be doing. I cannot call my club Nekkid. Nekkid does not exist."

"Or it's invisible to you."

"Invisible?"

Tanya looks as if she doesn't understand the word. She just doesn't get the way I've used it. I will not play word games with this child-woman in her second language. It isn't nice—and I am not winning by a large enough margin.

Tanya's not stupid. She's just the antithesis of my existence. A stripper, a white poor illiterate Russian stripper, is dating my black rich brilliant educated American football player. Stripper and football player go together, maybe. Does that mean football player eclipses everything else—including black, rich, brilliant, educated, and American?

"What's your act like?" I ask.

"It's not a thing to explain. I don't dance much to the old school you probably know. It's Cee-Lo, 'Closet Freak,' Benzino, 'Rock the Party,' Busta Rhymes, 'Make It Clap.' That's what people want to hear. But I think I do something with it. You must come watch sometime. I want to know about what you do."

"What can I tell you?"

"What do you teach?"

"I'm a professor."

"Of?"

"Russian studies."

"What did you write your dissertation on?"

"You know about dissertations?"

"I have a friend at the university."

"Didn't Pushkin bring you to Nashville, from . . . ?"

"Florida, we met in Florida."

"At a club called Mons Venus?"

"Funny name, no?"

"Hilarious."

"It would have been nicer to meet somewhere else. What did you write on?"

"Images of Russia and Russians in African American writings contrasted with images in Russian literature of Africans, Afro-Americans, Afro-Russians, and Africa, particularly literature available in America in translation."

"Primarily Pushkin?"

"Primarily Pushkin."

"That's nice."

"Your turn. What do you do that's so different?"

"I mix Middle Eastern women's dancing—"

"Belly dancing?"

"Belly dancing, with elements of Russian folk dance, especially the footwork, with tap, except I use isolated muscle contractions all over my body to hit the beat. I hit it visually instead of with sound. I can do stair-step ripples on my belly and wave ripples across the inside of my thighs."

She's animated and unashamed. Tanya considers the rap songs to be poetry. I ask more questions, not because I want to hear her but because I want to confront Pushkin.

The longer she talks, the more fluid her talking becomes. When she gains speed, she has an eloquence. Not standard diction, not standard perspective, not standard theme, not standard content in support of theme; but she's saying something, something that somehow, in some way wholly unexpected by me, has some kind of truth and beauty to it.

I come too much from a people who too often depart from standards of diction, perspective, theme, content, and development to deny the truth—she is trying to do something, even if I don't understand what it is.

Tanya explains that when she performs, she does a very subtle syncopation with her body parts off the beat of the song, creating a kind of corporal scansion of the meter, of the poem. She uses the word *meter*. She uses the phrase *iambic pentameter*. I am wondering who she has been talking to. Or maybe she's been reading. I sense I'm catching an echo or a streak of someone else's thought in her discourse. And I'm catching an echo of something else entirely. She is evoking an old and abandoned memory of mine. This troubles me. She reminds me of someone I once knew. For a moment I wonder if she reminds me of me at her age. This is easily dismissible. She is reminding me of something I have forgotten that I thought I would never need to know again.

She's talking about dancing. She's talking about writing songs that she can dance to instead of dancing to CDs that anyone can buy. She's talking about creating a performance that involves her naked body and her naked language. I ask her if she intends to write in Russian or in English. She quickly replies, "English." "Who would listen to me in Russian?" she asks.

Russian is irrelevant again. No one outside Russia read Russian before Alexander Pushkin. European nobles learned Russian to read Pushkin, to read *Eugene Onegin* and *Boris Godunov*. Later, Hemingway wrote, "First there are the Russians." Not for this girl. She is turning my world upside down.

As Tanya talks, a name and a name and another name come to me from my early childhood. Like dead bodies in a lake, the names rise to the surface of my brain, Lottie the Body. Lottie Graves or Claibourne. Lottie Somebody. Tanya. How many names did I teach myself not to speak after I moved from Motown to Washington? Lottie the Body is one of the names. Tanya is another.

All the days I have lived in Nashville, I have allowed myself to encounter no one and nothing to remind me of Lottie or Motown. At Harvard, there was Diana and nothing else. In Leningrad of the eighties, there was nothing. By the time I got to Nashville, Lottie's name was forgotten and irrelevant. But there had been a time in Washington when I had to remind myself not to talk about Lottie the Body and other people, nearer and dearer, who inhabited the world she inhabited, inhabited the place where I was born.

I am almost glad Pushkin met Tanya. If he had not met Tanya, I might not have remembered Lottie. Once I got to Nashville, I had no good reason to remember Lottie and her amazing body. Memory was lost, unsought, and forgotten.

Sometimes the only balm in Gilead is forget.

I ask Tanya if she's ever heard of Lottie the Body. She shakes her head, but she doesn't look blank. She looks interested. I don't tell her that Lottie was a friend of the people who spawned me, Leo and

Lena. I want to tell her this, but don't. I don't tell her that Lottie was the dancer in Motown when Deee-troit put the *d* in dance. I don't say, "Whatever that Blue Angel is or is trying to be, it ain't a Motown show bar. Lottie the Body was an exotic dancer, not a stripper, not a whore." To tell Tanya this I would have to toss off the words *stripper* and *whore* in an everyday job-description way, in a blasé way I don't remotely feel.

To tell her that would be to give her the term *exotic dancer*, and that would be more benediction than I know.

I wonder what it would be to tell Tanya what little I am letting myself remember. That little girls at Ziggy Johnson's dancing school on a Saturday morning sneaked into Ziggy's office to get a look at publicity glossies of Lottie that someone had taped to his wall. That these little girls, myself included, looked at Lottie and thanked God for big brown legs and round brown arms. That some members of the Motown Records rhythm section, the Funk Brothers, were inspired by the way Lottie worked her body against a beat.

Now, Tanya is reciting some of her lyrics to me. Dancing just a little bit in her seat. With the bouncing and bumping required by the pulse of the hip-hop songs she's creating, I don't dare ask what-all body parts she uses. There's a lot to syncopate. I don't want to know with what.

She's slowing down. She's figured out that I'm not following her any longer. Maybe she thinks it's because I don't like rap. I tell her I don't know enough about rap to like it or not to like it. That's not true. I know enough about rap to be vaguely ashamed of it. She promises to get me some Tupac CDs. She prefers P. Diddy, but she thinks Tupac will be just my speed.

I thank her for the thought and turn the conversation to Pushkin—the poet, not her man, not my boy.

I am giving her a chance to close the doors she has started to open, the door to the back alley of black low culture. She steps to her chance.

She has a story that dazzles me. On her seventh birthday, her mother took her to see the most famous statue in Russia, the Bronze Horseman, a gi-normous statue of a rearing horse and a fearless rider standing on an immense boulder looking from St. Petersburg out toward Europe. When they arrived in Senate Square, the child Tanya was struck mute by the beauty of the thing, the portrayal of Czar Peter the Great protecting Petersburg for all the world to see.

Into this silence her mother poured more beauty, a poem written by Alexander Pushkin about the statue. Tanya's mother didn't know "The Bronze Horseman" by heart, but she had a copy. As they walked round and round Senate Square, eying the sculpture from all directions, her mother washed over Tanya with Pushkin's language, bathed Tanya in Pushkin.

I am amazed. Pushkin and I did that too. Except I knew the poem by heart and didn't need a book. Tanya is less surprised. "People in Petersburg take their children to see the statue. People in Petersburg, even visitors, know poetry."

"I'm still amazed."

"I was amazed when Pushkin told me that he did it. Then I told him how my mother and I had done it."

Had they? Or did this girl just tell Pushkin they had to make a bond? I am suspicious. Suspicion is a hard habit to break. It is an old Motown way, and this girl has reminded me of old Motown ways.

I'm thinking of sculptures: of the Bronze Horseman in Petersburg, of the standing Du Bois on the campus of Fisk in Music City; of a sitting John Harvard on the campus of my alma mater in Massachusetts. I so quickly and clearly know the sculpted monuments that signify to me the significance of the cities I have called home, except Detroit. Do I choose the Jolly Green Giant, the spirit of Detroit, a classical giant of a white-looking green man with a sphere to represent the image of God in one hand and a family in the other? Or do I choose the giant tire? The eighty-foot-tall tire parked on I-94, the tire I rode when it still had seats, when it was a Ferris wheel at the 1964 World's Fair? Of course it must be the tire.

When that tire was a moving machine, before it was a sculpture, my parents were still married. When that tire was a working toy, Leo and Lena were the king and queen of Detroit. When that Ferris wheel disguised as a tire whirled above the throng, giving some of the two million people it rode a ride, I was a five-year-old girl in a shell-pink silk-satin dress with a scalloped bateau neckline, sitting ringside with the king and queen the night the Supremes opened at the CopaCabana.

I am thinking about how a flesh-and-blood female is always more than a statue.

And I am thinking about erecting an American monument to Pushkin, the poet, for protecting the intellectual pride of ebony princesses everywhere just by being black and beautiful and brilliant.

Tanya takes a last bite of her peppermint ice cream. She has already devoured the chocolate cake. She's thinking about something too. Her blond and silver hair shines bright white now. Her eyes are kohled black. She holds her knife and fork in the European manner. She places her cutlery down carefully.

"I think Alexander Pushkin would have loved rap. Tupac especially."

I cannot listen to this. I have heard too many losses foretold for a single day. She's imperiled my love of Pushkin X. Now she's imperiling my respect for Alexander Pushkin. I don't like rap. I find it hard to believe that Pushkin would like rap. I find it hard to believe that this little lap dancer feels so free to tell me what Pushkin would think about any artifact of black culture. I am the scholar. Then again, she's Russian. The Russians believe it is their birthright to understand Pushkin better than anyone else in the world.

Another thing. Every time Tanya calls the poet's name, it rings in my brain as if she's calling my son, and I shut down. My brain is shutting down. She's got a great big garnet ring on her finger. One day he might change it for a diamond. I can't think.

Now she's going on about the legend surrounding the statue of Peter the Great, as if I might not know it. As if I didn't tell it to my Pushkin, walking around the square. As she told the tale to me, I could hear an echo of my younger voice telling it to Pushkin all those years ago.

The siege of Leningrad lasted nine hundred days. For nine hundred nights, the city by the sea that had been St. Petersburg and would become St. Petersburg again, Leningrad, was battered by bombs.

The people were cold and hungry, but they were not hopeless. A belief born in the nineteenth century, in the days of the czars, crossed into the twentieth-century Soviet, providing succor. It passed from the lips of mothers and fathers standing in Senate Square into the ears of their gaping sons and daughters, who in turn as parents stood in Senate Square with their children at their knees, as the little ones of Leningrad were told in no uncertain terms that enemy forces would never take Petersburg while the Bronze Horseman stood.

Sculptures of less significance were relocated to comparative safety. The Bronze Horseman could not be moved. It was understood that he had to remain standing in his place to assure the safety of the city. To move him would have broken the spirit of the people.

The people wanted consolation. They needed encouragement. They held fast to the belief that their city was safe as long as the statue stood. They protected it with sandbags and wooden scaffolding. It did stand—and Leningrad never was occupied. Though Hitler made elaborate plans for his first night in St. Petersburg, plans to drink champagne and sleep in the lavish Astoria Hotel, he never entered the city. People believed it was because Peter, present in the Bronze Horseman, prevailed.

Erected by Catherine the Great to honor her ancestor Peter the Great—the same Peter who was the poet Pushkin's grandfather's benefactor and godfather—the Bronze Horseman survived World War II.

Catherine honored Peter with a statue. Pushkin honored Peter, the man who honored his ancestor, with a poem inspired by the statue.

"The Bronze Horseman" gallops from the bolt of lightning and clap of thunder that splits a sixteen-hundred-ton boulder from a Scandinavian mountain to arrive (more than one thousand lines later) at the seaside burial of Pushkin's crazy hero, Yevgeny. Yevgeny thinks he is being pursued through Senate Square by the deceased czar on the back of his long-dead horse. Or does Yevgeny think he is being pursued by the statue Peter on his imperial horse? Either is a powerful delusion.

"Pushkin blessed the crazy hero pursued by ghosts well," says Tanya. The just schoolteacher in me can't help but acknowledge that this is a good thought. Competition provokes me to assert that her good thought provoked a better one. I keep this acknowledgment to myself.

Was Pushkin thinking of his great-grandfather Abraham Hannibal's sister, the girl who swam after the slave ship that carried Abraham from Africa's shore, the girl who drowned without monument, when he imagined, in the final climactic lines of the poem, a hero at sea and unburied? Did he translate that girl in life to that man in fiction? What am I to translate?

Should the day come, I know just what this girl who loves Pushkin and the Wu-Tang Clan should have from me as a wedding present. There is something I know I can do for her, if I will. Something I can do for Pushkin.

I wonder if the bitch thinks about her Pushkin when she touches mine.

THREE

DIANA, PUSHKIN, AND ME.

That's how it used to be. Diana is my sister, my half-sister. I love me some Diana.

My sister spent the first half of her life sharing her name with an unforgettable skinny girl from the Brewster Projects and the second half of her life sharing her name with an unforgettable skinny girl from British royalty. Both Dianas branded the name, leaving every Diana after to seem to be borrowing it from them. Diana was unfortunate in her naming. She didn't care. I cared for her. Unlike both those women who seemed starved for something, my Diana was deeply well fed and skinny too. That's how being a lone and able huntress will do you. She alone I have not forgotten. Detroit Diana, Diana Detroit, my sole unforgotten one.

The first time I needed my sister, she was stepping across Harvard Yard in real Motown gaiters, wearing khaki pants and a gray sharkskin jacket. If you didn't see her that day, you've never seen anything like it. Diana didn't repeat herself. She looked like a very pretty boy who was ready to dance somebody across a humid room or kick somebody down a humid stair. She looked like somebody who could rescue somebody. Diana looked like our daddy.

What had been spilled on and dripped across those shoes? Diana's gaiters were made to be wiped off and shined up. Crocodile is a whole lot like patent leather, and patent leather is more than a little like plastic. Semen, blood, scotch? My sister led an exciting life, too exciting by half, the kind of life you lead in crocodile shoes. Gaiters keep your secrets. White canvas tennies tell, *Lawd*, show all their stains. Lord have mercy on me in my Keds. How many times had I prayed "Mercy, Lord!" till I didn't know if there was a Lord? Then there was Diana, standing in the path, looking just like mercy.

Trailing whiffs of Old Spice and Cutty Sark (back then she drank in the daytime), Diana stopped in her tracks as I approached her on one of the paths crossing Harvard Yard. She stuck her hands in her pockets and reared back, flashing the red silk lining of our daddy's suit jacket, as if leaning on some old and invisible wall. Love is largely a matter of paying attention. She had the essence of that matter down. She greeted me with a question: "What you know good, girl? What you know good?"

If I had turned the question around and asked her, she would have answered simply and frankly, saying, "We escaped!" or "Harvard." I had escaped craziness and she had escaped near-to-poverty. We had landed someplace peculiarly capable of protection. Harvard. That is what I still love about the place Pushkin hates. That is what I loved so soon. Harvard, antidote to and antithesis of the peculiar institution, slavery. That's what Diana knew good.

I had been robbed of one legacy, the Detroit street legacy of bravado and swagger that Diana so clearly possessed. Here was Harvard promising another, the academy legacies of read and write, safety and security.

After falling asleep over a volume of Shakespeare on a couch in a room where someone else fell asleep over a volume of chemistry, I would shake myself and make my way back home to Pennypacker, a four-story mid-last-century brick almost-tenement purchased by Harvard when the freshman class got too large for the Yard.

In the after-three stillness, walking between the well-wishing piles of brick, the respectful gaslights, the shining green lawns, all the surfaces with all their weight of wealth, I felt like a second-chance heiress. Breaking through the frigid silence of winter term, I heard the voices of Harvard policemen as they radioed from car to car, describing my movement from quadrant to quadrant, watching over me as I made my way back to my room. I had time to notice my breath appearing in little clouds before my face. I could ponder the clouds because I didn't have to monitor my surroundings. Watching over me with guns in regular issue, wearing drab uniforms, were the Harvard Police, my new knights in shining armor. Of course I love Harvard. It possesses the only sweet police force in America. A sweet police force is a revelation to a black girl.

I would walk across the Yard—after the libraries closed at eleven, after the coffee shops and bars closed at two, after the keys had been turned in the locks of all the places to gather and places to worry, places to anticipate—more than half high on possibilities, permanently three sheets to every intellectual wind, and, simply put, simple as I can put it, I felt like I had made it to the promised land, made it to the more-than-promised land.

I was prepared for, provided for, I was contained within a benign and omnipotent power. It was a return to a new and better womb. Harvard was poised to be proud of me. Harvard wished me well.

I learned to dance, those first days in Cambridge, in the upstairs bar at the Hasty Pudding. Harvard was as safe as it got, but reality was growing inside me. I disappeared in the sensual moment. Moving in response to rich boys who had never been pretty wearing smoky, junk-shop tuxedos purchased with the interest accrued, boys who swung me wild, or moving in relation to earnest-brained boys with more heart than land, from the middle of the heartland, armed with their public school truths, blathering about girls they matter-of-factly called Hoovers, embarrassing me to death, I danced, rocking the bundle within me.

Days before I arrived at Harvard I had been raped. It was an unfortunate few hours I was determined to forget, a few hours I quickly edited from the text of my life—by not telling. The man had said "I love you" as he came. The words hurt more than his penis. My vagina was number than my ears.

In those first days in Cambridge, I discovered a semblance of serenity. I didn't know yet I was pregnant. I couldn't conceive of that and pushed the new bad memory away into a space shared with the old ones. I discovered the Houghton Library's collection of the works of Alexander Pushkin. I wanted to swoon. To touch the volumes of Pushkin that the great American minds of the nineteenth and twentieth centuries had touched transported me surprisingly far from my rather alarming troubles.

Tripping up to the Emily Dickinson room, on the second floor of Houghton, I discovered my fetish for fortified architecture. I was beginning to find all safe places erotic. Holding the most precious papers, these rooms were protected from earthquake, fire, and flood. I like the idea of walls that protect their contents. I like the covers of books. They say the Houghton Library will survive the end of the world. I bought a membership to it. It was uncommon for undergraduates to buy memberships. I told friends that I enjoyed the free cocktails. I bought my membership on the chance that I might be in the library when the world ended. I became a frequent visitor.

Having experienced two catastrophes, a kidnapping at eight and a rape at eighteen, I could not discount the possibility of a third.

As no bombs were dropped in Cambridge during my stay, I can't say whether the walls of Houghton hold. I do know that I discovered within them the pleasure of breathing in the dust of Emily Dickinson's books. The physical books her hands had touched were decaying as slowly as the Houghton could contrive, but they were decaying still. Invisible bits that had touched her hands entered my nostrils. I breathed deeply, willing the essence of Emily to penetrate the essence of me. I liked tiptoeing up the serene green staircase that snaked above the round vestibule of the library. It was my own little stairway to my own little heaven.

Of sixteen hundred freshmen, I was one of fewer than one hundred who enjoyed the luxury of a semiprivate bathtub. It had been a prerequisite. When I accepted my place in the class of '81, I scribbled the condition that I be given a bathtub on the acceptance postcard. In part I was angling for rejection. In part I was looking for a soft place to fall. I knew how far I was falling and how soft the place had to be.

My mother, Lena, allowed me to apply to only one college. She said if I couldn't get into Harvard, I didn't deserve to go anywhere. After she made the statement, she tore the envelopes with my applications to Stanford and Princeton and Amherst into halves, then into quarters. Then she smiled and I started to cry. Only one of us was surprised when April rolled around and I was admitted.

Harvard would not have been soft enough without Diana.

On the day I told her I was pregnant, I smelled my sister before I saw her. I caught her scent and stood hunting-field still. I closed my eyes, inhaled deeply. That faint, sweet cloud of cologne and liquor entered my lungs. I opened my eyes and there she was, asking her Motown question: "What you know good, girl? What you know good?"

I should have said, "You." But I didn't. Scared rabbits run. I know that. Scared rabbits run. Love is ugly as a motherfucker—and scared rabbits run. How easy it would be to say, "I know I'm almost finished with the paper due Monday, I know that." How easy to talk about work and give myself a schedule rather than to acknowledge this: what I know good is you. Here is this creature dressed in my daddy's clothes with soft small shoulders and little pillowy bosoms and a grin that says she don't want nothing from me but for me to let her be my resting place. I can linger my while in her smile.

Our daddy was her steppingstone. She said, "His back was my bridge," and I was jealous. She said it over and over. He lay down across the sharky waters of her life and she tiptoed across, never soaking the soles of those crocodile gaiters. If I were wearing boots, there would be two inches of water in them. Our daddy's back was Diana's bridge, and she would be that for me. Learned it at our daddy's knee. I could hate her for that. Probably do. Certainly did. But I needed her more than I hated her, so I said, "I know my sister's going to buy me some supper tonight. That's what I know good." She didn't let me down.

Daddy did. He had a stroke and started to die. Diana got the call just days after she took me to supper and I told her some small part of the mess I was in. She banged on my door. Told me, looking in my face. We flew from Logan to Metro, from Boston to Detroit. We sat beside his bed in the CICU, the cardiac intensive care unit. We stroked his gray and wavy hair. We kissed his hands. His eyes were clear and huge and green. His skin was warm and brown. He was so young and too beautiful to die. He was forty-eight years old. He knocked Diana on the head with the knuckles of his hand. He said, "You ready. You ready." I thought it was a statement, she thought it was a question.

Leo let his chin fall to the left. He turned toward me. With pointer and middle finger, he thumped me hard and rhythmically on the forehead. "I'm going to take that brain of yours and give it a new home—in the skull of the Frankenstein monster," he said. He had said this many times. It had become one of the choruses of our life. The doctors thought this was the stroke talking, but I knew it wasn't. I would say something he would call off-the-wall, something I would describe as out-of-the-box, and he would say, "I'm going to take this brain of yours and give it a new home in the skull of the Frankenstein monster." I have no idea what he meant by this. We were running out of time for me to know. He was thumping my head, over and over. I was ready for him to say the words, to sing the chorus. He kept thumping. I thought maybe the stroke was talking in that silence. Finally he spoke: "Little heifer, I guess you get to keep your brain."

"I'm going to need it," I said.

He smiled and said, "A boy." It was not a question. It was a declaration, a dying declaration. He closed his eyes as if he were trying to remember something important. A sound went strange.

"You killed him," Diana accused. I said nothing. She repeated, "You killed him."

"I guess it's going to be a boy," I said.

We heard one of the old licensed practical nurses whisper, "Ruint."

Diana and I, we fell into friendship in college. Between our daddy dying and my son being born, it was easy to do. As children, half-siblings, we had not found friendship. Her mother, Portia, hated my mother, Lena. Portia hated Lena for her light skin and for her arrogant walk and for stealing Leo from her arms. Diana hated me because Lena had thrown her infant self out of Leo's arms to place me in them. And I hated Diana because her mother, Portia, loved her and she got our daddy all the time. I would say she was too fortunate, except she shared her good fortune so freely. Immediately upon seeing that I needed her friendship, Diana gave it to me. I was the last, best piece of our daddy she had left.

As I said, we fell into friendship in college. Between how much we knew about each other and how much was secret there was this electric space, and I liked to get down in it. She was always there.

I had two lives. One helped me hold on to the other. In one life, after freshman year, I lived in Eliot House, down by the river in a sturdy brick pentagon enclosing a courtyard overlooked by a clock-tower of gilded gold and sky-rivaling blue. Diana's suite was on the third floor. I was actually assigned to a room up at Radcliffe in a house then called North. The name has since been changed, but I didn't live there. I lived in Eliot, in the suite Diana shared, up three flights of stairs. In another life, in another city, in Detroit, I was the negligent mama who sometimes visited and seldom sent for her son. Sometimes I would sneak my son Pushkin up for a weekend and give him a nap on my bed. But he always went back. Later in the week, it would feel good to rest in the bed that had held him. This was good enough; it had to be. Diana said so.

What exactly did Diana say? She said so many things, even before he was born. I remember standing amid the green and brown geometry of Harvard Yard, not far from the statue of John Harvard, think-

32

ing I would borrow from my Diana money for an abortion. Then I caught the scent of her. Her strength allowed me to be strong. She laughed. And I laughed with her.

It changed things.

I would call him Pushkin. Pushkin X and I were transferring to the University of the District of Columbia.

But I didn't.

Pushkin was born bright and early on a June morning in the District of Columbia.

I birthed my son in Washington. I wanted my mother to be the first to see the child. She took the cigarette from her mouth and said, "A daughter's a daughter the rest of your life. A son's a son until he takes a wife." I thought she might be trying to rise to the occasion. Then she said, "I am the mother of an unwed black teen mother, the grandmother of a bastard." I said nothing. "You're just doing this to embarrass me." Again I said nothing. Embarrassing her was just a side benefit. "You can't keep this baby," she said. I had finally managed to get under my mother's skin.

After all those years of her insisting that black people were all hoodlums and whores and worthless, I decided to let her be right. She was defeated.

Sometimes I think of Pushkin's birthplace as the Emerald City, a magical land of excitement. Sometimes I think of the Potomac, the river that runs through it, as my River Styx, and Washington is just a place where I forgot what I would need to remember, what I am only remembering now.

I was an eighteen-year-old with a one-month-old baby and a day-old plan when Diana arrived. She arrived in response to the plan. My plan was to transfer to UDC, the University of the District of Columbia, get some kind of job, get some kind of apartment, and somehow get on with my life in an environment where lots and lots of girls with babies were trying to move on with theirs. I would be part of a group. Be like the group. Diana, who had jitterbugged around poverty all her life, didn't see the romance in the thing at all.

"Won't work, baby girl. Nothing easy gonna work. Maybe nothing gonna work. For sure, nothing easy."

I was annoyed, with her, with myself, but mostly with the baby.

Diana wanted Pushkin to go to Harvard with us. With a half-pint of scotch in her, she believed we could do anything. I knew I couldn't. Walking around D.C. was embarrassing my mother. Walking around Cambridge was embarrassing myself. I would go to UDC. Diana drank her second half-pint and figured out that I needed to take Pushkin back to Detroit, where the family could keep a watch on him. I said I'd see. I thought, She's drinking too hard.

Classes at UDC start before classes at Harvard. I went one morning to register and threw up all afternoon. I was a brat and I had a brat. I was embarrassed beyond my ability to think. It wasn't going to work. I called Diana. Diana said, "Get on the next thing flying."

I remember many things I would like to forget. I remember a day when I was eighteen years old when I took my baby in arms to a house, a semiprosperous two-family house with a postage-stamp lawn. I didn't pay the respect of attention to those two boys throwing a football or to the three-month-old in the grass between them, a dark black baby with immense purple-black eyes: Quimby. I didn't think a thing about those two boys in blue too-big faux pro jerseys, throwing the ball. As I walked up the walk to the house, did I bother to look those boys in the face? I only remember the baby-wash odor rising off my son, rising into the air through which the football flew.

It was my first venture into the world with my boy and I was leaving him stranded. I didn't know it yet, but I was. I know it now. When I replay the scene in my mind, I know it. When I remember his weight in my arms as I shuffled up the walk, my shoes, postpartum, too big for my feet, I see the spiral of the ball flying through the air but don't see the arc. His first rainbow. I know now what I did not know then. I had no idea at all that those little boys would be the face of the world for my infant son, no idea at all. If I had known, I would not have left him there.

I left him in the cracked-sidewalk world of black Detroit of my own early childhood and went off to Harvard. The divide I created that day I have filled with tears, tears that invite me to drown and tears that invite me to swim.

But maybe you never truly leave anything behind. Two of those boys I didn't see that day, Tyrone and Quimby, are coming to the wedding. They are invited. They are even welcome to bring some footballs for Pushkin to sign, which they can sell when they get back to Detroit. I'm sure Mrs. Perkins would be invited if she were living. So would Dwayne, except he's dead. How is it that Pushkin remembers them? I wish I had dropped Pushkin on his head. I wish he had developed amnesia. Why does he have to remember what will do neither of us good?

What do I remember?

Mrs. Perkins was "shocked as shit" to see us on her doorstep, when Diana told the story. She liked to tell the story.

"I'm Diana."

"I know who you is."

"Then you know why I'm here."

Mrs. Perkins didn't look like she knew any such thing. Diana just pushed on through the aluminum screen door and I pushed on after her, carrying my weight of Pushkin all wrapped up in cotton, then wool. He hated the feel of wool against his skin. A soft layer, then a warm layer. I took care of him like that, holding on to details: a soft layer, then a warm one. One foot in front of the other. Don't hit the baby. Don't throw him across the room. Be sweet. Speak nice. A soft layer, then a warm layer. We'd gotten through eighty-nine days.

My brain was bruised with holding on—squeezing so hard to facts, squeezing harder still on sanity, all my thoughts were bloody. Do you know what it feels like to have a dream so overdue you wake up in the morning and the dream is killing you? Ever try to lie down in your night, try to rest your head, somehow to discover you can't get easy in your bed? I remember that. Pregnancy gave me a son and a metaphor.

More than rape, pregnancy blots out innocence. A rape can last just ten minutes. Pregnancy is ten months long. Everyone says it's nine months. But it's forty weeks, and that is ten months. Mrs. Perkins was peeking into my bundle, peeking in and smiling. Pushkin didn't smile back, but he squirmed as if he wanted to.

Diana plopped down into an upholstered chair. It squeaked. There was some kind of plastic casing zipped around the cushion. "At least Pushkin won't mess up the furniture," remarked Diana to no one in particular. Of course not. We weren't staying long enough for that. I was just discovering the sublime qualities of projectile vomiting; strange prides mothers develop. Pushkin didn't seem to aim, but he had a way of reaching out and touching whatever or whoever was most seddity in a room. There was no one for him to vomit on in this room. Diana shifted in her seat; the chair squeaked again. She said nothing. Perhaps she was waiting for Mrs. Perkins to begin.

Cotton candy. My thoughts no longer felt bruised, they felt airy and falsely sweet. In my cotton-candy fog I could see my baby's toes. Little sausage toes. These fat little brown things: one, two, three, four, five, six, seven, eight, nine, ten brown things. Good enough to eat. A wave of nausea struck me. I was a cannibal mother. I wanted to devour my sweet baby's toes. Foreign crazy thought. Foreign crazy thought. This was my alarm mantra. On the other side of the cotton candy, Diana was talking. I could listen to her. I could listen to my sister and hold the baby. If we didn't leave this room, if she kept talking, I could listen to my sister and hold the baby and we would be all right.

The nausea began to subside. I loved Pushkin. It was not a tenet but the body of my faith. I looked at Diana and Mrs. Perkins. They were negotiating. The stakes were high. The room was hot. I unwrapped my bundle. Why did I do that? Pushkin started in to hollering.

I wanted to put him down and walk away. Put him down gently. Walk away quickly. It seemed so much like the best that I could do. What I wished my own mama had done. Put me down gently. Walk away quickly. That was better than she could do. *First, do no harm.* And me, what was my best? Pushkin was howling louder than I thought little lungs would allow. Mrs. Perkins rose. She walked over, calm, curious, as if whatever it was he wanted, she was about to give it to him and he was about to smile. As if this hollering could be a good thing.

It occurred to me that Mrs. Perkins was crazy. Diana was looking impatient, as if she expected me to quiet the baby or expected Mrs. Perkins to do it quicker. Mrs. Perkins took Pushkin from my hands. I should have snatched him back and run out her overornate front door. This was the day my life took a wrong turn. This is the day that haunts me now.

Pushkin stopped crying. I think Mrs. Perkins made him a little bottle of sugar water. Days of trying had taught me that I couldn't do any better, differently but not better. I had tried to breast-feed him. I couldn't do it. Couldn't find any way to let the milk flow and my love flow at the same time. Trying to let him latch on with his little mouth, I would start turning to stone. Too much for the body to feel, too much for the heart to feel, too much. So I bought him some soy-based formula and smiled as he sucked on that. I laid him on my belly to feed. I wanted him to have something. I wanted to give him something—just not me.

Mrs. Perkins held herself as if she wanted the baby to take something from her, take something of her. I began to remember Mrs. Perkins, remember the times I had met her before. I remember hearing Aunt Sara lavish her with praise for the way she kept Sara's son, Simon. I remember seeing Mrs. Perkins the summers I spent in Detroit with my daddy. She was what some white folks call a fixture, a domestic servant so familiar as to recede toward invisibility. Back then, she lived in a two-family factory worker's flat just a hop, skip, and a jump from Spady's corner store. Then, all of a sudden, we never heard anything more about Mrs. Perkins. She vanished, and I guess I guessed she had had a stroke. Back in the days when all the black women I knew to vanish stroked out.

I watched Diana watch Mrs. Perkins watch Pushkin. Diana was making some kind of evaluation, sizing her up. Mrs. Perkins was a tall woman with a straight-up-and-down bigness. She didn't carry fat. She carried muscle, and she didn't cook bacon. She cooked steak—with eggs and grits—for breakfast, with juice. And somehow she had come up in the world. I remember visiting her house a few times in the late sixties, coming to pick up or drop off Simon, my cousin she watched. Back then she lived in the downstairs apartment of a two-family flat. Now she lived out Seven Mile Road in a neighborhood of single-family homes with faux gothic ironwork and faux Tudor triangular roofs. From the crumbs and spatters and the jars and tins on the kitchen table, I could see she still ate anchovies and crackers, still drank papaya juice and ginger ale. She had moved out of Black Bottom, but Black Bottom was still in her.

Diana cleared her throat. "Hit the number big, Mrs. Perkins?"

Mrs. Perkins grunted, shaking her head, turning away from Diana.

"You'd a heard about it."

"That's Sara's nephew."

"Great-nephew."

"We're the nieces."

"I know who you is. Ain't yo daddy died? And one of you banged up."

"I'm the banged-up chick," I said.

I said this and some D.C. schoolyard joke started playing and replaying in my mind: "Ain't, ain't Jemima on a pancake box?" asks the playground inquisitor, and you say nothing and the kids taunt, "Don't you know nothing at all? Ain't you done ever seen a pancake box?" You've seen that brown and beaming face on the box and you don't know what she has to do with you, then or now, but you know the answer, you always know the answer at school, so you are not even scared when you say yes. And all the kids shake in their tennies, laughing at you and pointing. "Aunt Jemima's yo' mama. Aunt Jemima your mama," and you know that you don't even have the sense to be as embarrassed as you're supposed to be.

Pushkin will never hear that joke. They've changed the pancake boxes. Aunt Jemima had a makeover. Aunt Sara had a breakdown. And now Mrs. Perkins wore little pearl earrings. I wondered if they were fake. I wondered if she stole some real ones from her employer.

"Who's this baby's daddy?"

I wished the baby in the bunting was my daddy's. This was a strange thought. Not mine and some unnamed creature's Daddy would have stabbed and gutted while smiling. I didn't answer. Diana filled my silence.

"We need you to watch Pushkin."

"Too old for that now."

"You've been paid. No choice but do the work."

Diana rose to her feet and rocked back on her heels. She made a show of looking around. "Just three years. Summers and many weekends off," said my sister. Mrs. Perkins said nothing.

"I don't think this is going to work," I yelped.

"You got money for day care?"

"No."

"Miz Perkins's sharper than she lets on. He'll be fine."

"You can't leave yo' troubles here."

"Read your cards, Miz Perkins."

"What you think I'm holding?"

"An empty jacket."

Mrs. Perkins lifted her chin. She was defiant, determined, defeated. "I guess I know payback when I see it."

"Teach that to him."

That's how it began. My half-sister blackmailed a robber-woman into taking care of my son. Extraordinary problems need extraordinary solutions. Negroes who survive to thrive evidence extremely original adaptations to life.

"When will you bring him?" Mrs. Perkins asked.

"Today," Diana responded.

I surprised us all by yelping again. Pushkin hollered again, louder.

"We're leaving him today," Diana said. This time she was talking to me.

She wouldn't tell me again. I knew this about her. What she wanted to give, she offered. "This is not a restaurant," she said about herself. "I am a family kitchen." You ate what she put on your plate — or you ate somewhere else.

I needed a break from this baby. Diana would have preferred for me not to need to leave Pushkin. But I did, and she was dealing with it. She would have preferred that we rent a little apartment off-campus, someplace "real sharp," and raise Pushkin up under us. She thought we could handle it. I knew I couldn't.

Diana said lack of confidence smells like blood and draws the sharks toward you in the water and the bears toward you in the woods. If I could fly, I would wonder what this smelly lack of mine brings toward you in the air. I can't fly. I can barely walk and don't know if I can still swim and there are sharks and bears all around me now. I want my own glass of papaya juice and ginger ale.

I stepped toward Pushkin. I took the little booty Diana had knitted off his little foot and I kissed his little toes. Diana and I, we walked out Mrs. Perkins's door. My sister whispered in my ear, "He won't remember that you left, he'll remember that you came back." We were so young.

Diana and I taxied out to Metro. I was waking up. "How are you making her do this?" I asked. I asked because I needed to know. I didn't want Diana to have done anything extreme or evil, certainly nothing extremely evil.

" 'Member when Perkins used to keep Simon for Sara? 'Member that coat that used to hang in the hall?"

This is the beginning of a long story. That coat was Sara's bank. She kept thousands and thousands of dollars in that coat, and after a while maybe it was tens and tens of thousands. Mrs. Perkins robbed Sara. Took the money and the coat.

"How do you know all this?" I asked.

"Sara. There was more than a hundred thousand dollars."

"Whose money?"

"Sara thought it was hers."

A sliver, just a sliver, of the money that passed through Spady's corner store Sara siphoned off for herself. On all the Now and Laters and Good & Plentys, all the Jack Daniel's and Jim Beam, on every kind of candy for every kind of child, on every kind of bottle for every kind of after-hours club, Sara imposed her tax. Spady was branching out of numbers. This was Sara's idea, and it was fortified with Sara's labor. She felt justified in taking her sliver. Spady would not see it this way.

Spady would have had to enforce strict discipline. He would have had to for sure kill Mrs. Perkins, or how would any numbers bank be safe? How would little old walnut-faced ladies walk thousands of dollars safely down the block in Kroger sacks if he let anybody get away with robbery? A good beating would have to have been enough for Sara.

The thing, the only thing, that would have kept Spady from killing Sara was knowing that if he killed her, her brother, Leo, our daddy, would kill him. And then maybe one of Spady's crew would kill Leo.

Turning my mind back to this place gets me thinking about the song Tanya played me in the car after our first Martha's lunch, Tupac singing "Breathing," and I don't even want to like rap. But eighteen months in the company, even the sporadic company, of Tanya gets you exposed. This year for my birthday she and Pushkin gave me a two-CD Tupac set. It had "Breathing" on it and "Happy Home." "Happy Home" completely irritated me. It had a line celebrating moving out of his mom's house. I found the lyric threatening. I started switching the station whenever I got into Pushkin's car. There is only so much Fifty Cent I can listen to. My heart is conflicted on the subject of gangsters.

Sara was married to a gangster and knew about unacceptable risks. She knew she had to take the hit. She took it in a feminine fashion; she absorbed her loss.

"Miz Perkins plays life like we play chess," said Diana. "Boldly. You got to admire that. She was good to Simon and she didn't really hurt anybody. Coulda but didn't. It's strange how life kinda works out."

Worked out because a mama kept her mouth shut. If the truth had outed, someone would have died. Outlaw life is severe.

We boarded the plane from Detroit to Boston. We were wearing complementary ensembles Diana had run up for us: shiny silk tailor-made shifts topped with tailor-made swing coats, traveling outfits the Supremes might have worn in their heyday. Somebody had left the suits at the dry cleaners' and Diana had altered them to fit us.

As I have remembered that day, the day I left my son in the care of an old robber-woman, the moments unfold with studied cautiousness. I did this because that happened. That happened and I did this. But it wasn't like that. We were in a big hurry. I had an almost-three-month-old and I was sick and tired. Of him and me. Me more than him. I was empty. Outplayed. I had had the baby at least in part to upset my mother, and she had already forgotten about me and the baby. The baby cried, and I could hear his sobs becoming muffled in my ears. The baby wailed, and the muscles girdling my eyeballs relaxed until my retinas lost focus and everything came hazy. The baby wailed, and I willed the baby to disappear. I couldn't stand my vanishing sight; I rushed to give Pushkin away, rushed to give him away before I became blind to him. Diana wished I was better than that, but I wasn't. The baby cried and I did that. The baby cried and she did this.

Mrs. Perkins kept my son for three years. They ate canned anchovies and soda crackers in Detroit while I ate granola and yogurt in Cambridge. Mrs. Perkins and I grew close over time. Sometimes I would fly in for the weekend. Eventually she told me about robbing Sara. It was something about the money just hanging there. And she didn't think Sara needed it. Sara had Spady. Mrs. Perkins had nobody. She hated the idea of the money coming from the money they made providing liquor to after-hours clubs. Miz Perkins didn't drink. She got over that hate. Hated the way Sara called it her "pussy tax." Mrs. Perkins never got over that. Sara would keep the small bills in the coat, then change them to larger and larger denominations. Miz Perkins watched all that. One day she just took the coat off the hook, walked into a bank, and emptied out Sara's pockets.

Over time I got scared for Mrs. Perkins. I had come to care for her. If Spady ever discovered Mrs. Perkins had his money, he would kill her once for distressing Sara and kill her twice for taking what was his.

What was mine, I gave away freely.

FOUR

I WANT PUSHKIN BACK.

I am starting to hate Tanya. I can pick my reasons. One would be for stealing my own Tanya's name. Would Pushkin the poet hate me for giving Pushkin the football player his name? Am I a thief? When I claimed the poet's name, what did I steal to bestow upon my son? Can I begrudge a living girl a dead dog?

Can a tart be a madeleine? Can I forgive Tanya for evoking a discarded memory? Let me slow down!

My Tanya was a white toy poodle who preferred to wear a turquoise turtleneck sweater rather than her red raincoat with black piping. She slept on the second pillow of my girlhood double bed (faux French Provincial painted white and trimmed in gray-blue). When I rolled over onto her in my sleep, she startled me awake with snaps and snarls.

Whenever I say "Pushkin and Tanya" I think of my dark prince walking a teeny-tiny intelligent poodle wearing a turquoise sweater. And when I think of a tall dark man walking a tiny white poodle, the term *ferocious fluffball* comes to mind and I have to laugh at myself. And when I start to laugh at myself, I know that Pushkin's right: I'm thinking too much.

Tanya lived with me in Detroit, where my bed had a canopy. Later, after flying in the cold, unpressurized belly of a plane in a crate-cell, she lived with me in Washington, where my bed had no canopy. The frame to support the canopy had been inadvertently incinerated. I remember my mother's laugh and shrug. Carelessness was an aspect of Lena's glamour. Fierce loyalty was an aspect of the dog's. I loved Tanya in a singular fashion.

The fiancée/lap dancer cannot be named Tanya. I will not call her Tanya. It is too unfortunate.

Pushkin has renounced my aesthetic.

He would never own a poodle. Elvis, Whitefolks, and Tanya. Poodles figure large in my life. Each of them was whelped in Detroit. I respect the beauty of Detroit poodles. Pushkin thinks poodles are prissy and ridiculous. Pushkin never met my Tanya. Lena put Tanya "to sleep" the week Pushkin was born.

Three months ago I invited Pushkin and his Tanya to dinner to discuss the wedding. This was when I was still invited. Can it be as long ago as that since he has spoken civilly to me? She arrived wearing I-need-my-sunglasses-bright Lilly Pulitzer beach-print pants and a turquoise sleeveless silk Lilly turtleneck in January. A joke started to take form in my brain involving the proper noun *Tanya*, the noun *bitch*, and the articles indicating possession. I was certain the joke would not be appreciated. I silently amused myself.

Margot's, in East Nashville, across the river from my home and my university, is one of my favorite spots. It's near Adelphia Stadium, where Pushkin performs on Sundays; near Demonbreun's cave, where the first white native of Nashville was born; near Shelby Bottoms, sheltering the charred remains of an old plantation. Margot's has become our crossroads. Sometimes when I bike through Shelby Bottoms along the river, I imagine I can hear the baby's cries rising above the sound of water rushing over rock. Louder than the cries I hear the screams of his mother. Her voice, her birthing screams, resound through my head, reminding me of someone else's from my long-ago past, my dearly loved aunt Martha Rachel.

Margot's is a funky place. There's something about the building that suggests it might once have been a service station. Across the road is the High Bar. This is a good thing. Instead of eating dessert, you can ramble across the road and hear dark and gritty music in a dank and dirty club with glass windows that let the night in. The High Bar is the best bar in Nashville. This is convenient. After dinner with Pushkin, I often need a drink.

Our group is seated downstairs, prominently at the front table, visible to passersby. We are in one of the handful of tables sandwiched in front of the open kitchen between the ladderlike staircase leading to the second-story dining loft and a glass wall directly next to Margot's bar.

I keep glancing over at Margot, who has her hair tied up in a bandana like a mammy rag. Her scrubbed-clean, pale face is peacefully concentrated by preparation. She calms me. This is the New South. White folks at the stove, black folks at the table. We are further than geography from old plantation land. Or in this case, black and white folks at the table—and this is newer still.

Margot's, like Martha's, is one of the new chef-owned bistros beginning to speckle the suburban South, challenging the sovereignty of peppery hot chicken, steaming green beans, fatback kale, of corn bread and yeast rolls, of tea punch and congealed salad—challenging the sovereignty of meat and three (meat and three sides or vegetables) as the preeminent expression of eating in community with strangers.

The meal is going well. I have acquiesced to the inevitable; there is soon to be a wedding. Tanya was not a lap dancer in Russia. She has had some education. She has some conversation. She is amusing. This may not be an absolute disaster. I've spent some time with her and think it might work. Certainly I have survived worse. Then she asks Pushkin, "Is your father coming to the wedding?"

She is eating a winter vegetable soup made with fresh vegetable broth. I know because I am eating it too. The soup is finished off with a kind of onion marmalade. Tanya's spooning it in so quickly now that her question stays in the air. Pushkin has put down his fork.

Coffee shops, cafés, lunch counters, restaurants, are peculiarly important to the South. In the North, workers took blows to the head to defend their right to work for a living wage. In the South, students took blows to the head to defend their right to eat a hamburger next to somebody of a different color eating the same red meat.

I try hard to think about this. I try hard to think of anything but the question Tanya the bitch, but not Tanya my female dog, has left hanging in the air: "Is your father coming?"

Pushkin doesn't answer this question the first time he hears it. We both ignore it. I am sure it will disappear. It has always disappeared. The question is reliable that way. Then it emerges again, and this time Pushkin answers with a question of his own: "Are we inviting him, Windsor?" I stir my soup with my spoon. This is not quite polite. I think about the sugared fruit that Natalia spooned into the poet Pushkin's mouth as his time ran out. I wonder what words he had for the children he was so soon to leave half orphaned. I have the same words for my son—none.

"I would like to meet your father," says Tanya.

"So would I," says Pushkin.

Pushkin is looking good. He is handsome and he is well built. People would notice him if he were not famous. And he is famous. We are sitting at the front table in the window. He has trained us both to keep our voices down in public, to keep our faces mute. We are well trained. Still, Pushkin's eyes survey the faces of our fellow diners, looking to see if any one of those feasting on his celebrity from a distance, on the excitement of eating in the same place, eating at the same time, as the Phenom, have noticed the change at our table. There is a change at our table. Pushkin and I both see it. The creature Tanya is too sated to notice. Well fed, well fucked, well kept, she is too content... grateful... distracted? Too something to notice anything but Pushkin. Too something I have never been.

No one but Pushkin and I has noticed anything other than what Pushkin ordered. Three quarters of the customers have ordered what he ordered—duck. Soon that dish will be gone. When did he start eating duck? There is a ghetto champagne having nothing to do with fowl called cold duck. Is this what he recalls, lifting the crispy skin to his mouth? He says, "They don't barbecue in Nashville. Meat's too dry or the meat's too soft. Sauce too peppery. Closest I can get to Motown ribs in Nashville is Margot's duck."

I want to laugh, but I do not. Pushkin will think I am laughing at him. And he won't know why. I am laughing at his ability to translate one essence into another. I am laughing at myself for rocking him to sleep intoning "Two plus two equals four, eight divided by two equals four," and now Motown ribs equal Music City duck. Crisp, savory, and sweet equals crisp, savory, and sweet, does not equal soft and sweet. Pushkin is an able translator. He perceives the identity that must be conveyed. Crisp, Savory, and Sweet. Strange the canvases he chooses to manifest his discernment. The outside of good barbecue is crisp, inside the meat is soft and savory, and the sauce is sweet. He was such a strange child, and I have filled him with eccentricities.

And yet he has managed to transform into the simplest of stereotypes—strong black body, black athlete.

What does he fear the other patrons might see? I see what they cannot see. I see vulnerability. They can't see that. They see nothing except the hot white girl curling into his arm, extraordinary muscle, extraordinary beauty. They see that. He turns to me with a question. "Or have I met him already?"

What did Pushkin the poet say as he lay dying? Did he say, "Why have I done this thing?" Or did he say something far more labyrinthine? Did he say, "You would have had to be me to step out in that street, to lift that pistol against that man and not imagine the possibility of a funeral shroud at journey's end"? Did he say, "But I am me and I did not think life would come to death now"? Did he say, "It is worth dying to know you desire me"? To whom was he speaking?

And me, what did I imagine when I chose to let the embryo growing in me live, chose to allow him to be born half orphaned, like Pip? I laughed when he was born about just one thing. I laughed because he was born with a caul veiling his face. I laugh now to think of all my great expectations for this fatherless boy with a childish mother. And here, all these many years later, remembering the vestigial membrane that veiled his face and soiled the early pages of my favorite Dickens—one detail too visceral. Or was it as dark ladies in flowered dresses on front porches in metal chairs used to say, "Born with the veil, see beyond and behind"? Or was it as Du Bois feared, the black race is "shut out from their world by a vast veil"? I think beyond W.E.B. to the statue down at Tuskegee of Booker T. Washington lifting the veil of ignorance from the crouching slave's face. Again the veil. My son was born with a veil. Outside of books, outside of the nineteenth century, I do not know how to get even a few pennies for his veil. Unsold it remained, and now he is exhausted of it. He is tearing his veil off. He thinks it is time for nakedness.

He wants a name. Silently I try to cobble a translation. Tanya wants dessert. Someone wants an autograph. Bowls of coffee appear before us.

Pushkin waves the waiter over. He reads the bill. He insists on paying. He's making money now. More than regular money. He has a crocodile wallet. How can you be twenty-two years old and exhausted? Tanya looks exhausted now. Was I exhausted then? When I was twenty-two and he was four? Be my child. I have exhausted him. No, worse than that, I have bored him. I want to cry. I want to tell him that Negroes who survive to thrive exhibit highly original adaptations to life. I have told him this before. He shakes his head. I say nothing. He says, "Moms, you think too much." Pushkin signs the check, throws a wad of bills on the table for a tip. Tanya squeezes my hand as if she didn't mean to get me in trouble and she's sorry. I try to find the gesture patronizing.

We have had this discussion a number of times, Pushkin and I. He asked me the question before his engagement to Tanya, before he met Tanya, always in private, not even in front of Gabriel. On more than one occasion he asked me at the Sunset Grill, with Paul Harmon paintings (cheerful, sensual, dashes and patches of color) hanging on the wall and Randy Rayburn beaming at the door.

Gabriel and I eat at Sunset every week, but it's been more than two years since I last sat across from Pushkin at Sunset. The last time it was as if we were squared off for battle on some chessboard. I was at a disadvantage. I have no sense of space, I have no antenna that allows me to navigate distances with intelligence. He has the ability. I see him. I know he is going to make a move, but I don't know in what direction. I know he's going to win and I can't participate. We were talking about an upcoming game, and then he asked me about his father. I did what I've always done: said nothing. He sat back in his chair and watched me, not staring, not pleading, just watching. I remained mute. I was uncomfortable. Then he leaned forward and reached toward my face, extending his fingers toward me, batting back locks of my curls, tangling the tips of his fingers in my hair, pushing the springy tendrils behind my ear.

"What?" I snarled.

"You should get a haircut."

"When you were a baby you used to pull it out in baby handfuls."

"Miz Perkins used ta unwind strands of your hair from around my fingers."

"I don't remember that."

"You're too young to jump old, Moms."

"I'm not too young."

"We're the same, Moms."

"I'm an old woman and you're a young man."

"Eighteen years. We're the same generation."

"I'm your mother."

"I've gone with women older'n you."

"Somehow I don't find that reassuring."

"I didn't say it to reassure you."

"Thank you, Pushkin."

"I sat here to reassure you."

"Thank you, Pushkin."

"Welcome."

"Who?"

"Some lady who loved the desert."

"A lady who loved the desert?"

"A trainer in a spa in southwest Utah."

"Older than me?"

"She, like you, was looking good."

"What she like?"

"What would she be like?"

"Smart."

"Beautiful."

He reached toward me again. He separated a single strand from a lock tumbling toward my face. He grasped the strand between his pointer and thumb and began winding the hair around his finger. It hurt. He's so big it felt cruel and scary. He's my boy and I didn't know what it meant. I closed my eyes. I remember the pull. I remember little soft weak hands grabbing up for me, all the weight of his little body tugging with those chubby, stubby fingers, claiming me by some blood birthright, yanking the very hairs from the head he claims as his. I opened my eyes and wondered if he remembers this at all. Or does he only remember Perkins telling him that she unwound the hair from his fingers so the blood would flow and they wouldn't fall off? Does he remember my being there? Or does he only remember what Perkins told him about the aftermath of my visits?

Pushkin stroked the side of my cheek as if I were a baby and he were trying to feed me, trying to provoke me to root.

"In the religion of football, the black mama is an icon."

"Of highest significance."

"It's a good thing my religion is football, where the black mama is elevated beyond examination."

"You could forgive me."

"But then somebody would win and that would mean it was just a game."

"Will you leave me tickets? Maybe I'll come see you tomorrow."

"Not if it's maybe."

I ended up going to the game. Even then I needed to do something to atone for my inability to speak. I went to the game and I sat with Renita. I am jealous of Renita. I am jealous of a brownie-colored woman with curling-iron burns scarring her forehead and Vaselined tendrils plastered to her cheeks, whose son rarely gets to walk onto the field. She walks with her feet splayed, toes pointing out, one hand caressing an ear, one hand rubbing an eyebrow. When she smiles, she has the most perfect teeth I have ever seen. She smiles a lot, flashing the crowns her prince bought her. During the games she drinks Pepsi after Pepsi—always straight from the can—and she never gets fat. I am jealous of this as well. And I'm jealous of the way she seems able to watch the game when I can only watch my boy. I never know the score. I only know the points Push earned, the plays Push made, or the fumbles he caused. I resent the surety she has that her ambitions are fulfilled. She reached the pinnacle of her ambition the day her son signed his first NFL contract. His best days are long behind him. She has more than everything she ever wanted. She is richer than me. Every boy she knows idolizes her son. Every man she knows wants to be him. Everyone she knows understands how the game he plays works. She has no colleagues to be vaguely embarrassed by his immensity in a tight, too-vivid uniform, no colleagues who make uneasy jokes about coliseums and lions and Christians, no neighbors who turn their noses up at tickets she can't use and wants to get rid of. Renita has no tickets she wants to get rid of. Renita's always scamming tickets off somebody—she always knows one more person who just gots to see Teddy do that Teddy thang, if he gets to do it. Who do I know who wants to see my boy play? Renita never blinks back tears of fear to see her son walking down the field, to see him walking onto the field. She always knows what to say to the other mothers—they like her and invite her to go shopping with them at the mall or take over the soft chairs in the hotel lobby after a win. You never see Teddy out on the field looking for her up in the stands. He just knows she is there. Just like he knows she has no place else to go. Push thinks I have better places to go. I am jealous of Renita.

I went to the game that day and drank coffee up in the stands. Renita kept up a swirl of talk about my head. She likes me 'cause I'm usually good for some tickets. She and I turn our attention to the field. I come rarely because I care in some strange way too much.

I cannot watch with detachment Pushkin tackling his man. I have heard commentators on television talk about his tackling, and I have heard men he has pulled into the ground talk about it. One player said simply, "He claimed me." I want him to do that to me. I want him to claim me. How do I get that when I cannot suit up and walk onto the field? I must get that without suiting up and walking onto a field.

It is painful for me to watch him. I went only because I couldn't give him what he really wanted. It was a stopgap measure. It held for two years and then some. I want him to claim me, but he has again put this question I can't answer between us.

. . .

49

A few days after our Margot's debacle, about three months ago, Pushkin called me for lunch. I suggested Vandyland—a haven of the bland. He suggested Prince's Hot Chicken. A few hours later, I'm sitting in a splintery booth drinking purple Nehi between bites of peppered poultry. Another meal turns into an express train to Detroit. Washing down hot chicken with a carbonated drink is like throwing water on a grease fire—you create an explosion. In the case of hot chicken and Nehi, an explosion of fiery herbs and sweetness. Once I ate hot chicken with Gabriel. Walking out, he grabbed me and kissed my cheek. My cheek stung where his mouth touched me, my waist stung where his fingers touched me. Prince's chicken is hot. Nonconnoisseurs are warned not to attempt to accompany their meals with soda. If you didn't grow up on it, you should stick to milk or flat water. I can just about stand the blast. The pleasure evoked by the intensity of the hot and cold sweet and spicy loosens the tongue like liquor. The whole thing, including the woman with a head full of rollers in the next booth, is much too real for truth not to be said. I am far too busy trying to manage the heat to hear all of what Pushkin has said to me. I'm just glad to be with him in this place, glad I'm with him in this place because he makes it safe. Nobody off the field would think of trying to hurt the Phenom. No Nashvillian, at least.

He breaks through my pleasure/pain fog with a question. "What the fuck you want with me?"

"You tell me."

"No other motherfucker in the NFL or the NBA puts up with this shit."

"Nice word choice."

"You're a fucking archaic artifact of a mother."

"Who's fucking offended by your bastard language."

"You fucking taught me to cuss."

"I taught you to use your words."

"And gave me so many of them."

"Which you refuse to use."

"I ain't nothing but what you wanted me to be."

"I don't even remember what I wanted."

"The smartest little boy in the world."

"That's what I said?"

"Over and over . . ."

"You were . . ."

"What?"

"Worthy of the name Pushkin X."

"You told me I was conceived from some descendant of Push-kin's."

"You believed me?"

"No."

"You were the smartest little boy in my world."

"Were . . ."

"I don't know who you are."

"You don't know who you are."

"What?"

"You do not know anything that is not in a book. You probably keep the Kama Sutra by your bed . . ."

"You are insane."

"Who- or whatever the fuck I am wants your blessing."

"No."

"Break off a little piece of your love and give it to her. For me."

"I'm taking back what I gave you."

"You're gonna stop loving me?"

"I'm gonna try."

"Then give me back my fucking invitation."

He reaches across the table and grabs my shoulder as if to hold me before I disappear. His fingers hurt. Bad. Tears are in my eyes.

"Sorry."

I am silent.

"You're trying not to love me?"

I remain silent.

"Bring on the howling wilderness."

"Exit pursued by bear."

"You're fucking crazy."

We finish the meal in silence. Pushkin and I pile into his black Escalade. He mumbles along with Tupac singing, "Breathing . . . I'll be the last motherfucker breathing."

It isn't long before we're back in Hillsboro Village. Every time he drives through my neighborhood he says something about helping me and Gabriel get into something bigger. He says it this time, like throwing me a bone. I throw the bone back at his head. "I think one member of this family living in a McMansion is a sufficiency."

Pushkin lives in Brentwood. He lives in a gi-normous house he bought on almost no acreage. He's lived there almost three years. I don't believe this. It's just a fact I know.

"McMansion?" Pushkin quotes me back to me. Then he gets a funny look on his face. I almost expect him to lift up his finger and start thumping me on the head like my father did so many years ago. He does not say, "I'm going to take that brain of yours and give it a new home in the skull of the Frankenstein monster." He says something far scarier. He says, "I'm tired of being, I don't want to be, the son of, or the nephew of, or the grandson of any—" Then he stops. Sometimes Pushkin's words come slow and jerky. He runs like a pouring stream of water, and it's hard for me to tell if he's deliberating or vaulting over impediments. I can't tell if he can't find the word or is holding back the word he knows. Whichever way it is, the swift silence ends and he spits out, "Intellectual black boogie eccentrics." Or did he say "Eccentric black boogie intellectuals"?

If he had slapped me, it would have hurt less and surprised me no more. I wish I had never taught him to speak the English language. Then I remember that I didn't. He was taught by that other woman, and now she is claiming him, down all the distance.

I cannot allow this. I cannot figure out if in this moment I hate Pushkin or Mrs. Perkins or Tanya more. I should have challenged Mrs. Perkins to a duel. Same with Tanya. In fact, I am dueling now. I want to ask my son if he knows that the poet Pushkin died in a duel. I'm no longer sure he knows who the poet Pushkin is. It took Pushkin days to pass over. He bled for hours in his own apartment with his beautiful, untrusted wife. I wonder if I stand up, will he sack me? I wonder how his opponents feel. On top of it all, I wonder why in the fuck he didn't play basketball like my daddy. If he was going to be an athlete, why couldn't he have been an athlete? A Will Robinson–coached, Brewster Center–playing basketball player. How sad can I be? Where did this boy come from?

I am extinguished. I laugh. I guffaw. "How intellectual, bohemian, and eccentric to say so. Only the spawn of an intellectual black bohemian boogie eccentric would call his mother one." I laugh at my own joke. Pushkin doesn't. He stares as if he is seeing me for the very first time.

Then he leans across my body and pushes the truck door open. He isn't getting out. He isn't coming in. He is already on the interstate, headed south to the superior suburbs.

He bought a McMansion on what was once a cow pasture. It is landscaped with immature trees. He parks an SUV up a curling drive. His house says, "I am regular." He has stopped speaking to me at all. He gestures.

FIVE

WHY DIDN'T I CLAIM HIM THEN?

Why didn't I say, "Be my son"? Why didn't I say, I am not so very black, or intellectual, or eccentric. I am not boogie. I am actually bohemian. Be my son, my precious one. Dark as the sky on a moonless night. Dark as black velvet. Dark as eternity with eyes shining as bright as now. Dark as creation, dark as love, dark as layer upon layer must be. I was instructed by my mother to leave you in the hospital, instructed to leave you and go back to Cambridge and forget, forget and move forward, as always. As she knew I could, as she knew I should, as she knew I would. Mama ain't always right. The weight of life was in you, and you were dark as the ace of spades. I could not let you go.

Something of my history unknown to me was tattooed upon your skin, and I would not let you go. As I ached with love for you, my ambition sagged. It seemed more likely that I would one day be president of these United States than that I would be a good mother. Usually the apple don't fall too far from the tree; that's what I knew then.

I know something more now. Usually ain't always. Usually the apple don't fall too far from the tree, unless it falls upon a hillside and rolls. You were my hillside, and I come from a long line of fine rollers on my daddy's side.

I looked at you and saw those tiny fingers, saw you wiggle those miniature fat long fingers, and I thought, Let me be wrapped around those. Let them tease through my hair. Let them grab for my breast.

53

It was a shocking surrender. Let me be wound round your finger tight as my hair that you will soon grasp. Be my son.

Be my son. I am saying it again after all these years. I'm not sure I know you. You think you know me too well. Let us meet again. I am just a colored gal from Detroit City who sat on her father's shoulders and watched the Thanksgiving parade pass her by. I am a woman who was a girl awed by a department store dining-room dessert of an ice cream ball crowned with an ice cream cone, trimmed at the neck with meringue lace, chocolate drops forming the eyes and the mouth of a cone-hatted clown. I am the woman who was the girl awed by that trick. I prefer Vernor's ginger ale to champagne. How did I forget to make you a Friday plate of red snapper dredged in flour and fried in Crisco? Where, in all the glasses of champagne I have poured for you, was the cocktail of corner-store papaya juice and Michigan ginger ale? Where is your slice of juicy fruit from the plugged melon? What must I prepare for you to provoke the remembrance of my scent? Why have you moved to Brentwood?

What did I tell you about Pushkin?

Push, let me say it right—let me call you in the name you have chosen for yourself. Ain't that like my boy to christen himself—ain't it like Pushkin's own great-grandfather to possess a known name and more than a name: Jesus, Christ, Emmanuel; Abraham, Ibraham, Peter, Hannibal; Pushkin, Little Man, Push, Pea, My Boy, Sweet Pea. Sweet Pea, I can't call you that anymore. It belongs to her, to your dark, to the middle of your night. When you need it to be church, does she construct for you a temple, a time out of time, with her thighs and her whispers?

I cannot go further down this road of my imagining—even the possibilities belong to you and her, not to you and any former mommy. But I pray that together you create a territory in which time is erased and space expands. Have that power or veer away here, veer away from her.

And if you cannot build that temple, maybe it's not she who is the problem. Maybe it's I. Maybe my boy heard too much silence in the dark of my night. Or was it not enough? What do you remember about St. Petersburg?

You say you need the name of your father. I gave you Pushkin. I gave you Du Bois. I married Gabriel. How much more daddy do you want?

When do my sexual choices get liberated from your developmental needs, or should they never have been tied? How many mistakes have I made?

What did I tell you about Pushkin?

I know I told you about the duel. I remember that we saw his nightshirt stained with blood in a little house off a square in downtown St. Petersburg. Or did I see it later?

I told you he invented the modern Russian language. The way millions and millions of white men talk. I told you he invented the language of Tolstoy, the language of Chekhov and Nabokov, the language of Dostoyevsky. Of Turgenev, the language of *Fathers and Sons*.

Can you imagine the dimensions of his mind's geography? Pushkin had a mind as vast as Russia. Mother Russia. Father Pushkin. Did Pushkin love and admire the way Russia protects herself from invasions with her vastness and her cold? I know he did. I have emulated Mother Russia and felt his love, felt his admiration. You may violate her, you may wipe your feet upon her vulnerable Spring, nibble from the vine fruit of her abundant Summer, trampling fragile grasses, but you will not escape safely. You cannot reach Moscow and get out of Russia before winter. Your unburied but frozen bones will drape across her belly like so many sequins in a glistening belt of death adorning the lightness of her snow. You can violate Mother Russia, but it's your doom, not hers, you will conceive—at least it was so in the fairy tale I told Pushkin.

Push, does the vastness of you, the immensity of the territory covered by your speed and strength, have anything to do with the vastness of Pushkin's brain, the vastness of the Siberian plain, the vastness of my body undisciplined?

Why is Pushkin not enough? Pushkin has fed us and clothed us and housed us for many more years than football and far better than most fathers.

Do you remember that his mother's father's father was a slave given as a present to Czar Peter the Great? Do you remember that the czar, impressed by the intelligence of the slave, raised him to the nobility and gave him a noble wife? And that wife bore him a son, who was educated in France and in Russia, and that son's daughter spawned Pushkin? And Pushkin invented the modern Russian language and fell in love and married. But he feared that his wife did not love him. Feared that she could not love his kinky hair, inky skin, and broad nose. He believed that she was unfaithful. He challenged the man he thought was her lover to a duel. Pushkin was shot in the duel and took days to die. In the days in which he was dying, he discovered that his wife had been faithful, had loved him all the time. Do you remember this?

Pushkin began bleeding in a white shirt. I've seen the shirt. It is romantic, a white shirt with ruffles and a rust-colored stain. Life leaked slowly out of him. Or is the shirt I remember his nightshirt, soaked through from a wound that would not heal in the days that belonged to him between his duel and his death? Do you remember any of this?

I have always imagined in those days he came to understand that his wife did love him, that the duel had been unnecessary. I believe he would have believed it worth coming that close to death to know this.

On my first trip to Petersburg, our only trip to Petersburg—it was called Leningrad then—on the trip during which we saw the shirt in which Pushkin died, I met a woman in the Kirov Theater. In fact, we met her; you were so young I suspect you don't remember. She was a very old woman, part of the landscape now, sweeping here, smoothing costumes there.

I cannot remember her because I have never forgotten her.

When she was young she had been a scenic painter. There is a room at the top of the building, in the dome of the Kirov, that is round and magnificent, a room not unlike the center hall of the Houghton Library at Harvard. The room was used for the painting of scenery. Spread across the wide and curving floor had lain, painted on canvas, walls of castles and fields of stars. But her job had changed with the war. Now the floor was covered in camouflage—sheets of painted grass to drape over buildings, paintings of buildings to stretch over grass, all in an effort to disorient and confuse the airborne enemy.

The young painter had to relieve herself. She walked away. She was pretty back then. As she painted, she dreamed of dancing on the stage beneath the stars she had painted in front of the castle gates she had brought into being. Painting illusion. She could not imagine, or understand, what the government would do with acre after acre of grass that ached her back, ached her mind, and ached her hand. Still, she painted. She was on the toilet when she heard a very loud sound. She finished her business, then walked back toward where she had been. It was gone. It had vanished. The dome, the floor, the wall, the people, the paintings—gone. A German bomb had taken them away.

Inside that woman's story I discovered a story of my own. Her theme of sudden loss, at first so foreign, provoked a dull psychic pain and a frisson of déjà vu. I identified myself with the young scenic painter; I identified my mother with the German bomb. There had been a moment when my world vanished: the watermelon trucks, love, Daddy, Spady, Dear, Sun, the canopy above my bed, Tanya, everything I cared about or counted on—small or large—eradicated from my existence. Talking to the old sweeper lady, I remembered loss.

I associate this lady with the quintessential Russian curios called matryoshka dolls. When I met her, she had bright painted-on apples for cheeks and a silhouette like a pear. She looked just like the nesting dolls one can buy all over St. Petersburg. I started laughing inappropriately before I parted from her, thinking, she is a curio and this is a curiosity: life is a series of stories within stories, surprisingly hidden, surprisingly revealed. Who'd a thunk she contained me? At twenty-two, I didn't ask who I contained. I was just amused to find myself inside the Russian woman.

Years later, on a trip to Moscow, I bought a matryoshka in which a figure of Dennis Rodman nested inside a figure of Michael Jordan. I don't remember who was inside Dennis, but there must have been three other identities. There must have been a Pippin. I gave the figures to Push one Christmas. He didn't understand the gesture. He screwed Jordan open, pulled out the next figure, screwed it open, and continued until he had an entire glazed team shining before him. Then he said, "They never do football players."

It was an absurd comment. Almost as absurd as my gift. How would he know they don't do football players? I was wondering when he answered aloud, "Russkies do football players, you'd a bought me one of 'em." It wasn't the truth, but I didn't tell him. My son tells himself such sweet lies about me that I am tempted to maintain my distance. He knows me better, he will lose his innocence; he doesn't get to know me more, I will lose his love. This is a predicament.

I am like that woman. There are stories within stories within me and vanishings about me. Who will I show you? Who do you really need to see?

Pushkin's getting on with his life and leaving me behind. I taught him to do that. This is my achievement. I sensed this before he took up with Tanya. Sensed this the last year he played college ball. I never told him that it would be better for me if he played basketball. He thinks that somehow football is too ghetto for me. This is an incorrect understanding. Football is too Coliseum for me. In a stadium seat, looking down to the field with its clear markings, his game on a map, when I look at the opposing team, I don't see men, I see lions. This shames me. And I fear for Pushkin. He is my Christian. Staring at the lions, I fear he will be devoured.

My fear shames my son. Don't I see how I made him crazy? Detroit was his patrimony and I stole it from him with silence. Miss Mary Mack . . . mosquito in a wrestling jacket . . . they said the best was Sugar Ray, that's before they all saw Clay. Mama's little baby; Daddy's little maybe. How he know who this man Clay be? He don't know Clay. We all saw Clay.

I love the way I gave him Clay, the pretty pretty boy-man with power in his hands. If Pushkin remembers this, he will love me again. He must remember this.

I drove Pushkin to Louisville to have his first haircut in the barbershop where Muhammad Ali got his hair cut. It was four hours there and four hours back, time I didn't have midsemester and money I didn't have midmonth for gas. If I had no father to offer him, I was determined to give him the ceremonies of men. Have I played Delilah to his Samson? Samson's power was shorn with his locks. I wish I had never cut Pushkin's hair. I wish I had taken him into that barbershop and said, "Sir, you cut Ali's hair? You can anoint this boy's hair with oil." But maybe I did this better thing. Let a haircut be a haircut. Let a haircut be a crowning. Take him to the barber who snipped upon the head of the boy Cassius Clay and let it be a blessing. Choose Pushkin's present over my past: I did that. Maybe that's why he is so strong.

For a time I chose my past over his present. For years I never cut his hair, never let anyone else cut it either. I said I was letting it grow Samson long and strong into a wild and dark brown cloud of beauty. The truth was I had a fear of barbers, ever since my mother walked into a Washington barbershop with a photograph of Mia Farrow in one hand and one of Twiggy in the other and got a barber to hack off my long brown braids, relax the remaining curls board straight, then peroxide the whole mess white. I looked like a humiliated duckling. I wanted Pushkin to have the biggest Afro in the world as a celebration of my hair that had been shorn.

He wanted something else. He came into my room early one morning clipped like a poor hedge. He came in self-butchered, with little art scissors dangling from his hand, explaining, "Mommy, can't keep hair this long . . . Mommy needs to fix Little Man's hair." The kids at school had been teasing him. Did I weep at the marring of his beauty, or at the rejection of the symbol I had chosen for him? What cold words did I say? Tainted words, tainted words. I should have wept, because I didn't do what he needed me to do.

Then I did it. We walked silently into the barbershop and waited for his turn to be shorn. This is love. This is love with all its hope and ambition. This is love. I love this child enough to get his hair cut and let it be a haircut. It bit me to the quick, each snip, snip, snip of the scissors. It was a busy Saturday morning. My boy waited for his turn in the chair long enough for me to concoct five different reasons and ways for us to walk out without a haircut, but none would be acceptable to Pushkin. I started imagining it was my father's head that was getting shorn. Then I imagined Pushkin up in the chair and my daddy touching his kinky head, the tight springy density that was his hair, and Daddy saying, "Jesus was black. Had hair like a lamb, tight curly hair. You don't see no lamb with straight silk for hair, no sir. Jesus was black, had hair just like me." My son has hair like Daddy's and Jesus'. Nothing like the father's at all.

Then it was Pushkin's turn. The barber was eager to tell someone new all about his most famous client. It didn't hurt to see Pushkin sitting in the chair that Cassius Clay had sat in. It may have been decisive, but it wasn't painful. It almost didn't hurt to watch his beautiful brown kink fall to the floor and get swept away. That barbershop, that special place, was just enough blessing, just enough reassurance, just enough break with the bad past and just enough connection to the good past to get us moving on down the road.

As we crossed the Kentucky border back into Tennessee, I amused Pushkin and me by playing the *Smithsonian Collection of Country Classics* in the tape player. I was looking for translations of my experience that I could share without damaging him.

Our favorite song was "Detroit City." It felt strange to be singing hillbilly songs, maybe even vaguely disloyal, but we sang along together and struck a pretty harmony. "By day I make the cars, by night I make the bars, if only they could read between the lines." "Detroit City." If only they *could* read between the lines. My daddy made the bars, day and night. That was enough for him.

59

Only during summers did he ever work on the assembly line. He worked at Kiles's. Old man Kiles was what black folk down in Alabama call "one of the big mules." He ran Detroit. They named things after him. When I was at Harvard I slept with his relation who was attending the law school. He was earnest, with blue eyes and a motorcycle. He thought I was someone to run away to. I thought he was someone to run away through. I had no idea in the world then how rich he was or how much money mattered. He gave me his driver's license as some kind of token, because nobody in my family could believe we were together.

And we weren't, really. Lying beside each other, we threatened to change the world as we both knew it, my belly flat again and anonymous. I was too much a coward to tell him about the son I had already. He couldn't imagine him; couldn't imagine anything at all but me, which was fine by me. He was a place where I discovered I had lost my words. Wanted another word, a clean word, for everything that mattered. Lying beside him, I wanted to forget, but I kept remembering the story Leo had told me of the summer he worked flipping auto bodies at Kiles's. Remembering, I held that boy tighter and I became committed to the notion of abandoning English in favor of Russian. There seemed to be no middle way.

Pumpin' iron, my ass. Pumping iron, my narrow black ass. How strong the grip of the symbol upon me! Pumping iron. You don't pump it, you flip it, you pull it; weight is not an abstraction, it can kill you if you are not strong enough to push it off your leg or your neck, your arm.

Push it off. Summers were enough for Daddy. Auto bodies came down the line belly up at Kiles's and they had to be manually flipped over. Thousands of pounds flipped by maybe six men, maybe twelve hundred pounds of men. Thousands of pounds ready to land on somebody's shoulder or leg, thousands of pounds to lift if it did, and how quickly you did the lifting determined whether the limb was saved. It was just a thing a farmboy from Alabama, from Montgomery County, Alabama, did to survive life in Motown. My father worked on that line for only a few summers, but seven of his ten toes were smashed.

Daddy's toes weren't so smashed he couldn't play basketball. Leo had a basketball scholarship to college, and a football scholarship too. He was captain of the first black high school team to be state champions in the history of Michigan. He went down to Atlanta and didn't last a year. He didn't go to the fancy Morehouse; he went somewhere else south—for a minute—is how they told it. He couldn't stand it, couldn't go back to being county, poor, and colored again. Not the way they be it in Georgia in the late forties. He caught the train to Chicago, switched, then rode on to Detroit. He got in an enameled tub and washed the red Georgia clay off him, put on a suit, filled his pockets with folding money, and went to work for his daddy and his oldest brother, Bob. The Country Boy had become a City Man.

The first thing I remember, my very first memory with words, is Leo jogging slowly up a court, dribble-step, dribble-step, taking his shot from way out in the three-point zone 'cause you can't ally-oop with a baby in your scoop. You don't get under the basket. Dribble-step, dribble-step, he dribbles with one hand and holds me in the other arm. He makes his basket. "It goes where I look," he says. He kisses me on the head.

I saw Leo's ball go in many times. I saw it from his arms, I saw it from the sidewalk, and I saw it from the grass. Then I never saw it again.

I remember clearly the last day I ever saw my father touch a ball. I was a little girl in a neat little back yard with a patch of concrete and a patch of grass leading up to the garage. Over the door of the garage was a basketball hoop. I was maybe five or six or seven. I picked up the orange ball from the grass, walked toward Leo, stopped, looked back at the basket, and threw that ball up in the air. It went right through the hoop, as if it knew where I wanted it to go. "It went where I looked too," I said.

After I made the basket, my daddy took the ball from my hands. "This is not for you," he said. He tossed it onto the lawn.

"I want it!" I grabbed up the ball and made another basket. He caught my rebound and pitched the ball over the garage and into the alley.

"I went to college and nobody wanted to teach me a goddamn thing and nobody taught me, Mr. Michigan State Champion team captain, a goddamn thing. All anybody cared about was how I threw a round ball and how I caught a pointed oval one."

I have seen my son pumping iron. It is a sight to see. It is one of the things I have disdained about him. I see him out on the Astroturf and

I can't help but let my mind scream "Faux field, faux field!" and "Don't the referee look like an overseer!" I never wanted him to bulk up like that. Never wanted him to carry any ball.

"Big and strong," that's about all he said to me when he was very little. "Big and strong." These are the three syllables I got. Not "I love you." He was even miserly with the word *Mama*. Big. Strong. Ma. That's how I know he was talking to me. He hoards his words like treasure. He beefs up. I hate that expression. He is not a bull. He was a boy. He is a man and he's doing this thing called beefing up and I say, I wanted nothing practical for you, Pushkin, nothing useful, Pushkin, nothing utilitarian, darling, didn't want there to be any way at all they could use you, baby.

If you are a miser, I was a miser first. Instead of saying "I love you" I said, "Ya blu a." And my voice in your ear is so small, so small. Too small for you to hear me.

I told Pushkin the joke my daddy told me about old man Kiles's funeral. Men, big men, strong men, are carrying the casket to the grave and Kiles himself rises up from the coffin, sits straight up on the silk, and says, "How many carry my pall?" The mourners are afraid of Kiles. They are afraid there are not enough men to provide sufficient honor. They are afraid to tell the truth and they are afraid not to. They tell the truth. They scream in one voice, "Eight." Kiles, white as a sheet, white as death, is silent for a moment. Then he thunders, "Lay off four."

Dead white men retain their power. What is the power of John Henry in the grave, body expired, exploited, depleted? Is it the power of myth reinvented, is it the truth of Colson Whitehead's novel? Why, my son, did I not give you the skills to read it? Or did I give them to you, only to watch you put them down? It is easier to think that I failed in giving them to you than it is to know that you have put them down.

God help us all, and our fear of being laid off by dead men.

We laughed so hard in the long trailing wake of my father's joke I started to cry. This made Pushkin laugh harder. I teasingly slapped him upside his clean-shaven head. We had finally returned from our sojourn in the Soviet Union.

This was when Pushkin and I had fallen into mother-son love and I believed he had forgotten Detroit and Mrs. Perkins. This was when I was flying my way through the tenure track and easing into a different romantic love of my own; this is when I started seeing an architect named Gabriel. I believed I had finally made it across some kind of border. The life I was living felt finally my own. I rarely thought about your father and the circumstances of your conception. I thought about Gabriel. I thought about you. I loved my mommy-mobile. I sat in the driver's seat like I was sitting on a throne from which to look down on and over all the other cars that might imperil my precious cargo. Strange the illusions that sustain you. An ability to see a far piece down the road made me feel willing to propel my little family along in a tin can on wheels. For the first time in our lives together, I knew we were headed home.

That winter I drove us to Ann Arbor, for a conference at the University of Michigan. How quickly my mommy-mobile got cold when I turned off the heat. The air just breezed on into it. Yep. My Saab isn't like that. Your Escalade ain't either. It's sealed up tight. You leave it warm, two hours later, two hours later in thirty-degree weather, the car's still warm. And it has side airbags and driver airbags and passenger front airbags. Thank God there were no passenger front airbags then, or Pushkin might have been suffocated. I used to strap my boy into the front seat of the Jeep, before we knew that front seats were dangerous, and just drive where we needed to go. Drive like the Motown girl I wanted to be. Drive like I would get a new car every year. That Jeep had the brains blown out. Sunroof baby. Moonroof, maybe. Mammy's little baby, Daddy's little maybe. Nursery rhymes. I try to remember my first words. Words that bounced about my early days.

My first word was *Scoobydoobydobaby*, in imitation of Frank Sinatra. I spoke it to Martha Rachel.

I am trying to remember what I withheld from Pushkin that I must give him now and trying not to remember why I forgot.

SIX

MOTHER STOOD BETWEEN ME AND DADDY.

Now she's standing between me and you. Sometimes I think my best choice would be to fucking shoot her, but that would be Detroit talking. And besides, I don't even know where she is. I think her company relocated her to Europe. She's probably the world's last tragic mulatto passing for white.

Didn't I say, when you were a kid, that a hellhound guards the gates to paradise? I was talking about Lena, I was talking about Detroit. You can't say I didn't tell you something about it. But I'm not sure I ever really told you about Martha Rachel. She was a sweet, sweet love of mine the hellhound kept at bay.

I never wanted Detroit to whisper its hard truths into your ear. That's another reason I never talked to you much about Leo and Motown—about a place where all it takes is forty dollars nailed to a dope-house door to get somebody killed. I was just a little girl when Daddy explained that to me, as if it was something I might need to know. "There's always another junkie who will kill a name at an address for his or her next fix. When you can't rely on anything else, you can rely on that."

How many Russian professors or Russian studies professors know that? What have I given for you not to know it?

Leo was seven years older than Lena. When I asked her once why she had married my father, she replied matter-of-factly, "He was the handsomest, smartest, richest man I knew at the time." When the times changed, she changed men. I asked her that after she'd taken me to D.C. Around that same time she would look at me and wonder aloud, "It's hard to believe you're not even taller or even prettier, with me for a mother and Leo for a father." Then she would smile, adding, perhaps to console, "Your brain came in as expected." I never knew in those moments quite what she wanted me to say. But that was Washington.

Motown was something else. Back in the day Leo and Lena were a golden couple in black Detroit. He had a pocket full of money, she had shoulders covered in fur and ears dripping with rhinestones. They had a dangerous swagger, a way of holding their heads up higher and their feelings in deeper than anyone else. Each thought the other was the most exquisite being obtainable. Lena loved Leo because he was lightbrightalmostwhite. Leo loved Lena because she was so clearly original, like no one he had ever met before.

For eight years the king and queen of Detroit were my parents. They were always busy working or playing. Even in bed they barely slept. I didn't quite know what they were doing, but it was too noisy to be sleeping. When they walked, he kept an arm draped around her waist. Then they were linked at the hip.

Other times he was all mine. I loved him intimately. I loved her from a distance and from around a corner, from the laps and porches of aunts and grandmother.

Early days. Knew you when. Back in the day. I was a skinny little brown girl in a place where big-legged women were the sirens that screamed in the dreams of sweet dark daddies.

Black Bottom felt like the bottom of the world to a six-year-old girl on a Saturday night any summer in the sixties. My grandmother, Dear, would open up the windows after the streetlights came on, and the smell of old roses would mix with the smell of Raid bug spray and my grandfather's urine, and you would wish you were anyplace else, someplace not so forgotten. Someplace where everybody wasn't too old or too young.

Somewhere out there in the night, at the Top of the Flame, at the Twenty Grand, at any of the show bars, in the final echoes of Paradise Valley, was the love Dear and Sun, my grandfather, had made, was Leo, was my daddy, rolling in a burgundy-red Riviera with Lena wearing silk and smelling like one true thing, carrying an alligator bag, wearing alligator shoes. Sharp. Somewhere beyond the orbit of Alabama, somewhere out there in the night, my parents, Leo and Lena, were gallivanting in ways my grandparents could not imagine.

Leo and Lena had moved beyond the pull of the porch and the pull of the South; they strutted to the rhythms of the assembly line. Leo laid his bets on a ball team named the Pistons. These players, some so lately cotton pickers, almost all the descendants of cotton pickers, smiled wide, held chins high to display themselves as moving parts of a powerful engine. They were almost invincible. They were all but visible. They do not tell the story of John Henry to little children in Detroit. They do not tell that tale in the streets. They don't proclaim the truth that machines kill the men that best them, that you work yourself to death faster in a factory than in a field.

They said the best was Sugar Ray, that's before they all saw Clay . . . Last night, night before, twenty-four robbers at my door . . . I got up to let 'em in, hit 'em on the head with a rolling pin . . . Miss Mary Mack Mack Mack, all dressed in black black black, with silver buttons, buttons, buttons all down her back back back.

These are the words that echo in your head when you sit at the bottom of the world in cotton underwear, when you are little more than mosquito bait. You feel hot, abandoned, itchy, damp; you toss in the darkness that has not yet brought sleep. But some hour deep in the night Dear slips out of her bed, past Sun's door, she slides into the back room and dabs perfume on every single red bite raised upon your brown body and behind your little ear. As the alcohol evaporates, the bites stop itching and start to sting. It is a calmer thing.

Dear never spoke of Martha Rachel, her eldest daughter, my aunt, my real mother, but the way she poked her head in that back room all night long was a quiet tribute to disappearing children. Perhaps Dear watched me and my cousin and bathed our mosquito bites with perfume hoping it could wake the dead, but Martha Rachel's children kept on sleeping beneath their slate headstones in Elmwood cemetery.

I haven't spoken Martha Rachel's name aloud in years. She died not long after Lena snatched me from Detroit. Diana told me one of the last things Martha Rachel said before she died: "She blasted out of Detroit like a hell-bat out of heaven with my baby in her beak." She thought Martha Rachel was hallucinating. Martha Rachel knew exactly what she was talking about. Lena had settled a score; she used me to kill Martha Rachel. If there is a best reason to risk all the injuries associated with gangsters and crazy mothers and memory, it's to grab back Martha Rachel.

Pushkin, if you called me child, claimed me kin, till the wrinkles round my neck were deep enough to lose dimes in, I could not love you more than that woman loved me.

Martha Rachel was a whiskey-drinking, finger-popping, slurred-word-sneering, white-looking black broad. My aunt was a dame. She wore severely tailored dresses, fur stoles, and dark lipstick. She had a neat if not narrow waist that separated neat but ample swells of hip and breast. She knew Billie Holiday personally. Martha Rachel liked to sit in a club next to her brother, sipping on a Seagram's, dropping deep into her dark bag as Lady Day crooned, "You don't know what love is till you've learned the meaning of the blues." Martha Rachel knew what love was. She would drink till she started talking too much, embarrassing my mother. My father refused to be embarrassed; he adored this sister. The chatter irritated Lady Day, who sometimes walked off the stage. When Lady walked off the stage before the show was over, Martha Rachel would go home and put a Billie Holiday record on her hi-fi.

All the drive home my mother would glare coldly at Martha Rachel and my daddy would sip from a bottle he kept in a bag on the seat beside him. Later in the week Martha Rachel would sew a tight skirt or a strange blouse with a side bow or deep inverted pleats and take it to my mother. The next Saturday night they'd be back in the clubs and Lady Day would be back on the road.

Martha Rachel was the oldest child, my father's big sister. She was born in a section where everyone, black or white, understood that no matter how light Martha Rachel was, she was a nigra. Martha Rachel was painfully pale. She was a colored country girl, but shopping downtown in New York or Detroit she a white city woman. Not that she tried to pass; she didn't. But she couldn't help but notice in the moments before she identified herself a different self. She always identified her true self.

Dear did not love Martha Rachel. Or if she did, I don't remember it. She never talked about Martha Rachel, and Martha Rachel never came to her house. Never. There was Oakwood, the street Dear lived on, and Riverside, the street Martha Rachel lived on, and in the life of my childhood Oakwood and Riverside were separate principalities, discrete and divided. At Martha Rachel's I climbed into a cherry tree and watched the world from its branches while greedily nibbling on car-color-candy-apple-red, sweet, sweet maraschino cherries plucked from a small jar. The jar was small enough for me to eat every last cherry in one snack.

High up in those limbs, I felt like Eve. And I felt like I had something better to do than eat the apple, someone better to listen to than the snake. Martha Rachel had chosen me, she proclaimed me to be the one child in the world chosen to taste the fruit of her trees. Every other child was chased away. I ate the warm fruit that fell from the apricot branches. The flesh, feathery soft and buttery sweet, furry on the lips, tasted like a tomorrow I did not yet know existed.

When I had tasted that tomorrow and longed to return to my garden, to taste again the apricots of my childhood, I could not think of myself up in the tree without thinking of a completely different girl up a tree in Mississippi, eating a different fruit, wearing different and soiled drawers. Caddy. My panties were clean. I thank God I encountered the tree in Martha Rachel's garden before the tree in Mr. Faulkner's, or the knowledge of my relatives who ate from its fruit.

I took my first steps holding Martha Rachel's fingers. I spoke my first word to her. She sewed me lovely dresses. She cut my sandwiches into shapes and baked teeny-tiny princess-sized lemon meringue pies for me. She dyed dress boxes full of peeled and baked apples striking shades of blue and purple to amuse me, and I was amused. Martha Rachel was my first love. She was my father's sister, and that's what I called her, Sister.

My urban chatelaine auntie's house on Riverside Road abutted a freeway called the John C. Lodge. When I was a mere child, I didn't appreciate the irony. The Lodge was wide and deep and altogether urban and ugly. It was separated from my Eden by only a grim chainlink fence and a grimmer narrow street. A house so close to the freeway and a child about might have scared other people. Martha Rachel was beyond scared. She was convinced God would do no more to her because he could do no more to her.

The house had yard on all four sides. The side yard farthest from the freeway, the refuge orchard with four fruit trees, was my domain. The back yard was Martha Rachel's. It was a place for us to visit and a place to receive the few guests she received, usually cousins from down South who remembered Martha Rachel from before she'd been truly kissed, let alone had babies. She was easy with those folk, because they seemed not to know her affliction. To know her affliction was to embarrass her and make a demand. But these Alabama cousins were merely thirsty. She could pour lemonade from a glass pitcher, wearing an embroidered apron over one of her tailored dresses, sporting a lipstick smile, as if nothing had ever happened to her—except she grew older and moved up North into a great big house with yard on all four sides. She could play chatelaine of the urban manse easiest with folk who hadn't known Bullock, folks who'd never seen the babies. For those folk she had a place on a glider couch beneath the apricot tree. Other afternoons she splashed me in a blue blow-up pool she inflated with her own breath, or taught me to cha-cha in her living room.

The story went, one morning soon after coming North, Martha Rachel fell in love with an older man, a very dark man. Dear and Sun would have none of it. The man was too old. Martha Rachel would have no less. She ran off with Mr. Bullock. They ran all the way to California. But finally they came back. And Martha Rachel set up housekeeping and having babies in Black Bottom.

Misfortune flashed down on a rainy day in February. Martha Rachel was out to the store, Bullock was working. One of his girl cousins was napping on their bed in the downstairs front bedroom while the babies slept, one on its cot, the other in its crib, in the upstairs back bedroom. No one knew exactly what happened. Lightning struck somewhere, and something in the electricity exploded. No one knew why the fire truck took so long. The cousin got out. The babies burned up in the house.

It was impossibly sad.

The sadness took hold of Mr. Bullock's body. He came down with cancer. Martha Rachel didn't know why she didn't get it too. She wished that she had. Too quickly he died. Too quickly she discovered piles and piles of hundred-dollar bills, some of them molding, in the safe he kept. Life was strangling Martha Rachel and she was too tired to gasp for air. She had lost her children and now her man. She inherited a small colored cab company and a funeral parlor. She bought a big house and prepared to die.

She put her pistol in her brother Leo's hand. He placed it back on the kitchen table. She said, "They shoot horses, don't they." Leo walked away.

She drank whiskey by the pint, then quart, and listened to Lady Day by the hour and night. Five or six years passed.

Then brother Leo knocked his woman up. Lena was going to have a baby. The year before, or was it the year before the year before, Martha Rachel's sister Sara had had a baby. Martha Rachel hated that baby. With empty arms, she could not stand to see Sara's full. Dear took to Sara's baby like a calf takes to milk. And his daddy was a numbers runner. Martha Rachel didn't get it. Dear hadn't let her man, Bullock, in through the back door and now she was doting on this black-as-the-ace-of-spades number runner's child. Dear was doting on Simon, Sara's child, as if Martha Rachel's babies had never existed.

Now this girl of Leo's was swelling up big. Everybody was having babies except her. Leo's woman, ain't that a joke—the girl was no kind of woman, was vain beyond imagining, couldn't stand getting big. Martha Rachel watched her tottering on high heels and hoped she'd break her neck and bleed the baby out. The intensity of her wish startled Martha Rachel awake.

She had been sleepwalking a while. Now she was roused but not quite awake. She could hear, she could see, and she could remember, as if in a dream, love. She had had two children, a son and a daughter, and they had died in a house fire. She had loved the man who had put them in her and he was dead too. And the parents who had made her had cast her off. She didn't know for sure why.

She had a suspicion. Everything remaining that mattered to her depended on her suspicion's not being true. Had they begrudged her a trip back down South the summer . . . what summer was it? Sometime before she met Bullock. She had gone back down to Montgomery, stood looking at the thousands of stars in the Alabama sky that blanketed the heavens above their fields. She had done that in the company of her brothers, her younger brothers. They called on their grandfather.

Their grandfather was a big mule in Montgomery, the descendant of one of Alabama's richest planters. Things were named after him: wings of schools, playgrounds. He was white, of course, and had gone to Harvard. It was the war now; maybe it was the same day they bombed the Kirov Theater in St. Petersburg. No, it would have been the Korean War.

On the occasion of this visit, her first return to the South, Martha Rachel sat for the first time in the parlor of the old house—for just a minute. When the men headed out back to look at the hunting dogs, she darted from the kitchen into the parlor.

She had never stood in this parlor in a fresh and pretty storebought blouse and skirt. Never walked through that parlor without work to do. She wanted a taste of that. She slid into a hard, deep chair and looked at herself in a carved wood and gilded mirror festooned with apples and cherries. She saw herself reflected in the mirror along with another face, the reflection of the portrait that hung on the wall behind her. The painting was of her great-grandmother, the woman whose hair she had combed when she had been a very little girl. The shape of the face, the shape of the mouth, the shape of the eye, were almost exactly her own. Only something about the nose was different.

Martha Rachel turned to look at the painting behind her, and her back appeared reflected in the mirror with long waves of curls streaming down it. This is what her uncle saw walking into the parlor—a sea of lovely dark curls tumbling down a back toward a narrow waist, lily-white hands dangling at the gently swelling hips. He saw someone exquisite and untouchable. He cleared his throat, and Martha Rachel turned to him. Her father's half-brother had not seen Martha Rachel in years. A northern man might not have noticed the ever-so-slight broadness of the nose. Her uncle did. And though he could not see a trace of shadow in her lily skin, he knew who and what she was. She was exquisite yet colored, thus touchable, so he touched her.

He was her uncle, her father's youngest half-brother, and his boldness shackled her as much as her beauty unhinged him. He covered her mouth with his hand and whispered, "I don't care if they watch. Make a sound if you want your brothers to see this." She started to dart away. He grabbed her by the shoulder and pulled her back, knocking over a chair. He laughed. "So you want them to see. Holler and they'll come running." She got very silent. He unbuttoned the front of her blouse. He unbuttoned the fly of his pants. He pulled out his thing. It was sticking straight out and straight up. It was big. She dropped down on her knees. He smiled. "Now, that's more like it." She took him into her mouth and he pushed toward the back of her throat. Her gagging seemed to bring him pleasure. He grunted some kind of appreciation. She stroked his balls. He made another sound and she squeezed them as hard as she could. She worked her hand like a vise and her teeth like blades. He howled. She tried to bite it off. She didn't let go.

Her younger brothers, John, Jack, and Leo, ran into the room. Her grandfather walked in behind them. Reflected in the mirror was the image of a girl with a man's thing jammed into her mouth as his whole torso arched and twisted away from the pain. His hands were in the air. Later she wondered if he was reaching up to Jesus or surrendering. Filling the room was the sound of his screeches. She dropped his thing from her teeth. The uncle fell to the floor, grabbing at himself. She spat.

No one said a word. She began to button her blouse. Her grandfather walked toward her, then turned away. He stepped to his son and slapped his face. Then he turned back to the girl and he slapped her. Martha Rachel did not say a word, but tears ran down her cheeks. The uncle buttoned his pants and walked out of the room. Her grandfather reached into his pocket and pulled out a roll of bills held together by a silver clip. He pulled off a ten and then another and another and handed one to each of the three brothers. He pulled off a twenty and handed it to Martha Rachel. "You boys should keep better watch over your sister. This is not a New Orleans bawdyhouse."

The people on the porch waved goodbye as the car pulled away. The people in the car looked straight ahead, down the road, not at each other. Each was counting the seconds until somebody said something. Pulling into Montgomery, she said, "His skin is no whiter than mine." Leo said nothing. He just took the bill that was still in his hands, tore it in half, and threw it out the window.

The brothers were passing a bottle in the basement on Oakwood when Martha Rachel, stone sober, told them her part of the story. Leo's voice got loud and angry. He wanted Dear and Sun to hear it. He wanted Dear and Sun to fix it, wanted Sun to renounce his father.

Instead, they shunned Martha Rachel and she started drinking. Then her husband died and her children burned to death in a house fire. Then a child needed love and she rose from her dead to give it. My father told me this story, but I have no words to tell it to Push.

If he cannot weigh Martha Rachel's love for me, how can he weigh my love for him?

SEVEN

PUSH CALLED ME PRINCESS MOMMY.

He was three turning toward four. I had redeemed him from Miz Perkins and taken him to Russia. We were staying in St. Petersburg. It was the year I was a Fulbright. The year after I graduated from Harvard. I packed him away with me like a kitten or a puppy, but what landed in the airport was a curious boy delighted by the novelty of voices he could not understand and faces he had never seen. As I watched him toddle-dash across the great plaza in front of the Hermitage Museum, I saw him. I saw you. I saw that you moved in a herky-jerky way that reminded me of the first being called *Homo erectus*, who claimed his humanity in his gait—the carriage of his body. You moved with genius.

Too bad the nature of hypercompetence is sporadic.

We were in the square in front of the Hermitage Museum. Our fingers were braided together and we were running in a circle. He was swinging out into the air as I turned around and around and around. He was looking into my face and smiling.

It wasn't complexion that distinguished Push from the Russian children. It was so cold, he was so mittened and gloved and scarved, rarely was more than a patch of brown skin visible. His speed distinguished him. He was faster than any child on the plaza, faster than any person on the plaza, decorum and frost slow-dragging the adults like chains. Zip-zap he was here, then he was there, flashing his gap-toothed grin, his teeth so little and perfect, so brightly white, and parted precisely down the middle. I couldn't catch him. He dashed back and grabbed my hand. We were holding hands, running in a circle. He was screaming, "Faster, faster, faster," and he believed that I would never fall down. "Princess Mommy, faster, faster."

We didn't go faster. I kept finding brakes, stutter-stomp-romping, images of bruised knees and bloody knees swirling before me, images of chipped teeth and Cola bottles, of his baby tooth chipped, displaying the adult tooth erupting behind.

When we had exhausted ourselves, I lifted him onto my hip and started the long walk home. Tugging at one of my curls, he pulled my head to his face. He kissed the crown of my head, then he turned his little dark face toward the sky, toward Pushkin's sky and Tolstoy's sky, toward the sky that was about to be ours. He blew out a little stream of air. "What you doin', Little Man?"

"Kissing the dirt up to heaven."

"What?"

"Like when you drop a piece of candy you really want to eat. First you blow on it."

"You blow on it?"

"Blow off the dirt."

"Dirt?"

"You kiss the dirt you can't see up to heaven."

"Kiss it up to heaven?"

"God eats it."

"God eats the dirt and the little boys eat candy."

I say this as a joke. I tickle his sides, but he doesn't laugh. Pushkin believes this. It is a tenet of his ghetto Sunday school theology. I have heard this idea before. God eats the dirt so the little children can eat the candy. Kiss it up to Jesus.

I remember this. A Motown sacrament performed by playmates, passed along on Detroit schoolyards. I can still recall a Now and Later—was it green? Was it apple? A piece of candy dropped in a gravel yard. I remember a girl with five thick twists sprouting from her head stooping over to pick the dirt-flecked bit of flavor off that gravel. She blew the dirt to heaven and offered one of her two pieces to me. I declined the invitation and she did not ask again.

"You see dirt on me?"

"No." He shakes his head. "That's why I ain't blow on you first."

"Don't say *ain't*, son, don't say *ain't*."

Pushkin doesn't say *ain't* again for years. He says, "You always taking baths."

"No, I don't."

"Yes, you do."

"All the perfumes of Araby could not make this little hand clean."

Pushkin ignores the nonsense and kisses me again. This time he blows harder when he blows toward heaven.

What do you do with a person who kisses your dirt up to heaven? You take off the brakes. You shut your eyes to images of bruised knees and chipped teeth. You swing him faster and faster, and you don't fall down and you don't get tired until he's ready to go in. And when he is ready to go in, you kiss his forehead and turn your face to the sky, blowing that kiss toward the heavens into which you lift your son, and you hold him up to the sky. You kiss him up to heaven, and for the first time in forever you are defiant, proud. This is my precious one. See him shine brighter than your sun. This is primal idolatry. Watch this mother love this child. I don't even want to do right. I want to do right by him.

I remember the day I fell in love with my son. He was kissing me up to Jesus.

We turned back toward the Hermitage. There was too much feeling rising between us to be contained in the walls of our tiny apartment. Too many reasons to weep, and one eclipsing reason not to, my boy. We walked through the Hermitage together. I don't remember the paintings. I remember it was warm inside. I remember a gigantic clock, something like a Fabergé egg, something mechanical and ornate, a box of mechanical ornate time counting with carved and jeweled animals, perhaps an owl. I don't remember. Everything that was not Pushkin was too light to see. With all the wealth of the czars before me, I knew I was richer.

It was then that I remembered some particular words of my daddy's: "White men may have everything else in the world, the Senate, the moon, but if they don't have you, they have less. I balance my little brown baby against all the rest of the world." Daddy was leaning against a wall with a glass of scotch in his slowly swaying hand. The amber liquid rose in little waves over the ice cubes. He took a long swig from his glass. "Let 'em have the moon, keep the Senate." He kissed my head and pulled me into his arms.

I am sweating my daddy's truth.

I did not wish for my father, his memory or his ghost, to join us in Petersburg, but he came, uninvited, recalling to me the marrow of pleasure in the bone of love—even the broken bone.

We exit from the museum in the bright of day. We return to the square. The exterior of the Hermitage is blue and gold. I take Push-kin in my arms and hold him up to the sky. I swing him round and around, his fingers braided tightly to mine, his feet high off the ground. I turn and turn us both around. I was the fulcrum and he was the angel on the day we fell in love.

I kissed him up to God and he was clean.

He has forgotten all this. If Pushkin can set me aside, he has for-gotten all this.

Later, another year, another city, another hemisphere, we are living in Nashville on Woodlawn Boulevard. We are up in his room, the front bedroom that overlooks a courtyard ornamented with tulip poplars, sprawled on wall-to-wall beige carpeting. In the spring, lacy white flowers that stink cover these trees. In the fall, orange and yel-low leaves bash against his window in the wind; in the winter, the limbs are so bare and harshly hacked back that their sharp angles and thick branches have a lunar-landscape starkness. In the summer all is green. This happened on a summer day.

He is stumble-reading to me. I am listening as he reads aloud, praying for something to switch on in his brain and make it easier. Praying for him to let me read to him till it does. Neither prayer is obviously answered. Finally Push closes the book. He has earned his treat, a GooGoo Supreme, some mixture of chocolates and pecans and caramel and maybe marshmallow. He unwraps it from its enve-lope of golden foil. We step out of his room and into mine, through mine onto my back balcony, which overlooks blacktop parking and other townhouses, to get a view of wood and sky. We want to get a better look at the evening sun coming down. It's a streaky-pretty af-ternoon. There's purple in the clouds, which hide the sun until it sinks beneath them and appears.

"Look," says Pushkin. He is seven or eight. A piece of candy falls out of his mouth. He picks it up. I snatch the candy from his hand. The saliva and sugar stick my fingers together.

"Don't eat that!"

"Kissed it up to God."

"God has better things to do than clean candy."

"What things?"

"That's just a lie poor kids believe."

"Are we poor?"

"Let me get you a clean piece, Man."

"Uncle Spady believes it."

"Spady."

"Uncle Spady."

"Uncle Spady is illiterate and superstitious."

"What's illiterate?"

"Unable to read."

"I'm illiterate."

"You are preliterate. You will be able to read."

"Uncle Spady can't read?"

"No, he can't."

"Then I don't need to learn to read either."

"What does Spady have to do with us?"

"He smart."

"If he was so smart, he wouldn't eat dirty candy."

"After you kiss it up to God it's not dirty."

"End of discussion. You're not eating dirty candy."

I grab the candy from the ground. I look at him as if he is dangerous. He remembers Spady. I had not intended this.

"You're not eating the dirty candy and you're not basing your life on the abilities, inabilities, eccentricities, rituals, or superstitions of aging gangsters."

"Is Uncle Spady an aging gangster?"

"Yes."

"What's an aging gangster?"

"An illiterate, illegitimate mess."

The brothers liked Spady because he returned their sister, their younger sister, and her Buick with a full tank of gas, a fool tank of fuel. This is what Leo remembered. That's what he called it later when he told me the story, lying on his side in a hotel room in undershorts, skinny long legs demurely crossed at his ankles. With seven of his ten toes smashed; most of his nails were opaque, white, rough. I remember staring at those nails the first time he told me this story, and I remember noticing the nails that day too.

Daddy said, All the girls 'cept Sara, all the other girls in the neighborhood, found Spady too scary to be thrilling. He was black as the ace of spades. Fine-featured. Diamond-chiseled. One could imagine God taking a breath after he made him.

Why I wanted to lie to my son about my uncle it's hard to put down. Why I avoided Spady, why I never took Pushkin to visit Detroit even when we went to Ann Arbor, is hard to admit.

In Motown, where schoolteachers and the preachers were put up as being the great minds, worthy of the rare deference the community allowed, it scared me to find my little heart lurching toward this ebony beanpole of a man at whom my mother spit the word *illiterate*, who worked down at the smokestacks, wherever that was. But if you saw things with any level of exceptional detail, if discrimination was any part of a habit of your mind, you had only to eat a frozen Salisbury steak TV dinner with Spady to be dazzled by his ability to observe, discern, shift perspectives, distinguish what was important, what was problematic, where the potential profit lay, where the breach of loyalty might be, what beauty or evil a thing or a moment might contain.

I have eaten that Salisbury steak, that highfalutin hamburger with pretensions. Cells of my body are made from that steak. There used to be a company named Swanson's—maybe there still is—that made frozen dinners served in sectioned rectangular tin containers. There was a place for the meat, a place for the starch, a place for the vegetable, and a place for the dessert. The Salisbury steak dinner came with tapioca pudding with a maraschino cherry slice on top. There were peas in the vegetable section and mashed potatoes in the starch section. The whole thing resembled the meals then served on airplanes. This was a glamorous association. In Motown people looked forward to plane food and served TV dinners on tin TV tables as a feast of celebration of how far they had come, from hard rows to hoe in Alabama to moving pistons in an assembly-line engine in Michigan. A TV dinner was a good thing.

Spady and I both had Salisbury steak dinners in front of us. Having never milked a cow, picked collards or corn, or ground corn for meal, I had no reason to celebrate industrial food. And I was sick. The grandparents were sick too, having caught the flu from me. Everybody else was working. Mother in the library at the psychiatric hospital, Daddy in his cleaners', Sara at the corner store. Martha Rachel had some cab runs to do. That's why Spady was watching me.

This was also during a vicious period of territorial conflict between the old mob and the new hoodlums, in which a child or two had been snatched for an hour or three to make a point—so nobody was taking chances. I was up under Spady, and Spady was tucked inside a house where some of his boys stood sentry outside and some of them walked. We were secure.

Spady ate his portion quickly. I played with mine. I was nursing the tail end of a virus, but my nose had cleared enough for me to taste my food. I didn't like the taste. As Spady ate, he watched me not eating.

"I tell you how many peas in the dinner, you eat what you got?"

"And if you don't?"

"I'll eat it for you and tell your mama you cleaned your plate."

" 'Kay."

"Deal."

He put out his hand for me to shake. His fingernails were neat, shiny even. We shook hands. Quickly I covered the peas with my hands so he couldn't see.

"Ninety-six."

I counted the peas. There were ninety-six. I started eating my dinner. Halfway through, he interrupted the greasy silence.

"You know how many peas you have left?"

"No," I snapped.

"I do," he said.

"How many?" I challenged, shooting out my hand to cover the vegetable slot.

"Twenty-three."

I counted again. There were twenty-three peas. I said nothing. He already knew he was right. Spady said, "A man gots to see what going on 'round him, how it's changin' and how quick it's changin'. Gotta notice. A girl, a smart girl like you, do well to do that too."

"What's the diff? How many peas."

"Ain't no such thing as useless information! I know useless people—some's trifling, disloyal, skeered, some just weak. They is plenty useless people in this world and I met quite a few of 'em. I ain't yet come up with a piece of information didn't make a good soldier in the right situation."

I smiled at the idea of facts being soldiers. A picture came into my head of Spady moving facts around a checkerboard.

"You a smart girl. It ain't never too early to start collecting soldiers."

He had said it again, "smart girl," like he was patting the head of a puppy or anointing the head of a priest, like I was Miss It. I had heard it once and I wanted to hear it again. "Smart girl."

Spady said it, so I thought it might be true.

Life was Spady's study. No saltshaker, nor all the grains in it clumping and unclumping, was beneath or beyond his notice, no dope dealer growing bored. In all my life, in all the universities I have passed through, I have never known a person more able to hold at one time more complex and contradictory analyses of a moment. It breaks my heart that he must be considered by most a common hoodlum. Hardly any arrests, not one conviction, and decades and decades of doing illegal business is not common. It breaks my heart to know that I cannot find a way to allow myself to hold him before Pushkin as an example. Spady is the unacceptable exceptional.

There was nothing common about Spady. He carried a roll of cash that could choke a horse. Lounging about in a striped silk robe and a nylon stocking cap, the better to keep his conk conked, Spady looked authoritative. It's no small feat to look authoritative in a stocking cap. He kept his bank like he kept his books, without ever writing anything down.

I loved him, though I did not want to. Pushkin loves him, though I do not want him to. Spady wasn't safe and he isn't respectable. But I loved him all the same and admired him—this was how I first came to know I was attracted to brilliance, and my attraction to brilliance was stronger than my attraction to safety or respectability. If I had not met Spady, I would not have known so soon. If I had not met Spady, I might not have gone to Harvard. Though he did not know the word, he developed a kind of arbitrage. I would explain it to you, but he might shoot me. Gangsters don't retire, they die, or go to prison, or get older working in a smaller and smaller territory, till their bank is a kitchen table and their fiefdom is a suburban block where old folks with money in the bank and pensions and retirement plans play the numbers to remember who they used to be, as a way of saying to themselves, "I knew you when."

If I had been Spady's mother, if penicillin had been available at the first, he might have been—I dare say Spady would have been—a mathematician at some great university. Or maybe I dare not say it. I am Pushkin's mother, and he is a defensive lineman. If Spady had become a mathematician, it is not his life that would have been improved but the life of America. He would not have had his mohair suits or alpaca golf sweaters, but he also would not have had his pistols in his waistband. He would not have worked at the smokestacks.

I would still be able to say, He was a numbers man. He was in numbers. I would still be able to imagine Spady in a giant fishbowl of digits, of sevens and nines, of twos and eights, of threes and fours, fives and sixes, and ones, a gargantuan version of the bowl you find in pet stores and calm, cool homes where goldfish gills suck air from water. Spady sucked more than money from the numbers. He sucked an exuberance to keep thinking. He sucked in life from numbers. Had the numbers he was counting been more than abstractions, more than poor folks' dreams, more than strange byzantine equations and computations created by the results of races, the order the nags came in, there are people who are dead who might be living today. With a different mother, in a different America, Spady would have been calculating the probability of the placement of electrons as they floated around the nuclei of cells, or noting the geometry of spots on a mammogram, creating complex calculations that prolong life. He would have added more to the days he counted and counted more days.

That I ever heard tell of, Spady had no family. I thought he was from the blue-black South, someplace distant, isolated, and African where black folks tended indigo or rice, vanquished crops on ten-thousand-acre plantations where malaria was a watchdog, where sickle cells sat sentry, where mosquitoes kept the white folks at bay— from South Carolina, south Georgia, or lower Alabama.

Years after malaria had all but vanished in the United States, the charity hospitals of Detroit and Chicago and Washington echoed with the screams of the descendants of slaves who suffered bone-bursting pain, paying their ancestors' debt, paying for their ancestors' privilege of not being susceptible to malaria, with sickle-cell anemia.

Spady reminded me of these people, both because of the rich blackness of his skin and because I associate Spady with hospitals. But this was a false connection. Just a few years ago, I learned that Spady was from Texas, from Galveston, where rich folk were cotton brokers. O wicked propriety! Spady was bred among the cotton brokers. It was there, in Galveston, that Spady learned the beauty of a bank, of money made from money rather than money made from labor. And it was there, in Galveston, beneath the tall and languid palms, that Spady learned his undulating stroll. He walked the way the fronds of the palms rolled.

Spady grew up and turned grown in a ghetto TB ward before antibiotics were understood, in his own magic mountain of bedpans and dark hands, of sputum and numbers. He was so skinny, so lean, when he rubbed his belly he could feel beneath the skin the place where one, two, three, four ribs broke after four, five, six coughs. He took the measure of the ratio of the thing and remembered more coughs than breaks. He counted the days in which his spit was not flecked with near-black red and he remembered the number of days since he had coughed up blood. There was a ratio, and though he did not know this word, he knew the principle of the dynamic.

Quickly and quietly, men around him died. Spady began to keep a count in his mind. First it was just the beds beside him on either side. How many days till they died? Then it was, how much water did they drink? How many basins did they pee into? Then it was ten beds on either side. Finally it was the ward. He had all the men's numbers in his head.

He could detect the nurses' lies and idiocies. He knew the probability of life in a particular bed with a particular cough. He knew the probability of life as the patient of a particular nurse. The nurses were more idiots than liars. The numbers told him who to avoid and who to cling to.

When Spady left the hospital, he got a job as a numbers runner. One of the first bets he took was twenty dollars on 020 for Sun. He never wrote anything down and didn't have to. This one of his lesser attributes. When the police, suspicious, stopped him, they never found any evidence. Over time he became the numbers king of Detroit. Letters were another story.

Spady's most prized possession was his driver's license. Because he could not read or write, the written portion of the Michigan State driver's license examination was a mountain to be crossed. In the city, illiterate men do not drive. They walk or ride the bus.

Unless you are Spady. If you are Spady, one of your boys drives you anywhere you want to go. Eventually a favorite emerged: Lynx, a sleek boy with catlike eyes and milk chocolate skin. Spady had a chauffeur but no license. His boys thought it a great joke. Spady would snap, "With all you niggers, what I need a driver's license fo'?" That's what he said, but I am suspecting he felt something else.

When Spady got slick and rich enough, he bought himself a license, no written test required. He could drive. Spady learned by watching and thinking all the time he had been riding. He didn't need to practice. He just got behind the wheel and did it. He started memorizing new numbers, the number of his driver's license, the number of his car off the assembly line (seven), the number of miles or fractions of miles from here to there. He always left his keys on the seat. There was not nigger in Detroit fool enough to boost Spady's ride — and Spady never left the black side of town.

No, God did not make people that stupid. You didn't take any-thing from Spady without repercussions. Even children knew that. God only knew what he would do if you took something he loved as much as his new car. That day he was all ivory teeth and brown-lipped joy. Nobody except Sara and some of his outside women had seen his teeth in years. Spady was more exuberant than a boy. He was as exuberant as an old man to whom something stolen has been returned—after he has abandoned hope of ever seeing it again.

That day he didn't stop driving until everyone on the street had taken a ride. He paid out on 225, a deuce and a quarter, even though that number hadn't hit.

Later, when driving was no longer a novelty for him, when we were no longer surprised to see him behind the wheel, I came to no-tice that there was always a little gang in Spady's car. He had learned to drive, but he never learned to ride alone.

To this day, I wear a fine gold watch, thin, reliable, handsome, bought from a pawnshop by Spady for my father. To this day, Spady cannot read or write, yet the first luxury goods I ever enjoyed were purchased by the engine of his brain.

Spady bought that watch for my father the weekend an aspirant to the title of numbers king was shot dead, by an unknown assailant, while Spady played golf. There was a picture of my father, unidenti-fied, and Spady walking out of the man's funeral in the newspaper. Daddy was wearing the watch. I am terrified when Pushkin reminds me of Spady.

I wish I had long ago taken the watch from my wrist and pitched it into the Detroit River. Spady's watch, the watch Spady gave Daddy, makes it impossible for me to forget that once I couldn't be-lieve all death threats were rhetorical.

There was something that Leo used to say to me that terrified me when I was a girl. Leo would say, "You bring home a white boy, and the only question is whether I'm going to shoot him first or you. For sure I'm going to shoot you both."

The law I broke my son has broken too. And I owed Daddy too much to break any of his laws. Or maybe I'm just scared. Maybe I think Leo can set up hits from heaven.

My mother left my father on a cold day in January. Snow and ice were on the ground. I wore leather go-go boots with thin soles that rose just to the ankle. I slid and twisted my ankle walking with her to the car that would take us to the airport. Motown was trying to hold me home. Lena and I kept stepping.

Later that year, using detectives, the address books my mother left behind, and both his and Spady's good brains, my father finally found me. Eventually he dragged Lena back to Michigan and into court. Eventually a judge ordered that the minor child should immediately visit her father. I was startled when my mother told me the news. I just *knew* my daddy was dead. Daddy hadn't called, he hadn't come for 162 days. The only explanation I, Windsor of Motown, could imagine was that they had all been killed. Suddenly I was introduced to a different reality. I was returned to Detroit, to the house on Iowa Avenue, to an empty room lined with royal blue carpet. Sudden shivers me.

My father looked into the room and said, "I came in after work and Tanya was sitting there whimpering." He pointed to a particular spot on the rug. Gone were my bed, my dresser, my night table, my clothes. All that remained was a whimpering white poodle named Tanya. When I returned to Washington, Tanya was with me on the plane. It was a small good thing for me, paid for by another loss for Daddy.

I kept waiting, I am still waiting, for someone with wand enough to reverse the trick and have me show back up, with my gray-blue French Provincial furniture, canopy intact, having risen like Martha Rachel from the ashes. Maybe that's what accepting Tanya the girl would be.

Visits back were strange. The room my parents had shared was still there, except my daddy had pulled the twin beds apart and placed them at right angles. Out on the glassed-in sleeping porch, in the room my mother had used for her dressing room, was her chest of drawers—something on the Swedish modern order. In the drawers I found black padded bras. I found falsies. I found bits and pieces of Lena's come-hither aura. In the bathroom I found tube after tube of jettisoned lipstick. I climbed from the toilet seat to the sink, sat on the sink, and tried color after color. The tube I liked best turned my lips a "going to a go-go" shade of white. When I looked carefully at the tube, it wasn't a lipstick at all but something called a concealer.

She had never been a queen. I would never be a princess. There had been no reason in the world to traipse after her.

When January came around again, a court had given my mother my life and my father my holidays: Christmas, Easter, and summer.

Courts are dumb and vicious. They should have sent me back to Detroit to live with my hoodlum daddy. There would have been no more crime in Detroit and fewer crimes perpetrated on me.

The next Christmas my father and I stood at the window of my empty bedroom, near the place my pillow had once been, in the space where I had rewritten the Batman show in my sleepy brain, inserting a Negro girl as ally to the caped crusader into each and every episode. My body had returned to the place where I had first begun to imagine, where I first observed, out a window not meant to be opened, that the stars looked distant. I would never sleep in that room again.

But there was something Daddy and I needed to do there. It was the last day of the year. I was shaking. Daddy had pried the window open. Heat was flowing out and cold was blasting in. He stuck the barrel of a rifle through the slit. He tried to get me to hold the butt of the rifle close into my shoulder so it wouldn't kick back. He tried to get me to hold the rifle and pull the trigger. I had vague memories of purple and blue flowers blooming on his chest on the coldest days of the year, and so I crinkled my nose, kept my eyes wide and silent. He put the rifle to his shoulder, nestled the butt into the crook, then reached for my hand and pulled it to the trigger. My fingers reached for his. In my mind the Beatles were singing "I Want to Hold Your Hand." The five years it had been since I carried my Beatles lunchbox off to kindergarten seemed an evil eternity. I had reached double digits. I was ten years old. In my head the Beatles were no longer singing. I was singing: "I still want to hold your hand, Daddy. Please say you understand, Daddy." We squeezed off a shot of welcome round about midnight. I pulled the trigger with my fingers wrapped around his. It was the first day of a New Year.

Later, down South, in Washington, in Nashville, I would learn to eat collard greens on New Year's Day to insure prosperity, and black-eyed peas to assure good luck, and I would come to despise these rituals, saying, "Anything all black people are doin' can't be gettin' anybody any good luck." Back then I didn't know collard greens and black-eyed peas, I knew gunsmoke and charcoal hope. I fell asleep to gunsmoke.

Soon the scent of Alabama, family barbecue to family barbecue, would rise to embrace the city of Detroit. Like a wife returning to the bed of her cuckolded husband before morning, the scent of Alabama, like hope, would fall upon that hungry, angry, lonely town.

Then the town, Motown, my town, would inhale deeply and eat a bellyful while there was eating to be done. This wife didn't come home often. On New Year's Day morning, the past met the present in Detroit.

Later, in the bright light of day, beneath the gray plate of the Detroit sky, when Daddy walked around the house in his trousers and his undershirt, I saw a bruise beginning to bloom. He could not hold the rifle close enough and help me pull the trigger. Concentric circles of mauve and blue and purple marked the moment when he could not help himself and me at the same time.

EIGHT

F OOTBALL IS FOR FORGETTING.

There is a thing, a singular thing, I have loved about football. Football made Pushkin's adolescence look more different from mine. The high school I attended had a Communist Club and Ultimate Frisbee, but no football. Football is an unyieldingly unfamiliar country to me.

Having Gabriel in the mix made it different too. The simple fact of being a family of three created an extravagant difference—space to breathe. As different as a triangle is from a line is the difference between Gabriel, Pushkin, and Windsor from Lena and me.

And Gabriel Michael played Texas high school football, second string to be sure, but head-banging Texas football. He never wanted to see Push get hurt, but Gabriel loved to watch him play. It was where they connected.

Friday nights in west Nashville, young families of the old guard go to the institute football game. Some park Volvo station wagons and Range Rovers (many of which have been driven out of two of the five wealthiest Zip Codes in the nation) in front of basic brick houses of the suburban southern sort on the streets surrounding the school. Gabriel's 1967 Lincoln with suicide doors didn't exactly fit in, but it was there. In four years I don't believe he missed a game, home or otherwise. The neighbors (some who are elderly and have been planted forever, some who are young and will move as their families grow) park minivans and Audis and New Yorkers and Cherokees.

In the fecund dimness of autumn south of the Mason-Dixon line, the slouching silhouette of a fifty-pound bag of mulch and the shadow of shovels leaning against a porch column are familiar sights. Walking through the neighborhood on the way to the games, Gabriel and I would smell the bulbs buried alive to sleep through winter and pop up awakened in the spring. The students at the institute, I once noted, were not unlike the bulbs, buried alive and sleeping, waiting to bloom brilliantly one spring or another. Gabriel disagreed. "The boys are like the neighborhood, square and sensible," and I finished his sentence for him, finished it as he would not have finished it, saying, as I thought of my son, "Lacking in all pretension, possessing a lean but real charm." We both laughed at me; he started laughing first. I like that about Gabriel.

It was worth watching football and putting up with bad weather to walk in the dark with my husband those autumn nights. I thought football was some part, an amusingly traditional part, of our bohemian intellectual world. It never once occurred to me that it would become Pushkin's life. The institute prided itself both on its ability to bestow a classical education and on its ability to field an excellent football team. As far as I was concerned, he was there for the Latin. And it was somehow emotionally convenient for me to locate Pushkin in a place that starkly contrasted with Paliprep and Washington. That felt safer for Pushkin and safer for me.

I have thanked God that Pushkin was not a girl. When he was in his mid-teens I weekly thanked God that he was not a girl. Each time I prayed those words I recalled the daily prayer of Orthodox Jewish men that shamed the Reform Jewish boys of my adolescence. Inspired by orthodoxy, I made myself remember that everything that is preference is not prejudice, and continued my prayer. One go-round in the mother-daughter relationship ring was more than enough for me. Pushkin's being a boy made mommying easier.

If the institute with its green lawns and white columns, its blue blazers and khaki pants, seemed far from Spady's bronze suits and red sweaters in Motown, and far from my cream painter's pants and purple granny dresses in Georgetown, it also seemed far from injury, hurt, and loss. The distance between Pushkin's institute and my Paliprep was almost as great as the distance between boyhood and girlhood. Yet and still they were and are both points on the same spinning earth. There was a familiarity to be recognized as I watched Pushkin stumble around and into and through adolescence, achy, bruised, and bruising, watched his power appear as he took to the field and did not vanish.

Pushkin is an invincible man. Pushkin is the ultimate visible man. A hundred thousand people have held their breath, unblinking, waiting to watch him make his move. I have sat in my skybox and watched them watch him. I see that they see him. Sometimes I will be sitting home on a Sunday afternoon or a Monday night, and my phone will ring, or an instant message will appear on my computer screen, as I try to prepare for the week's classes. Someone I know is looking at him on television and trying to decode some twitch or lean or wince they have seen. They want to know what I think it means. I think it means my son is highly visible.

Watch and see and think. They look at his eyes and his hands. They study his gait. They notice if he has lost or gained a pound, if he is favoring a shoulder. In my childhood, dark men of power made use of the fact of their invisibility to cloak their actions and intents, exploited invisibility to do what they needed to do. Gabriel is a master of this. Pushkin knows nothing of the privacy invisibility provides or the alienation visibility provokes. They see you. Every "they" this country contains and defines. They all see you.

Before you were the visible man you were the visible boy.

The institute felt linked to Cambridge. All those boys wandering around, a very few half lost, carrying books, wearing Brooks Brothers shirts and khakis with their regulation ties dangling, reminded me of the days I wore chinos and Brooks Brothers shirts with my tie dangling, in some boy's wool vest, dressed in the image of Annie Hall. Dressed to look like someone I didn't know. I thought the institute would be Pushkin's road to Harvard. I hoped it would be a road that would curve back to me, after you curved appropriately away during your sojourn in male adolescence.

You parked and then you walked. So many people went to the game we usually walked for blocks and blocks, right down the middle of the road, or on the edges of lawns. There are few sidewalks in Nashville. Even if you stick to the asphalt, you smell the lawns. The scent of wild onion rises from the grass. The neighborhood looks its welcoming best. There is a subtle caste within class pride at work. The enveloping lawns of thick-bladed grass sprouted through with onions and clover and tiny wild strawberries are fresh-mown into respectability. This is southern city safe. Arriving at the field, Gabriel would give a parent working for the booster club three dollars and someone would stamp our hands.

Four years of fall Friday nights I stood on the sidelines in the same clothes I taught in, gray wool pants and oatmeal cashmere turtleneck, a tweed jacket, a Burberry raincoat on top of all of that and maybe a Hermès scarf around my neck. Nashville is a conservative but stylish place with an Anglophile bent. Sometimes my pants were chocolate brown and the sweater was black. Sometimes the pants were black and the sweater was brown, but the rest of it never, ever changed. If I was going to a dinner party, I just had to put on my pearls, take off the jacket, and tie the Hermès scarf directly around my neck instead of over the Burberry.

I worked hard at being invisible. I wore the uniform. I even had my hair straightened again. I wore it in a long flipped-under page-boy, not very different from the style of hair Condoleezza Rice wears now. I had it done the year before I faced tenure review. Someone significant in the world of universities said the straight hair made me look smarter. I replied that research suggested IQ doesn't change with age—or hairstyle. They didn't laugh, so I didn't either. I just wondered for the few seconds it took me to come up with the answer and stop wondering if the someone significant had ever seen a photograph of Pushkin's or W.E.B.'s nappy, nappy heads.

At most games Gabriel and I would eventually take seats in the stands, a little off by ourselves by choice. Our marriage was young, and I wanted to savor the thing my Pushkin had that the first Pushkin hadn't, the thing Pushkin was developing that W.E.B. Du Bois only partly achieved: true visibility. First I took pride in his projectile vomiting. Then I took pride in his very visibility.

Sometimes we sat with other parents. I always made an effort to avoid sitting with the handful of overly rah-rah football families. I could bear voices saying how wonderful it would be to see Pushkin playing at some first-rate football power with second-rate academics. I couldn't bear hearing it come out of the mouths of people whose sons had SAT scores far lower than mine did but were going on to Virginia or Sewanee or North Carolina or Princeton. When rah-rah football folk blithely banished Pushkin to Alabama or Auburn or Tennessee, some football powerhouse, I just tucked my Mary Tyler Moore hair behind my ears and smiled my biggest smile.

I knew where my boy was going. Or I thought I knew. When I spoke of attending Pushkin's future games with a crimson scarf tied around my neck, I was thinking cashmere, not silk, I was thinking Cambridge, not Tuscaloosa. Unless the Bear were still alive. If my daddy and Bear Bryant had still been alive, I might have begged Pushkin to attend the University of Alabama.

I believe it would have broken the Bear's mind to know my boy. To meet someone from his defensive line who could outthink him, whose vocabulary was larger than his own, whose diction was of a higher caste and class—this would have surprised the Bear. To get inside a colored boy's mind and find no shame in it, no sense, at top or bottom, of any natural inferiority, no acknowledgment of the Bear's innate superiority, to get that far into a black man's mind and find no submission—I believe that would have scared the shit out of the Bear. And it would have been a nice tribute to Leo.

My hiney was almost always cold on those aluminum benches. I would usually choose a spot more than halfway up, the closer to heaven in case Pushkin seemed in need of intercessory prayer. He rarely required aid. I did spend time praying. Every game, almost every play he was out on the field, unless he intercepted and stripped the ball from a confused player's hand or returned a fumble for a touchdown, every play he sacked the quarterback, whoever he was, I would pray for them to get up unhurt. They always did. For a while Pushkin was dubbed the "Angel of Mercy" in honor of how painlessly but profoundly he took his opponents out. I didn't like it when they called him that. Gabriel Michael was enough angel name for one family.

Still, I did not want Pushkin to hurt anyone. I was terrified of inherited thug tendencies. It was very important to me that he did not injure. He could knock them down, but I wanted them to get up walking. And if he didn't go to Harvard, I surely wanted him to go to Princeton or Virginia.

Once the boy Pushkin tackled didn't get up. It was the beginning of an ordinary night, which I now see as a breaking place and blending place. It was a night the boundaries didn't hold, and the past, in spits and sputters, contaminated our present.

One Friday night, after he knocked his man down and the play was over, Pushkin held his hand out for the fallen opposing player to grab while standing. The kid just stayed down. I held my breath. Players from the visiting team were jogging quickly toward their teammate, but they were still a long way off. Pushkin offered his hand again. A few words seemed to be spoken. His opponent's head rolled on the ground. Pushkin waited until the visitors got to their fallen comrade, shrugged, and turned away. I started breathing when I saw the boy take one of their hands, rise, and walk like Lazarus to the sidelines.

After the game Gabriel and I took Pushkin to Dalt's. The second win of the season it was our tradition to go out, just the three of us, to this stylized diner of a place with black-and-white tile floor and fancy meat-and-three and other comfort foods. It had the advantage of being close. The game had been a good win. Pushkin and Gabriel were going over plays. I was still puzzled about Lazarus. I broke into their conversation as we took our seats in a highly visible booth.

"What did that kid say to you?"

"Which one?"

"The one who stayed down so long."

"He called me a name."

"What name?"

"Assassin."

"Assassin?"

"Assassin."

"What did you say to him?"

"'I just assassinated your ass. Now let me resurrect you.'"

"What does that mean?"

"Just messing with him."

"That's funny. I thought he looked like Lazarus."

"The two of you think too much alike," Gabriel said, yawning.

A gaggle of girls, cheerleaders from the local Catholic girls' school, approached the table to congratulate Pushkin on the game. They looked like they were in the tenth or eleventh grade. Four of the five girls were white, one was wearing braces. All of the girls were pretty. The prettiest of the girls was black. I had vaguely known each of these girls for a very long time. Nashville is a small town.

"Great game!"

"My dad says you could go to State."

"Time will tell."

I took a sip of bitter coffee and blushed. If you have a baby at eighteen, can you have a hot flash at thirty-four? Does it work that way? I was looking around this overgrown diner. All these blond girls standing by our table made me nervous. Especially when my son was spouting my daddy's old lines. "Time will tell." Did I say it that often? When did I start saying it? When did he?

I noticed the other patrons noticing our table. I was alert for disapproval. None was evident. Many of the tables of Friday-faced families were taking an interest in the goings-on at our table. All who were, were smiling. If they didn't go to the games themselves, most people in Nashville had seen Pushkin's picture in the sports section of the *Tennessean*. They saw the pretty brown girl in the middle of the clique. Saw her cocking her head away from Pushkin in a way that gave him a better view of her eyes. Saw her turn her toes in to make her legs prettier. Saw her trying to get him to notice her. Without a seat at the table, they didn't see the little strawberry blonde. This girl, whose nose was sprinkled with reddish freckles, had eyes shiny with reckless disregard for established decorum. She was breathing down her brown friend's neck, furious that the brown girl had put her body between the redhead's freckled self and Pushkin's coffee-and-cream smoothness. You couldn't see this from a distance.

The restaurant saw a perfect pair: a chocolate brown cheerleader and a coffee-colored football player. They silently cheered Pushkin on in the diner, like they cheered for him on the field.

I was recalculating the price I had paid for the life I had led. Recalculated in the light of this swift and sudden realization that I had raised Pushkin in a place where you don't have to be ashamed to have a conversation with a cheerleader. I was not raised in such a place. I was ashamed that my son was talking to a cheerleader. Gabriel looked proud and amused. In my mind I began to plan a very chilly night for Gabriel.

"After what he said. Next time you tackle him. I hope you break his leg."

"Me too."

"He deserved it."

"I think calling Pushkin an assassin was clever," I chimed in.

"I'm not allowed to say what he said, but it wasn't *assassin*."

"Oh." I looked at the black girl. I raised my eyebrows. I knew her parents. She didn't want me to call them, but she wasn't talking.

"He called Pushkin a nigger," said the strawberry blonde.

"He was just advertising Dick Gregory's autobiography," quipped Pushkin, deflecting.

All the girls except the redhead dropped their heads and started staring at their gym shoes.

"Really" was all I said.

I wanted to say, "Next time you play him, I hope you do break his leg." I didn't. I knew enough about the high school football season to know if they played that team again, it would be because those fools had made it to the playoffs. The girls knew it was time to get back to their table. They were not ready yet. Pushkin lifted up his burger and stuffed it into his mouth. We all saw it as a signal for the girls to move on. They didn't. He chewed. I took a sip of wine. The girls fidgeted. Gabriel Michael squeezed my hand.

"Has anybody asked you to the winter formal yet?" the freckled girl asked. Pushkin stopped chewing. He wiped his face with his napkin.

"Is someone asking me now?"

"I am," the black girl responded.

"No and yes. Haven't been asked and glad to go."

The girls squealed with delight. Mission accomplished. They scurried back to their table, back to half-drunk Diet Cokes and half-eaten brownies. They had the busy look of people with a lot to plan.

Pushkin was chewing another bit of hamburger. I was staring at him, moving macaroni and cheese around on my plate without looking at it.

"What?"

"I wish you wouldn't play football."

"I don't play football . . . I inhabit it."

I tried not to be amused. It was hard. When he smiles and flexes a few of his muscles, when he flexes his brain, when he thinks and winks and talks that sweet trash talk he talks, it's more than hard not to adore him. It's impossible.

"If you didn't play football, you wouldn't be around people like that."

"Like who? The peckerwood that called me nigger or that peckerwood cheerleader?"

"Peckerwood?"

"Like you never heard that word."

"Take a step back, now," Gabriel instructed.

"You have never heard me speak that word."

"I've heard tell of it."

"I am cursed with a son with a memory."

"I know what you're thinking."

"You don't know what I'm thinking."

"I know everything about you, Moms."

This stopped me. I liked the idea of this. It was a lie, or a fairy tale, but it was a pretty lie, a seductive fairy tale. I said one of those strange and silly things I say to him when I don't want him to understand. I said, "It's a privilege to bore you, my darling."

"You never like it when I talk to white girls."

"No, I don't."

"You dated white boys when you were in high school."

"That was completely different."

"Yeah, that was you and this is me."

"That was Washington."

"Yeah."

"I dated brilliant boys who happened to be white."

"Who am I going to the winter formal with?"

"Ashley."

"Thank you."

"Thank you."

Gabriel took money from his wallet, laid it on the table, wiped his mouth with his napkin. He was needed back at the office. "I think Pushkin should date absolutely who he wants. Huey Newton said it was the black man's responsibility, the political black man's burden, to date—he didn't say date, but we'll leave it at date—as many white women as possible. To even the score."

"Huey said that?"

"Huey Newton didn't say that."

"Are you and Huey on a first-name basis?"

"Aren't you due back at the office? Don't you have a presentation to get ready?"

"I'm just messin' with you."

"Gabe, thank you, man."

"Push, when the time is right, you got to do yours and mine too. With all these fine sisters about, I never could bring myself to do my share."

I got a kiss on the lips. Pushkin got a shoulder bang. Gabriel was off. I was rapidly changing my mind. He would not have a chilly night. I took my fork out of the macaroni and cheese and started sipping on my black coffee. Pushkin startled me into a cough.

"What color was my daddy?"

"I don't remember."

"Grandma Lena said—"

"Mention of Lena does not help my memory."

"Black, white, Japanese?"

"What color do you want him to be?"

Pushkin set his darker arm next to my lighter one. He softly banged shoulders with me.

"I guess I know what color my daddy was," he said, smiling.

I waved the waiter down and ordered another glass of red wine, even though I was driving.

"As far as I can discern, your father was a relation of Malcolm X's or a descendant of Pushkin's. I was a promiscuous teenager."

"Moms, you're telling stories."

"Sometimes the truth is insufficient."

"I'm going to keep asking."

"No, you won't."

"Yeah, I will."

"No, you won't."

"Who's going to stop me?"

"Me."

"How you gonna do that?"

"One day I'm going to give you an answer."

"Yeah?"

"If you promise to let me choose the day. Don't ask again."

He shrugged and smiled. The muscles in his upper arms flexed. His dimples showed. The little teeth were big. The gap was gone. He reached across the table and pulled at a little hunk of my straightened hair. He wrapped it like a ribbon around his agile finger.

"Ya lyublyu tebya."

"Ya lyublyu tebya."

We were together again. There was no separating these syllables from the sound and fact of our affection. He remembered his Russian. He remembered my love. He gave me his word.

I didn't lose you at the white girls; I lost you at adolescence. For all I tried not to let it, your adolescence reminded me of mine. The white girls just showed up at the same time, and, adding insult to injury, they looked just like what Lena had wanted to slide miraculously out of her body—a white girl baby. When I remembered my mother and my adolescence, I could not wish to be a mommy. That was a break between us.

It was the best I could do to keep the promise I had made to you and me when you were a baby: first, second, third, do no harm. Put him down slowly, walk away quickly—don't hurt the baby. If I was Lena's child, I was Leo's child too. If anybody hurt the baby, I would blow his brains out and let the matter splatter on my feet, even if it was my own brains, even if it was my own feet.

Later, in bed, I tried to turn it over in my head. I tried to determine there and then whether it served you well or poorly to think that I had been a little bourgeois girl in Washington, that my disdain for my mother was the disdain of a spoiled brat for a hard-pressed mother. I remembered that I asked you what the boy had said to you and you lied to me. It seemed a sign. Pushkin had lied to protect me. Could I do less than lie to protect him?

I rolled over in my bed toward reprieve and distraction, toward an erotic exorcism of sorts, and Gabriel provided. He tasted in my kiss that I needed this night a secular sacrament.

Later, as Gabriel slept, I was fitful; the acts I thought would distract me had in fact provoked undesired memories.

Every time Pushkin asks about his father, I remember being raped. And when I remember being raped, I wonder about my mother's part in it. I am worried not about the past but about the present. About how near to impossible it is for me to want to be a mommy. How it is possible only because Pushkin is so lovable. I am thinking about how you will never know how compelling you are because you don't know how unwilling I have been. That all the darkness that has not happened is an amazement to me.

There were some things I understood about Lena when I got older; most of it I didn't. Thinking about Lena is like trying to calculate the square root of pi. With or without a computer, you just get stuck on it. Lured deeper and deeper by a next possible step, a doable step, and another step after it, with no answer in sight, you are distracted from more significant, if less attractive, equations.

I tried hard, in years to come, not to wince when I heard yummy mummies cluck to delicious but undevoured daughters, "You'll understand when you're a mother." When I heard breast-fed mouths, newly wet with their own baby-powdered sweat, their eyes first crinkling in the sunlight, screech to each other in feigned horror, masking a milk-into-bones self-satisfaction, "I've turned into my mother," then I felt beyond the map. I was in some uncharted territory of emotion, a place without identified landmarks. Not a place untrammeled or unexplored or unknown, but a place without demarcations, beyond compass, as if each previous traveler had vanished, leaving nothing behind, discerning nothing but loss.

Grown folks forgive. Grown folks get on with their lives. Grown folks understand. How would I know when I was grown? How would I know without being able to say, I have forgiven? Without saying, I have turned into my mother? Would I have to lie sprawled across a summer-bed, silver dangling from my earlobes, my child strangling in the heat of moist sheets and department-store White Shoulders perfume, before I was grown? Would I have to gaze down at my own butter-hued flanks and say to the fruit of my womb, Crawl back in but kiss me first, before I could say I had turned into my mother? This I would not do.

People usually go to high school football games to see what the offense can do, to see the quarterback, to see the receivers, to see somebody put on a show. But those days they went to see something else. They went to see Pushkin shut the opposing team's offense down. Sometimes what doesn't happen is more important than what does. I should have paid more attention to that.

I was never comfortable in those stands. I don't believe I was ever comfortable with all those eyes on Pushkin.

While I worked at invisibility, he worked at invincibility. That was a difference between us.

NINE

H OW DO I TRANSLATE *lap dancer?*

When Tanya tells me she was a lap dancer, am I to understand that Tanya was a whore?

How many tarts are in this tale; how many tales are in the tart?

When I think of Tanya, I think of poodles and whoring. When I think of poodles and whoring, I think of Whitefolks. When I think of Whitefolks, I think of Delicious and Daddy.

Whitefolks was a vicious apricot poodle.

Delicious was a pimp from Paradise Valley. He ran white whores and walked a ferocious fluffball. He wore his hair in an absurd style, straightened and lacquered, the front jutting out above his forehead in a triangular pouf reminiscent of the triangle between a woman's thighs. It was something like Little Richard's hair.

Delicious was on the slight side of medium-built, with narrow shoulders and short legs. The women he worked had once been farmgirls who knelt in German Lutheran churches, reciting words from Luther's *Small Catechism*. Their noses and lips and asses were narrow, but sometimes their minds were broad.

Delicious was my father's friend. He was my daddy's teammate. Him 'n' Dexter and Sammy, four of the five starters. Delicious was the screw-up in the bunch, even back then. Opposing teams never guarded him too hard, and sometimes that meant they could be on you like white on rice, but there was this thing about Delicious. When you really needed a basket, just so as it wasn't the last throw of the night, he would get you one. He came through when it was least expected. Balls that rolled around the rim and bounced out for other folks fell in for Delicious.

Sammy was Dennis Rodman before Dennis Rodman. He scrambled after every loose ball. He kept those elbows flying. He was tireless as an ox up and down the court, and faster than most. He was the only freshman starter the year they were state champions.

The year after my father graduated from high school, after he abandoned college to work with his father and brother in the cleaners', Daddy was drafted into the army. He had one girl pregnant and another had just delivered a baby, so he thought maybe that was a good thing. Angry mamas and angry grandmamas made a neighborhood tiny. Even Sun and Dear thought Korea might be the right next step for Leo. His family was smiling the day he got on the bus. They didn't allow themselves to imagine that he might be hurt or killed. No one they knew had ever died in Korea. Folks, black folks, died in Mississippi, in Alabama, in places like that. Sun barely knew what leaving the country was, but he thought he knew he wanted to do it. He was smiling when my father got on the bus. The mothers with babies were scowling. Dear was walking back to her chair on her porch. She wanted her favorite son, her middle one, to know where he could find her upon his return.

Standing in the center of the street, all six foot five inches of him, was Sammy, his shoulders hunched around his ears. His immense hands pulling down at the sleeves of his jacket. Tears rolling down his face, sobs cracking like thunder through light. He cried with his eyes wide open and his mouth closed. Standing straight up in the center of the street. His face was the last face my daddy saw before the bus turned off his block.

My father always loved Sammy. After his kids, I suspect he loved Sammy more than anyone else. Sammy showed up; Sammy showed love; he was ready to have the party and ready to pay the price.

The poet Pushkin's ancestor had his sister; Daddy had Sammy. If these pages do nothing else, Pushkin, know that I am crying and screaming as she takes you away. I am standing in the middle of the road, and I am crying. Anybody who wants to can watch.

I loved Sammy too; he was easy to love, he was like a third dip of my daddy on a double-dip cone. His wife, Glenda, was a secretary. His children were sharp-smart. Sammy gave me my first dolls that had professions, a doctor doll and a nurse doll. They were both white, of course. There were no black dolls in my childhood. My father didn't believe in dolls. My mother didn't believe in black. The nurse doll had a little navy blue cape that she wore, and she carried a satchel. The nurse doll looked professional. She was the size of a large baby doll but proportioned to represent a grown woman. I was playing with her the day Kennedy was shot. I would love to see her again, but she was something else that got left in Detroit, then got lost, never to be found.

Strange enough, good enough, Sammy's son, my play cousin, Dominick, became a professor too. He teaches sociology someplace out West. We lost track of each other for many years. One afternoon I was reading an academic article that spoke to me, preached from its pages to my soul. I looked back to the title page for the author's name. I wanted to ask him a few questions. I smiled to see Dominick's name. I assumed it was another Dominick, but a lovely association. I looked up the author's number, using the Internet white pages. I made the call. When I heard the voice, my heart flipped over. My Dominick was speaking again. He remembered who I was. Sammy was blessing our family again. Sammy was easy to love.

Delicious is an altogether different story. Some say Delicious was the sweetest pimp who ever took a whore out on the stroll. I say, how sweet can a pimp be?

What do you do, what does a Harvard-graduate Vanderbilt professor do, with memories of a gangster daddy and his wild-assed friends? A Paliprep teenager does nothing. She forgets. Maybe a middle-aged professor can do something different and better. Maybe this remembering is the first step to this better thing.

How sweet can a pimp be? Once when I was a young girl, long before I thought to ask that question, I asked my daddy, "Who's white folks?" He said, "Why you wanna know?" And I said, "I heard somebody saying, 'White folks always keep us down.' And I heard somebody else say, 'White folks always be around.' I just want to know who or what these white folks be."

To understand these questions, you must remember, understand, or be taught that Motown was an almost all black community. Except to go downtown, to the department store, to Hudson's, to the big library, or to the Art Institute, except to go to the doctor or the dentist, I barely ever saw white people when I was a young child.

There is, in fact, a story my family liked to tell of a Sunday afternoon when my father, dressed in a proper gray silk suit, took my mother and me downtown for an ice cream sundae at a place called

Saunders. I was small. My father carried me into the ice cream parlor hiked up on his hip. From this princess's perch I extended a beige arm and pointed a beige finger toward the crowd. "Look at all the little peck-a-woods, Daddy," I exclaimed.

My mother was embarrassed and furious. The crowd was shocked, perhaps. I don't know—no one in my family knew. No one in my family stayed to know. My mother turned on her heel and left. My father followed quickly behind Mother. When he stopped walking, she snatched me from his hip. "You teach her any more of this Malcolm X mess, we're gone." He wanted to laugh. He wanted to take me onto his hip and tell me I had more courage than any man he knew. But first we had to get the hell out of Dodge. You don't call a room full of peckerwoods peck-a-woods with impunity.

How can I tell this story to Tanya? Is there another true way to tell this tale? How do I parse the poignancy of knowing that the story which helped me might hurt her? If the story bruises her, does the story blacken her? And if one cultural essence of blackness is to be bruised, is another to transform bruising into beauty?

My daddy transformed bruising into beauty on more than one occasion. It is the nicest necessity of negritude. I remember the day Daddy tried to teach the skill to me. He asked if I remembered Delicious. I nodded, yes.

Daddy spoke. He said, "Delicious was the sweetest pimp who ever took a whore out on the stroll, and Delicious had a dog, a vicious poodle he called Whitefolks. He guarded his girls with that dog. Whitefolks," said my daddy, "became notorious throughout the neighborhood. He'd bite through your meat to your bone, but every day he strolled his girls safe home." My daddy said to me, "Wherever you go, whatever you see, commit this thought to your memory. White folks ain't nothing but a broken-down black pimp's dog."

Vicious, racist thought, vicious, racist thought.

How simple it is to announce that. How complex it is to realize that that vicious racist thought has walked me safe home through tenure reviews at Vanderbilt and the pursuit of honors degrees at Harvard. If white folks ain't nothing but a broken-down black pimp's dog, they can't scare me.

I have no idea in the world whether Delicious had a dog named Whitefolks or my daddy just thought that he should have. I only know that in spinning the tale, he understood himself to be weaving me a girdle of protective gold.

My family had a wealth of racialist doggy legends. My grandmother, Dear, had a standard poodle named Elvis. He was either chocolate brown or black. One day Dear stopped referring to the poodle and put her Elvis scrapbook on the heater behind the wing chair in the front room. She had heard the rumor bouncing around the nation's black communities that Elvis had spit on a black girl trying to get his autograph. She put the scrapbook away and cut off Elvis's table scraps just in case the story was true.

So what am I to make of Tanya, anointed as I am with vicious racist thoughts?

"Don't be this way."

"Don't be this way."

We say these words to each other. What way does he think I'm being? I am here for my son. And if I'm not ready to share with him the name of his father, I'm ready to tell him about my own. He can listen or not, read or not. I am not ready to tell the whole truth, but I am scribbling my way to some part or translation of the truth that might be useful to him. I'm not ready to tell the whole truth, but perhaps he'll accept what I can offer.

If I cannot give him his father, I will begin to give him mine.

My name is Windsor Armstrong.

Being a man of modest means, powerful imagination, and substantial wisdom, Leo understood that the name he chose for his child would be a significant portion, perhaps the whole, of his daughter's dowry. I was trying to be like my father when I named you Pushkin.

Before I knew Windsor to be a castle in England I knew it to be a town in Canada, a place across a border. Before I knew Windsor to be a town in Canada I knew it to be my name, and before I knew it to be my name my father, fascinated by borders and boundaries, gifted it to me.

When I was small, only me and Tennessee Williams had a place for a name. Me and Tennessee, reason to be proud.

Pushkin is a place name.

Leo wished to bestow not merely a sense that I was unique, rare, but a destination to obtain, distant, desirable, not present, cold, longed for: Windsor Armstrong. Windsor; he had thought to name me Star, after the North Star guiding the slaves through darkness, but the North Star was disconnected guidance, not participant, and that was not as he wanted it to be. Discovering love to be larcenous,

Leo was amused to name his unborn daughter for the scene of the crime.

Leo met Lena, Daddy met Mommy, in Windsor, Ontario, in Canada. Back then Windsor was a hotspot, a border town beyond the grasp of United States of American history, offering to my father, a refugee from Confederate Alabama, the promise of North American equality. Windsor was a place where the Negro had never been counted as three fifths of a man, defined by the law as not a man, even if on occasion its government had allowed a man to own another man. In his mind, it was a town across the Puritan line, a place of money and whores, of, nearer to, Catholic pleasures and forgiveness bought by confession. In honor of Windsor, Leo ate fish every Friday, red snapper dredged in flour, then fried, or catfish when he couldn't find snapper. Ate it until the pope said you didn't have to.

Windsor was all mobbed up—ever since Prohibition. If Leo had known the poem "Kubla Khan," he might have named me Xanadu. "In Xanadu did Kubla Khan a stately pleasure dome decree." There was a club on the lake named Xanadu, but everyone called it X, 'cause no one knew how to pronounce that neon word. It was in that club Leo first saw Lena dangling off Fatty Mo's wrist. Leo didn't know any Coleridge. But he knew women. He gave two hundred dollars to two blond twins to flap their pussies in Fatty Mo's direction, whispered in the gangster's ear that Lena was probably over the clap, took her in a car, and kissed her where she had never been kissed. Lena was Miss It, then Lena was his.

Two or three Saturdays later, when Lena saw the blondes dangling puny gold bracelets and sporting great big purple bruises, she was grateful.

Leo was thrilled: by her height, by her narrow waist, by her cantaloupe breasts, by her ham-hock thighs, by the sweet jelly curve of her belly and the just-a-little-more-than-a-handful size of her ass. He loved the way she talked like a Lutheran lady from the sticks, how she almost had a German accent. She had been the only inkspot in St. Phillip's Lutheran School, and she had been the valedictorian of the eighth-grade farming town class. Leo loved her big brown cowlike eyes and the way she cast them down so casually, gazing upon those chocolate-tipped melons. He fucked her the very first night in the stall of the ladies' bathroom. He lifted her out of her shoes. She wrapped her legs around his waist and her arms around his neck and he bucked till she came. When they were finished, she wiped herself off with her panties and threw them into the trash. He zipped his joint into his pants and said he wasn't gonna wash it till it had tasted her again.

I know all this because she wrote it down. In one of several hundred steno pads, spiral notebooks bound across the top, the page divided in two down the middle with a red line. She kept these pads as diaries and tokens of a time when she tried to learn shorthand. I read, uninvited, pages upon pages from what she called her "flip books."

This is a thing I inherited from my mother, the habit of confessing onto paper what one cannot speak aloud. I warn you that most of my mother's habits are dangerous. I was twelve or thirteen, in Washington, when I first studied one of her tablets. Reading the progression of her insights and experiences almost broke my mind. Still, I was lured back time and time again. Every time opportunity presented itself, I peeked. The raw carnality and unblinking intelligence coupled with her childishly simple commitment to having exactly what she wanted exactly when she wanted were riveting. What weird wants grow in the forest of ever-heeded sighs.

If I knew where Lena was, if I visited her right now, somewhere across an ocean where everybody thinks she is white, I would sneak into her office or library or bedroom and search for the flip book with damp ink.

I wish you would come upon these notes of mine. I am not certain whether I have the courage to give them to you, or whether I should give them to you. I remember both the shock of knowing too much about my mother and the satisfaction of knowing something about my mother. My mother believed that paper absolved. She thought that by committing her sins to paper she achieved a kind of absolution. I don't believe that. I have read too many of her lines to believe that. What I know is what the Puritans knew long before Freud—we are changed by the way we talk about ourselves.

My mother's words on paper transformed her into a hell-bat and then a hellhound. Reading her scrawls, I learned that a bad woman can lead a good man to hell by his cock, or his joint, or his johnson, or his whatever you want to call it—except, maybe, magic flute. A woman who calls it a magic flute will take you to heaven.

Did I hear Tanya whispering those two words at you? Is Tanya somehow breaking my mother's spell? Did I once whisper those words in someone else's ear? Must you know who your daddy is? I think I am going crazy. You want to know who your daddy is and I keep writing about my mother. She stands between me and remembering Daddy and me and loving you and your Tanya.

As strange as it sounds, I wish my daddy was your daddy. I write all this to give you my daddy as your daddy. He's better than you would get with the truth. And I keep hearing my daddy ask me, "You wanna know the truth or you want fo' me to tell you a story?" "Don't tell no story now," I hear Dear admonishing me after posing a hard question. And I hear you saying it too: "Don't tell no story now."

We have both said it. Sometimes me first, sometimes him. The request is earnest and urgent on both our parts. I can't help feeling I am the mother, I am his mother, my request takes precedence, white folks in the lexicon of my childhood ain't nothing but a broken-down black pimp's dog, don't be this way. And he looks at me as if I'm some dyed-black version of the ghost that rides through Alabama in sheets. He looks at me and he takes his love away. He withdraws it like a deposit he made in a bank. He takes his love from me and he gives it to her. I am smaller than I have ever been, small and hot with anger.

But there is something else here, something else here, so much else here.

I understand they are decorating the wedding cake with sugared blackberries. I find this hopeful. It means Pushkin remembers his childhood. Blackberries in syrup was the dessert I most often fed my son, and I also fed them to him for breakfast. I knew it was a strange thing to do, but I kept doing it. I told myself blackberries in syrup are sweet and delicious, but I knew I was doing it because they were historical and literary. I knew it was risky. You don't have to dig that deep to find the negative part of the Pushkin legacy. Fueled with Lena's diatribes and disgust, I found it so easy to recognize the poison in my patrimony, to reject hog head cheese, fried bologna, and Vernor's ginger ale. How did I fail to see that the toxic tensions in the Petersburg poet would not be sugared over?

Contrary to what most scholars declare, I believe Pushkin doubted Natalia, his wife. And somehow because Pushkin doubted Natalia, I doubt Tanya. Many scholars have written about the death of Pushkin. I take issue with most of them.

Of course Pushkin doubted Natalia. He doubted Natalia because he doubted himself. He doubted his own sexual attractiveness. He doubted his own beauty. He doubted his great-grandfather's beauty. He doubted his great-grandfather's erotic grace. What a thing it would be to transform all that! In Pushkin's unfinished novella, "The Negro of Peter the Great," about which I have been thinking so much lately, it is clearly evident that Pushkin doubted his own humanity. Pushkin doubted his great-grandfather's humanity. Pushkin is a pleasure because we don't doubt him.

It has been written that on his deathbed Pushkin called for blackberries in liquid sugar. I served blackberries in my special cinnamon sauce too many mornings of my son's life. I understood it to be his favorite food. I fed a little boy, my little boy, a last supper over and over for breakfast.

My father taught me to say *peckerwood*, told me the story about Delicious and Whitefolks. I have carried these words from my past into my future, carry them in my mind as a kind of amulet I do not understand but understand to work. My daddy packed a lot of things into words.

He intended his racist epithets as antidotes, not poison. The impetus of his racist language was a loving protection for infant dark souls from racist ideology. He practiced a kind of psychological homeopathy. I who have been poisoned and revived am grateful to his racist signs, lies, and attitudes.

There was another story my father told me about Delicious and the girls. It's a story about whores. I am suspecting *lap dancer* is a euphemism for whore, but who knows. I surely know that things aren't always what they seem to be, and that's what it seems like, so maybe it ain't so.

I once heard Delicious boast, "When I turned them out, they didn't go back in." I asked my daddy what "turned out" meant. I was getting older then; it was after I was abducted from paradise; I think I might have been eleven. I was just beginning to notice my body changing, but the changes were still small: a few silks of hair, a rising wave of ripple across my chest. My period had not yet begun, and neither had it for any of my friends such as I knew about.

Years later I discovered that one of my best friends, Jael, who was destined to be five-foot-nothing with big boobs, skinny legs, black hair, and gray eyes, had had hers start in the fourth grade, but she hadn't told me. She told Hopii, a girl with blond hair and blue eyes, and that girl told me later to make me feel small and out of the inner circle of the circle. Anyway, I was back in Detroit on a visit, and Detroit was changing even more dramatically than I was. You couldn't call it Motown anymore. Motown Records had moved out of Detroit, out West to Los Angeles. There were rumors, never substantiated, that Barry Gordy no longer controlled the company. When I would mention Motown with awe in Washington or New York, after a while the response was not curiosity and jealousy but "Gordy's sold out. So sad. Too bad." I didn't believe it. I don't believe it. I believe Whitefolks is not only a broken-down black pimp's dog, but white folks will always try to keep you down . . . but they can't because they ain't nothing but a broken-down black pimp's dog . . .

As I started writing, I see I am losing my thread here—I always lose my thread here, because I find it hard to look at all my cards, let alone play them. It is hard to discard what I wish to discard, knowing that someone at the table may pick up my cards and see what I had in my hand, see what I held in my hand for so long.

Anyway, back about the time Motown Records moved to California and Japanese cars, fuel-efficient cars, began to dominate the domestic car market, after the Detroit riots, after the deaths of Martin Luther King and John F. Kennedy and Robert Fitzgerald Kennedy, by the time Jimmy Hoffa disappeared, before the Renaissance Center towers were erected, housing the hotel in which my daddy and I holed up, him lying on the bed, me sitting in a chair, a movie on the television, trays of room service on the bed, a view across the river into Canada through the window as we visited—about that time I heard Delicious say, "When I turned them out, they didn't go back in." I thought I knew what he meant.

There are prostitutes in Washington, D.C. Streetwalkers, when I first moved to Washington, congregated around Logan Circle. Left-leaning children in D.C. don't know prostitutes or pimps, they know about them. They know that pimps exploit prostitutes, sending them to sell their wares, sex without the detail of love, on cold and rainy days, the kind of days when left-leaning children would prefer to be eating crepes from Brittany on Wisconsin Avenue in Georgetown. Preferably a lemon crepe, crackling with broiled sugar, preceded by a crock of delicious onion soup topped with a giant crouton and an inch of melted cheese, served to you in a dark room by white women with ample bosoms wearing peasant shirts and broad navy blue gathered skirts and odd little white hats, like shower caps, that keep their hair tucked up.

Back to the whores. They are so easy to avoid and so unavoidable.

I want to avoid them, but I remember this. If I didn't remember this, all the onion soup and lemon crepes, tasted and remembered, could not return the sense of savor to my life.

So I say to my father, "'Turning out'—that means he doesn't let those poor women come back in till they make some money for him." My father looks at me as if he's trying to figure out whether I will ever need to know this. I look at him as if "Why doesn't he just acknowledge I'm a grown and sophisticated girl who has now seen more than he's seen?" Daddy's starting to look a lot more like a gangster and a farm boy now that I'm living in Washington. He's starting to look a little inadequate. He stares at me, but he can't see into my future. He says what he usually says aloud at moments like this; he says, "Only time will tell." He doesn't have time to let time tell it. Somehow he seems to know this. He does what he always does; he tells me the truth.

He says, "That ain't what Delicious means by that. That's not what 'turning out' means. 'Turning out' is the process by which you take a female and you turn her into a whore, usually a girl who's pretty innocent. Life turns more whores than any pimp, but when life turns 'em out, they're hard from the get-go, ain't no softness or love in them. When a pimp turns a woman out, if he does it right, he takes her and he teaches her to love sex, then he looks around her mind with her for her body's strangest desire, and whatever that desire is, he fulfills it, and when she steps out of his bed she's jonesin' for his body. She knows herself in ways she ain't prepared to know, and she knows her own mama, let alone her daddy, could never love her if they had seen what she had done. A turned-out girl can never go back in, into the safe, sweet love. She can only stay out in the streets with the kind of love you can find there."

I didn't know much about sex when my father told me this. Couldn't imagine many specifics of what one might do on that dark journey to desire, but I was scared. Not specifically scared that someone would do this to me, scared that the world was a darker and more complex place than I understood it to be and Daddy, who was swimming deeper and deeper into his bottle, wasn't around to explain stuff to me. Daddy, who had for so long been so close, was now far away and in a different city. I was even wondering, If Daddy was sober, would he have told me all this? My Washington ears were becoming attuned to a different tenor of parental disclosure. This struck me as possibly an inappropriate conversation. I certainly knew it made me feel uncomfortable. I was ready to forget all about Delicious and his whores. I had already forgotten about that poodle named Whitefolks, eclipsed as he was by all the white folks in the flesh I was meeting. I was feeling like I had bitten off more than I could chew with my question when my father said, "No one could ever turn you out. There's nothing you could do, nothing anyone could do to you, that would cause me to turn away from you. Nothing your body could know. Nothing your body could want would make me shut my eyes to you. You a sweet child. Only time will tell if you start screwing like a rabbit and leave your heart out of the bed. If you're screwing some bastard ain't ever take his heart into the bed, they'll be a heart in bed. My heart wrapped around your little fingers, going wherever your fingers go, even if it's up some son-a-bitch's ass."

There was nothing I could do with that sentence except forget it. Nothing I could do with those words on the day they were spoken but pretend they hadn't been. I could not even imagine what he might be talking about. But a day came, days came, in which I had reason to remember, and in those days to come, I had reason to thank God that my daddy had told me the lie, white folks ain't nothing but a broken-down black pimp's dog, and his truth, I will love you no matter what you do or what is done to you.

The one great shame of my daddy's life was snatching his love back from Martha Rachel and raining some shame down on her for no good reason. Somewhere between Martha Rachel and me, my daddy recognized that we couldn't all be Dear, we wouldn't all be pure, unsullied, untouched except by love. Remembering how he severed his mother from his sister, how he made his sister cry, he had determined never to be that way again to a woman he loved. He was speaking to me, but he was talking to his sister. He was putting those words into the air hoping they would carry back in time, and forward in time, expecting and accepting in that moment that his heart would go places he never wanted it to go, places that could break his mind.

His mind might break, but he wouldn't send another woman he loved out into the world without his unshameable love. He wrapped that love around me like a girdle of gold. I discovered at once that it constrained me. Only time will tell, and time has told: that girdle of gold has sustained me—and it is shot through and through with Daddy's racist preference for everything brilliant and black and beautiful.

To break off a piece of my love for Tanya, I'm gonna have to unweave the cloth from which my girdle of gold is made. How can I do that when I know, when I am knowing, that girdle of gold has saved me from the cold? What is enough? I let you hold on to me, I put you on my hip and said, "Stay close. You have my heart. Can you hear it beat?" I should have been tying my heart to your wrists, nailing it to your lips, telling you what Daddy told me. I am not that vulgar. I am not that fierce. I am not that loving at all.

When I think of poodles and whores, I think of Daddy's mercy and me. Maybe I can let Tanya be Tanya. There's only one whore in this story, and it ain't Tanya and it ain't Windsor.

I want to love Pushkin the way my daddy loved me.

I did not give you my heart; I just held you close to it.

My father ran with gangsters and outlaws, the predecessors of thugz. He told a far too little girl far too real stories about far too many whores. He loved me with naked simplicity. I do not love you like my daddy loved me. Before you were born, my heart blushed and took up a veil.

Maybe Tanya can teach me to strip.

TEN

WATER WASHES CLEAN.
I like the Jekyll Island Club. I like the Greystone Inn on Cumberland Island. I like the funky old lodgings that began life as places people like me have not always been able to stay—be it Jekyll's millionaires' club or Greystone, the hunting lodge Andrew Carnegie built on Cumberland, when he wasn't allowed to join Jekyll. They both kept *us* out—except to serve. I like to sleep in rooms with character and quirks and high ceilings and food that tastes, or at least tries to taste, like someplace in particular, not every place in the world.

Pushkin likes something else altogether. He likes new hotels with immense marble bathrooms and feather beds, hotels with DVD libraries and fast Internet access, places where people like us have always been. He would not consider staying in a hotel without pay-per-view movies and gourmet mini-bars, without biscotti and Terra Chips. He likes the stark and sleek W chain with its bright chrome bathrooms and its dim hallways. He loves pushing the whatever, whenever button and ordering whatever, whenever.

I like Ritz-Carltons. I remember when I thought the Hilton was fancy. The only vision of heaven my father ever saw on this earth that he shared with me was seeing black and white children swimming together in a Howard Johnson's swimming pool outside Montgomery, Alabama, the summer before my freshman year at college.

Ever since he joined the NFL, Pushkin has given me a trip for my birthday. He tries to take me somewhere I have long wanted to go. One way or another, we always seem to end up on an island. I like islands and he likes me.

Shortly after they got together, I invited Pushkin to bring Tanya over for Sunday brunch. Pushkin and I were gently fussing over alternative destinations for our yearly trip when Tanya broke into the conversation and suggested San Juan. We were sitting in my living room. It was strange to see Tanya in my barrel chair, the one that was Adam Clayton Powell's favorite seat when he visited a family on 145th Street, according to the Harlem antique dealer who sold it to me. Almost too strange for me, but Pushkin didn't seem to notice. He just continued to read the travel section of the *New York Times*. It was Tanya's first visit to my house. I'm rather sure I brought up our annual trip as a subtle form of exclusion Pushkin wouldn't recognize. For the first time in a tiny while, Pushkin and I shared a coded look, a look that both of us understood to mean "I'm glad she's not going on vacation with us."

This pleased me. Over the years there have been two things I have done well with Pushkin, travel and eat. Now he does them better than I. He is a sophisticated traveler and he is a sophisticated eater. I want my payback. I'm ready for him to show me what I don't know. He says when he retires from the NFL he's going to create a whole series of on-line travel guidebooks with up-to-the-day suggestions for restaurants, hotels, clubs, galleries, everything. He's going to be the more than Fodor or Fielding or Zagat. Post-Zagat and Fodor and Fielding, more than Insight or Inside, will be his X guides. They will not only clue you in to the history and the literature of a place, they will hook you up to the best corner to watch street hoops, the bar of the moment, the particular rhythms of each city's particular rappers, to the massage therapist with the best hands.

He has no interest in going to San Juan. He might go to that little island, Vieques, that used to be a military base, which people are flocking to now. Vieques, yes. San Juan, no. San Juan is not someplace we would go.

"Mom's mother took her to San Juan when she was a kid. The only good food was black bean soup. She got robbed on the beach."

Tanya bit her bottom lip, then the thumb of her right hand. She was not wearing much makeup. What was there was there to heighten contrast. Her skin is very white. Her lips are very red. Her eyelashes are very black. Her hair is silver. Someone needs to take her out of her misery.

"Who's hungry for lunch?"

I asked this finally feeling amicable. I wished I had prepared something Pushkin might actually like to eat. I hadn't. Instead, there was almost warm chicken salad and a chilled half-bottle of bad champagne waiting. Once a month, when it wasn't football season, before Tanya, Pushkin came over on Sunday for bloody marys and omelets. He loves omelets. I had not made omelets. I was trying to make an impression of hospitality, provide a measure of intimidating sophistication, without providing food that would attract a guest to return. Half-warm champagne hit the perfect note. It's horrible; it's flattering; it intimidates.

Tanya refused the champagne and asked for something non-alcoholic. I wondered if she could be pregnant. Pushkin asked for some Pellegrino. I was wondering if he knew she was pregnant. I eyeballed her belly, trying not to look purposeful. Her eyes caught mine as I glanced up from glancing down. Somehow it felt significant. She slowly smoothed her ringless hand over the thin cotton of her T-shirt, over her protruding hipbone, over her glove-snug capri pants.

It was still early days in their relation. Tanya had yet to adopt her signature style, but she had a look. I liked the trousers. Thought I might try getting a pair for myself.

"Where'd you get your pants?"

"Target." She pronounced the word *Tar-jay*, and I didn't know if she was making a joke or mispronouncing. "I buy many of my clothes at Target."

"Frugality or style preference?"

"Decency."

"Decency?"

"Target clothes are decent."

"You get them at a decent price?"

"Not cheap. Decent. When I first came to this country, all the women I was around, they dressed a certain way. Everything is primary colors, very tight, very small. I dressed like that too. Petersburg is so cold, we stay wrapped up in layers on layers. Here I walk around half naked. Of course, I work nearly all naked, so half naked seems dressed."

I was amused; I was glowing. This girl was not going to last long, but she would provide admirable entertainment while she was here. Behind his *New York Times Sophisticated Traveler* magazine insert, Pushkin cleared his throat. He wanted Tanya to stop talking.

"Now I dress like you." Tanya stared at the back of his paper.

"Everything at Target is decent." She pronounced this second sentence as if she were both unsure of its veracity and desperately desirous that it be true. She was right, up to a point. Or should I say two points. The buyers for Target were not imagining Tanya's 34Ds or double Ds set high and perky on the chest when the buyer for boys bought undershirts. Target's mass-market sensibility usually doesn't lead to sartorial sensationalism, but the store's finest rarely finds its way to a body like Tanya's. Then again, she was clearly wearing an opaque padded bra—very Tar-jay rather than Victoria's Secret. Her headlights were not showing. The high beams were not on. Discretion, not nipples, was in evidence.

"You'd look good in a paper sack," I said, giving her the compliment for which she was not fishing. It was hard to know if this was a facetious remark. Tanya couldn't tell. Pushkin couldn't tell. I could barely tell, and I'm not telling, even now. Pushkin looked up from the piece he was reading on travel to southern Chile. I knew because I had walked behind him—the better to read over his shoulder and see where we would be going without this girl—on my way across the room to pour myself another cup of coffee.

An expression appeared on his face that I had seen before in my parlor. Nervous. It's an expression he never wears on the football field. Tanya rose from the antique barrel chair upholstered in white denim. She walked over to my stiff-backed Egyptian-revival sofa upholstered in black and gold, on which Pushkin was sprawled, and dropped into his lap. The *Times* magazine fell to the black slate tile floor with a quiet flap. "On the other hand," she said without looking at me, "the more clothes you are wearing, the more clothes you get to take off." For half a second the nervous look on Pushkin's face got more pronounced; then it vanished. I saw this and Tanya saw it. I saw it from across the room. Tanya saw it from Pushkin's lap. She bent her head to kiss the crown of his kinky head. Her white hair fell onto his shoulders. She completely obscured my view of my boy's face.

Pushkin was clearing his throat again and pulling away from her—but none too fast. There was something as unconscious as a kitten about this girl. She turned to me, giggling. "Sometimes I forget you are his mother, you look so young. You are so pretty."

It was my turn not to know whether the compliment was facetious.

At that moment I would have given the world to slap Tanya. I wondered if it was possible to walk the few steps across the room and

slap her and somehow continue on with my relationship with Pushkin. It should be possible, I thought then. She had all but told me she
thought of me as a rival. Why couldn't I tell her that I saw her as a
tramp trying to steal my boy? He may not be my man, but he's my
boy. If letting that girl keep sitting on his lap was Pushkin's way of
telling me he was no longer a boy, I was starting to get the message.

Hoping he'd get the bitch off his lap if I signaled my awareness of
his manhood, I smiled sweetly. I put on a mask I rarely wear. I would
play southern black hostess in a quasi-academic setting. I would go
get the drinks. I would serve a properly chilled bottle of apple cider. I
remember shocking myself with a strange chain of thought: I will
not slap her. If she's pregnant, I will push her down the flight of
stairs. Even in that moment I realized this was crazy cannibal mother
thought. After all those years, another one. Regression was complete. I got the drinks.

Two weeks later the three of us were in a house off Lopez Island, far
out in the ocean between Seattle and Vancouver. Gabriel was off
building something for somebody. Lopez is the tiniest of the significant San Juans. Tanya was not angling to go to Puerto Rico. She
was arching toward Seattle. She had her words just a few letters off,
but her ideas were clear. And it was not a bad idea. She wanted to see
the Northwest. She was in on the annual mother-son birthday trip. I
had little to say. We flew from Nashville to Seattle on a nonstop
Southwest flight, laughed at the jokes, ate the peanuts, saved money.
We stayed in the W in downtown Seattle and slept in what Pushkin
says are the most comfortable beds anywhere. Then we took a Port
Authority ferry out to Lopez.

Puget Sound is one of the loveliest watery places in America.
Looking at the surface of the water, I blinked at the deep, cold, clean,
and wondered if Tanya could be pregnant with my grandchild. We
live our lives suspended between limited vastness below and limitless
vastness above, only ever half knowing what is going on even in the
immediate vicinity of ourselves. It is a generosity of the sea that it
lulls us into knowing that darkness is finite and perhaps more precious than the light. On the deck of the ferry I felt the cold meeting
warmth. I saw islands exploding into life and picturesque silhouettes.
The wind across the sound was a bold and invited caress. To stand
on the deck and motor out to Lopez was to be wind-blasted clean
of psychology, history, and complexity. At least it was that way
for me.

Pushkin and I stood out on the foredeck in matching bright yellow field jackets we had bought separately years before, when he was at Michigan, exclaiming "Great minds think alike," then "Fools seldom differ" when we both showed up in Ann Arbor in them.

We got off at little Lopez Island. This tiny place was not our destination. When we walked down the gangplank of the ferryboat, Pushkin had a fishing boat, not a car, waiting. We were going farther on, to a tinier island without a name. It had a beautiful house. This was a surprise to me. I thought we were going to Lopez.

On this boat, open and small, we felt the swells beneath us, felt ourselves rising brightly and abruptly. I wasn't queasy. Tanya wore one antinausea patch on her shoulder and plastered a second to her thigh. She waved Pushkin off. The boatman kept his eyes on the near distance across the open sea. There was something on the horizon. It looked like a birthday cake. It looked like a castle. It looked like something in a little girl's dream. It was the island Pushkin had rented.

As we pulled in to the pier, the fisherman hand-pumped an air horn. This was an unnecessary formality. We could already see a golf cart flying down the one visible road toward the pier. I noticed as we disembarked from the flaking wooden boat that the name painted in flowing black script across the bow was *The Queen of Spades.* I shivered in the rising cold. The housekeeper and her husband pulled up on the golf cart, introduced themselves, welcomed us, and started transferring luggage. The sun was going slowly down and darkness was rising. The couple led our way up to the house.

It was a spectacular place with dramatic views in all directions. Framed in the front hall were pages of *Architectural Digest* documenting the construction. All weathered wood and wonder, the house was a work of love and money, built by someone, according to the indiscreet real estate agent, who got in at Microsoft early and enjoyed more good fortune than he knew existed—until his wife decided she was gay and requested half the funds from his Pacific palace and a divorce. It was up for sale, and Pushkin was vaguely thinking of purchase. There were six thousand square feet. Four bathrooms. There was an inner courtyard with a heated pool. There were three different private beaches on the fourteen acres. The live-in couple lived in a converted barn at the far end of the island.

After a dinner of Pacific oysters and Orcas Island lamb, we retired to our bedrooms.

• • •

In the days that came I would see otters and seals, I would see many, many things, but I cannot tell you what they were. I remember perhaps fiddlehead ferns. I remember very little except this:

One night I drank and ate too much and woke up thirsty. Ridiculously thirsty. Passing Pushkin and Tanya's closed door, I wondered how late it was before they finally got to sleep. I shuffled down to the kitchen, awakening to the possibility of watching the sun rise.

I ground beans and boiled water, waiting for the dawn, for the veil to lift from the earth. I was eager for morning. Looking out on the porch, I saw the silhouette of what looked to be a beached seal. I walked out to get a better look. There was no seal.

Pushkin and Tanya were sleeping on the beach. Pushkin was lying naked on a towel. Tanya was lying on top of him. They were stomach to stomach but crotch to face. Her head gently rested in the cleft where his thighs parted. Her legs were splayed one over each of his shoulders. Except for her feet and ankles, they were both completely naked. She wore pink satin toe shoes laced with broad shiny silk ribbon round her ankles. There was a towel thrown across her back. The sun cracked the horizon, dividing light from shadow. Place after place in the sand were the prints of her palms, the impress of her toes, and his footprints. The beach was studded with love.

The towel blew off. Tanya stirred. She kissed the skin closest to her mouth. Her hair was blowing straight with the wind. Her head was a spiky blond cloud that was dancing above my son's body. He was rolling onto his side and struggling to his feet. He was pulling her up with him. She was standing on the wooden blocks of her ballerina toes, inches and inches taller than she was in naked feet. Her arms levitated from her sides until they were around his neck. They began to waltz in circles as the sun rose over the hill of the next island and the moon splashed down into the sound, as the last stars of morning twinkled on, as Pushkin lifted Tanya into the air and twirled her around as he twirled into her. She yelped into his twirl and his eyes opened. He saw me watching him. He made her scream again and then again until I turned and did what I should have done at first awareness of sight: closed my eyes and walked away.

Later I took solace in being told that the strange girl had put Ecstasy into my wine, thinking I shouldn't be left out of the party. I want to think this explains why I didn't look away. I am not so sure it does.

Throughout the rest of the week, breaking through the quiet clamor and buzz of the island, I heard and heard again her screams turning to whimpers, then moans into screams again. I wondered if Pushkin had remembered an old anger. I worried that Tanya was falling in love.

Once upon a time a long time ago I had been the girl falling in love and Pushkin had been the betrayed beloved who stumbled upon the waking lovers. It was in Petersburg, with the man from Tsarkoe Selo, the little town that was once called Pushkin.

He was a Russian scholar. He cared little for Pushkin the writer and perhaps little for Pushkin my boy. *The Master and Margarita* was his favorite novel. He warned me against the Ginsburg translation. Ginsburg, he thought, took too many liberties. He loved the moderns. He didn't like my beloved Turgenev. He thought *Fathers and Sons* was ideological. I thought he thought too much. I can't even imagine thinking a man could think too much today. But this was yesterday, many yesterdays ago. It was, in fact, before the day I fell in love with Pushkin, before the day we twirled together in front of the Hermitage and he kissed me up to Jesus.

I had not made the connection. After all these years. I just accepted my son's kiss. I did not ask what paved its way.

Like all Russians, my Russian, Alexander, knew Pushkin, knew his work directly and knew his tone, knew his aesthetic because it blew through the modern Russian language into the modern Russian mind. The modern Russian language is shot through with Pushkin's love of folklore and clarity, as brightly and boldly as Shakespeare blows through the King James version of the Bible. That is bold and bright blowing.

Like most, Alexander thought Pushkin's great achievements were *Eugene Onegin* and *Boris Gudunov*. In contrast with most, he preferred *Gudunov*. We saw the opera of *Eugene Onegin* performed at the Kirov Theater from the czar's box.

Though Alexander knew Pushkin had African ancestors, the idea of his "being black" he dismissed as "not a Russian concept." He amused me when he declared, "Even a tree cannot be black in Russian, in the sense of the verb *to be*—I am, she was. A tree is not black. Black is not an adjective in Russian, it is a verb. There is a sense not that a tree is black but that a tree emanates blackness.

"My people were serfs," Alexander told me more than once. "Serfs were sold with land. They were little different from slaves." I begged to differ, but I didn't want him to know the difference. I thought of Spady so far away, Spady who could not imagine Alexander or how I might find my way to amusing him in my bed. I didn't want to tell Alexander that the difference between slavery in America and slavery almost everywhere else through time—the defense that Americans gave for the legitimacy of owning slaves—was the fiction that the slave was not human. I didn't want that idea to enter Alexander's mind.

A few months ago, a Nashville gallery owner who knew my son was engaged phoned me up about a painting he thought might make an excellent wedding present. I was excited about the painting, because I thought it might save me some labor and some pride. I had started a project that could become a present, a present that could serve as blessing or curse. But it was a hard row to hoe, the work I had undertaken, and I wasn't particularly good at it. I was looking at other presents in case I didn't have the humility to step away from my expertise, to lay myself down as a rough bridge between Motown and Petersburg. That day, with my labor unfinished, an easier but still profound present seemed a very good thing.

The gallery, on the outskirts of Nashville, is bijou—tiny but full of fine paintings of local interest. The painting the art dealer had called me to see was of a brown girl and a lamb. There was almost something realer about the lamb than about the girl. The gallery owner wanted eighteen thousand dollars for it. I wouldn't have given him eighteen hundred. It was a silent argument against the humanity of the black child. Maybe I would have given him eighteen hundred dollars. Given it for the privilege of buying the painting, then burning it up.

That day I decided to complete the writing project that could be a wedding gift.

Alexander has written two books. Both have done fairly well in the States. While a graduate student, he was a visiting fellow at Harvard. He knows some people I know. He teases me and tells me that he used to see Diana and me walking across Harvard Yard. He says that he had twin fantasies about us. I forgive him because I know it is not true. Diana and I were at Harvard more than a little after Alexander. He is almost twelve years older than I am. It is his fiction that he saw us.

Alexander has dark hair and dark eyes. He says they are getting lighter with age. He has the darkest white skin possible. I tell him that Pushkin is not the only black blood in Russia. He says, "Yes, but all the black blood in Russia is noble, and I am not noble." I tell him this is ridiculous. I say, "Pushkin and his progeny, I know they planted some wild oats among the serfs." I tell him it is possible that he just might be part black. He laughs at me again, and I don't mind.

I am writing a paper on "The African American Intellectual and the Image of Russia." He is translating my paper into Russian. I am flattered that he thinks any native Russian speakers would want to read my work. He does not take a fee.

Over and above the difference in age, race, mother tongue, and mother-tongue alphabet, my friends in the expatriate community taunt me with the possibility that Alexander is a spy. Some think he's a spy for the CIA; others think he's a spy for the KGB. It crosses my mind that this is a possibility, but I don't think it's probable. He allows too much poetry to seep into and out of his soul. I grew up in Washington. That is not the CIA way. Beneath the surface, CIA homes are fundamentally dry. I smile to think I learned something of use to me in Washington.

Alexander does freelance translations for some political agency to pay for our luxuries. He has far too little money and far too much time to be a secret agent man. When we meet, usually it is only for a few hours, because that's all the time I can afford away from my little Pushkin and my literary studies. Alexander takes me to the Hotel Europa. He is very old-fashioned. First he buys me a meal, doses me with vodka; finally he takes me upstairs and ravishes me.

Every so often an edged-in hour of play-love-play does not feel like enough. I get hungry to explore Alexander for more hours on end. It amuses him to be explored. He takes connecting rooms at the Hotel Europa. On these occasions, we—Alexander, Pushkin, and I—take up residence in Old World elegance, escaping our respective cramped hovels. For these weekends we are like an old aristocratic family where the father sees the children only from the distance but provides for mother and child abundantly, while the mother provides the child and father with abundant love and kisses.

I pack carefully for these excursions. As we never leave the hotel and seldom leave our rooms, we need very little in the way of changes of clothes. The valises are heavy with books. I also take drawing materials and watercolors, if I can get my hands on any, and a pack of cards, and a rubber stopper for the tub. The hotel provides plentiful hot water but no way to plug the drain. We take luscious baths in the clove-scented bathing oil I made. I tuck Pushkin up, warm from his bath, in the heavy covers beneath the counterpane and start reading to him in English. He is so surrounded by Russian, so able in Russian, that I have begun to worry about his English.

I am trying to remember what his favorite book was at age four. I believe it was *Winnie-the-Pooh*. I dutifully skipped over the Christopher Robin bits—the child was far too skinny and blond. The community of animals was our concern. When Pushkin got a little bit older we would play a game dividing people into Pooh categories, into Owls and Eeyores and Piglets, into Poohs. Pushkin said Alexander was an Eeyore. I thought he was an Owl.

On those nights I would read to Pushkin until he fell asleep, however long it took. I didn't want to rush him. I didn't want him to feel rushed. I loved the weight of abundant time on my heart. Excitement rose from not being able to have Alexander the very first moment I thought to have him but being able to have him abundantly in moments to come.

While Pushkin and I read up in our room, Alexander drank down in the hotel bar with whatever flotsam and jetsam from the expat community was lying and sniffing about. When Pushkin fell asleep, I would ring down to the bar.

Soon I would hear Alexander's key in the lock of the door to my connecting room. I would wait a few minutes; then I would unlock my side and enter. As he washed himself in his bathroom, I would let myself in and snuggle beneath his sheets. I would hear the flush of the toilet, then the shush of the shower. He was as clean as a cat. Tooth-brushing, then gargling. I couldn't hear the splash of cologne, but it was on him, thick clouds of scent around his neck, around his belly. When I kissed him in certain places, my tongue stung from alcohol and the soapy taste of cologne.

Exhausted of sobriety, I poured vodka over his belly and lapped up the little rivulets that formed and flowed. I whispered the French number between sixty-eight and seventy into his ear and watched him smile. He turned to his side and I eased myself into a most erotic posture that left me feeling connected to the universe and the possibility of satiation. Tears of pleasure in my eyes washed out tears of other remembering. I closed my eyes and Alexander climbed onto me in a different way. My ankles were on his shoulders and my hands were around his neck when I opened my eyes and saw Pushkin standing at the door, a book in his hand. I closed my eyes to think, to find a word to say. When I opened my eyes, the door was closed.

Pushkin had vanished, and Alexander was whispering verses of *Eugene Onegin* into my ear. I was twenty-three years young, and Pushkin was four years old.

ELEVEN

ONCE UPON A TIME, I was four years old.

When I was four years old, my grandmother would send me out into the garden just to see the four o'clock flowers open. After the flowers opened, I would peer into the shed, hoping to catch a glimpse of the presses at play.

Leo had Sun's old presses. Kept them for years in a shed on Oakwood that was tucked between a rose bed and a picnic table. The shed was really a garage, but my grandparents no longer kept a car, they kept gardening supplies and clothes presses. Daddy said presses kill men but presses don't die. He said presses break men down but they don't break. He said it so often and with such intensity it kept me peeking into that shed window, hoping to see them do something. He left the presses to me in his will.

What would it mean if I pressed a twenty-dollar bill and put it in a wedding card for you? Do you ever wonder what your check with lots of zeroes in a Christmas card means to me? Would Tanya marry you if you were black and broke?

All through high school Leo wrote to me, slanting bold print, all capital letters, dashed on yellow lined paper which he would fold into plain white envelopes. Into the folds he would tuck a ten-dollar bill or two fives or a twenty that he would press flat and shiny but not new, a hot bill he had found in the pocket of pants he was pressing.

Daddy had complex ideas about thieving. Basically, he didn't believe in it. But little of his life was basic. He said there were three kinds of employees: those who were dumb enough to steal, those who were too dumb to steal, and those who were smart enough to steal just as much as they could get away with without the loss being noticed. This latter group, the smart thieves, were the employees my daddy sought to hire. He didn't begrudge the thief his taste. He considered that to be the price of having someone intelligent work for him.

I like to imagine that those hot dollars were dollars he had in fact earned but did not like for me to think of him laboring to earn. How strange to suspect that he believed it was better for me to think of him picking his customers' pockets than to think of him standing over a press.

I cringe to think of you laboring so hard with your body, because Leo labored too hard.

Looking back toward his predawn migration to his cleaning shop, to stand at the counter or at the press, sweeping the floor to make sure his place was clean, I cannot visualize my father in less than arduous labor. Those presses in the shed were what my father inherited from Sun. I'm not sure Daddy ever moved them anywhere. He always seemed to buy or lease a building that had presses, but the knowledge that he owned these behemoth machines seemed to him a promise from the grave that he could always begin again, would always be able to make a living.

I never think of my daddy as a dry cleaner. I think of him as a presser and a spotter. He said that he could get anything off clothes except okra—okra was so slimy it would slip off before you could get it off. Okra was different, and Daddy found a way to recognize the difference in his mythology of the cleaners'. To this day I love the chemical smell of just-cleaned clothes. I love the odor of gasoline fumes. I do not love it ironically. I love it like a woman whose day crib was a canvas cart full of the newly cleaned garments of strangers. I love it like a being who was conceived of on a hot day in the cleaners', by a man who would stand over the presses bringing the big hood down and up over and over and over again.

To press clothes takes your whole body, your arms on the hood, your legs standing you up and on the pedals, your hands smoothing, your skin absorbing the heat. You bend over and you rear back a hundred, hundred times a day, many thousand times a lifetime, a piston in the engine of clean. Standing at his daddy's presses, exerting his strength against a tide of pants and skirts and blouses, of suits and dresses, canvas carts of clean but wrinkled clothes waiting to be pressed and hung and filed and returned to customers, who wore and soiled them and returned them to him to be cleaned, to be pressed again, kept my daddy lean.

Dirty clothes looked just like the Mississippi River to my father, like the way the Mississippi River looks to a fisherman or a gambler, like a way to put coins in your pocket, like a chance to take.

I have tried to remember how it is he claimed me, and I cannot. If I could remember how he did it, maybe I could do that same thing to my son. What keeps coming back to me is the place where he rejected me. That is the place where I am rejecting Push.

I am thinking again about my father's question. "You bring a white boy home, and the only question be, should I shoot him first or you?" Him first or you? Did I prefer to live a few moments longer, or prefer to know for a few seconds fewer that my father could kill me? At seven I wanted to die first. At thirteen I wanted to go second. It strikes me strong after all these years: my father repeatedly threatened me with death; my father questioned how to kill me. Some competing forces will not balance or reconcile. I felt certain Daddy could not, would never kill me, despite his question. I also can't remember a time when the killing question wasn't in my life. Certainty can be so closely braided to confusion. I knew my daddy wouldn't kill me and I thought he might.

I remember wondering why I would bring a white boy home, wondering what we might do when we got there. White boys felt like exotic pets, like Bengal tigers or Peruvian lions. My father used to say that none of the elephants we saw in circuses were African elephants. African elephants refused to be trained, he said. Circus elephants were from a different continent. In those days, the notion that I might meet such a person, a white person, seemed as unlikely as the possibility of seeing an African elephant in the circus, but somehow I started wondering if my daddy would shoot me with his pistol or his rifle. Perhaps because I had pulled the trigger of the rifle, I imagined he would choose the pistol.

My father was a racist, and I am coming to suspect that I am one too. This is a painful suspicion. Pushkin, you call me a racist. Your Tanya is certain I am racist. I like to think of myself as an ancestor honorer. And I know I loved a little white poodle. Does that count for anything? Maybe it shouldn't. How is it I know Tanya was a Negro dog? I rather hope I'm just some kind of advanced aficionado of African American culture.

If the French poodle Tanya is a Negro dog because a Negro girl loved her, could that mean that the Russian woman Tanya is a Negro girl because a Negro man loves her? Can we torture reason and race far enough to accommodate that? I am way past beginning to think that all the constructions around race in America are good for is a belly laugh.

Once when I was in Oakland, California, touring behind my book on African Americans in Russia, *Black on Red*, I spoke at a bookstore, where I mentioned that my father was a racist. Several members of the audience took issue with that description. Someone stated that by definition it was impossible for a black person to be a racist, because racism required the ability to exert power over another being and African Americans do not exert power over European Americans in America, except perhaps in the armed services.

I know my daddy was a racist. He called white people bad words like *peckerwood* and told me that white folks ain't nothing but a broken-down black pimp's dog, and he told me that he would shoot me, first or last, if I ever brought a person home. He told me Jesus had kinky hair, like a lamb; he told me white folks had light eyes and skin like rats. My father was a racist.

To be a woman is to know that racism has more to do with beauty than with power, and everything to do with a refusal to see, a refusal to recognize, a refusal to be beautiful. "Black Is Beautiful" was the clarion cry of the civil rights movement. My father was a racist. He refused to recognize the beauty in white women or children or men. He told me about taking his own father down to temple number one, or was it two—the Muslim temple built in Detroit in the late fifties or the early sixties. He told me about taking his daddy, taking Sun down to hear Malcolm X speak. Sun said, "They be getting on the white folks worse 'n the white folks usta be gettin' on us." Malcolm's talk scared Sun. Malcolm made my daddy happy. Malcolm makes me happy too. Malcolm was beautiful.

I find it easiest to appreciate my daddy's racist soul when I remember that both his grandfathers were white and that my mother's father was white. He hated white men in general, but his hate began in intimate particulars. The main white person my daddy hated was his paternal grandfather. One of the things he hated his daddy's daddy for was making it so nobody taught his gold-colored son, my daddy's daddy, to read or write.

I am recalling the day Sun died. I was living in Washington.

Daddy called to tell me before I left for school. It was the ninth grade, and I had just finished reading *Gatsby* for the first time. I was reviewing for a test, holding a paperback copy in my hand, when he said the words "Sun died." Blue eyes eerily like Sun's stared back at me from the cover of Fitzgerald's book.

My grandfather was dead. He would never read any book. I think I had thought I would be the one to teach him to read, as payback for teaching me how to express myself without words on paper. A few days before I had baked a glossy chocolate cake to represent some of the vagaries of Gatsby's glamorous personality and turned it in instead of an essay. I baked something wholesome to represent Nick. The teacher was impressed. I received two *A*'s. Looking back, I understand now what I didn't get then: those cakes were a way of trying to stay connected to the gesture culture of my childhood.

After I hung up the phone, after my daddy's sad voice said goodbye, I changed clothes. I put on a red plaid workshirt and blue jeans. It was a kind of homage to the land of Sun's birth, to the state of Alabama, to land on which I had not yet stepped. Somewhere in the day, the image of me sitting with him in the morning kitchen flashed across the screen inside my eyelids. A picture of us, Sun and Windsor, drinking coffee from pink plastic cups on turquoise saucers, eating slices of his black-skillet yellow cornbread. I felt through time the thump of his fingers on my forehead saying, "Education is the only thing they can't take away from you," the sound of him saying, "Life ain't fair, be twice as good, or three times as good, and get what you want." I started crying, crying as if I intended to cry two buckets full and carry them across a celestial field, the field I had dressed for, or tote him water in case he was going to hell. My algebra teacher banished me to the quiet of the health room.

When I didn't show up in English, the teacher came to find me. That white boy—he probably was barely thirty—sat on the cot patting my back. He seemed to be thinking, It cannot be as bad as all this; I could feel it in his hand. But it was. Sun was dead and all my mother had to say was "If you had all the money that pathetic old man bet on zero-two-zero, you'd be rich." It was a hard day.

It was a day like a hot day in the cleaners', a day like the day I was conceived. In a convoluted sense, this was the day I determined to conceive my Pushkin, to conceive you, to conceive a child who would be a destination for me to attain. It was the day I knew someone fierce must be born again. Someone my mother could not deny or denigrate. Someone more than me or Daddy. The day Sun died, I conceived of you—my fierce, black, brilliant one.

My father took a little, but only a little, pride in telling me that each of my grandfather's white half-brothers had written to express sympathy. One letter, penned by a half-brother who was then a judge down in Florida, was particularly vivid and floral. I read it only once, but it created a sense of a boyhood they had shared hunting and fishing in some kind of prelapsarian Eden, if the lawyer were to be believed.

My father took the handwritten pages from my hands and touched that letter to the tip of his cigarette and "set the mother-fucker on fire." I watched it flame. I heard Daddy recount the event to others later. I watched Daddy hold on to the letter until the fire was licking at his fingertips and the words on paper started to vanish. A ragged sneer tangled his lips as phrases and memories of the past died in the present of our presence. He was doing a good deed. He was being the good and faithful servant of his father. He was stabbing his grandfather, the literal motherfucker, in the groin by burning that man's literate, licentious progeny's letter. Leo dropped the char onto the marble top of a cocktail table and watched the small flame devour the rest of the paper, then fall down into ash.

I was annoyed. I had wanted to read the words again. Writing this now, I feel hip-hop oral poetry seeping into my prose, and that's another way of honoring Sun, now. Then I wanted those words on paper. I wanted to know Sun as a boy, I wanted to see and feel him as a member of a pack of wild Alabama privilege, bringing down birds and deer on his father's land, their daddy's land, doing for his half-brothers, hanging back, keeping quiet, watching his mother stand at the stove stirring the pot. Sun's mother was the cook on the place.

For once in my life, this once only, Leo derided my desire. Daddy wouldn't allow it. He kept shaking his head mutely. I knew what he was not saying. Sun could leave no words on paper of his own. Daddy would obliterate Sun's brother's. Daddy's muteness was his way of honoring his daddy, and maybe Martha Rachel. It was a way of diluting the power of Sun's literate white half-brothers. Sun's life on earth was recorded on air, in the vanishing flesh of his heir's brains. Where and when he was born, they didn't issue birth certificates to colored babies. There was no proof of Sun's birth. No proof of his existence. No photograph of us in the morning kitchen.

No proof except the engraving of his heft on our hearts. My father would not allow the literate brother, the documented brother, the brother with birth certificate and college diploma and law certificate, the brother who could put words on paper, to become the authority on his illiterate brother's life.

If Sun's words were to vanish into air, so would the judge's. My father assured me it would be no great loss. What is written on paper is not necessarily the truth. In truth, what is written on paper is necessarily distortion.

And Daddy was making amends for Martha Rachel.

As the smoke of his half-uncle's epistle rose in the air, the story of my grandfather's death foretold rose with it. As the ash floated to the floor, smoke and words rose in the air. Daddy turned to the window and began another story—maybe hoping to justify in my eyes what he'd done. He told me the story of Martha Rachel, and why he shouldn't have told his daddy. He said Sun was never the same after he knew.

Sun was never the same after Daddy told.

Daddy knew Sun as a strong man; I knew him shuffling. And the telling of the Martha Rachel tale made the difference. The telling of the young Sun tales made a different difference.

"Your daddy cussed a white man, now he's gonna get kilt." My father had heard those words many years before, but Sun had survived. All those times Sun walked across lines, he only seemed to grow in strength. Daddy learned fearlessness from his own father's improbable victories. Sun had bought a car from a white man in Montgomery. After driving the car for a few days, he thought he'd been gypped. He took the car back, but the man wouldn't return his money. Sun cussed him out. The news passed through the white part of town into the colored. It passed from the grown folks to the children. "Your daddy cussed a white man, now he's gonna get kilt" was all Daddy heard at school. Sun didn't get killed.

Sun was fearless. He couldn't play low, wouldn't hang his head, shuffle, or fetch. Sun robbed trains and factories for pure spite and audacity. In honor of the enslaved by law he broke every law he might enjoy breaking. He robbed and stole, cussed and pissed and howled till he exhausted himself. The white man who cheated him in the car deal didn't kill Sun. He was just the place Sun discovered who he was—a bad nigger, not a shady Confederate aristocrat.

His white family was seeing it too. The patriarch protected Sun, but he knew that soon he would have to let him go, hobbled or not. He had thought Sun would stay in the sweet South, that he would play shadow and suffering servant to his half-brothers. Toward that future, the white patriarch had maimed his mulatto son's intelligence with illiteracy. Soon he would have to let him go, crippled or not. But not yet. He loved the boy.

Sun's father protected him. His son had cussed out a white man, and a prominent white man at that, but the man would have to accept his disgrace. Sun would walk away whole. The son of the biggest mule in Montgomery would walk away. Sun's father wrapped all the nobility of the Confederacy he could muster, and that was considerable, all the arrogance of the southern aristocracy, wrapped the fact his people had been the biggest planters in Alabama and his mother was a Virginian—he wrapped all that around his shoulders and he pulled the grown man his son to his flat chest and invited the wealth of the town to dine at his table. He had the boy's own mother cook. When the guests arrived, the patriarch was standing on his columned porch with his arm around his big boy's waist. Sun didn't nod or drop his eyes. He kissed his daddy's cheeks and walked away slowly. He was beloved.

Sun was an outlaw, pure if not simple. There were few notes of grace in him. There was bravado and courage and intelligence. Sun's daddy should have wept.

Sun left and he never went back South. Not once. Never called. Couldn't write. Probably Sun's daddy did weep. He had reason to feel abandoned. Maybe that's why he slapped Martha Rachel those years later. White or black, children make parents vulnerable. That white man had loved his black son. Daddy swept all of this away when he told Sun about Martha Rachel.

Sun took the bluest blood of the Confederacy north and started his little dry-cleaning business. He made change by slowly laying the coins and bills in his patrons' hands. He could tell by the eyes when to stop laying his money down. He hit the one-cent key of his cash register and made a fortune. Yours is not the first fortune in our family. Sun's businesses prospered. Then Sun, reeling silently from the Martha Rachel mess, let his firstborn, Bob, take over the business.

At that time, in the fifties, there was an idea at the Internal Revenue Service that Negro businesses were peculiarly vulnerable to audits. Oral cultures aren't big on records. People could construct bills for them to pay and they couldn't defend against it. The IRS determined that Sun owed eighty thousand dollars. Bob went to work to pay the bill. He worked his self into the hospital, where he died for want of a drink of liquor. For the first time in his life Sun shuffled; he hung his head and stumbled.

My father stood on the corner outside the hospital with an acute pain in his side. His appendix was bursting. As the pain stabbed through him, he thought, "Gotta get to Bob." Then he said, right out loud, appendix bursting, pus and poison moving into his blood, "I'm Bob now. I am Bob."

Sun went down to some office and put in for Social Security. He had no birth certificate or record of employment. He was pathetic. Someone took pity on him and certified him qualified. They gave him a Social Security card. He started to get a check. He said he was riding the streetcar downtown. There was no streetcar. He started pulling down his pants to show people his hernia. Martha Rachel was soiled; Bob was buried; Sun was broken.

I do not want to lose you, child.

TWELVE

I HAVE LOST TOO MANY dear to me to lose another.

Dear was dear. She was tender and she was loved. She was our beloved. In a family of warriors, outlaws, and knights errant, in a family of fast-twitching muscles, elastic tendons, a family of narrow behinds and callused minds, Dear was something else altogether. She was roundly female, and she was tenderly, meticulously, and patiently loved by all her angular males.

She stood just at five feet. She was probably more than five feet around. I am guessing that maybe she weighed 280 pounds. She wore flowered dresses almost all the time cinched in at the waist with fabric belts. Martha Rachel made a majestic butter-colored brocade dress for Dear and a minute matching silk brocade frock for me, because yellow was Dear's favorite color. Martha Rachel was trying to make up for hoarding me; she didn't relinquish my little hand quickly. "Lena and Leo asked me to watch Windsor," she said. And everybody knew, because she said it so often, "it isn't good to haul babies across town!" Still, when Dear begged long and sweet enough, Martha Rachel left me with my grandmother for an afternoon or a night.

Once, standing by the side of the tub, watching me bathe my skinny body, Dear lifted her skirt just a little and shuffled off a few agile dance steps. "All that's left is my ankles." I found these words confusing. Her ankles, which were so small, almost unable to hold up her luscious bulk, seemed to be the thing she didn't have left, the thing that was changing by dwindling.

I had never imagined Dear young. That day she just showed it to me. I saw a girl turning into a woman with European features set in an oval face, a girl with hooded eyes and generous mouth, with jaunty figure, crook in her elbow, hand on her hip, a girl trying to look like a woman, with something in her eyes that acknowledged she had seen what a wife sees, she knew what a wife knows: an explosion took place in my mind. I saw the edifice of my grandmother young, I saw a fading photograph.

All such days are combustions. The price of a life of revelations is a pock-scarred brain. The moment when a lie vanishes is nothing like the moment when a caterpillar turns into a butterfly or when some other gentle metamorphosis occurs. The moment a well-treasured lie ceases to be believed is something like the first moment the universe began. Science has redeemed the theory of the Big Bang. Good. I have experienced its reality. The moment a well-treasured lie ceases to be believed is like the moment two half-cells collide in a tawdry bang and a sacred soul is conceived. It is no gentle thing.

That day, that exploding day, it was almost a hundred degrees outside. All the windows were open. Dear had settled me into the tub for a long afternoon of splashing in cool water. She had a shoebox full of pictures and a paper fan on her lap. I kept asking her to stop fanning and show me more pictures, tell me more stories. Then she held one up and asked a question. Dear asked, "Do you believe that's me?" And I, being the smart girl, said, "No." I waited for a moment for the smile I thought I knew was hiding in her eyes to emerge, the smile that said, "You can't fool my grandbaby." The smile didn't come. She shimmied her shoulders and lifted her chin. For the one and only time in our life together she looked right through me, looked through me as if I weren't there. She stared straight off. When I stare like that, it's into a kind of blindness. Then Dear sort of crumpled, her chin dropping to her chest, her shoulders hunching forward as if they were trying to meet. She closed her eyes. She took the shoebox off her lap and set it on the medicine shelf. She stood. Her hands dangled by her sides. She grabbed at the skirt of her dress. She opened her eyes. Now she was looking at me and I was feeling scared. Pulling her fists full of fabric toward her hips, she hiked her dress above her ankles. The pointer finger of each fist was popped out, pointing south. Dear shifted her weight to her right foot, bent her left knee, and raised her left foot up till it almost reached her right knee, then she gently touched down. "That's all I have left," she said.

For a moment I wondered if she meant the dance step, that little ball and shuffle. Then I knew, I let myself know, from the bent note of pain in her voice, the whine that even toddlers understand, that she was not talking about something she could do. She was talking about somebody, the body she had once inhabited. Looking down from her immense breasts pouring over her vast stomach, pressing closed gargantuan thighs so that no cloud of scent (of aging ovaries and yeast) would rise to mingle with the perfume at her neck and on the insides of her wrists, her eyes rested on the piece that had not inflated. She was talking about the remnants of her beauty.

Slim ankles. An exquisite territory of limb, connecting feet to calf, was all she had left. Shame rose up in my eyes like hurry-home drops. If the girl in the picture had been large and awkward, if her features had been muted with flesh and fat, I might have gazed upon her in recognition. I didn't recognize Dear as the girl in the picture because the girl in the picture was beautiful.

Yes, my seven-year-old brain knew Dear was beautiful in some God's-in-the-sky-and-everyone's-beautiful way. I didn't know she had been beautiful in a Miss-America-Pageant-Barbie-doll kind of way. The Dear I was looking at was pretty, pretty. And I hadn't known it, guessed it, or imagined it. Whether it was beyond the scope of my imagination or beyond the longings of my heart for her once to have been other than she was, I cannot now say for certain. I prefer to think I could not wish for her to be other than she was. I sat naked in the bathwater looking at Dear in her dress, wishing for something to cover the starkness of her age, wishing to undress her of the sheets of fat and skin and cloth and age that hung off her. I was no longer splashing. The water was no longer cool and nice. The air was too hot and the water was too cold until Dear's smile finally returned.

"I was beautiful in Alabama." Mariah tapped at the picture, then returned it to the box on the shelf with the others. Mariah was Dear's name in Alabama. She pulled a towel from the bar bolted to the wall, then dried me till my beige turned red. She kissed the top of my head. "This is me here." "Now," she should have added. "This is me now," she should have said. She was drying behind my ears. She eagerly attacked each lobe. Things were not as they had always been. Now, we both knew. While she pondered how beauty fled, I pondered that beauty had been. I looked at her ankles and thought they were so very much like my own, strong and beige and skinny. I picked up the picture from the shelf and wondered if one day I would look like the girl Dear used to be.

In that picture she's taller than five feet, perhaps five foot two or three in little boots that lace up. She has a superb figure, almost an hourglass, without an excess of tits or ass, a flat stomach stretched across baby-breeding broad hipbones. A long neck that drops down to a high and curving swell and points up a perfect oval of a face with a thin straight nose and huge dark eyes that stare frankly into the camera. Her lips are just a little full, but still delicate, as if in fact they had been stung by bees. There's a jauntiness to her stance; her body is slightly turned away from the camera, but her face is turned full toward it. A hip is thrust forward. A hand is on that hip, and a smile seems to suggest that she knows things. At the same time it's a fearless smile. I feel certain that if I stood before that girl and lifted my hand to slap her cheek, she would not flinch. She would expect the hand to come down and caress her lovely face. Dear knew and trusted her own beauty.

Sun knew and honored it. He was very protective of Dear. He knocked a man down with a crowbar for cursing in front of her. Almost killed the man. He had warned the man. In those days Dear sometimes accompanied Sun to the dry cleaners', occasionally making herself useful with a bit of mending, more often being useful by scolding and schooling the girl who did the mending. Primarily she was simply present. It was lonely at home in those years between children at home and grandchildren at home. The man had dropped off some slacks and made a reference to the "motherfuckin' rain." Sun warned him. He had picked up his clothes and referred to the "goddamned . . ." No one remembered what he cursed. They just remembered he cursed. Sun didn't warn him again. He picked up the crowbar that he kept behind the counter next to the cash register. He stepped out from behind the counter; he brought the crowbar down toward the profane creature's shoulder. The victim flinched and turned, caught part of the blow with the side of his head. Sun had knocked him down to the ground. The man writhed in pain. Dear shut her eyes. Sun said, "I told you not to curse in front of my wife."

The man didn't call the police. He knew he had transgressed. He knew who Sun was and what he was like. The community condemned the man for acting a fool.

Sun loved Dear like the Russians love Pushkin. She was his everything. And Dear loved Leo like that. Leo loved me that way. When I lived in D.C., Leo would send me telegrams. One read, "You are the alpha and omega, you are the beginning and the end, you are my everything." You don't forget words like that. "Pushkin is my world," I say. "You are my everything," and it is true.

Pushkin says, "Get a life, Moms!"

He doesn't want to be my life, he wants to be a true love. Leo had a life and he loved me truly. How do I get to there?

Sun loved and honored Dear as I have seen few women loved or honored. He also betrayed her—but that was before I was born. When I knew them, love was restored.

But I know the story of her betrayal. Know it enough to be puzzled by it. I have an uncle Jack and an uncle John, both on my father's side. This made sense to me until I learned that Jack was a nickname for John. I asked my daddy why his parents gave two of their children the same name. There was that familiar hesitation. That hesitation that arose whenever he started his answer off with a question. "You wanna know the truth or you want me to tell you a story?"

Because my grandfather could not read or write, Dear would read Sun's letters to him. It was his habit to join her in the front room after his breakfast of cornbread and coffee. She would sit in her big chair facing the window; he would sit to her left on the sofa, the whatnot between them. This was before they moved to a brick house on Oakwood, when the family was still in a wooden house in Black Bottom. This was back in the days before Martha Rachel's girl and boy had been killed in the fire, before any of them had met Spady, back when he was still alone in his TB ward.

Maybe it was 1940. I know they were still down in Alabama in 1937, the year Joe Louis became the heavyweight champion of the world. I know my father and his brothers heard the fight on their white neighbor's radio. I know they were too afraid to show excitement when the white man lost. They slouched home whispering, "Joe Louis won, Joe Louis won," till they could contain themselves no longer, till they shouted to the stars above Alabama, "Joe Louis won!"

Sun was already up in Detroit, starting to make his way, dry-cleaning clothes in a bathtub. Maybe he had just met a brown-skinned beauty. Working to send money South to Dear, working to establish his northern outpost, perhaps he was not immune to all distractions. It was an achy, awkward time in the life of Dear and Sun's family. Then they moved to Detroit, stopping first in New York.

My father never forgot his first days in the North. Until a blood clot took away his speech, until inflammation set in motion by years of poor dental hygiene slew each and every one of his syllables, he would tell the tale of standing on the sidewalk wearing his first pair of shoes, trying to twist his mouth up to ask a man for a hot dog, until the man said, "Speak up, son, you're not down South." And when my father asked for the hot dog, the man gave him one with plenty of mustard and relish and ketchup. And he wouldn't take my father's coins. He tipped his cap to my father and bid him on his way, made welcome. The words stayed with my father and he said them to me. He couldn't even imagine staying South and speaking up.

Sometimes the South is silence.

Words in air are full of life. And words on paper are a kind of death and a kind of immortality. My father was born into an oral culture: a world without reading and writing, a world of sound and memory, a world of listening to a fight on the radio.

Detroit was a different kind of world. In Detroit, Dear read. She taught herself by squinting at the pages as she got the children to read to her from the *Michigan Chronicle*, the green-colored newspaper written for and about the Negro community. After a time she could read Sun's mail to him: the water bill, the light bill, the house note. He didn't get social letters. And then one day a letter came.

The letter said, "I know you love your wife. I know you can't be with me. I know. You don't know I came back home. We had a son. His name is John." Sun's ears were on fire. What was he hearing? "Times were hard. Now times are harder." Sun could not walk away. Was the boy still living? Did the woman still love him? Where did they be? He couldn't walk away and he couldn't listen. My grandfather was speechless. He hung his head in shame. He walked away.

Two weeks later my grandmother, Dear, started meeting the Saturday bus from Montgomery. One day a child got off that looked like a dark version of Sun. She brought him home and raised John alongside Jack.

Dear had written words on paper and sent them to a woman she had never met. Did she write, "If he's my Sun's son, I will know him"? Did she write, "I will hold your boy if you let go my man"? Did she write, "Do that for me and I will do this for you"? I only know one black woman put words on paper and sent them North and another black woman responded with words on paper of her own. Together they saved a child's life.

I'm putting these words on paper hoping to save mine.

Dear said to Sun, "Anything that is yours I love." A wail flew from Sun's throat. Dear said, "Where you go, I go. Don't lay me down in another nasty place."

She let it go. She didn't mention it again. Sun grew fiercer in his love for her until the day he struck that man down with a crowbar for cursing in front of her.

Like a general leading an army, Sun loved Dear, and his boys followed behind him. When they were grown and tall, when they owned houses of their own, they kept keys to her house on their rings and made frequent use of them. They stayed in and out of her house, each son having his day of the week to bring himself, or his family, over for dinner.

Leo had Sunday. There was always a pound cake ready before noon and steak and gravy with onions for Leo. On a Saturday afternoon any one or all of the boys could be found in the dining room chairs dragged into the arch that separated the dining room from the living room, pulled up to a torchère while Dear trimmed the corns that crowned their toes and the calluses that padded the bottoms of their feet. She could deftly wield a razor blade and her eyes were sharp. What she couldn't see she could feel.

The boys brought her trinkets. They brought her perfume. They carried her to the dime store. They brought her their children. They carried her out to the old cemetery. They wrapped themselves in the quilts she made from her old dresses. But mostly they brought her their attention. And they reached up to her titties for the hundred-dollar bills she kept folded and hidden in her cleavage as if they needed them. As if they didn't have so much money in the bank. Spady's son said, "Dear's house has everystuff," and the boys repeated it time after time because it was true.

My father loved his mother, but, more significantly, he treasured the love she bathed him in as his most precious birthright. If later he would tie his heart to my fingers and wait, accepting what came, perhaps it was because Leo had moved through his life with Dear's love tethered to his leg.

Leo did not question whether he waited in vain for my love. He would not ask himself that question. He stood near me as long as he was breathing, offering love abundant without regard to reciprocation. He said, "It ain't a two-way track, chile. It's all goin' in one direction."

I was his direction. And now Pushkin is mine.

Dear's daddy was a poor white boy from West Virginia who found himself down in Alabama. He was a guitar player and a song maker who hung out in jukes. Everybody was surprised when he actually married his colored gal, in front of a Negro preacher and God, except maybe the colored gal, who had discovered him to be a pure-hearted true hillbilly. He called the baby Dear because, he said, "that's just what she is."

He taught his woman, Dear's mother, to play the banjo. They made a little money when people liked the songs and threw nickels and dimes and pennies. He put food on the table. He taught his daughter to tie her shoes, the letters he knew, and quite a few songs. Dear's mama and papa died in a car crash. The whole family was walking home from church in the rain and a car crashed into them when the driver had a heart attack. Dear was unhurt because she had stopped to tie her shoe.

So much depends on a shoelace. Dear loved her sons like she loved their father—abundantly. She tended her sons' feet; her father had tended hers. When I think on Tanya, I am reminded of the evils of white culture. I have something to hang against the sins of white folks: Dear's white daddy got down on his knees and taught his brown daughter to tie her shoes with a rhyme about rabbit ears and rabbits chasing each other around, under, and over a hedge. He was a patient teacher with a way of getting and keeping his pupil's attention. So much depends on gesture, a gift of teaching. He taught her to tie her shoes and blow her nose.

On this act of mercy I will build my grace.

THIRTEEN

W<small>HERE'S THEIR GRACE?</small>
I have never liked whiny children. Somehow it seems so perfect, so perfectly awful, that the school chosen to be the place for the first great race-based shootout of the twenty-first century was the university where Pushkin chose to attend college, Michigan, Big Blue.

I've seen those whiny undergrown children complain. I've read their complaints too. I believe in the *New York Times* one girl said she had come home from cheerleading practice when she saw the thin envelope and she just knew she hadn't gotten in. Poor little entitled baby. Knew and decided to sue.

That's the whiny girl's right. It is mine to recognize, to note and question, the significance of whom she decided to sue. Some fine editorials were written on this subject. Did she challenge the alumni children with lower scores and grades who got in ahead of her? Did she challenge the athletes with lower scores? Did she challenge the children of large donors who cut in line? None of the above. She challenged only the black kids, many of whom came from inferior schools in the Detroit ghetto, kids from deep in the cut.

On that CD Pushkin and Tanya gave me for my birthday, Tupac sang, "If one of us got it, some of us got it." The white and whiny ones who could not compete successfully against others of similar backgrounds subject to similar privileges and adversities are too spoiled to understand this concept. I see them in Tanya's face and I want to turn away from her.

And Tanya loves college football; I hate college football. She says it's purer than the pro game. She has memorized all of Pushkin's college stats. I know something about college football. I know enough to know I do not know that very much about college football. Perhaps I refused to learn. When I look at the diagrams of the plays, my mind sees geometry and time colliding. I get tangled up in space amid the X's and O's.

There is one play I remember. One play I comprehend. One play I diagrammed on a cocktail napkin at the Dearborn Inn. It was a play from Pushkin's Senior Day. It was the game they call the Little Brown Jug. There is one play I will never forget.

They call the University of Michigan stadium "the Big House." Every year at Michigan the biggest game is Michigan versus Ohio State. Every year. People come from Chicago to see it. People come from all over the Midwest. Every other year this is the last home game of the season. When Michigan versus Ohio State takes place in Columbus, the final game at the Big House is against the University of Minnesota. The Golden Gophers versus the Wolverines. Minnesota against Michigan. Michigan wins every year. Pushkin wasn't even born the last time Michigan lost and Minnesota had possession of the Little Brown Jug.

Senior Day at Michigan, parents wear their sons' jerseys. Pushkin's jersey reads "59." Middle linebackers always have numbers in the fifties. I don't know why. I saw Pushkin a lot in college, but not especially at football games. I let Gabriel fly up for the games. We couldn't afford to send both of us, and Gabriel loved to watch Push play. On weekends I was reading and grading papers, preparing for class, dreading getting a phone call that my beloved was brain-damaged.

I showed up for Senior Day. I even arrived at the stadium wearing his jersey. There was no way not to do it. It wasn't the most flattering of outfits, but it was customary and appropriate, and I am big on customary and appropriate when it is possible. And Gabriel Michael wouldn't let me not wear it.

It was in no way comfortable.

It was awkward for me to arrive at an academic institution as a football mom and former teen parent rather than as an academic and a tenured colleague. It looked worse than it was. I looked young for my age, and Pushkin looks old for his. If you saw us together his senior year, you might have thought I had him when I was fourteen. It was almost embarrassing, but in honor of the occasion of his last college game I refused to be embarrassed. Even when I ran into colleagues.

I prefer the high school game. For four years in high school he played offense and defense. For four years in college he only played defense. Senior year, Pushkin was up for the Butkus Award, given annually to the most outstanding defensive player of the year. You could call it a Pulitzer Prize of college football. The award for the best college player of the year is supposed to be the Heisman Award. This is their Nobel Prize. The Heisman never goes to a defensive player. College football felt limiting.

I had wanted Pushkin's high school to be different from mine, and football helped make it so. I wanted Pushkin's college to be like mine. Football made that impossible. Gabriel Michael was beginning to think Pushkin might be a big-time player, the kind for whom football blasts new worlds of opportunities. I was getting irritated with Gabriel. I was over football.

In these stands, at Michigan, you never sit alone. Every single seat is taken. The parents sit together. Our section was not as good as the one they save for the big donors and boosters, but it was very nice. Gabriel Michael had managed to snag an even better seat near the scouts. Anything that could be overheard or read on a face, he wanted to know.

Diana took Gabriel's assigned ticket and sat in our second parent seat. Whenever I needed to go to a game Gabriel Michael couldn't make, Diana would go with me. We'd sit in the stands and cheer on "our baby." She would grab my hand and hold tight in third-down situations. Saturday nights I would find the crescent curve of her fingernails indented on the back of my hand, over and over. These were little curves of worry and joy.

Diana still looked sharp, only now it was an early-middle-age size-ten St.-John's-knit-and-Longchamps-bag kind of smart. She had reversed the great migration and moved back South, marrying an ob-gyn from our Harvard class whom she had never met during college. They met at Howard Medical School. She was a psychiatrist with a tiny private practice who was transforming herself into a political activist. After serving as president of the local NAACP, she had gotten herself elected to the city council. She was contemplating a run for Congress. Her husband practiced with his father. When his father had opened his office in the sixties, he had been the only black doctor in the county. He was good, he was kind, he was funny. His son was very much like him. They never turned away a patient for lack of insurance or money. Half the county was indebted to Diana's husband's family. The only things stopping her from making the run for Congress were three kids, a man with a thriving practice he couldn't move to D.C., and the memory that I hated the city of Washington. Diana too was acting on our daddy's words after death. She was working on "I want you to speak for those who cannot speak for themselves."

I sat in the stands beside my sister half on her way to Congress, looking down on the field at my son more than half on his way to the NFL. Pushkin was on his way to being a gazillionaire. If he made it through to the third week in April, he *would* be a gazillionaire. The three of us had come a long way. Still, I couldn't help but think something was one beat off.

Pushkin was playing just a little erratically. Or maybe he was playing too confidently. Michigan always won this game. I knew how Pushkin's body looked on the field when the game had his full attention, and I knew how it looked when it didn't. This game had his full attention, but he wasn't quite playing right. I didn't want to imagine what Gabriel Michael was overhearing the scouts say about it.

It crossed my mind that Pushkin was having second thoughts about the NFL. If that's what his almost-goofs meant, I wanted to applaud every almost-misstep. I couldn't help but think there were better ways for my son. I wanted him to stand in Diana's shoes. I wanted him to be on his way to Congress. If not now, someday.

Strangely, this rare appearance of vulnerability in Pushkin's play provoked me to be protective of his ambitions. I thought of J. C. Watts from Oklahoma, congressman and college football star. I thought of Alan Page, who is a Supreme Court justice for the state of Minnesota and a member of the Football Hall of Fame. I had heard his name in my childhood. Heard it all the way up in Washington. We knew of the Minnesota Vikings and their Purple People Eaters. They were psychedelic and superior enough for us nonsports people at Paliprep. For the first and only time in my life I closed my eyes and sent up a little prayer for the quality of Pushkin's play.

Halftime.

Nobody but me was worried. Michigan was way ahead. Pushkin had made some great sacks. It was time to drink and remember. My sister wanted to get nostalgic. I wanted to know about what. Gabriel started pouring champagne to chase the coffee and Courvoisier I had already downed.

Diana and I went to three football games during our college days.

We went to the two Harvard-Yale games held in Cambridge during our years and one of the ones in New Haven. "The Game" is always in November. We tailgated with other kids whose parents were not showing up.

Our first "The Game," I was the buffer for Diana. It was the least I could do. All semester she had been the ballast for me, scheming and dreaming and believing about the baby. Polite, tactful, knowing my way around the privileged and the powerful, I made a way for her into the center of their elite pack, where she was appreciated for her unabashed originality.

We served soup. The wind blew it back into our faces when we tried to eat it with spoons. Finally we abandoned the spoons and drank straight from the cup. We always served soup. It was too cold not to, but it always burned us.

Watching Diana in her perfect St. John's knit, looking at her powerful body and her perfect bob, I remembered discovering that she was the place where I learned that what I thought I valued about Washington wasn't necessary. We were the near-twins separated at birth. We both ended up at Harvard. I hadn't needed the independent school. I hadn't needed the brilliant spoiled classmates. Hadn't needed the recommendation from my mother's boss, Harvard grad and large donor. Hadn't needed any of those things for which I had paid so high a price. None of this was necessary. This was a revelation.

What I needed was some of what Diana had—street political sense of how to be a student. For me, student was still an idealistic pursuit, the one pure thing I had left. I studied for the love of learning. Harvard was a good place for this. I did not work to a schedule or for a grade. I did not go to class. I did not worry, at least not about my education. I had graduated near the top of my class in one of the best day schools in the country. I had nothing to prove except the fact that I would not go insane. Nothing at all.

Diana was different. She had what she called the "dumb-ass rule." I had never heard of such a thing. The rule was, you register for a class; you go the first day. You look around, you listen, you talk to people. If at least a quarter of the class are not dumb asses, you don't stay. She told about walking into some kind of modernist poetry class the first day, about looking around and around at the other folk till she realized that in that room, at that moment, she was the dumb ass. That insight took anything but a dumb ass to recognize.

Seeing Diana in action at Harvard was having a ringside seat at a powerful intellectual show. All the games with numbers she had played on Spady's knee, on my father's knee, came into play. All my father's raw intelligence was coming into focus. It was a sight to see.

Still, so far from the faces she loved, the values and probabilities that had teased her mind into action, she got bored. Math had been for her, without her knowing, a language to share with the men in her life. At Harvard the men with whom she could share advanced algebra did not interest her. She switched her concentration to biology and decided to go to medical school. No one took particular notice. Nice little black girls from Harvard went to medical school every year. It happened without anyone's having to pay particular attention or take particular notice.

When some horrible boy from a private school in New York City said to both of us, "If you had been me, you wouldn't have gotten into Harvard," implying that he had higher SAT scores than we did, Diana didn't let that bother her. She expected white folks to be foolish. The boy had just finished a problem for her, just put a number on the other side of the equal sign. Whitefolks + Harvard education = still foolish, is what she told me, laughing, later in her room. And I said, "White folks ain't nothing but a broken-down black pimp's dog."

Diana looked at me blankly. She had had a very different relationship with our father. She had had a conservative and protective mother. Daddy had not been as raw with Diana as he had been with me. He had not thought he had to be. I ache in my heart and my throat, recognizing the pure genius of his love.

"Our daddy told that to me." I wanted her to be curious. I wanted to tell her the story.

"When you make racist statements like that, you just give them permission to be racist. Our power is less than their power. Don't give them permission to do what we can't do. Don't do that to me. Don't do it to the baby."

"What about not doing it to me?"

"You barely black, baby, barely black."

"Who died and made you the negritude police?"

"Our daddy."

It was supposed to be a joke, but it wasn't. Even today I can feel the incision. These words don't cut close to the bone, these words cut into the bone. I am bleeding some kind of marrow. So much was at stake in that moment. I could feel different pieces of myself and my relation to Diana struggling to pull apart or stay together. We were on an old street corner in Motown that maybe she doesn't know about. We were Leo and we were Jack and we were trying to figure out which one of us was Bob now, which one of us was heading the family in the wake of death. Diana knew it was her. I didn't know who the hell I was. After that moment I didn't even know I was black. I didn't even know if it was me who got to decide if I was black, or some bitch in Washington, or my dead daddy hopefully in heaven, or the Negroes in the Freshman Union who clumped together at the same table, who stared at me when I didn't sit with them and made a place for me when I went to sit with Diana. Today, those same Negroes send great big checks down South to support Diana's various political causes. These same people, who are running parts of this country, are not surprised that I have fallen off the face of the earth. Isn't being an African American woman in Nashville, at Vanderbilt, isn't that off the face of the planet?

None of the people from Harvard, even the ones I still keep up with, none of them e-mail me about Pushkin. They cannot imagine he's my child. When he was a baby, when I was in Cambridge, when I was with anybody but Diana, we always just called him "our baby," if we referred to him at all. I wanted to keep his identity private, safe. Didn't want stories about him wafting down to Washington. Wanted a complete and punitive embargo of news. Maybe I was a little afraid Lena would snatch him. She had snatched me under cover of a question. She might snatch him. I had developed a healthy fear of the Queen of Spades.

It was in my junior year, when I was looking for a specific topic for my junior paper, that I reread "The Queen of Spades" and "The Negro of Peter the Great." I loved reading the tale of the black man in Paris, the black man in court. It was like a fairy tale I had been missing, like my Snow White and my Cinderella—only I didn't get a girl. There is no beautiful black woman figure in the Pushkin I knew then. It was later I came across the sister. Later I came to contemplate the existence of his dusky mother. All this was later.

Then, I was hating hearing from my sister stories about my father that differed so greatly from my own. Then, I was reeling with the knowledge that the one great thing I thought I had gotten from Washington, my superior education, didn't matter after all—I would still have ended up at Harvard. Diana did. I would have had more work to do once I got there, would have known fewer of the preppie kids, but I would not have had to endure the comment and the misperception that I was barely black. I envied Diana both her easy knowledge of where and to whom she belonged and the fact that her identity as she perceived it was recognized by others.

Halftime is over. Between my sister and me we've killed a bottle of White Star.

Pushkin back on the field. Third quarter flies. Something strange is going on, but most of the crowd is too high and too happy to notice. And then they do. Suddenly the crowd sees. What I thought was projection was perception. The crowd is screaming, they are shocked, Diana grips my hand so hard she breaks my skin. My blood is beneath her fingernails.

Pushkin let his man go.

A wide receiver scored on Pushkin.

A hundred thousand people in the stadium. Ultimate visibility. After so many tackles. The Phenom, the one who claims his opponents as he braces them with his chest, dropping his legs, the one who never grabs with his arms, grabbed like a girl for a hug.

Pushkin stood so visible on the field, as visible as failure.

This is love, in all its audacity and ambition, as Pushkin watches the scoreboard change. This is love. As Diana lets tears of shame roll down her face, muttering, "Our boy is no half-doer." This is love. As Spady, who took the under on a forty-five over/under, watched the combine score tally up to forty-nine, demand-swearing "Motherfuck this!" even as he shook his head, smiling and saying, "Motherfuck that." This is love too.

There are days you have to lose when you could win. Days you lose so someone else can win. Days to see the mercy beyond justice. This is love. These are the days when you know that "if one of us got it, some of us got it" is not enough. You wait, holding the door open for somebody else, even if the door is heavy, even when the body is slow.

Pushkin saw an old friend coming and he kept the door open long enough for his friend to slip in. All afternoon Pushkin had been cracking the door a peep to beckon that old friend home. That's why his play looked so strange.

Spady had to respect that, even if it cost him forty-three thousand and two dollars.

It happened in a few moments. It was forgotten in the minutes after the win, when the Little Brown Jug stayed at Michigan. It didn't affect the third week in April, except maybe a little bit the money. Some folks looked at the film later and said, Pushkin's a little slow or maybe lazy late in the game, when he's done a whole lot of tackling. Some folks said Pushkin didn't want to risk a big hit so close to the combine, so close to the end of his college career. He was saving himself for the NFL. He had been, they said, a shoo-in for the Butkus Award. Now that was over. Folks say a lot of things.

Other folks said, "That boy, that wide receiver, got more go than give, got more than we thought he did." People said, "Everybody gets one lucky day. And everybody gets more unlucky ones. Quimby Jones ain't gonna be about nothing."

Me, I was thinking about my second most unlucky day ever. And I was thinking about my first. I was thinking about the drive up to Harvard with my big trunk and all my things. I was thinking about a restaurant on the Cape. He let me drink a glass of white wine, Vouvray, and then another glass. My mother was up in her room, allegedly ill. I was thinking about telling Mr. Andersson that my mother has . . . he knows what she has done. I think he has put this together. I think he has come to deliver me and protect me, to lift and carry my burden. He walks me back to my room. I have managed not to cry. He holds me at the door gently, as my father might have done. I whisper into his ear one hard thing I need someone to know, and a sob breaks from my throat. As I gasp, my mouth opens. He sticks his tongue into it and pushes me through the door. She has told him that I want him. She has told him that I'm cold and I need him. She has told him too much about me altogether, and he's heard it all, believed it all. He's been waiting for the tears to make it good. A virgin without the tears would not be as tasty.

That was the most unlucky day of my life.

And then there was that day at Harvard. The day after the days I had been throwing up. The day I sat at UHS, the University Health Service, after walking through a modern glass box of an arcade, sat and waited for the results of a pregnancy test, saw something swirled. Was it into my blood or into my urine? I know there was a piece of paper and the technician swirled it in her hand, then said, "The rabbit died." But there was no rabbit at all, and she could see that this was no place for jokes. She had tried to foreshadow the death she thought she knew had to come.

But it was not to be like that. Not at all.

There was another weary young woman in that room. She was wearing a flowery English print to upholster her ripeness. There was a gold band on her hand. She had a French shopping bag full of manuscript. She looked like a graduate student. As I passed, the woman suddenly smiled. She asked me if I was pregnant. I didn't speak. She rested her ringed hand on her big belly. "My baby just jumped," she said. She could feel her baby leap in her womb. It was my own private annunciation. It was a sign. I would not wash this child down the drain. Maybe unborn souls can sense each other. This was love. This was a day I had to lose. For the baby to be, to win, I had to lose the rest of an incomplete childhood. This was love.

It was a third-down situation. Third and long. Minnesota has a three-receiver set, with two wide receivers and one flanker. Q. Jones is the flanker for Minnesota. Pushkin is the captain of the Michigan defense. In defense you either play a man-to-man or a zone. Pushkin calls the huddle in. We don't know what he said, but Michigan lines up in a zone defense. The Gopher quarterback comes to the line, takes the snap, and the play begins. The two other linebackers blitz the quarterback, one from the left and the other from the right, leaving Pushkin the only defender over the middle as the safety goes deep. Jones runs a three-step slant over the middle. He catches the ball and is headed for his touchdown attempt. Pushkin is the only defender in the zone. It's Pushkin and Jones, and Pushkin is the most athletic player on the field. It's third and long. Pushkin reaches out to tackle Jones with his arms. Jones runs right through them. Scouts from half the teams in the NFL are there to see Pushkin, and he just fades away. They see Jones.

Quimby Jones, whom I first saw sitting in the grass in front of Miz Perkins's house, a football arcing and arcing over his head, will arrive at the combines with a buzz that allows him to be chosen on draft day, not at the beginning but before the end. Quimby's career could not end on Pushkin's senior day. Pushkin's senior day; everybody was looking at Quimby. That's how Pushkin wanted it.

It is the invisible man who is invincible.

FOURTEEN

M R. ANDERSSON DIED.
Sven Jude Andersson was hit by a car, a 1963 deuce-and-a-quarter, Saturday, March the sixth, shortly before sunrise. The driver did not stop. Upon impact, Mr. Andersson's body flew into the air, then abruptly fell to earth, or rather onto the turquoise nose of a fast-moving vehicle. Quickly becoming a corpse, his shell slid down the hood of the car onto the blacktop, where it was run over, first by the front wheels, then by the rear.

A nurse pulling into her driveway as she returned home from her graveyard shift at the county hospital reported that the driver of the car that hit and killed Mr. Andersson swerved dramatically to avoid hitting his dog. A single child's red go-go boot was found at the scene. Police have come to no ultimate conclusion as to how, if, or why the boot made its way from the car. The witness thought she saw it flung from the passenger-side window. The police said it only appeared that way. They believed it was rolling around forgotten somewhere in the car when it was propelled through the window during all the starting, stopping, and swerving. They declared the boot irrelevant.

Later, as Saturday night turned into Sunday morning, as his nurse and neighbor exchanged an empty bag of IV antibiotic solution for a full one, Sven Jude Andersson died. His skin hung about him loosely, as if he were deflating. He was eighty-two years old.

There was a long obituary in the *Washington Post*. A smaller one appeared in the *New York Times*. The Harper's Ferry newspaper ran a story on the front page, reporting the accident and featuring a picture of the shoe.

This is all I know for sure. This, and what comes in the mail has been strange of late.

Today an envelope engraved with the initials of a friend from schooldays and "Eventide" arrived in my letterbox. Eventide is an eighteenth-century house situated on a bluff above the C&O Canal outside Harper's Ferry, West Virginia. Inside the envelope were three clippings.

It's easy to imagine Eve, my best friend from Paliprep days, sitting in her wheelchair, looking through the wavy glass of old windows down to the banks of the canal at the bikers and the canoes. On a good day she's out there with them on her electric scooter. She used to be one of the runners. I remember her teaching me to say "I'm sorry" in Russian. *Mne ochen' zhal'*. I'm hoping for cool days for Eve. She moves so much better in the cool. I am wondering if the skin on her legs is healing up fast enough for her to continue her injections of Betaseron. Is the flesh still too hot and too red? A withered sympathy becomes wet again. She has picked up the scissors, scribbled the note, mailed the envelope.

She remembers that I do not read the papers every day as well as I remember that she does. The habits of our codenizens of adolescence are not easily forgotten.

The police believe that the event was an accident, a random act of recklessness. They suspect the inhabitants of the car were drunk or high and lost. They are surprised that the witness remembers them as being old. Interviewed on local television, the patrolman at the scene can think of no possible link between a conservative (he snaps the word to imply Caucasian) retired entrepreneur and two colored dudes, of whatever age, in a rolling wreck. He doesn't say pimp-mobile, but he gets the idea into the air. The officer in charge attempts to mitigate the rookie patrolman's graphic if graceless rendering of the facts with leaderlike cosmic bullshit. "Sometimes the country gets lost in the city, usually to disastrous results. Sometimes the city gets lost out into the country, usually to disastrous results." One of the neighbors differs. "This isn't the kind of place where it's unsafe to take your dog for a walk," he says. I fear he is right.

The local paper notes that the nurse and neighbor will be adopting Mr. Andersson's dog, reporting that she said, "That's the least I could do for the man who helped invent gourmet ice cream." I laugh so hard I have to lie down.

He is dead.

This was a day I have prayed for. I wonder what Eve makes of this. If she sent me the clippings without words of condolence, perhaps she knows the news is good. I thank God print journalists are now reporting on television coverage or I might have missed some of the details.

A dead man, a red boot—a signature? Or could this much good luck happen by accident? I wonder what the dog's name is. Whatever his name is, he is no Whitefolks. Whitefolks would have died with his teeth in a tire.

I am ready to cry.

The other strange piece of mail arrived the day before Eve's envelope. It was a Federal Express packet that contained an invitation to your wedding. This will take you by surprise, as you did not send me a second invitation to your wedding. It took me by surprise. There was no calligraphic outer envelope. There was no inner envelope at all, just the precious square, which looked like it had been passed around and toasted over. Drops of some sort—scotch, champagne, tears—spattered the fine board. Carefully printed on the bottom right corner were the numbers 0-2-0, separated by dashes. I knew what the numbers signified, but I was confounded by the invitation. Now I understand.

I am crying now.

Leo has reached up out of the grave and touched me. Do I know whose hands he used? I think I do. But it would not be like him. It is not his way. I wish it were not he, but it cannot be anyone else. There is the matter of the car.

I rode around in that car so many hours so many years ago, down Grand Boulevard, down Twelfth, down the John C. Lodge, out to Belle Isle, on toward the Boblo boats. I rode in that car to Windsor the first time I ever rolled to Canada. It was well after the lights had gone off in Paradise Valley, in the middle of the night in the middle of a summer. I rode in it to get a taste of plugged melon. Juicy fruit. We saw falling stars that night. I rode in it when there was a big funeral and extra runs to make to the blind pigs, the illegal after-hours joints. Dropping off cases of Seagram's and Courvoisier and Black Label and Yago Sangria. In the days between death and burial, we lubricated the wakes, providing death support for an overgrown town on life support. Laughing along the way. Jingle bells. Especially at Christmastime. When people died around Christmas, everybody wanted to get especially drunk.

I'm ready for a drink of my own. Vodka. I pour myself a shot and pull up a chair to my kitchen table. There's a porcelain basket of eggs in the center of the table. It is not coming on Christmas now, it is coming on Easter. You have chosen the first Saturday after Easter to be wed. I believe this is fortunate. I remember teaching you to dye eggs in the Russian manner, drizzling the eggs with hot wax dropped from the tip of a straight pen, then immersing the eggs in color, then covering the colored patches with fresh wax and immersing again till there is no white, till the colorful pattern is all that appears.

Did Tanya dye you a basket of eggs? Did she make for you a cross and a heart? I imagine that she did. There's something missing from the bowl on the table. I walk up the stairs to my bedroom. In my closet, high up on a shelf, atop an inlaid mahogany box in which I keep my good jewelry, on a golden stand, I spy my most significant material treasure. It's a fragile, brittle bit of a thing, flimsy really: a colored egg. I smuggled it out of Russia in the toebox of a shoe wrapped in thin, hard Russian toilet paper. It is the egg you blew out for me, piercing first the broad end, then the narrow end of the delicate oval with my knitting needle. Do you still have the scarf I knitted for you in Pushkin? I still have the egg. The purple has faded to red, the green has faded to blue, but the letters of the Cyrillic alphabet that I did not know you knew how to use are still visible. They still announce to me your love.

And I am still longing for what I will not allow myself to have. I am in my prairie house in the city; I am on the phone to Detroit. All I have said is "Hello."

I am thinking, when I was a girl I thought there was a *w* at the end of that word. I am trying to distract myself from the emotion of the moment.

"Bootsie, Bootsie, Bootsie, how's Leo's Red?"

"How should I be?"

"Better 'n' better e'ry day."

"I don't know what to say."

"Thank you works."

"I'm too scared to thank you."

"Everything's cool. Copacetic."

"Nothing's copacetic—now."

"You got your invitation?"

"It's not that simple."

"Yeah, it is."

"Not for me."

"It didn't take the card, did it?"

"What?"

"For you to know."

"It didn't take the card."

"Didn' think it would. Card was insurance."

"When I read that the car that struck him down was a two-tone deuce-and-a-quarter, *who* wasn't a question."

"Then you still Bootsie and it's simple, Red."

"Why now?"

"I'd a done it a long time ago if I'd a thought you coulda stood it."

"I don't want this."

"That's why you can stand it. If he had got himself killed when you were wishing every hour he was dead, you be sad now."

"I didn't want this."

"Now you can tell your son who his daddy is."

I start to cry. I am sobbing. I blubberbubble into the phone. What I was afraid would happen has happened, but in a way I did not imagine. Someone I love has murdered to avenge me. This is too strange. This is beyond the ken of bohemian black life, beyond the sphere of Harvard, beyond the world I have constructed, beyond my desire to know. I have turned a first true love into a killer. I was afraid of this particular thing. I was afraid of this, afraid if I told, someone I loved would kill Sven Jude Andersson, and I am afraid of loving a killer. I don't want to love a killer.

"You nailed forty dollars to a dope-house door."

"Better me than him."

The statement makes no sense. I am thinking that Spady means better that he killed Sven Jude Andersson than that Sven Jude Andersson killed him. Then I realize that Spady is not comparing himself to Sven Jude Andersson, he is comparing himself to Pushkin. He is saying it is better that Spady killed Andersson than that Pushkin killed him. My uncle is swallowing our sin.

I sob again. I was afraid this was who my son would become. I would lose him before I turned him into this. I have withheld all his fathers from him because I was afraid of this moment, and now this day has come.

"Why?"

"Because they shouldn't be no son of a bitch left in the world dumb enough to do what that baby-fucker did to Leo's Red, to Spady's Bootsie."

"Now they ain't."

"Now they ain't."

"How long have you known?"

"Almost from the git-go."

"How?"

"They ain't but so many things can go that wrong in a girl's life."
I'm crying harder now.

"Leo loved him some you. 'I love Red like the sun loves the
moon, like the moon loves the stars,' that's what he say. You were his
one thing and his all the rest. 'She my moon and she my stars.' That's
what he say."

"He sent that to me in a telegram once. My moon and all my
stars. I love Pushkin like that."

"Naw, you don't."

"Yes, I do."

"You got Push all jammed up. You messin' up all the lines."

"I was afraid of what he would do."

"They ain't nothing to do but sit quiet now."

"I can tell my son who his father is now."

"Yep."

"I love you, Spady."

"You should. I paid a high price for you."

"Spady!"

"Didn't pop Perkins. Now this?"

"You know about Perkins?"

"Eventually."

"Why she breathing?"

"You and Pushkin needed her."

"Aunt Sara?"

"I would a given that bitch anything."

"She robbed herself."

"She picked my pocket and showed me she wadn't me."

"Thank you."

"For what I did or did not do?"

"Both."

"Art ain't necessarily no esoteric shit, sometimes it's a perfect
hit."

I am quiet. I hear breathing, but it is hard to remember to keep
the phone to my ear, hard to have the energy to keep my elbow bent.
I have been avenged.

"You comin' to the wedding?"

"Consorting with the likes of me, an NFL star? I won't be there.
'Sides, I hear you need my invitation."

"You hear everything."

"Once you tell him everything, it's gonna be rough days for white boys. I'm laying heavy green on him taking his team all the way next year."

"Time will tell."

"Time done told."

Time done told; time done tolled. And why am I so glad they didn't run the old dog down? So much depends on learning to tie a shoelace in the warmth of a daddy's smile, a shoelace being tied over, over, and over again until the skill is mastered; so much depends on a dog that got away. Little gestures of mercy light our way. Little gestures of mercy and little gestures of gratitude.

Oh-two-owe. Ode to woe. The number Sun played every day of his adult Detroit life. Spady could count on me 'memberin' Sun's old number. Since no word from me at all had been the best I could do, he wasn't sure I would hear him callin' my name. He wasn't sure I knew my names anymore. Spady had cleared up an old debt.

"Who rode with you?" I asked.

"You good. Almost good as me. Gots to go, Bootsie, gots to go. Gots to go and never can tell."

Spady hung up without answering another of my questions. It could have been Lynx in there with him, Lynx who used to chauffeur us all around the big D when Detroit was something, before they blew up Hudson's downtown and twenty-some stories crashed into the town. It would have been Sammy, 'cause Sammy would a had to go. Like Sammy couldn't he'p himself but tip his hat when he walked down the sidewalk in front of the porch on which Dear sat. Lynx might have driven the car down from Michigan to Maryland, but Spady and Sammy would have been alone in the car that day. If Dexter had been living—well, if Dexter or Leo had been living, Sven Jude Andersson would have been dead a long time ago. Neither Dexter nor Leo was as patient or as smart as Spady. And Delicious would have driven Sammy and Spady down. Lynx would have been left at home. This was personal.

Spady was right. I had wished Sven Jude Andersson dead too many times not to have felt guilt if he had died.

I think of my days in the fields of Middleburg, that horse town where Mr. Andersson rented a farm to entertain clients, where the stallions stand in stalls of gold. Middleburg, with its well-stocked bookstore and Red Fox Inn with its Rolls-Royces rolling onto other fields where ladies in hats watch point-to-points and gentlemen shuffle and deal cash at their races—how far the Virginia communities of horses and horse money and gambling feel from the community of horse money into which I was born. Sven Jude Andersson took me target shooting in the Virginia hunt country time after time. It's hard to comprehend the arrogance or the ignorance of the thing—to take a girl you are planning to rape out into the fields with you, arm her with a gun, and teach her to shoot.

I think this way and I wonder if I can ever let you, my Pushkin, read these pages. What is this thing I am writing: a prayer, a pleading, an explication of the text of my life? A manifest effort to convince myself that I have the courage to love and tell? Who am I writing to? With angel eyes, can Daddy look down from heaven and read inkspots on paper? Can God only do it, or can the angels do it? I'm praying Pushkin and Martha Rachel know each other in heaven. I am hoping they read these pages.

I remember thinking, knowing in my cells, how easy it would be just to make a mistake, to let myself make a mistake. How easy that would have been. He invited me to Middleburg *after*, that first fall break, for a riding and shooting weekend. Maybe he thought I would lose the baby. It would have been easy to take my shot, and it would not have been me. I would have been taking his shot, not mine. I thought about it. I even believed with the smug grandiosity of late adolescence that I would get away with it. I could not imagine any jury punishing me for executing that sinner. I was naive. Who would not believe that the muddled girl-woman I was then would not be likely to make a mistake? But I wasn't God, I wasn't judge, or jury, or killer.

I cannot say this for my father, I cannot say this for my son, but I can say it for myself, because I've been there and I didn't do that, say it not out of fear or weakness but out of some sweet tie to some sweet truth: I am not a killer.

I think of my daddy and Dexter. I think of how much I hated Dexter for preying on the black community, selling powder, emanating whiteness, making the women sing in the middle of the night when they needed to sleep. I think of my daddy saying, "You didn' know Dexter when he was a kid, before they sent him off to the—" I thought my daddy said "parrot troopers." When Daddy told this story, it always had the same raggedy refrain: "One, two, three, jump!" When Dexter came back from the paratroopers, for weeks turning into months, all he ever said was "One, two, three, jump.

One, two, three, jump." Like a parrot, over and over Dexter said, "One, two, three, jump!" Something had gotten broken in his brain. When it was mended and other words again began to be spoken, his brain had realigned, turning efficient and cruel. Most of the time, toward most of the people, Dexter maintained a posture of stern indifference, but not to my daddy. Daddy remembered a different Dexter, and Dexter lived within that difference for the duration of his life.

I recall without difficulty, though it is thirty years past, the week Dexter died. He was visiting one of his boys in the hospital. One of his crew had got shot sticking up a dope house with some of Honeyboy Jackson's crew. Honeyboy was a kind of Robin Hood in those days in that place. Dexter would let his boys off to run with him and cop some spare change. This time his boy got popped, but they made off with the dough and nobody got arrested, so Dexter went up to visit his boy with a bottle of cold duck in his hand. Dexter had on his cashmere coat and his cashmere muffler, had him on some sharp shoes. He was walking down the hospital steps when the tiny fox of a girl he'd been trying to hit on, a girl who owed him forty-seven dollars, a girl whose debt he was offering to forgive if she would only just show him some love, stepped out in front of him. This girl had a lover of her own. He was the only man she'd ever had, or ever wanted to have. She was a dangerous girl, but Dexter didn't see it. Dexter had been pushing her hard, like she didn't want to be pushed, and she was afraid her man would see and try to do something to Dexter and Dexter would turn and get him. This girl met Dexter on the hospital steps, but not with the forty-seven dollars. She knew she'd be owing Dexter again; she was getting to like the white powder. Her best hope was that the next drug man wouldn't think she was so pretty. Truth be told and the truth showed, the little fox saw it in her mirror: she was getting less pretty by the day. So she met Dexter on the steps with a gun, not the forty-seven dollars. She shot him down in front of his boys, because none of them had the sense to be afraid of a desperate woman. That girl is still in jail. She never did have another man for a lover.

The little fox didn't have Spady for an uncle.

And I am realizing this about Pushkin—the writer, not my son: he picked up the pen and the gun. He picked up the pen and the gun and that is why he had my heart.

Pushkin is my everything.

FIFTEEN

I DIDN'T KNOW what an area code was.

I knew Sun's favorite number, 020, but I didn't know the area code for Detroit was 313. I knew my phone number. I was the star student of the third grade, but I couldn't phone home.

I have not forgotten the day Lena arrived at the door of my little all-black Lutheran school, St. Peter's, asking to have a word with me. She was wearing a pantsuit with snowflakes appliquéd on the shoulder and four gold bangles. She was wearing pumps. I stepped out of the classroom into the quiet hall. The door clicked shut behind me. She said, "I'm leaving your father. You can stay here or you can go with me. If you stay here, he will take good care of you. If you stay here, you will never see me again."

Her sociopathetic detachment was contagious. That's how it looks to me now. What it felt like then was that the queen was quitting the castle and the princess felt compelled to run after her.

"Where are you going?" I asked.

"I'm not saying till we get on the plane. In case you change your mind."

The worst decision of my life was not hard to make.

Lena and I landed in what is now called Reagan Airport, which was then called National, the first week of the year Martin Luther King would be gunned down in Memphis, 1968. The day before I attended a segregated private school in the North; the day after I attended an integrated public school in the South.

I have told you, Pushkin, of the bright minds, the ambassadors, the Foreign Service officers and journalists and politicians, the congressmen and secretaries of this or that, the celebrity shrinks and lobbying Georgetown matrons and superlawyers, who populated my childhood. I have told you about the schools, the fine doctors, the porcelain, the paintings, Pablo Casals at the Kennedy Center, the American Ballet Theatre's *Nutcracker* at Christmas, the avant-garde *Midsummer Night's Dream* from London on a jungle gym, with all the dancers wearing white unitards. I have not told you too much about Lena, about Lena and me.

We walked off the plane, not holding hands. The ankle I had twisted on the Michigan ice was half numb, half acutely painful. I scrambled behind my mother, trying to keep up, trying not to limp.

Our plane arrived in early evening. The terminal was filled with commuters and businessmen. Midweek in January there were precious few families passing through—and there were almost no black men.

The clip, clip of her heels on the hard surface of the National Airport is the remembered sound that I allow to take me back. For a few minutes in the National Airport I was sure everything was going to be all right. I was full up with Leo's daddy-love and Martha Rachel's mommy-love, and the queen was taking the princess on a journey. Finally it was my time to be with Mommy.

The flight that took me from Detroit to Washington was my third plane ride. I had flown with my mother and father to New York for the World's Fair the week the Beatles played Shea Stadium and the Supremes sang at the Copa. We had ringside seats. What I knew was, you got on a plane, had an adventure, then returned home. When I stepped on the plane that would fly from Detroit to Washington, I thought I would soon return home.

Home would be a very long time coming.

Here were my first volumes of businessmen. Younger men wore blue jackets with metal buttons that I had never seen before. They wore light tan pants that I had never seen before either. I didn't know the word *blazer*. For the very first time in my life, I saw plenty of white men. Many were wearing suits, gray suits and blue suits mainly. Here and there a brown suit. The cloth didn't shine. The suits were dull and fine. This surprised me.

Even Lena herself, as I remember, seemed surprised by the number of men. She had stopped at the gate when we deplaned, rested her traveling case in a seat, removed her cosmetic bag from her alligator contraption, and reapplied lipstick with martial intensity. Her eyes were big and bright. She was ready.

As she was clip-clip-clipping down the corridor, I was wish-wish-wishing for my great adventure. Lena looked like a general surveying the land and the people she intended to conquer, and she was taking me with her to do it. I felt like a powerful warrior-princess. We, she and I, had walked into the world of the movies. The only thing I found familiar in the faces and the clothes now surrounding me were flashing images from James Bond movies and from *The FBI* and *Perry Mason*. The entire cast and characters of *Perry Mason* courtroom scenes seemed to circle around us.

My mother stepped boldly, chin up, switching her hips, letting her hands, encased in black kid gloves, fall to her side, letting her fur fall open to reveal a carefully tailored white wool pantsuit. She strutted through the middle of the crowd, and men almost bumped into her.

At first I thought they were doing it on purpose, bumping into her, shuffling near to grab a whiff of her scent, White Shoulders. I thought they were brushing up against her body with intention and not by accident. In Detroit, men took and made opportunities to careen into my mother. I had noticed that. This was different.

When the collisions occurred, there was a startled apology and a brushoff—a hurried going on about business that suggested the stumbles were not intended. She smiled indulgently into the faces of the bunglers, and they looked away. Her smiles were not returned. This was something new too. When Lena walked by in Detroit, men, black men, whistled or looked like they wanted to.

My mother walked through this sea of men and it did not part. This was beyond novelty. It was almost as if they didn't see her, almost as if she were invisible.

I was struck salt-still in my tracks. I watched Lena's face turn a little red. She didn't drop her chin. She didn't stop switching. She didn't stop smiling. To my surprise, her smile got broader. If she was losing the first skirmish of her war on Washington, she was in the battle. It was my first moment of knowing, of beginning to know, that she liked battles. If her vanity was injured, she would find a way to assuage it. She would be seen.

I tried to scramble up beside her before she noticed I was lagging too far behind to be an effective courtier. I had an ankle again. A pain shot through it into me. I winced. A young man in a suit stopped. "What's this?" The man smiled at me; I smiled at the man. "Lost your mom?"

"Yes."

"I think I see her."

"My ankle hurts."

I had been waiting to tell someone ever since my ankle twisted as my little go-go boot slipped on the ice in Detroit. I was waiting to tell Daddy. I had waited so long I told this man instead.

"How about a piggyback ride?"

I said nothing. My daddy always hitched me up on his hip or slung me across his shoulders. I didn't know about piggyback rides. The man—he must have been thirty or so—reminded me of Darrin on *Bewitched*.

"She must think you ran ahead of her."

"Maybe."

Briefcase in hand, he crouched down to his knees.

"Climb on."

I climbed on this man's back. People smiled at us. A Robert Kennedy–looking man was carrying a clean-faced black kid down the airport corridor. This was not an unwelcome sight in the District of Columbia in 1968.

The man tapped on my mother's shoulder. She turned on her heels. She was pleased to see a handsome face smiling back—until she noticed me on his shoulders. Her eyebrows rose. Her smile froze.

"Pardon me. I think you lost something." He crouched to the ground. I scrambled off his back. I could see that she was displeased. I stood beside him. I didn't move toward her.

"It's my first time traveling with a child alone." She flicked at her lips with her tongue as if flecks of tobacco from an invisible cigarette she had invisibly lit had gotten stuck in her lipstick.

"They're hard to keep up with."

He pushed me gently toward my mother. I stood beside her, staring at a novelty—a man abandoning me. I needed this man, and he was about to run off. I had never seen a man do that before. Lena dug her fingernails into my shoulder until I didn't have a shoulder.

"Can you point the way to baggage claim?"

"I live at this airport."

The man pointed down the hall and to the right. He seemed to be appraising Mother. She lifted her hand to push the hair back from her face. He shifted his gaze from my mother to me. Maybe he noticed her fingernails digging into my shoulder. Maybe he noticed the white band of skin where the band of gold had been earlier in the day. He patted me on the top of the head. Her eyes got wider.

"Take care of your mother."

His eyes shifted back to Lena. He was cheerful, professional; he was on his way. "I'm going to miss my plane." He nodded and walked off toward his gate. My mother dug her other hand into my other shoulder.

"That was an A-number-one performance," she sneered. I didn't know what she was talking about. I barely knew who she was. I was about to find out.

We spent our first months in Washington in a townhouse in Southwest, where my mother had a friend. The friend, a psychiatrist, had a husband, a psychologist, and fraternal twin girls, Erin and Siobhan. They were white and do-gooding, lapsed Irish Catholics. Their place was decorated with Marimekko fabrics and they cooked in Dansk, the colorful enameled cookware in organic forms. I tasted my first chocolate mousse from that refrigerator, a modern affair composed of melted chocolate chips folded into whipped cream and spooned into a champagne glass. I felt embarrassed by my mother for the first time in that house. As our stay stretched on too long, from weeks into months, the psychiatrist asked if I could use a towel more than once, even if my mother couldn't.

Once when she, the psychiatrist, was called to the hospital, when he, the psychologist, had a session with a patient in his home office, he paid me six dollars, in quarters and dimes, to keep the twins absolutely quiet for fifty minutes. I was intrigued. It was clearly understood that something very important went on in his room. Usually the twins were allowed to chase around the house screaming louder than banshees. That night when the house was asleep I sneaked down to his office and sat in both black leather chairs. I lay on the black couch. I looked at the bookshelves and drew a finger across a shiny leaf of one of the green plants. The room felt sturdy. I had the sense that something important had gone on inside its walls.

Yet and still I have never been in more than a session or two of therapy. I write instead. I attempt my own psychoanalysis. When I think of psychotherapy, I think of the therapists who helped my mother kidnap me from the father they didn't know and the culture they didn't understand, and I have nothing to say aloud on a leather couch at all.

The black kids in my new third grade were nothing like the spunky, jaunty children I had known in my little all-black Lutheran school.

There was hungry dullness in the classroom and ashy anger on the playground, none of the shiny, bright blackness, the tenderly Vaselined knees and faces of boys and girls that shone all over my Detroit. Before I knew *nigger* to be a bad word, my daddy had said, "Detroit niggers hold their heads up higher," lifting my chin. My D.C. schoolyard was populated, my mother said, "by black kids from the new Negro-removal housing projects whose mamas cashed New Society welfare checks and by white kids whose mamas were newly minted baby bureaucrats fresh out of graduate school, come to Washington to save the world." I didn't know exactly what Lena meant by all that, but I knew it wasn't good. I saw a lot of drooping dark chins. One of them was my own. Daddy was right.

My Washington third-grade class was released early when rioting began the day King was assassinated. I was grateful for a reprieve from the seemingly endless parade of slanting lines and ovals we drew on endless sheets of faintly green lined paper, practicing cursive letters while we waited to see whether I would be admitted to private school. It seemed that I had lived through the Detroit riots in the summer of 1967 only to make it to Washington for its lesser lights.

Things only grew dimmer when we moved into an apartment of our own.

Most days she didn't speak to me at all. She wrote out a schedule with five-minute intervals, dictating how I was to get dressed in the morning. Six-forty-five, pull on panties; six-forty-six, pull on undershirt; six-forty-seven through six-fifty, lotion body; six-fifty through six-fifty-six, brush hair. I had six minutes to brush hair. It gave me time to think. Over and over I kept thinking about the same few minutes, the moment I twisted my ankle and had an excuse to stay, when the frozen surface of the city of Motown tried to hold me safe, tried to hold me home. Over and over I kept wondering how I could get back to then.

There was a day, there came a day, when Daddy asked me why I had gone with her. It was the summer I turned ten. I was playing in the bathtub in a swimming suit. It was too hot to play outside. I had my head covered in an old-fashioned, curl-pulling rubber swim cap. Daddy was surprised to find me dressed like that, splashing in the bathroom. Maybe he had had a drink. His question excited me. It was a cool, sweet invitation to speak, to cry, "Rescue me, Daddy! Daddy, why didn't you tell me she was a witch?"

I started by telling him what I had thought on the day she snatched me. Since that day I have learned to put the emotion in the facts. Then I told the truth in a cold, factual way that betrayed us both. I don't remember the beginning of the conversation, because it wasn't important to me. I was so eager to tell him about my first days in Washington—how I wondered why he didn't call, why he didn't come. I wanted to say again, "I didn't know you didn't know where I was." I needed to tell him that the queen had turned into an evil witch.

He took his turn first, asking, "Why did you go with her? How could you choose her?" Even after all these years, after his death, I can hear the incredulity in his voice, I can hear his question and the dying in his voice as he realized, as his brain came to know that I had in fact chosen her.

It was something he could not believe. It was something he would not have believed unless he had heard it from me. He formed the question "How?" so that I would answer "Didn't," but that was not my answer. My answer was more complicated and insufficient. I was nine years old. He wanted something adult from me. He wanted a woman's answer to that question. With small ears, I didn't hear the desperation in his query. He wanted me to say I hadn't done it, whether or not I had. He needed me to be woman enough to lie. And I wasn't. But I wasn't. I gave him a little girl's answer. I gave him my answer.

I told him he had everybody and she had no one. He raised his hand above his shoulder. I looked to see what he was doing. He slapped my naked thigh. His grown-man eyes were filling up with tears. "You almost made me hit you. Do you see how close you are to getting hit?" He hit me, then he lied about it. I started to cry. The fact of my daddy slapping my thigh shattered everything I knew. The idea that I had chosen her shattered everything he knew. The lying about it was at once irrelevant and the worst thing of all. We both knew it. I cried harder. He gathered me up in a towel and stopped talking.

He didn't let me tell him it was the worst decision of my life. He didn't let me tell him how she had transformed from a queen to a witch. Didn't let me say that I had quickly come to realize he had sheltered me from her for so long that I didn't know who she was. Didn't let me say that the touches he used to give her the men in Washington didn't want to give her. Didn't give me space to tell him what she wanted from me.

165

He didn't ask the question I wanted to answer: "Who do you love?" If he had asked, "Who do you love?" I would have responded, "You, Daddy, you, only you." He didn't ask that. He asked "How? How could you choose her when I had been your mama and your daddy? I wiped your ass and your nose and drove you to school, did everything but cook your dinner." I am hearing the tom-tom beat in "I heard it through the grapevine" as I recall this. Danadundun . . . "I'm just about, just-about, just-about gonna lose my mind." I think he stammered those words in that bruising conversation. Between the time he lifted his hand and the time he wrapped me in a towel, I think he said, "I'm just about, just about to lose my mind." Then he didn't say anything to me for a good long time. That hurt more than the slap.

I think back on Daddy having heard through the grapevine — through my mother's boastings, through her friend's friends talking — that I had had a choice and I had chosen her. I imagine him refusing to believe. And then my words gave life to his nightmare. Then and there I learned silence, my love. Then and there.

And when you hide behind the defense of silence once, it is almost certain you will crouch behind it again. It is a deceptively safe-feeling space.

But that was later. I was trying not to think about my father those early days in Washington. I tried to ask my mother, but she just glared and told me not to "act simple." She left me with neighbors and went out or pulled me by the hand and took me to an art gallery or a political rally, wherever a child would be an intriguing accessory.

I started learning how to cook. There were a whole lot of worldly kids who came home to empty houses who went to my new school. They knew some things about taking care of themselves that they were willing to share. I learned to make a lemon pie by stirring a bottle of lemon juice into two cans of sweetened condensed milk and pouring the whole bowl into a ready-made graham cracker crust. I learned to eat cheddar cheese from a spray can on a Triscuit for dinner and call it a canapé. I learned to melt a slice of cheese on an English muffin. I learned to mash an avocado into guacamole. I savored the hot meal provided in the lunchroom.

When we first got to Washington, I told my mother that I missed Tanya and she bought me a stuffed Snoopy. This surprised me. First, this was an act of kindness. Second, something in Washington was like something in Detroit. The funny papers. The cartoons were almost the same. I grabbed my Snoopy and held him tight. Everything else had changed. Even the taxicabs. We didn't have a car yet, and when you rode in a cab somebody else could get in, somebody you didn't know, and there was no meter ticking away, let alone no Aunt Martha Rachel who owned the cab company.

I tried to pretend that Daddy was dead and that I had to get over it. It was easier than fearing Daddy was dead and believing I couldn't get over it. I tried not to want what I could not have. I dialed our old phone number, but someone else answered, someone who lived in the city of Washington. I wondered if everyone in the world hadn't just gotten up and moved to the nation's capital on some Northwest flight.

SIXTEEN

WASHINGTON WAS DAZZLING PLENTY.
At the Smithsonian, a beleaguered classroom teacher rushed forty of us past the Hope Diamond. I returned on my own when I was supposed to be going to the bathroom. I rested my eyes on that blue stone, the largest diamond in the world, and knew what it was like to be a potentate. I walked along the Potomac River, hypnotized by the rowers sculling their muddy way; I skipped home from public school and the "Veep," as they called the vice president then, said hello to me. I heard Mozart's *Magic Flute* and read *The Hobbit*, and this was just in the first four months.

Lena easily landed a job with a consulting firm. Negroes were in vogue, literally and figuratively, in Washington in the late sixties and early seventies. It didn't take long for her to discover two superficially contradictory truths. She could be a professional Negro, paid to provide the Negro perspective, but she didn't have to be black all the time. She didn't have to live in a black neighborhood, go to black restaurants or clubs, or know any black people. So she didn't. The problem was me. "What," she inquired laughingly, looking at me one afternoon, "am I going to do with this little pickaninny?"

She had forgotten why she had brought me. Then she remembered. She had brought me to hurt Martha Rachel and Leo. Unfortunately, she wasn't getting the pleasure of watching them writhe. Lena lived in a never-ending now. What could she do with me now?

Her simplest, least imaginative idea was to teach me to wash and iron and cook and clean. More than saving her the cost of a maid, it gave me a role, it gave her a reason to have brought me. And, perhaps most satisfyingly, this is what fine ladies did with pickaninnies. You exert power without limit. She was enjoying the novelty.

In Detroit, in Motown, if Lena had dug her fingernails into my shoulder, Leo would have knocked her to the ground. My innocence and her ignorance ended before we got in the cab leaving National Airport. She had dug her fingernails into my shoulder and the sky hadn't fallen in on her. She could do what she liked with me. No one would interfere. The white man had seen, but he hadn't interfered. And I hadn't screamed. I wasn't as feisty away from the family. This was a revelation for both of us. Lena could do what she liked. She would spend the better part of a decade exploring the details of her desires.

I cried myself to sleep, thinking I deserved her for leaving him. Wishes don't come true. You just get punished for having them.

Punishment requires distraction to endure. My first refuge was a tiny glamorous playground, two supremely large wooden sandboxes filled with shining white sand. I had never seen white sand before. Inside the sandboxes were two elaborately carved saddlehorses whose bridles were festooned with finely chiseled wooden flowers. The horses were mounted on giant springs. You climbed on, then threw your body backward and forward and the horse responded. I would rock myself past memory into the rolling hills of forgetfulness. So far from my Detroit, from the postage-stamp lawns and the chainlink fences, so far from warm, wide laps, cool, strong shoulders, so far from familiar comfort and familiar joy, that white sand stood somehow in the long shadow of home.

To reach the sandboxes from our apartment, you walked across a reflecting pool on what appeared to be a poured concrete floating bridge, then up a curving cast-iron stair. The approach was enchanting.

I appreciated, I appreciate, every construction of *approach*. Sudden shivers me. I still dream of tree-lined gravel drives leading to houses not yet visible and arching bridges connecting place to place. Those elegant playpens struck me then as pristine and magical—a destination to obtain, to compensate for a home lost.

Sometimes when I think of my father I say to myself, On that bridge called his back I walked across the water. I think when I say that I am thinking of that bridge to the sandboxes. It was sometimes like that for me. More often it was like a nightmare I had over and over in the nights of those days.

I would walk back alone from the sandboxes. Let myself in with my key. Eat dinner, do my homework, and go to bed. Along the way Lena would check in by phone. My bedtimes were always very early. Lena wanted me asleep before she came home. I'd climb into bed— remarkably, the same bed that had been in Detroit—grab hold of the Snoopy, and wonder again what I had done to make her nice the day she got the Snoopy and how I could do it again if I didn't know what it was. Then I would fall asleep. On unlucky nights I had the dream.

We were swimming from one place to another, Daddy and me, swimming back to where we belonged. My mother stood on the shore and threw rocks at Daddy's head. I tried to hold on to his back and my mother threw rocks at him and Daddy and I almost drowned and he almost got killed until I got off his back and she stopped throwing rocks at him.

Then Daddy would begin to swim toward me, careful to keep his body between me and the rocks, which began flying again. Rock after rock hit his head until I turned back to shore and started swimming toward Lena. Then the rocks stopped.

Every time I mentioned my father or anyone from Detroit, Lena would look puzzled and ask me why I was referring to "that worthless yellow nigger and all his hoodlum friends." I stopped mentioning his name. She showed me an article in one of the national dailies discussing the Washington riots in the context of other, earlier urban disturbances, including the "inferno in the Detroit ghetto." I looked up *ghetto* and *inferno* in my classroom dictionary. This was how I discovered that the world thought my little piece of paradise a hell on earth.

Sometimes she took me along with her to cocktail parties. I would hear her screeching to her friends, "My brother-in-law was a policy banker, an illegitimate gambler. Imagine a black mafia. This is what I was married to. I'd go to Saks and pick out an outfit. He'd send someone to go and steal it for me—in the right size. Thank God I saved the child."

I began to feel puny and vile from a vile and puny place.

My mother discovered a public use for me: social climbing. She enrolled me in Paliprep.

Palisades Preparatory is one of the great American institutions. A progressive school with a conservative name, it is reputed to be the first independent school in the country founded as an integrated school. I don't know if that is true. I do know it was founded in the late forties and it was founded integrated. In one legend the school tells about itself, the anthropologist Margaret Mead was involved with the inception and the plan was to attempt to create a kind of ideal coming of age in the federal city. In an alternative legend, the school was founded by Holocaust survivors with the intention of raising a group of kids who would never design, drive, or ride on the trains to Auschwitz. Paliprep celebrates people who would die before they would do certain things. The Jews at Masada and Romeo and Juliet were put before us as examples of how a human being will choose death before a certain kind of life. Inspired by my environment, I considered running in front of a car.

The way you swept me off my feet, you know you could have been a broomstick. None of them knew the words to this song. The Temptations were on *The Today Show* one morning and I gathered some friends to watch. They laughed at all the gestures and the spinning. I switched off the TV. I couldn't stand to hear them laugh. I didn't have the words to tell them how beautiful it was.

I didn't have the words to tell and they didn't have the soul to see. Even liberals have severe cultural limits when it comes to cool.

About the same time I remember reading or hearing that the Rolling Stones had taken the Supremes out on a group date. The Stones, so the story went, couldn't get past the Supremes' prim ghetto-girls-in-silk-with-mink-stoles-around-their-bony-shouldered ways. I felt personally rejected.

A poster reading "Just because you have silenced a man does not mean you have converted him" hung on the walls alongside posters of Jimi Hendrix and Janis Joplin. That poster made me feel like someone had gone through what I was going through, and that made me feel better. At lunchtime they would close the door of our homeroom and play music loud on a stereo as they sang along with Country Joe and the Fish: "And it's a one, two, three, what are we fighting for?" None of these kids was curious about the world from which I came. They generously welcomed me into theirs, convinced and convincing that it was the center of an affluent universe. If I experienced being pulled out of Detroit and losing all my relationships as a kind of death, being enrolled at Paliprep and initiated into a new culture was starting to feel like a magnificent afterlife.

In Motown, my grandfather, Sun, had always said, "The world ain't fair. Be three times as good an' take what you want." Here I said, "That's not fair" and three people jumped to fix it. I had kind of died and gone to a kind of heaven.

Gentle beauty abounded. I was charmed. In the kindergarten room were transparent colorless glass vases filled with colored water. All eyes—brown eyes, green eyes, gray eyes, blue eyes—were delighted to watch the colors change in response to the clouds and the hour. This was so much quieter than watching synchronized dance steps and purple suits.

For the most part, prepsters called our teachers by their first names. We didn't get grades, we got comments. Report cards were no longer simple folded-over cards listing rows of *A*'s. They were portfolios attempting to discern my preferences and my predilections.

Even if home life was fraught—and the very idealism of the teachers and administrators made it impossible for them to see this almost too obvious truth—I loved my boogie bohemian days at Paliprep. Book report by book report, from *Little Women* in the fourth grade to *The Bell Jar* in the twelfth, I came to like being known and knowing.

And for the first time in my life, for the first time in the life of my family, the Armstrong family, it felt good to be an outlaw. The hippies were a kind of outlaw, and the Holocaust survivors were too. Both groups understood that just because a thing is done by the state, that does not necessarily mean it is right. Just because a thing is allowed by law, that does not make that thing just. Palisades Prep felt translated but familiar.

Of course, there were immense differences. The weekend the Pentagon Papers were stolen and every reporter, every Federal Bureau of Investigation agent, was looking for Daniel Ellsberg, I knew where he was. I was at the right sleepover to be an invisible sharer in that hour. Sitting in my new friend Jael's Adams Morgan living room along with Eve, listening to Jael's lefty-lawyer daddy predicting how the Supreme Court might rule, I felt important. How, the adults in the room asked again and again, would the Court balance the rights protected by the First Amendment and the needs of national security? On the television screen a reporter was saying that no one knew where Daniel Ellsberg was. We knew where he was. We were sprawled on a brightly colored couch better suited to smoking pot and listening to Iron Butterfly than to hearing this practical debate, taking it all in. The parents swore us to secrecy. They were so young they believed we wouldn't tell. We were so young we had no one to tell.

I liked the hippies for saying criminals weren't all bad—but I suspected, even grade school reason let me know, that the hippies would judge a criminal trying to stop the war differently from a criminal trying to make money. It was hard to love Spady in Washington. It was harder to think about him.

It was a very strange time.

I kept thinking about the Hope Diamond. The day I sneaked back to see it again I got caught. My overworked public school teacher assigned me to copy "I will not break away from the group under false pretenses" one hundred times, because that's what I confessed to. When I confessed, she snarled, "You have quite the vocabulary, young lady." She was wrong. I didn't have words to say how much trouble I would get into if Lena found out I had misbehaved. But I would have done it again. I was drawn to the stone. I thought it was the abandoned tear of an ancient giantess. As I copied my lines, I stopped and closed my eyes and remembered the stone. I knew loss was that large, that hard, that sparkling.

I loved the Gem Hall of the Museum of Natural History at the Smithsonian, case after case of sorrow solemnized into hard color and light. I went back time after time with various school groups. "Diamonds are the strongest thing on the planet," I was told on a Paliprep school tour.

All over Motown I had seen glitter. I had watched my mother clip various rhinestone earrings to her butter-colored ears. The Smithsonian seemed to scream that I had committed myself to weak materials.

I even fell asleep thinking of diamonds. Diamonds looked like something I hadn't seen before. They looked like more than what I knew. The sharkskin that prowled the Detroit night didn't shine as bright. The world as I had known it while I read *Heidi* in my little room in Detroit beneath the magenta canopy of my faux French Provincial bed was a colder, dimmer place.

I forgot who I was. I lost sight of who I would be. I forgot the ones who loved me.

I no longer watched *Batman*. I was no longer curious about pale people. I knew them.

• • •

Martha Rachel died. Leo sent for me. Lena cashed the money order, sent flowers instead of a niece, and bought herself a new outfit. She told Leo I would be waiting for him at the funeral home. Leo cussed me over the phone, as if my eleven- or twelve-year-old self could do anything about it.

There was a hole to fill. Madame, my French teacher, was a cute and lively graduate of one of the Seven Sisters. I loved Madame. I wanted her to be my mother. Madame taught her class songs. Lena never sang to me. Nor had my father, except the mockingbird song—at least, not yet. Later, once or twice when I was in high school, he sang me some Billie Holiday tunes, but he hadn't done that yet. Madame taught me the song of the bells of the cathedrals of France—Orléans, Beaugency, Notre Dame de Paris, Vendôme— and I sang it as if it meant something to me, and she sang "Dors, dors, l'enfant dors, l'enfant dormira bientôt, dors, dors, l'enfant dors," *Sleep, sleep, little baby, sleep,* and I started having sweeter dreams.

I was gathering up new pieces to fill in for missing parts; I was abandoning my first loves. In the terror times of intimate exile, amputation and amnesia make excellent allies. The songs Madame taught me are the songs I sang to Pushkin.

The way you swept me off my feet, you know you could have been a broomstick . . . Now, I was the kid you couldn't imagine wanting to be a broomstick. I was forgetting the words to this song. The Temptations were on a different television show, and I didn't watch. I listened to Simon and Garfunkel and Joni Mitchell, to Bob Dylan and the Allman Brothers.

My only touchstone with Detroit blackness in this new world was a friend called Isabella. Belle was smart as a whip. She was the only child in our school who dressed sharp. Belle never wore the same outfit twice. Her mother, a nurse, made all of her clothes, and they were magnificent. Belle could do everything. At least, being an athlete and a mathematician, she could do everything I could not—and that felt like everything in the world to me.

Belle lived in Northeast Washington, in an all-black area segregated and separated from the power precincts of the city. Her mother had a lovely rose garden that reminded me of my grandmother's. Every piece of furniture in their living room was encased in plastic. Her mother would cook us endless plates of food. I remember staying with her one weekend and eating and eating. Her mother had made us strawberry shortcake and apple pie, fried chicken and smothered steak, all in the same day. She cooked endlessly for us. Starved for Dear, I ate until I could eat no more and started throwing up.

Belle taught me to play and deal rummy 500, which was a little like putting Spady back into my life. I wonder where she is now. Mrs. Perkins reminded me of Belle's mother. Maybe that's why I could leave you there. I would like to think that was true.

James Taylor, sweet baby James, captured the mockingbird song, the one my daddy gave me: "Hush little baby, don't say a word, Daddy's gonna buy you a mockingbird, and if that mockingbird don't sing, Daddy's gonna buy you a diamond ring, and if that diamond ring turns glass, Daddy's gonna buy you a looking glass, and if that looking glass does break . . ." and I would set my jaw every time I heard it play.

The mockingbird didn't sing, the diamond was glass, and the only mirror I had was my mother's ever-mocking eyes. Yet and still I was getting acclimated to Washington.

I started wearing jeans and carpenter pants. My hair grew out. I washed it and let it do whatever it did, which was fuzz into a shaggy brown halo. I went for my summer visit to Detroit the year I turned thirteen and everybody said how changed I was. Cousins made fun of the way I talked and dressed. Dear was alarmed by my hair. Everybody was embarrassed by my raggedy hippie-girl clothes. Daddy alone still claimed me. Detroit was changing too, from Motown to Murder City, U.S.A.

Tragedy and promise were in the air. Everywhere.

Down in Alabama, the dogs and hoses had let up. Folk were beginning to vote. The poor people had come and marched on Washington, built their Resurrection City, even if Reverend King was dead.

Me, I didn't march with my cousins from Alabama. We had completely lost touch. I was too busy being a rising star at Paliprep, dashing through the curriculum from Egypt to Austen, from French to physics, with anthropology everywhere—waiting in line to see Haldeman testify at the Watergate hearings in person. It was the seventies.

I went to dinner at Eve's house, and there were magic people flying in the air. I stood staring transfixed on her stair landing. I was looking into the soul of Marc Chagall. I was nose and eyelash to his pigment and his power. I didn't know his name then. I just knew the power of the canvas. A vision from one of my deep dreams spoke aloud to me in the daytime. I wanted to know who the painter was. I wanted to know how he did it. I wanted to know everything.

Washington was more than the city. Some weekends I spent with a girl on an island in the Chesapeake Bay. Both of Mary-Stuart Storey's parents were descendants of southern generals. He was a writer and a drinker who wrote speeches for conservative senators. She was a member of the Junior League and the DAR and worked for a conservative congressman. They had oyster shells for ashtrays. When they got to fighting, the oyster shells would fly.

They lived in a stand-alone house quite close to downtown that was in anything but a good neighborhood. The house had been in her family since it had been built. Back then, the mother assured us, the neighborhood had been excellent. But the house in the city was the least of it. Friday nights we would drive to the Maryland shore, singing Woody Guthrie songs about America, packed into the back of an old station wagon, and we would get to the island and smell the salt air. All day Saturday we would swim and fish and dive for treasures, particularly water glass, pearly green jewels from the bay that began existence as broken pieces of Coke bottles. Once three of us— Mary-Stuart, her little sister, and I—dived off the same side of the same small sailboat at the same time and managed to flip the boat over. The crab bucket and my glasses were lost in the yelping confusion. The rest of the weekend was a blur.

Sunday night, when I told my mother, I remember being afraid that she would be mad about the lost expensive glasses, and then I saw a wistful look on her face that suggested to me that the glasses were not at that moment significant. Now I think she was thinking, "I almost lost her. I was almost relieved of this burden. She almost died." Lena encouraged me to go back to the beach.

Like children who wake up of a morning and discover that they are literally taller, there were nights after days on the bay that I closed my eyes and began to dream, only to discover that I had more images, more colors, more shapes than I had had the night before.

Many were the afternoons we walked across the scratchy clover lawn down to the pier, where we lashed a motor to a wooden dinghy and set off with Ben, the tenant who kept watch on the place in exchange for living in the dependency, a Johnny Cash–loving water-man, navigating us toward the Barron Islands. There were six or seven of these islands. Once, not so many years ago, I saw them for sale in the back of a magazine. If they went for sale now, maybe Pushkin could buy them. All of them.

One was surreally beautiful. This isle was long and narrow, so narrow that standing in the middle, you could see water lapping on both beaches. The white sand was dressed with pieces of driftwood bleached albino white by the sun. Some of the pieces were near-whole trees weather-changed into eye-commanding sculpture. The water around the sandbar was warmer than the water off the home pier. It invited; we accepted. We shed our shirts and shorts and pant-ies beneath a sun I was just beginning to think had not been created by God, a newly pagan sun, and tiptoed like young goddesses along the shore. Our throats got rough, and silence set in. We had no wa-ter and knew better than to drink from the sea. We were stung by nettles and cautious of men-of-war. The white sand, the heat, the salt, the whiteness of the wood, the very moonscape quality of the seascape, gave that place a sense of death and strandedness, close upon heat and wet. We each sensed there was nothing to be or do but become a warm-blooded animal pushing off land into the water, an animal with salt and wet on her skin, floating above oyster beds and crab cages. You don't forget weekends like that.

By Monday morning the nettle welts on the cheeks of our asses would turn red and itch. We would shift in our desk seats, starting in first-period French, trying to get comfortable, barely making it to seventh-period sports. Tuesdays were better. By Wednesday the welts were gone. The sense that there was nothing to do but take off our clothes and plunge into the sea as Ben looked away stayed with us.

Ben did not molest us in any way. Bellowing "Folsom Prison," "Ring of Fire," and "I Walk the Line," he left us to run naked and budding. He averted his eyes so we could have our good time, keep-ing his ears pricked in case we needed his good strength. Do you re-call the time I asked for tickets when you played Baltimore? They were for Ben's family.

Later those nights, as we sprawled sweating and naked on lady-mended two-hundred-year-old sheets in Mary-Stuart's antique beds, reading dusty fifty-cent paperbacks—*Delta Wedding, Look Home-ward, Angel, Member of the Wedding,* books nobody else in our world had or read anymore — the voice of Johnny Cash would blow in on us through the screen window, from the shack across the scratchy clover yard.

Leo could not imagine my knowing a man like Ben. Leo would not remember that children loved to play beneath the hot sun in the out-of-doors barefoot and naked, not strut in full-length rabbit coats mimicking the pages of *Children's Vogue*. Leo knew nothing of white sand and driftwood. He knew nothing of water glass. He was losing me and I was losing him.

When people meet me now, they think I'm from Washington.

SEVENTEEN

SOMETIMES FALLING DOWN in the dark is a good thing.

Next to nothing at all is what I knew about *Gone With the Wind* as I stood outside the Uptown Theater, on Connecticut Avenue in Cleveland Park. My mother had suggested it. Isabelle's mother had the good sense to forbid attendance, which of course guaranteed that Isabelle was there. Mary-Stuart's mother, the descendant of the Confederate general, was somewhat aghast that we wanted to go, but deferred, saying, "If the Negro girls' mothers think it's appropriate." Jael and Hopii's moms thought it would be instructive, in a what-not-to-do-let's-be-horrified kind of way. Eve's mother, born and raised in Europe, had never been South except to change planes in Miami. She didn't have a dog in the fight. We, the most popular clique in the middle school, the six-pack, went blithely off to the movie theater.

Afterward, as we marched back to Hopii's, where her doctor mom and doctor dad would collaborate in the preparation of our meal, Mary-Stuart said, "Windsor, you're not like Mammy—you're like Scarlett!" I wanted to cry right out on the street, but I wouldn't. I might have been trying to forget Leo, but I couldn't even begin to forget his lessons. He had schooled me stern. I remembered the one that went "Never let them see you cry."

I dropped back from the group. There were still six of us walking, the same six who had gone trick-or-treating for ourselves and UNICEF, the six of us who had passed around buttered grapes under a sheet and pretended they were eyeballs, the six of us who had been chased by boys until we divided into groups, the better to escape. But I no longer felt a part, I felt apart.

179

Eve hung back with me. Since Halloween night we had started to become an acknowledged minigroup within the group.

That October thirty-first, the six-pack had taken off from Hopii's house, shiny black sacks in one hand, orange UNICEF boxes in the other. Eve was dressed like a gypsy. I was dressed like a mermaid. I wore my mother's sleeveless shell, the one with giant blue and green sequins, and her long pink satin skirt, split way up the side. It was the one she had worn to see the Supremes. I twisted and knotted the hem into a very pretty tail, which I dragged through the Norman Rockwellish sidewalks of Cleveland Park that autumn night. If Lena could transform into a me-creature, I would transform into a sea creature. Two hours later, rich in coin and candy, we were on our way back to fondue at Hopii's.

I was thinking we were a long way from October thirtieth and Devil Night in Detroit when a group of boys started chasing us, boys from Hopii's neighborhood who went to the fancy Episcopal boys' school. It was all in good fun, but the six-pack's fun was to run and not get captured. Eve grabbed my hand and we both gained speed. We were headed for a corner. I could feel her pulling us into a curve. We were guessing the boys would go after the four and leave the two. We guessed wrong. The boys followed us around the corner, where the street came to an abrupt dead end. We were caught between the boys and the leaf pile. We dove straight in, screaming. The boys scattered, laughing.

Eve's bank, a folded, taped, half-pint milk carton of a thing, imploded on impact. Quarters and dimes intended for blighted children rolled off into the dark.

My bank was intact. I had held it above my head. Eve began feeling in the dark for her coins—a foolish trouble, I would have thought. She found one just as I was beginning to put her empty bank back together by tearing little notches in the cardboard. That nickel was only the first coin she found. She found a second, a dime. My foolish trouble was her hopeful effort—and she was rewarded, if only slightly. I wished her greater reward. I split the contents of my bank. Suddenly we were friends, and it did not shiver me. Back at the Halloween party, we laid our thin cloth sleeping bags down side by side and whispered as the other girls slept.

We both had secrets; we both were lonely. We both knew and loved places strange and wild. Eve had been bounced all over the globe, from Hong Kong to Moscow, to London, to Paris. Her father inherited from two fortunes, a department store chain in the Midwest and real estate in New York, then ran off to join the ranks of foreign correspondents. Eve was full of memories and ideas that would mean something only to another girl—full of playground ambitions and humiliations, playground triumphs and tragedies that she wanted to share. She carried within herself her history as a girl, and though she was careful to protect it, having experienced ridicule and lack of interest in response to certain earlier tellings, she was urgently eager to share it. It might vanish if it remained untold. Some of it had already vanished.

Eve explained all this to me that first night. She knew how she worked. She had been in therapy. And she was a good teller of tales. Eve reminded me of Leo. Eve reminded me of Daddy.

For the first time in a long while I began to think of Leo, albeit silently and secretly. I thought of him as a refugee—a man with an Alabama history divided from his Motown present, just as Eve was a girl with a Hong Kong history divided from her D.C. present. I was the place in the present where Leo and then Eve could locate themselves through the telling of their past, a place to put their past and visit it.

Eve was the place where I learned that I could continue knowing my daddy even if I wasn't with him. Reflecting on what I had already been told, what I had already seen, I could get to know him better. The idea charmed me. And the idea of charming me charmed Eve.

So when I dropped back, in the deepening dark of the street after the movie, and Eve dropped back with me, my reaction was surprising to me. I wished she hadn't. Her physical presence at that moment chastised me. She looked too much like Melanie, or Scarlett, or any of those white characters on the screen. They were all looking alike to me that night. I was thinking there was something about Hattie McDaniel that reminded me of my grandmother and something about Butterfly McQueen that reminded me of my aunt Sara.

I would not have any of these girls walking down Connecticut Avenue know this. Their idea of a black woman was Lena, my mother, in a knit suit and with a seddity accent. At the moment I would have it no other way. In the wake of watching *Gone With the Wind*, even Aretha embarrassed me. Anything country and colored felt idiotic, vulgar, undesired, and undesirable. You know you're starting to go crazy if you can think Aretha is undesired. You know you are close to crazy when you want to sing to your mother, "You're no good, heartbreaker. You're a liar and you're a cheat."

We were almost at Hopii's house. The others disappeared

through her front door. I sneaked a side glance at Eve. We were both wearing long granny dresses and granny glasses with thin gold rims. We both had kinky hair, only hers was bright red. When we had first seen each other, she had said that we could be twins. I was wondering if watching *Gone With the Wind* had changed her ability to see that when she broke into my thought with a question. "Did you know," she asked, "the man who invented the modern Russian language was black?"

"What?"

"The man who invented the modern Russian language."

"One man invented Russian?"

"Modern Russian."

"What's modern Russian?"

"What people speak today."

"Who?"

"Pushkin. Alexander Pushkin, the man who invented the modern Russian language."

"What kind of black?"

"Black, black. His great-grandfather was a slave."

"They don't have slaves in Russia."

"They had Pushkin. My mom says Pushkin is more important to the Russian language than Shakespeare is to the English language."

"The Russian Shakespeare is black?"

"The Russian more than Shakespeare is black."

Hattie and Butterfly were vanishing from my head. I closed my eyes and tried to imagine Pushkin. All I could see was Rasputin with a suntan. I got goose bumps.

"There's a picture of him in my dad's study."

And so I switched my allegiances.

A week later I rode home with Eve in her carpool. It was a Friday night and her parents were going out. Dinner would still be served in the dining room. Eve and I sat on either side of her brother, who positioned himself at the head of the table. Exams were coming up. My classmate and I were quiet with the realization of exactly how much work we really had to do. A lot. We were studying South America, and each of us had to choose three countries about which to give a large report. I chose Venezuela, Argentina, and Brazil. Eve had chosen Uruguay, having been to its splendid beach, and Chile, because her father was full of talk about the military dictatorship there, and

Bolivia. Her choices were interesting, but I didn't want to move on to the side stories when the main stories needed learning. We were considering the necessity of a trip to the Salvation Army bookstore. I was pushing for it. If we went while we were at Eve's, someone in her family, or a driver or the housekeeper, would take us. If I went from my house, I would have to take the bus, and the Salvation Army bookstore was in an iffy neighborhood. Having once had street skills, I knew mine were now lacking.

Eve's older brother, who liked to swagger about the house in what he claimed to be the manner of Young Werther, made an asinine remark. I pronounced him an ironic zero. Zack was squawking a repetition of my accusation when his father entered the dining room.

"Calling my boy 'ironic zero'—which one of you pretty creatures came up with that?" Eve's father's eyes surveyed the room. He nodded his head and smiled as if to indicate explicitly that the scene received his approval. His children were healthy, his fortune was good. No one was about to go off to war or someplace worse. He was grateful. The friend was exotic and articulate. The children and the guest were sipping asparagus soup from bowls that were just like a set in the Victoria and Albert Museum. He savored his guilty good fortune.

His son said, "I, sir, am the ironic zero. Windsor is the zeroer."

The father walked over to me, softly repeating my name, "Windsor, Windsor," as if he were trying to remember it or figure out something about it. "Windsor, Windsor, Windsor." I stopped sipping my soup but kept staring into the bowl. "Let me tell you something about Pushkin. The man who invented the modern Russian language was a black man. Black just like you."

That night, in the few minutes before Eve's mother entered the dining room, worried and beautiful, her thin, thin body slinging immense but somehow elegant breasts, before she stood in the doorway smiling vaguely at her children, who each seemed too large to have come out of her, before Eve's mother spirited him away, Eve's father showed us a drawing of Pushkin and rattled on to us for two brilliant minutes about the poet.

That night I went to sleep on Pratesi sheets, knowing that the man who invented the language of millions and millions of Russians, the man who invented the language of Tolstoy and Turgenev, was black like me.

It was a revolution in my brain.

Our house, the house where we moved as soon as my mother made vice president at her firm, the place where I lived until I left for college, was formerly the embassy of an Eastern European country. That sounds fancier than it was. The neighborhood, called Takoma Park, was interesting rather than fashionable. I liked that. It was also just inside the District line. My mother, who had some political ambitions, would have it no other way.

I slept in an upstairs back bedroom that had two walls of windows. It was on what I called the library side of the house. In winter, when the leaves were down, I could almost see my library through the trees.

The Takoma Park Library is a conventional building of no particular physical beauty. It was, however, the place I first encountered Pushkin. And Brontë. And Du Bois. And Vince Lombardi. If I were a pagan, I would pray to it.

It was and is a dark brick building of a design that was intended to suggest, with its traditional municipal construction, the promise to conservative society that the state would civilize the willing. Inside was a large wooden checkout desk flanked by stacks to the left and perhaps periodical and reading tables to the right. Beyond this front room, of equal if not slightly greater size, was the children's room. The children's room was not in fact a room at all but an area, identifiable by long low wooden tables with little wooden chairs. It had lots of low bookcases. In the back to the left were two thin-metal brown desks where the librarians sat.

In the back on the right was a very small enclosed room with windows and blinds. This was the young adult section. There was one table and big-people-sized chairs. My love affair with architecture began in that safe room.

One book from that young adult section and I was hooked. I remember vividly the day that I picked a volume of Brontë off the shelves, then a second. I was intending to begin with A and make my way through the shelves systematically. Something pulled my hand past Alcott and Austen, right to Brontë. No one had ever pronounced the name to me. If I had had to speak the word out loud, I would have made the *o* long and the *e* silent, as in *vote*. I didn't know it was pronounced as if it were spelled *Brawntay* or *Brawntae*.

It is easy to see why black girls love *Jane Eyre*. Jane works as a servant for other children in the fashion that black slave children worked as servants for other children. She worked as a nanny in the home of a wealthy man, taking care of his child in the fashion that mammies worked in homes taking care of children. Ultimately, Mr. Rochester tries to lure Jane into his bed without benefit of marriage, though Jane, the nanny, unlike her literary cousin, the mammy, doesn't know this. Rochester can't marry Jane because he is already married to a woman from the Caribbean—the famed madwoman in the attic.

Good little boogie black girls all over America have read and re-read *Jane Eyre*. Many experience it as a satisfactory, if incomplete, translation of their grandmothers' experiences in Georgia or Alabama or Virginia into the gentrified and gentling English countryside—and into the queen's English. They quicken with me at the possibility that Rochester's wife, albeit crazy and imprisoned in the attic, was a woman of color.

Though the English audience understood that Rochester had been talked into marrying for money a woman with at least one hidden stain on her bloodline, the stain of insanity, there is inherent in the text a second possible taint, the taint of darkness. The little black girl I was read this quite empathically. I read the possibilities of black beauty. Rochester met the beauty in the Caribbean. There was the possibility he was bewitched as much by her beauty as by her money. My heart fluttered at the possibility that the hero had been attracted to a woman who looked perhaps a little like me.

When I think back on my days in the Takoma Park Library, I recall them as the period I was hooked on a drug so good I didn't want even to think about giving it up. It once occurred to me that an entire and exciting life could consist of reading *The Lord of the Rings* over and over. Before long I had read every book in the young adult section and every book in which I was interested in the adult section. The Takoma Park Library sent me off looking for a bigger fix.

Harvard's Widener Library promised to be a needle straight to the vein. Lord knows I needed a needle straight to the vein.

Life at home was getting more and more complicated while remaining entirely unspeakable. Lena was hired by a rapidly expanding gourmet ice cream company to introduce its product in the nation's inner cities. Her boss, a Swede from Minnesota who began life as a dairy farmer, had a very fine Ivy League résumé and a very large brokerage account. He began sleeping over quite a lot, though he kept his apartment in the Watergate. Mr. Andersson had never been married and said he would never get married. He never had any children and he didn't want any children. He was the perfect boyfriend for Lena. I didn't tell him about the complications. I barely spoke to him. But I was grateful for his sporadic presence. He distracted her from me.

I was no longer the maid of all work. Lena was promoted and hired one. Or was it two? Now I was only the sometimes cook and personal lady's maid. She spent too much money on clothing to afford all the personal services she thought she needed. I learned to make crepes and soufflés and chicken with grapes and almonds. Every weekend night I had a friend over or I was over at a friend's house. *A* by *A*, seven hundred and something by seven hundred and something looking for eight hundreds that didn't come, page by page, test by test, paper by paper, I was crawling to a place of my own where I could close my eyes. Harvard. Until I got there, I availed myself of the intermittent refuge and shelter of books.

I skipped through the streets of Washington; I staggered through the halls of our house. I ran to and through the corridors of Paliprep. In the whiteness of Washington, Lena hated blackness more than before.

It was in the young adult room, with a thick volume from the adult section toted back to my designated and chosen sanctuary, that I first encountered Pushkin. Eve provided the introduction; the library provided the encounter. I recall that hour in the mood that one recalls an assignation, the hour in a hotel room of an affair that vanishes but does not go wrong. Pushkin's prose was that sweet to me.

First I read his unfinished novella, "The Negro of Peter the Great." It was a strange beginning. All my reading was a revelation, but this was a most delicious and difficult revelation. On Pushkin's pages, a black man, a man captured from Africa, is in Paris, getting educated, moving in the highest Parisian society. He is also being loved and desired by a woman of the nobility. I felt my own possibilities expanding. I borrowed a *New York Times Menu Cook Book* from the library and learned to make borscht and blini. I began to lust for a taste of caviar.

Of course I was heartbroken by the truncated ending. The African quits France to return to Russia. He determines, after being introduced and encouraged by Czar Peter, to marry a girl from the nobility. The girl is disgusted by his blackness. But before that there was the beautiful and rich countess who thought the Negro of Czar Peter the Great was the most dashing man in all of Paris, desiring him more than she desired her white count. And there was a secret baby! My adolescent self was riveted.

I looked up Pushkin in the encyclopedias, first in the *Britannica*, then in the *World Book*. I wanted his life. I wanted to marry one of his descendants. I wanted everybody in the world to know who and what Pushkin was. I was thrilled that most of the well-informed world already did know.

There are seven words in the first line of the tale "The Queen of Spades." I counted them and thought of Spady and the peas. I remembered them because they seemed the annotation of my life: "The Queen of Spades signifies secret ill-will." To read the story was to have literature announce the deal life had dealt me. Lena was my queen of spades; the Queen of Spades was my mother. I read and reread the line. Spades are black people, people like Spady and me. Signify is what a black person, particularly a black woman, does to communicate: "Don't be signifying at me." I didn't need to wait till Skip Gates wrote *The Signifying Monkey* to know this. I knew this. *Signify* was not a white word in my circle. It was a sharp black woman's word.

It was a word I had all but forgotten until Pushkin, in translation, called it back to me. Something was signifying to me.

Actually, it was two different memories.

I recall seeing a computer printout of a pregnancy test pinned to a bulletin board in the kitchen of our apartment in Southwest Washington when I was in the fifth grade. The test was positive. But there never appeared a baby. I have not always wondered what happened. I have not always known without asking. I simply refused to know or think—even when Jael, spending the night, noticed the same postcard, the card I was intended by my mother to notice. Even with Jael's straight black hair, sharp blue eyes, and aquiline nose leaning into me, giving urgency to the instruction, "Ask her, ask her!" I didn't. Even when it was clear my new friend was dismayed that I didn't already know the answer to her question—"What did she say, what did she say?" I didn't relent. No, "Ask her, ask her" did not propel me to confront my mother. I knew what she had done. I was just grateful she had not done it to me.

Lena was signifying that I should be grateful.

That was the story of my birth: gratitude that conception wasn't followed by vigorous cleansing. I asked my father what he had said when my mother told him they were going to have a baby. He responded with that question about stories and truth. I wanted to know the truth. He said, "I told your mother I wanted her to have an abortion." He didn't want a baby. Didn't think she was ready to have a baby. He drove her to a doctor's office. It wasn't legal, but it wasn't a back room. It was simply after hours. My father left my mother in the waiting room and shot off to have a drink.

I wonder what the doctor saw. Lovely long beige legs, a slim and tall but curving beauty, accompanied by a man of thirty, good-looking, fully grown, but as young as a full-grown man can be. I imagine Lena taking off her fur-trimmed coat, her good wool dress, her stockings. I imagine Lena sitting up on the examining table in her padded black lace bra and black nylon panties, her stomach soft but flat, her sloping breasts, her shining silvery pink toenails.

They say it was Halloween night. He remembered that later. Children darting in black costumes in front of cars whose drivers could not see them. Had Lena ever dressed up as anything? The holiday seemed to her foreign. It was nothing remembered from her childhood in the farming town, where the church service was in German and all the other families were white, white as the Michigan snow. This bit of gold in her skin was more costume than she would ever want. So strange to think of costumes now, she thought, recognizing she was naked on a doctor's examination table. She had an idea for a girl group. She wanted to dress them in imitation of the senator from Massachusetts's wife, hat and gloves, knit suit. She knew what the Supremes should look like before they knew they were the Supremes.

Lena couldn't open her legs. She could hear the doctor asking her to, but she couldn't do it. The doctor had given Leo a pill to give Lena before the procedure. It had done something to her. She was remembering a snowsuit she had abandoned on the way to school years before because it made her look black and round. Her knees clinched shut. The winter wind had touched her gently then — until her foster mother stirred Epsom salts into a glass of warm water. A torrent of filth had exploded from Lena's bowels. This is what lives inside you, she had been told. Now something else grew. She wouldn't open her legs. She had abandoned the snowsuit. And truth be told, she was cold. It was too cold in the white Michigan snow. Too cold then, too cold now. Too cold at ten, too cold at twenty-two.

Too cold in the room with the man wielding a shiny tool; too cold with that other man down the street in a bar. She was frozen stiff. Her knees would not part.

After the doctor left the room, she got dressed again. Stockings and slip and wool dress, coat with the fur around the collar. When my daddy returned, the doctor told him that the woman didn't want the procedure. He said he had neither tool nor strength to pry her legs apart. My daddy nodded. He took Lena for a whiskey shot. I was coming.

Plans had changed. Or they hadn't. My daddy never had a plan in his life, and Lena's plan was to whelp a slave—a pickaninny to loathe and hold. She said she wanted to have a little Lena.

Mama don't always tell the truth.

"The Queen of Spades signifies secret ill-will." I read these words and things were different. That's what I knew then. Now I laugh to understand that the reading of these words provided me with both a context and a con-text to read against and with the narrative I had received regarding my beginnings. It changed everything. It changes everything. I must be careful about what I tell Pushkin.

I had underestimated the pretty doll who was my mother. I would not have thought her a face card, could not have imagined her trumping Spady or Leo, let alone Spady and Leo. In Detroit, in Mo-town, with Leo calling her a motherless child, Lena seemed small. Small enough to be my child? In Detroit, Lena was largely an aching absence in an orbit of powerful maternal attractions: Dear, Martha Rachel, Aunt Sara. I have not yet read the line that precedes the tale. Seven words: "The Queen of Spades signifies secret ill-will." They struck and they stuck.

It was almost too late. She had all but vanquished me. I looked into the mirror and saw a being brown and unlovely. I looked back in time and saw a thug-life childhood and a ne'er-do-well drunk, maybe now sober father. I stopped looking. She gave me reason to want to put my eyes out.

It was a thing that I never had opportunity to tell my father, how I hadn't truly known who my mother was. Have I recreated an echo of this for you, an inverted echo? You do not know who your father is. All the silence I have heaped upon your head, all the wishing after Cordelia, it came down so softly to this: I didn't know who she was. Then I did. She bore me to have an intimate audience and per-haps an intimate mirror. And I will keep her secrets, because they are of no use to us. Mine I will share. My mother was the queen of spades.

All the hell we have walked through, the hell we are left to walk through yet, is but the ending of a trail that began when I followed after the shimmering and pale woman, the tall and slim lady, the one who, when striding the pavement of Motown, looked just like a fairy queen. I had utterly misread her significance.

You want to know who your father is. I wish I didn't know who my mother was. I wish all that I knew about her was that she was a girl brave enough to bear her burden and birth me. For years and years and years, until I read "The Queen of Spades," there was a story about my mother that I liked, a story about my mother that made me feel loved, the Halloween story. Then there wasn't.

I was confused by the Halloween story, because it seemed to say my mother wanted me. My father let it say, Your mother wanted you even before I did. Then I read "The Queen of Spades." It is the story of a woman who is apparently giving assistance but is in fact sealing doom. A woman who makes relationships to effect damage. Suddenly I knew why I was born. The Queen of Spades signifies secret ill-will. Lena had me to have someone to hurt. If my daddy didn't understand this, Pushkin did.

After having my library card suspended for refusing to return the volume of Pushkin's collected works, I finally got my own copy. All the six-pack had been keeping an eye out. Mary-Stuart found it for me one Saturday in the Savile Row Bookstore, a Modern Library Giant, *The Poems, Prose, and Plays of Alexander Pushkin*. Finally I could return the borrowed volume that was too many weeks overdue at the library. My copy was published in 1937, the same year as *Gone With the Wind*. When we paid the lady in gray tweed and cashmere the seven dollars, she thumped the book soundly and scowled. She said, "Pushkin, Shakespeare. That's all. Geniuses."

I loved a black man whom Washington respected, a black man whom the whole world revered, a black man whom my mother could not revile or defile, a genius bred from the loins of a kidnapped slave. Perhaps you are another. I was a child not long from having a child beginning to contemplate my complicated future.

After I started reading Pushkin, Eve taught me a few words of Russian. The class put on Chekhov's *The Cherry Orchard* and I couldn't stop smiling. Without Pushkin, there is no Chekhov.

I had something in common with another brilliant Russian.

EIGHTEEN

"APRIL BE the cruelest month," Pushkin said.

Nobody laughed except his mama—and I didn't laugh very loud. But first he said, "Whan that Aprille with his shoures soote the droghte of March hath perced to the roote."

Draft day falls in late April. The last year of the twentieth century, draft day for the National Football League fell on April seventeenth and eighteenth in New York City.

Pushkin was sitting with a group of primo prospects, college stars who had every reason to believe there would be some kind of place for them in the NFL. They nodded their heads gravely in agreement. Nothing was guaranteed. They didn't laugh, because they didn't know Chaucer. They didn't know how funny it was to compare the terrors of the draft to the tremors of the Crusades.

Me, I didn't laugh because I was scared my son had become the joke. A football player named Pushkin was something too much like a slave named Cicero. My son was some kind of strange blend of high and low. I kept waiting for the pieces to separate.

I had checked myself into the Paramount, an edgy little hostelry just off Times Square. In 1999, the Paramount was just, or a little more than just, beyond its heyday. Still, it had gorgeous boy doormen who smelled of botanical shampoos and tiny shiny dark rooms that made me feel like I was in a well-appointed womb. And it was cheap.

Cheap was important. Cheap was so important that week. I wanted my boy to know . . . well, I need to stop and tell you . . . what I didn't tell then. Going with a boy to the draft is like going with your daughter to her wedding. You go to give her away. You go in case she changes her mind. Most important, you go in case she gets left at the altar. In case he don't get chose.

I don't believe Pushkin ever knew why I went up to New York. Or maybe he did. Maybe he does. Maybe you do. It's time to get to me and you. Ain't it, baby?

Why do I write *ain't?* Because years and years ago it offended Lena to hear me say it?

All Pushkin remembers about draft day 1999 is that I was wishing against him. He couldn't figure out exactly what I was wishing for, but he knew it was against him. That and that the Tennessee team took him in the second round. Suspense didn't last that long.

He insisted that I check out of the Paramount the very next day and check into the Plaza. A hard new smile appeared on my face. The banality of my son's ambitions slayed me.

The room at the Plaza was sumptuous; it evoked a sense of mythic wealth. When the bellman, grave, gray, and solicitous, an old man from the Old World, left with ten dollars of Pushkin's cash money crossing his white-gloved palm, I locked and bolted the door, trying to shut out the reality of how quickly black wealth passes back into the white world.

The color—draped, upholstered, and painted—through the suite was intoxicating. There was so much eye candy, almost too much ease. I felt like Daisy when she first saw all of Gatsby's shirts. Knowing how that story of wealth after poverty ended, I worried for Pushkin.

I flashed back to my very first fancy New York hotel room, in 1964. My daddy bought it for me. I was five years old. In 1999 I was almost forty. I wanted to turn my back on this new room.

I wasn't taking care of Pushkin anymore. He was taking care of me. He had arrived in New York in clothes and shoes we had purchased for him on a professor's pay and an architect's wages. He would leave New York in clothes he purchased for himself on his salary as an NFL star. He was richer than Eve's father. He was richer than my mother's boss. He was very rich indeed.

Everything about this room shouted, more loudly than he had declared when I kissed him just after he slipped the Tennessee jersey on, "I'm gonna take care of you now, Moms. Gonna take care you now."

Why does he think I need taking care of? Who is it he reminds me of when he thinks we need so much money? Lena? Leo? Spady?

It was the one thing those three had in common. Why can't Pushkin see I have to reject that? Or is it I who can't see that I don't have to reject wealth now because of wealth then?

By the tub there was a gift basket of bath supplies from a very fancy shop. There was also a note. It read, "Now you can retire." The note was written in Pushkin's own hand. That new smile jumped onto my face again. How could I tell him that you don't scratch and scrape for tenure and get it to retire before forty? Did I tell him I suspected that I liked what I did a whole lot better than he would like what he was going to do?

I turned the water in the tub on, turned the hot on full blast and the cold on just enough. I stripped off my clothes. The tub was so big it would be running for minutes. I tied on one of the thick, soft Egyptian cotton robes and padded back out to turn on a television and find a book in my luggage. I remember thinking I needed a pedicure. My toes looked so raggedy on that carpet. I chastised myself for being trifling.

In possession of tenure for barely ten years, I was nowhere near ready to let it go. I loved Vanderbilt. It was poised to be the Harvard of the South. Yet and still Vanderbilt was no longer our nest, our safety net, the thing that provided for our food and shelter, for insurance and retirement down the road. When Pushkin put on that Tennessee jersey with the number 59 on it, all that changed.

The fabrics, the fabrics plastered to the walls, all the fabrics hanging off the walls, the fabrics in the curves of the drapes, the brocades and silks on the mattress, the linens and the lace on the pillows, the wool of the throw on the ottoman, called to me. I raised my hands to my face and contemplated the possibility that this was the moment I would become untethered. But what was I letting loose from?

I walked to the window and pulled the silk of the drape to my face. Leo had never, ever stood in a room like this, not in his forty-seven years. He took me to a fancy room in a fancy hotel, but not like this. But Leo could erase my tears from silk. I needed Leo.

When I was a girl and we came to New York, we stayed in a fine hotel. Daddy took us to the CopaCabana. Took me to see Sammy Davis on Broadway—*Golden Boy*, or was it *The Man with the Golden Arm*? He paid a scalper two hundred dollars for my seat in the front row. I sat in his lap and slept through almost the whole thing.

I needed to weep. This memory required tears. It would be an hour before I stopped. I would be in and out of the tub. I would cry with my eyes open and cry with my eyes closed. Cry staring at the ceiling above the tub and cry on my stomach into a feather-filled square. Every piece of marble, every inch of gilt, every anything Leo would have taken pleasure in seeing or touching or feeling or just knowing existed, caused me to sob again.

When Pushkin tried to be my daddy, I knew my daddy was no more. And when I recognized, let myself know, that he had been trying to be my daddy for a long, long time, I knew just how long Daddy been gone.

I cried for how far we had come from Alabama and how far we had to go.

I would have told Pushkin all that if I had slept first. If I had had time to pour myself a glass of wine, maybe throw back a shot of scotch, but that's not what happened. The phone rang, and I stopped crying before I was ready to stop crying.

I should never have picked up the phone. I guess I was still hoping you needed me. What I didn't get was this: it was time for me to let you know that I needed you. If I wasn't ready for that yet—and I wasn't ready for that yet—I shouldn't have picked up the phone.

You were excited. You were just checking on me. You were with a lot of people, your agent and your lawyer and your girl of the moment. It sounded like you were at a party. I wasn't saying much, because I didn't want you to hear that I had been crying. Didn't want to start crying again. Didn't want to interfere with the fun you were having. You thought I was irritated, with the room, or the day, or just being changed from my regular hotel.

Somewhere in the conversation, the background noise on your end faded away. You must have stepped out of the room you were in. When you spoke, it was so clear—like a whip, your words were, slicing and punishing and cutting.

"I could no more resist being a football player than you could resist having a baby at eighteen with no daddy. If you didn't ask for this, I didn't ask for that. You did the one thing that was unacceptable for you to do in the world you were in, and it looks like I did the one thing that was unacceptable for me to do in the world I'm in. Know payback when you see it, Moms."

I didn't have a word to say. That he could or would speak to me this way, with a bald kind of ugly truth, with a truth as ugly as homemade sin, stung me. I started laughing. It was my turn to tell the joke only I and my mother would understand. I said, "Homemade sin can be pretty too." Pushkin said nothing. I was thinking about Muhammad Ali and how pretty he used to say he was. How he loved to touch his own cheek and show off his beauty. My son is inspiringly beautiful. I was thinking that homemade sin can be beautiful. I finally found some more words to say aloud. I said, "I guess we're both fucking stereotypes."

"You don't get it."

"What might 'it' be?"

"We both did what wasn't expected."

"You could be anything."

"I'm the biggest thing."

"A football player?"

"I'm Bob now."

"What?"

"It's a Detroit story you wouldn't know. Diana told me."

It's not the moment to set the record straight, to tell Pushkin that Daddy told me the story and I told it to Diana. But there is something I am starting to want to know.

"Why did you pick the number fifty-nine for your jersey?"

"Middle linemen always get numbers in the fifties."

"Oh."

"And it was the year you were born."

"Thank you."

"It couldn't a been no easy thing to be a freshman at Harvard with a great big baby in your great big belly. I bet you were as wide as you were tall."

"Wider."

"You a stand-up girl, Moms."

"Why didn't you go to Harvard?"

"I hated the way people looked at you when I visited there."

"When you were three years old? You remember?"

"I'm a fucking genius."

"I know."

"I remember sliding out from between your legs."

"I remember being embarrassed."

There is silence at the other end of the line.

"I don't mean by you, darling, I mean by me. By being a baby having a baby."

"That's by me."

"That's by me. I have always been proud of you."

"You weren't proud of me today."

"Yes, I was."

"I saw women prouder of their bastard sons than you are of me."

"No, you didn't."

"Don't tell me what I saw."

"This is going sideways. I'm too tired."

"I want to know how you feel about my draft day."

"I don't know."

"I want you to know."

"We don't always get what we want."

"You should know better than most. Welcome to the NFL."

He's through with me. The conversation is over. There is endless hot water in a hotel bathtub. There's a CD player, but I brought no CDs. I have the wrong books with me. In fact, I have no books with me I can read in this tub. I have only the first edition of *The Souls of Black Folk* that I brought to give to Pushkin, however the weekend went, and now had to withhold because I feared that to give it to him in the context of this strange conversation would be to take something away.

And I ain't taking nothing from a defensive lineman who makes jokes in Middle English.

I should have brought him my Riverside Chaucer. I didn't think of it then, but it's true. He made the joke in Middle English. That signifies something. Chaucer braids the high to the low, the body to the mind, the bawdy to the spiritual — that signifies something too. Chaucer signifies.

Spring semester of my freshman year I took Chaucer from a visiting professor from Oxford. Diana took it with me to keep me company. We were both beginning to sense that the pregnancy was a kind of pilgrimage. I read lines and lines of Chaucer that semester, memorized and analyzed and theorized, but Chaucer was the least of what I learned in the Chaucer classroom.

Late in the semester I left a notebook in the room and went back to fetch it. The professor, a bespectacled hippie who always wore a tie with corduroy pants and hiking boots, was standing at his desk at the front of the room, gathering up papers and notebooks into a wine-colored satchel of indeterminate age. He looked up when I came into the room, then immediately went back to his task. I had the sense that even his hippie self found being in a room with an all-too-obviously sexually active teenager awkward.

A gaggle of girls gathered in the hall just beyond the door. I couldn't see their faces, but I could hear their voices. They were probably members of the next class to use the room. I collected my book. I was approaching the professor to ask one last question. Awkward or not, the final was approaching, and the sound of chatter from the hall made us less alone. The professor smiled. I opened my mouth. Before I could get a syllable out, a voice from the hall rose and carried clearly back into the classroom. A female voice announced, "You'd think a person smart enough to get into Harvard would be smart enough to know how not to get a baby." A different girl said, "Or know what to do about it if they did."

Tears wanted to leap into my eyes. But I didn't even think of letting them do it. I recognized the voices. They were girls I knew from the dining room. Girls who sat at one of the all-black tables near the salad bar in the Freshman Union. I had embarrassed them. Now they were attempting to embarrass me. Maybe if I had been getting better than a *B* in the dis-located don's course (again I feel my experiments with hip-hop poetry seeping into my prose), I wouldn't have felt utterly humiliated. But I was getting a *B* and I was pregnant and shunned. I was being dismissed from the world of black women in front of a white man.

It hurts being black, especially when you are an unwed teenage mother, and maybe more especially when you are not an unwed black teenage mother and some black fool in your class gets herself knocked up and walks all over the campus carrying her baby inside her black body for all the white world to see. Someone's always disgracing blackness, validating the stereotype somewhere it shouldn't be. At Harvard I was that fool.

I was that fool.

Bohemian hippie me from Paliprep wanted to think that carrying this baby reflected on nobody but me. That it was an individual decision reflecting an individual's sense or lack thereof. I had refused to recognize that what I did reflected on the community. This was a mistake with implications.

White friends of mine in the class were curious about the baby, about the pregnancy. None of them got worried that they would be guilty by association with me—that somehow because I was in their class and pregnant, people might think that they'd do it too.

After I started showing, I had fewer black women friends at Harvard. I made every single one of the ones I had, except for Diana, uncomfortable. Every single one of them thought that my disgrace reflected on her. I forgave them that, because I discovered it was true.

Yet and still, some of them, some precious few, thought that the unborn baby's survival, his or her thriving, would reflect on them as well. These black women taught me one truth of community. Community endures discomfort to maintain connection.

Some of my embarrassed but connected associates started into helping Pushkin before Pushkin was born. One played classical music to my belly; another played jazz. One encouraged me to eat high-quality protein, while a visual and environmental studies concentrator crocheted a mesmerizingly complicated and enchanting receiving blanket. Still, it was almost too hard being the pregnant black freshman in Cambridge.

At one of my first visits to the obstetrician, the nurse looked at me and said, "Why do you girls do this?" I was in a store and somebody said, "You're the reason we pay high taxes." I started carrying my Russian books around with me and talking about the poet Pushkin as often as possible, as fast and analytically as I could. People didn't know what to make of me, but they stopped confusing me with a welfare mother and you with a pre-welfare baby. They didn't know what they were dealing with, and that was important to me. All our life together my mother had secretly understood me to be and sometimes called me a "worthless nigger." My Washington world, my Motown world, the larger society, had always told me I was young, gifted, and black. Now, suddenly, shiveringly, the world was agreeing with my mother.

I saw it in so many eyes. I was a baby having a baby, a burden to the state, worthlessness breeding worthlessness. I looked for solace close at hand. I took my already needy love of Pushkin and made a discipline of it. I tied my stereotypical fat pregnant ass to an identity that exploded stereotypes—Russian scholar. I was afraid there wasn't enough high culture to balance out all my lowness. I worked hard and carefully. I hated to be late in case somebody called it CPT—colored people's time. I went crawling after that Harvard honors degree to keep myself from slipping back into the pit of worthlessness from which I had been expelled at birth. I went crawling from Cambridge to London through Petersburg.

And you, my son, have you reached for low culture and stereotype because I all but drowned you in high culture and eccentricity? I would not have you locked down into other people's narrow expectations. Perhaps this should include my own. Perhaps my own expectations for you are too narrow.

You quote Chaucer to me and I must smile. Chaucer was being spoken the first time you ever waved your powerful fist.

• • •

It was an April day in Harvard Yard. The black girls outside my Chaucer classroom, my fellow classmates, spoke with the intention of embarrassing me. They and I expected the visiting professor to be overwhelmed by intragender, intraracial strife, expected him to look away, to blush, to silently agree, to buy into the stereotype by distancing himself from me. I expected to look into his eyes and see my student self vanish and some idea of me as a social problem appear. Instead he stepped closer to me.

Just then the baby kicked. Hard. I was startled. It was as if my child was talking back to the girls talking to me. I thought for sure the burden in my belly was female. I was wearing a thin knit maternity dress. I could see the baby's little fist. The Chaucer scholar could see it too. We watched it move together. My eyes were still dry. The professor's eyes got shiny.

"May I?"

"Yes."

He reached out to touch my belly. The baby kicked again. The professor dropped to his knees. He growled into my navel:

> Whan that Aprille with his shoures soote
> The droghte of March hath perced to the roote
> And bathed every veyne in swich licour,
> Of which vertu engendred is the flour,
> Whan Zephirus eek with his swete breeth
> Inspired hath in every holt and heth
> Tender croppes, and the yonge sonne
> Hath in the ram his halve cours yronne,
> And smale foweles maken melodye,
> That slepen al the night with open yë,
> (So priketh hem nature in hir corages);
> Thanne longen folk to goon pilgrimages

The baby kicked again. The professor kept growling:

> And palmers for to seken straunge strondes
> To ferne halwes, kowthe in sundry londes . . .

After April with its showers of sweet fruit the drought of March has pierced to the root . . . when the quickening of Zephirus . . . when the little birds sing, wakening every sleeping being, then folk long to go on pilgrimages and start down strange roads that lead to places sacred and distant in other lands . . .

My Chaucer professor taught me a fine lesson. Sometimes the identity of your ally is not obvious.

That April night in New York, the weekend of his draft day, Pushkin rained down on me with journey's end. It had been a very long March. It had been a very long march. How long we had to go we were yet and still to measure. I arrived at his sacred place of draft day in the territory of the NFL with the wrong token—the wrong alms for my exhausted pilgrim.

The Souls of Black Folk would not do. He required the soul of his mother.

I had said before we left, before he left for New York, "Look at you—pants hanging down. Who do you think you are? Why are you doing this?"

I should have said, "I love you." I should have bought and brought *Up from Slavery* or, better still, Chaucer. Instead I took that moment to tell you that once I had been ashamed—of me and my baby. I should have spoken of the benediction an unabashed man whispered to my belly.

April is the cruelest month.

If Pushkin tells that joke another year, I'm going to laugh aloud and eat myself a piece of juicy-fruited watermelon while I do it.

NINETEEN

O MISSION IS ERROR.

There is a story about Pushkin I failed to recount to you.

Rather, it is about Pushkin's mother's father's father and his sister, about Pushkin's great-grandfather and Pushkin's great-great-aunt.

I told you certain pieces of Pushkin the poet's story over and over. When did you start rolling your eyes at me? I told you that Pushkin's great-grandfather was captured into slavery on the African continent. It is debated as to where. Long ago it was debated as to whether or not he was an African. That is no longer debated. It is ignored, but it is not debated. I saw a rather amusing article in a British society magazine (I think it was the *Tattler*; it might have been *Country Life*) concerning portraits of Pushkin's descendants. The article was illustrated with photographs of the paintings. The faces are all so rosy and pink. How much easier would it be, how possible would this thing be, if I could color your Tanya beige?

Is there any remote possibility? Could we be lucky like that? I am owed some luck. I wish that was the part of Tanya's story you failed to recount to me.

I imagine this incident is apocryphal. When I first read it, I did not know what *apocryphal* meant. I took the story into my heart. I give it to you from that place. I give it to you with my growing intuition that anecdotes make very fine antidotes.

Pushkin's great-grandfather chose for himself the name Abraham Hannibal. (This is particularly notable as Peter offered his own name to the slave.) It is thought that Abraham Hannibal was born in 1697, perhaps in Suriname, perhaps in Ethiopia. Before he took this name he was kidnapped and put on a boat.

I have imagined this occasion. The boat sets out to sea. Abraham Hannibal stands with the hundreds on the deck, with hundreds of newly enslaved, looking to shore. His sister can stand safely on the beach no longer. She throws herself into the water and swims after the ship until she swallows a last mouthful of seawater, feels the last sharp contraction of muscle in her leg, the last sting of the trailing tentacle of a man-of-war, the last wave crashing on her head, just before her last sight of the ship. The last lifting of her arm in a straining arc, a curve of power above the water, is her last act.

This girl was not eclipsed by economics or politics or psychology. She refused to be eclipsed by psychology, economics, or politics. Hannibal's sister swam behind the boat that carried him off until she drowned. She allowed nothing but death to part them. She forced life to keep its promise. Then she went under the waves and drowned.

How long did Hannibal wait to see his sister break through the surface of the water? Did he hold his breath? Did he mistake a bird bobbing on the sea for the crown of her dark head? When did he know his true loving one was dead?

It has been said in different languages, throughout time, that the first step of a journey is the hardest. She accompanied him at the first; it would change everything after. She gave her life to accompany him. He would ever after remember that there had been a witness and a rebel, one who would not see him stolen, one who refused to lose him. She held him in her eyes to the last.

His was a very different case. He lost her. He watched her go down and had to live after. He saw love enacted. He saw in her sacrifice both immeasurable love and how it ceased to be. He saw innocence impaled upon itself and vanish.

That girl is like Leo and I am like Abraham Hannibal.

I understand that kind of love, "Ain't no mountain high enough . . . to keep me from loving you" love. Love that sustains geographic separation but endures, diaspora love, Motown love, the love proclaimed by people who have walked across mountains and valleys and walked through rivers looking for a father, a mother, a sister, a brother.

The songs of Motown are the love songs of parents to children. They are the love songs of poor people whose wealth is to be found not in material things but in relationship; "I don't need no money, fortune, or fame, I got all the riches, baby, one man can claim." Pushkin, my Pushkin, you are so very far from that. When did that cease to be for you, or was it never in you? Did you not understand that I would have thrown myself into the sea like Pushkin's ancestor and swum until I reached you or died trying? Do you know that? Do you understand that that is the way black women love their men? Do you not believe it is so? Did I not show you it was so?

Can Tanya love you like that?

Every night now, in my dreams, a ship is taking you away. Every night now, I am drowning. It used to be I would reach the ship, climb on board, and sail to slavery with you. It used to be like that.

Pushkin was not a slave. Pushkin's great-grandfather was a slave. I am not a slave—we are the descendants of slaves. We are like Pushkin.

Pushkin, the black Shakespeare, thought over and over, How does this matter? Must this matter? Pushkin was a genius—the great genius with black blood in him. When Pushkin sat down at his desk, when he sat down at the very last desk he had, the desk that stood near the bed where he died, he used an inkwell that looked like two black men leaning on bales of cotton. He dipped his ink from an African well.

I dream that you are taken away on a boat. I dream that I swim after you. Just before I drown, I see the death of innocence in your eyes. Where it dies, I see the birth of staggering love. I awake and sleep again. I dream that you are taken away on a boat and I remain on the shore, watching you sail away, watching the innocence not die in your eyes, watching the knowledge of love not be born. This dream is a nightmare.

The first dream is a nightmare too.

I have asked myself the wrong question. I have asked, *Why* does race matter? I should have asked, *How?* How does it matter in the face of love? How does it matter beneath the fact of rape? Where must we go to have the questions vanish?

I have loved, do love, and will love the poet Pushkin because his poetry proves, his existence proved, to a teenage black girl, in an unassailable way, the fact of the black intellectual. And maybe I love him because he walks this earth as a restless shade, hungering to embrace a body like his own. I have felt him haunting my dreams, and I wonder if he doesn't haunt the dreams of bookish brown girls everywhere, as he aches for the bronze kiss he never had.

Who was it who first asked, "Where is the female Shakespeare?" Was it Virginia Woolf who responded, "The female Shakespeare died in childbirth"? How unsatisfying an answer is that? How much better is it to think, Virginia Woolf created a language of modernism?

Before Pushkin, without Pushkin, I would have to answer, "The black Shakespeare was whipped to death in an Alabama cotton field, or drowned during the Middle Passage." How much more is it to be able to say that Pushkin, a black man, invented the language of Tolstoy and Chekhov, and through them, whom did he not influence?

My father taught me to love blackness. My mother taught me to be ashamed of it. Both lessons took. I resolved the conflict by falling in love with a kind of hyperintellectual blackness wherever it occurred, from Spady's blue-black brain to Pushkin's omnipotent, omnivorous one.

My world has become impossibly narrow. Too small for Leo, too small for street language, too small for street poetry, too small for athleticism, too small for football, too small for Beethoven and Mozart as well, too small for anything that isn't brilliant and black, too small altogether, but dearly comfortable. We are about to blast it open.

When I factor the blackness out, I am left with these equations: father = love, mother = shame, father > mother, love > shame. It should be possible for me to correct the error of omission. And yet . . .

At the beginning of the day, we are shaped by the cradle in which we are rocked. Mine was a Malcolm X–loving, Black Panther–wannabe cradle thrown into a world where the only numbers that counted were IQ points. I am giving up on numbers. They have failed me. At the end of the day we are shaped by the beds in which we have lain.

My father's racism protected me and it protected Pushkin. I cannot regret it. I can put it down only if I am ready to tell you what I needed to protect you from. Only if I am prepared to love you not as boy but as son. Don Corleone never said, Look what they done to my boy! He said something more like, Look what they have done to my son! And I say, will I be able to say, Look how my son can take it!

If my racism honors my father and my people but it injures Pushkin, it's time to say, "Sorry, Daddy." Whatever I was at the beginning of the day, at the end of my day I'm Moms.

I have seen the cotton bales on Pushkin's desk. They are golden. They have redeemed, for me, the picking of cotton. Somehow with the absurd but not, I feel, ironic linking of his labor of writing with the slave's labor of picking, of harvesting, Pushkin mitigates the banality of sweat-back labor. Pushkin changed things. He dips his pen in the well of slavery and its servitude. He elevates the cotton bale. He elevates the cotton picker. He connects himself across geography and time to those who will later claim him. He invites the assessment, "How far he has come!" He invites the preposterous lie, "What a strange comparison. He is not really black at all."

The enemies of Pushkin used to say that his great-grandfather was bought off the auction block for a bottle of spirits. It is generally known in certain circles that two members of Pushkin's family married into the British royal family, one marrying into Prince Philip's line, the other marrying a descendant of Queen Victoria's. Prince Charles, Prince William, and Prince Harry are blood-related to Pushkin's blood but not descended from it. They are black through Queen Charlotte's blood. By the Old South rule, the one-drop rule, Charles and William and Harry could be sold on the same auction block where Abraham Hannibal was sold, where Pushkin could have been sold.

When I was a girl and expressed a certain fleeting romantic interest in Prince Charles, Leo said Charles was not smart or sharp enough for me. Then he said, "And he ain't possibly fixin' to be thinkin' 'bout marryin' a little Negro girl from Dee-troit." Little did Daddy know that the prince was a little Negro boy from Windsor. Or maybe he knew. Why did he name me Windsor?

I, Windsor, imagine Pushkin dipping his pen into the black black ink of his golden cotton bale inkwell and smiling down the years, dreaming of Queen Charlotte.

It is almost certainly not true, or perhaps, like so many things, it is strange and not commonly known but true, that Pushkin was thinking of Queen Charlotte when he titled "The Queen of Spades." I should rename the story "The Spady Queen." I call my own tale "Spady's Queen."

Have you seen *The Madness of King George*? It's a poem of a violent and lyrical film, all violet urine and powdered wigs. There is a love story in it: the queen is loyal to her impaired husband. In the movie the queen is so white, so unlike the real queen. I think the film should be remade, the face of the king's wife colorized beige, the title changed to *The Blackness of Queen Charlotte*. Had they cast this and a thousand films differently, might my son have chosen differently? If he had been shown the beautiful brown, might he have chosen a different wife?

Queen Charlotte was born a princess of Mecklenburg-Strelitz on May 19, 1744, in Mirow, Germany. She died at Kew Palace on November 17, 1818. She had accumulated seventy-four years. Her personal physician described her as having "a true mulatto face."

There is debate surrounding the ethnicity of Charlotte. I side with those who believe she was black. You have only to be black and look at Sir Allan Ramsay's painting of her to *know*. Pushkin would write, "Apparent blackness emanates from the generous Queen." And from this queen rose Victoria, and from Victoria rose her grandson George Battenberg, to be transformed into Mountbatten, and George married Pushkin's granddaughter Nadejda at Buckingham Palace.

In 1868 Pushkin's daughter Natalia married a royal, Prince Nicholas of Nassau, and became countess of Merenberg. Their daughter Sophie married Grand Duke Mikhail and became the countess of Torby. It was Sophie's daughter, Nadejda, who married a grandson of Queen Victoria's, George.

And where are any of them now? Why has Pushkin disappeared and turned white? Turned white and disappeared, as child after child married a pale European. What would these marriages have meant to me when I was a little girl wanting to play pretty princess and feeling too brown? What will it mean to Pushkin's children?

Why is it easier for them to forget their black blood than it is for us to forget our white? I believe it has much to do with how the blood got into us. Another thing I love about Pushkin: his dusky mother was not raped. Perhaps everyone in the world is secretly black, including your Tanya. Wouldn't it be nice?

Perhaps we can exchange your Tanya for Hannibal. We have long had Hannibal. It is known that the great general who conquered the Alps on elephant-back was black. But who black? How black? Arguments arise that he was Semitic, that he was a white North African; arguments arise that he was as black as that ace of spades. I will give them Hannibal in exchange for Tanya. I know I would do it. The absurdity of the thing breaks down on me like the waves crashing down on Abraham's sister's head.

I hope it only finally matters to me because that green-eyed yellow-black man I loved, Leo, said, "You bring home a white boy and you be dead." You were a reparation I wanted to offer my father. I am carrying you up a hill. My anger and my persistence sacrifice you. You were Isaac-innocent and you let me carry you up the hill. And I am down on my knees in my heart praying, "Lord, provide some other sacrifice."

What I need to do is stand the fuck up and refuse to sacrifice you. It is so hard for me to get off my knees. Am I willing to sacrifice you because Lena sacrificed me? Can I tell you everything and remain your mother?

I have sought fortress and shield. You stride the wide-open field in plain view. What do I owe you?

I remember a day no other sacrifice was provided. I was carried up the hill and the fire was carried in my own heart and I wondered where the lamb was and didn't know it was me. Isaac stayed Isaac, but I was a lamb.

What can this mean to you? I am cryptic. I am your mother; I must be cryptic. If I am to remain your mother, I cannot tell you everything.

Just about the time I started high school, Leo took to drinking very, very hard; then he took to psychotherapy and gave it up. A year into his sobriety he gave a party. They even had a little champagne fountain. His doctor, a young, thin, birdlike woman, came. He told me he enjoyed drinking and was sorry he had done all of his on the front end. He admonished me to pace myself. He said whatever else happened, "At least I'm not drunk."

At least I'm not drunk.

The week Dear died, so soon after Sun, that was all he could claim: "At least I'm not drunk." For a while after Leo got sober he kept a small mirror in the breast pocket of his suit, a little square wallet mirror in a leather sleeve. If anything went wrong, he reached to his breast pocket to see who the cause of the problem was. By the time I had left for Cambridge, I was avoiding mirrors altogether.

Looking-glass. It's time for me to look in the mirror. I hear a spin being put on the annotation of the reflection. I hear Martha Rachel saying, "Baby, there's the solution—you."

I have told you so many stories, bits and pieces thereof, but I have very little way to tell you the story you think you want to hear. I approach it and I back away, not from fear but from trepidation.

I am trying to weigh what I know of who you are and what I think you might want against what you tell me you want, and I come up powerfully, pitifully short, Man. Do you remember when I called you that? I don't know enough of who you are now to know what you would want. I know my love for you, but I don't know you. My love isn't protecting you now. It has raised an opaque veil between us.

I am remembering a morning almost forty years ago. I was three or four, and I had wet my bed. The maid was coming that day. She did our flat once or twice a week. Daddy told me he would tell her that he had wet the bed.

I knew what I knew. What I knew at three or four was that it was an even greater embarrassment to be the daddy, be the grown man, who wet the bed. And I knew he was strong enough to carry the weight of the heavier shame. And I knew that he knew the smaller shame would crush me. For the thousandth thousandth time I was grateful to be his daughter.

Of course he told the maid no such thing. How could he? How could a grown man explain being in a little girl's bed? A grown man in a girl's bed would be a far harder thing to explain, a far hotter shame, than pee in a little girl's bed. I didn't know that then. Daddy said he'd say he'd done it, and I stayed proud. My pride was a fragile thing, but it survived that day encased in lies and innocence.

Can yours survive truth?

If you were to know, I hope it would not feel like theft. I would not steal your innocence. Could you imagine what worse than theft I feared this truth-telling might feel like to you?

A chasm appears between the past and the present. In this moment, in this moment, which I can or cannot sustain, will or will not sustain, I choose now. I choose you. I choose today. I choose to know that though my words in air provoked soiling and desecration then, my words on paper consecrate us now.

I washed my hands before I touched Pushkin every single time. Stood before the faucet before I lifted him to my chest. I did that in D.C., I did it in Motown, did it in Cambridge. I did it in Petersburg, where Pushkin kissed me up to heaven. I did it in Music City. If you believe in dirt, there is too much filth, there are too many germs, to keep clean. How is it I know that soil is insignificant? I am the daughter of the dry cleaner. That is my good chance.

Maybe God is one good chance, a single good chance, in a sea of killing alternatives—one good chance crossing the chasm, offering you a way over, if you will but swim into the sea of filth and fear, of dying, dead, and rotting, to grab it.

Maybe you were the only good chance I ever had. No maybe, baby, about it, boy. You were the one good chance I ever had. I began life in a she-wolf's belly; I acquired a kind of aloofness at the get-go and maintained it until I came to carry you. You kicked me into sub-mission. You balled up your little fist and beat on the inside wall of my belly till I did what a mother will do. I surrendered to loving you.

What does the child owe the mother?

Nothing.

Not a thing.

I have made decisions all tied up in lies and worse than that, truths that should not be. If I could get down on my knees and not repel you, I would get down on my knees and start apologizing. I would crawl across broken-glass-strewn Astroturf if you, my first-born, my only born, but not my only child, would listen while I begged. I would crawl for the calm of confession.

I make my yards with no hope of forgiveness. There are betrayals beyond forgiveness, at least beyond the forgiveness of the just. I know this. But I would get down on my knees, make it harder for you to knock me down. Maybe I would lie on the ground stretched be-fore your face and say, "I loved her like I was mama and she was child. I did that blasphemous thing. Loved her like a child. Squan-dered what was rightfully yours, your birthright, while you were still an egg in my belly. It seemed so kind at the time."

So long ago I claimed her as my own to take care of. My daddy had everybody, including Dear, who had everystuff. He would be all right. My mother needed me. Any fool could see she wasn't right. She needed something. In my arrogance, I thought it had to be me.

You are my only child. The child owes the parent nothing. What do I owe you?

Long ago I wrote a little triplet poem, and it comes back to me now: "I thank my God for this / Jesus knew / the Judas kiss." Now I wince at the elegance of the construction: Jesus betrayed by a kiss.

I was betrayed by a kiss.

You believe you were too. I had you, then kept your daddy from you. I did what I did so that you would not discover your maleness in the mirror of his eyes. I did what I did because I wish, I wish so dearly, I had never known my mother. I wish I had not first come to know myself in the mirror of Lena's eyes.

And now he is dead. How do you or I write that thank-you note? Is this a suicide letter or a thank-you note? That's the question.

Once, when I was very little, perhaps four or five, Martha Rachel played a seventy-eight on her hi-fi that my daddy declared to be the most mournful record in the world. He said he couldn't stand to hear it. He made fun of the recording, saying that somebody had to be "pulling on her tittie" to get the singer to sing so sad. For a few weeks Martha Rachel played that disk all the time. I remember the woman's voice crooning and cracking and crying all the while she declared, "Sometimes I feel like a motherless child a long, long, long way from home."

I said the words over and over again to myself, and I tried to feel it the way the singer felt it. I couldn't do it. Not at all. Being a motherless child far, far from home sounded too much like a good thing.

Just today I am finally understanding this: Martha Rachel was moaning along as a childless mother.

Right or wrong, I'm swimming out to sea after you as Leo did for me, like Martha Rachel, like Pushkin the poet's great-great-aunt.

Pushkin, I love your name. There is a world included in it. There is pride. There is mystery. There is the assertion of blackness, of the something indomitable that is born in bought slavery. When I tell you the little bit I must tell you, remember that I am telling you nothing more than a few new details that could be put in the footnotes. I have not left out, in the whole of the dialogue between us, any central experience.

The central experience is love.

I would like to tell you that you are Leo's child, that I got him drunk and slept with him. Would that be so very horrible? Mommy and Daddy would be full of love for you and each other. Mommy would think Daddy brilliant and beautiful, and Daddy would think Mommy brilliant and beautiful. Your daddy would be black. It would be incest, but . . . what is that if he was drunk and I . . . what would I have had to have been to intoxicate my father and sleep with him? Biblical? None of the horrors are new.

Sven Jude Andersson is your father.

In twenty-five years of looking, I have been unable to find even one potential African ancestor for Mr. Andersson. I found one for Queen Elizabeth, looking for Sven Andersson's, but I didn't find one for Sven Andersson. I was hoping to find one before I told you. I was looking up to an hour ago. But that doesn't seem important now.

To get that one black ancestor for you, I could almost wish that Sweden had invaded and colonized the whole of Senegal.

When I told him I was pregnant and going to have the baby, he left me completely alone. She left me alone too.

You protected me. Who's the mommy now?

TWENTY

I NEED A DRINK.

Maybe I need one of those drinks Tanya says the strippers imbibe—I taught her that word—when they need to get blitzed because something really bad is going to happen. She called it a hypnotic. Maybe if I knew a bartender who could make me one of those, I could actually tell Pushkin that dark as his skin is, he's really mainly white.

Short one, or perhaps two or three, hypnotics, W.E.B. and bohemian hillbilly me are waiting for Gabriel, drinking Jack and Coke in the daytime. I am back to banging my head against my monument to Du Bois. It's a lot less painful than wondering if rape is an elemental part of the black mother's experience in America. I think I need another drink.

My bar of choice sits in an old trailer stuck up on cinder blocks that's been at the corner of Hillsboro and Blair since before—before desegregation, before Vanderbilt became a significant national university, before the country music craze of the seventies. Before the world as we know it now, my corner bar was serving hamburgers and fries and grilled cheese and coffee and beer and whiskey to the hungry and the thirsty. They don't sell wine. This is fine with me. I am searching for secular redemption. Or that hypnotic my bartender doesn't know how to make. Maybe it's time to change bars. Or maybe not. I like it here.

Like the beach, the place changes over the course of the day. Before noon you get the workmen, painters and carpenters whose days begin in darkness, men who drive old trucks and live out by the lake or down south of Franklin. These workingmen are hungry before eleven. At noon, businessmen from downtown who started eating at my bar when they were in law school, along with assorted professors and current graduate students, swarm the space to overflowing. At three, the boys who make the noise down on Music Row show up to start drinking an early dinner. By six, the striplings, boys tall and sallow, boys who have yet to be seen, let alone discovered, by the town, white boys from rich families in Chicago and poor families in north Georgia, sharing a vicinity, arrive. The striplings live in rented rooms throughout our neighborhood. The Village, our little community of bungalows, four-squares, duplex fill-ins, the odd Queen Anne Victorian, and our prairie house, is a place where neither a washing machine on a lawn nor men carrying guitars standing on a porch about to start the appointment that will change their lives is an unfamiliar sight.

I'm still waiting for Gabriel. Waiting for Gabriel is something I like doing. It's a lot better than waiting for Godot. Gabriel will arrive.

This bar is not the kind of place I took Pushkin to when he was growing up. It's the kind of place, translated, my daddy took me. I sometimes think I like sitting in the neon-lit dimness of twilight in my bar because it reminds me that some of them are poor and shuffling too.

I am more comfortable with my daddy's drinking and his bars when I separate them from blackness—or is it that I am more comfortable with blackness when I separate it from my daddy's drinking? However that goes, they broke apart.

Race is not a part of everything.

Now that I am allowing myself to fall back in daughter-love with Leo, I remember that he used to pull up in front of dark storefronts and dash in for a "quick minute," until one day I said, "Daddy, don't go in that b-a-r." And he didn't. That's how I learned the power of orthography.

My spelling has gone all to hell. Maybe I can hold on to that instead of racism as a gesture of perpetual mourning.

Mainly I like disappearing, and I like Hank Williams. My great-grandfather on Dear's side was a hillbilly guitar player. There's more to this equation than planters and slaves and rapists. There are hillbillies and Russians. But I am only admitting the poets. Masters of the poetry of motion as well as a poetry of language. I need to hear a

Hank Williams song right now and get in touch with my whiteness. Hank Williams is a great American poet known in the common culture more for dying in a car, smacked out and unnoticed, than for his evocative portrayals of despair beyond anxiety, that place where you smell the muzzling scent of the lilies somebody will bring to your grave. Something is gained by admitting Hank Williams into any cultural conversation. In honor of Pushkin's about-to-be-discovered more complex ethnicity, I won't point out that Hank Williams was largely influenced by a black street musician named Tee-Tot. It's so hard to put down the habits of Afrocentric mothering!

Maybe I'm just getting seriously high on hillbilly speedballs, Jack and Coke, but there is something I am wondering. Did the sight of me in Alexander's bed prepare you to love Tanya? Would it mean anything if I said, if it were true, that I never slept with a white man again?

It is true. Let it mean something.

But it's too late to let that mean something. Or maybe it is this different thing altogether. Maybe Alexander was my way of preparing you for the possibility your daddy could be white. Preparation is no longer required. I'm going to tell you who your father is. Maybe you and Tanya will make some babies, physically whiter than Queen Elizabeth but soul black as Du Bois. When I was far away from home, in D.C., when I was embarrassed by my daddy, made small by minutes alone in the street in front of a b-a-r, Du Bois lifted me to his hip and shifted me up to his shoulders across time with words. Reading him entailed a kind of rescue. I was shaped by my relationship to Du Bois before I was shaped by my relationship to Pushkin.

Du Bois was shaped by his relationship to a tall, stringy-headed white girl. A simple thing, a small event, hurt Du Bois and sent him spinning: a young white stranger refused to exchange visiting cards with him.

In a wee wooden schoolhouse, something put it into the boys' and girls' heads to buy gorgeous visiting-cards—ten cents a package—and exchange. The exchange was merry, till one girl, a tall newcomer, refused my card,—refused it peremptorily, with a glance. Then it dawned upon me with a certain suddenness that I was different from the others; or like, mayhap, in heart and life and longing, but shut out from their world by a vast veil. I had thereafter no desire to tear down the

veil, to creep through; I held all beyond it in common con-
tempt, and lived above it in a region of blue sky and great
wandering shadows.

What if that girl had accepted Du Bois's card? How would his life
have been different? Would he have written *The Souls of Black Folk*?
How would the world be different? Would I be less embarrassed
about your father? How would my life have been different if Leo
hadn't left me stranded in a car? Du Bois implies that his ambition in
the world was a response to his intimate rejection:

> . . . sky was bluest when I could beat my (white) mates at ex-
> amination time, or beat them at a foot-race, or even beat their
> stringy heads. Alas, with the years all this fine contempt began
> to fade; for the worlds I longed for, and all their dazzling op-
> portunities, were theirs, not mine. But they should not keep
> these prizes, I said; some, all I would wrest from them.

How like Du Bois my son is! All he has wrested from them! I
reached for what the slave held higher than gold—book-learning.
He reached for what white hearts were yearning for when they stole
Pushkin's great-grandfather from Africa's shore and sold him into
slavery—wealth. There is only one thing for me to despise in you,
Pushkin, and I won't tell it to you in your wedding week: you snatch
back red-stained, green, filthy, filthy lucre, all my tears can't wash it
clean.

I would rather you had not played their game. You cannot wash it
clean, red-stained green.

I remember being so disappointed with Daddy when he told me
why green was his favorite color. I thought, green is grass, green is
stems, thought, ". . . through the green fuse . . . drives my green age."
Then he said, "I love green because it's the color of money."

Have all the "dazzling opportunities" W.E.B. imagined come
down to this, kissing a white girl's lips and making lots of money?

We come down to the nitty-gritty.

In his choice of football and in his choice of Tanya, I see only the
base commonality of the thing, the stereotype come to life. It is common for black boys to have the ambition to be a football player. It is
common for black football players to have the ambition to marry
white women. A hundred years after Du Bois, too many souls are

still chasing after some stringy-headed girl who should be long forgotten.

Most women in America would take Pushkin's visiting card. Many stringy-heads would take him in their arms and welcome his most intimate "visiting card." This is something. What is it? What if the taking is progress but the offering is regress? Is the ambition to be able to love whom you wish to love, or is the ambition to be loved by a white woman because the love of the white woman is more significant? Don't answer too quickly. Is the light woman willing to love the dark man because she is openhearted? Or is she willing to love him because he is rich? Can I doubt the light lady's love without doubting the dark man's value?

What if Pushkin's choices, his choice of football and his choice of Tanya, are not driven by a desire to achieve what was thrust upon him as a black man or withheld from him as a black man? What if Pushkin's choices are shaped by his response to his unique sense of being abandoned by me, his mother—his sense of being abandoned and his memory of being claimed by two boys who slept clutching footballs to their chests?

What if Pushkin reaches for Tanya because I never let him know where he came from? Where I came from? And what he did know of my world, the highfalutin blackness of my ebony tower felt too small for him?

What if Pushkin reaches for Tanya because she calls to him in the middle of the night saying, "Ya lyublyu tebya"? She speaks as I spoke when I first loved him.

What if I resent Pushkin's crowning Tanya as sufficient because I was so long uncrowned and insufficient?

What does the child owe the mother?

A long time ago in D.C., in the Takoma Park Library, I read an introduction to Mark Twain's *Huckleberry Finn*. I have forgotten all but one sentence of that introduction. This is the line I remember, as I remember it. Memory alters everything but the gist of identity. It went, it goes, something like this: *Huckleberry had all of the vices except those that are unforgivable and none of the virtues except those that are absolutely necessary*. I wept when I read that and recognized my daddy in Huckleberry.

Today that line makes me think of the contrast between Detroit and Washington. My Motown had all the vices except those that were unforgivable and none of the virtues except those that were necessary. My D.C. had none of the vices except those that were un-forgivable and all the virtues except those that were necessary.

Prideful gangster Daddy and self-loathing psycho-bitch Mommy. I raised Pushkin between these poles of parenting, trying to avoid touching either. I have protected his innocence. Protected it because no one protected mine and because it is what a mother does for her child. I am a mother and he is my child. What must a child do for the mother? What is owed the good mother? What is owed the bad mother?

The good mother knows the child owes her nothing at all. The child of the good mother is free—and he knows it. The child of the bad mother believes she is in debt, believes she owes. She too is free; she too is redeemed—but she does not know this. She calculates and recalculates, pays and withdraws payment on a debt with accruing interest and poor bookkeeping until the end of the mother's life—and sometimes after that.

I have said Pushkin owed me this—said it without words, said it with words in air, said it with words on paper: I have said he owed me this thing, a black daughter-in-law.

This now is the truth. My truth. Not your truth. Not black truth. I am locating myself for you. You can stand south of it or north or east or west of it, stand near or stand far. You can eclipse, dilute, am-plify, or renounce it. I have placed my truth on the map of entwined souls. If you place yours, however you place yours, we will be in love.

Speak of love.

Gabriel hard-grabs a handful of my hair. I turn my face toward him and he gives me a closed-mouth kiss on the lips. He shifts his beautiful bulk into the place opposite me in the wooden booth. I am rapidly inserting another fry into my slowly rounding face. He takes it from my fingers and feeds it to me.

"Preeminent will be the eminent Russky, Pushkin the O.G.?"

"You've been in my papers!"

"You've been holding out on me in brand-new ways."

"I could move from holding out to punishing."

"Whose is it?"

"Mine."

"Who'd you get to do it?"

"Me."

"O.G.?"

"Original Gangster."

"Remember when that Marquis de Sade diary of Pushkin's was circulating? How shocked you were? How sure he didn't write it?"

"He didn't."

"That's how shocked and sure I am."

"I'm stepping back to my roots."

"Which roots might that be?"

"My Spady roots."

"Spady roots?"

"Raw intelligence."

"What is it?"

"Literally or figuratively?"

"Literally."

"My son's wedding present."

"Figuratively?"

"A bridge from me to Pushkin."

"They're going to revoke your tenure."

"I hope not."

"Remember what happened to Cornel at Harvard."

"I'm telling my son I love him in language he understands."

"Who's going to perform it?"

"Me. I'm calling myself thug-lit. I'm stepping down from my ebony tower."

"Is that where you been?"

"Yes and no."

"What's the no?"

"I've been back in Motown looking for my daddy."

"I was just about to get Tanya to hook me up with some of her friends."

"Honey babe, I'd cut it off."

"Lorena Bobbitt land, that's a white, white place. I thought sisters understood."

"I'm starting to transcend race."

"You're going to fuck who you love?"

"I'm changing the subject."

"I'm not going to let you."

"I love you."

"Let's go home."

"Not yet. Pushkin first."

"You don't know your son as well as I thought you did."

"I know my son."

"Did he ever tell you that Jesus stood at the foot of his bed and talked to him?"

"Right. What did Jesus say to Pushkin, pray tell?"

"Show your scared young mama everything's all right. Let it arc across the field in the game's green light. Pigskin rainbows in the sky, day and night."

"You remember the words?"

"How could I forget that?"

"I don't believe Jesus spoke to Pushkin."

"I think that was Pushkin talking to himself."

"I think that was Pushkin talking to Pushkin."

"He wants you to meet him at the bar at the Hermitage."

"He called?"

"Of course he called."

"Fuck Du Bois."

"Du Bois is dead. How 'bout me?"

TWENTY-ONE

I WILL MEET MY SON.

I am to meet Pushkin in the bar of the Hermitage Hotel. The Hermitage is a lavishly renovated, old-style, Old World grand lodge in downtown Nashville. It's at once very old and completely new. Anachronism is part of the charm. It is very Pushkin and me.

I have arrived. The lobby is not immense, but it is elaborate. The ceiling is decorated with extraordinary mythological creatures and colors. One approaches the lobby by walking up a flight of marble stairs. One enters the hotel and immediately ascends or descends. Ascension leads to the lobby. Dissension leads to the bar.

Most of their out-of-town guests are staying at the Hermitage. Later tonight, the rehearsal dinner will be held here. I am not invited—yet. Tomorrow, the wedding reception will be held here.

Standing in the door, I see the door to the room where the reception will be held. The Hermitage has a real ballroom, with mahogany floors and lemon-oiled, dark paneled walls that have been dusted over the past hundred years by hundreds, if not thousands, of hands. Rumor has it that Pushkin had them pull up the carpet to get his hardwood floors.

I like the bar at the Hermitage. It reminds me of Spady. It's a space that nurtures gambling. A veiling darkness abides. Nowadays the chairs are upholstered in beautiful leather. For years they were upholstered in a fabric that celebrated the suits of cards—spades, diamonds, clubs, and hearts. The dark clubbiness of the space creates a sense that this is a place for risk to be taken. When Minnesota Fats lived in the hotel, he traded pool lessons for his room and pool demonstrations for his board and slumped in the corner over a glass when he wasn't paying his way. In life he slept in his room; in death he slept at the last table in the corner of the bar.

If Spady can't be here in the flesh, I'm glad Minnesota will be here in the spirit. The oldness of the place may be a possible bow in my direction, but I am thinking something else altogether. I'm thinking of Pushkin and me in Petersburg—that the hotel allows Pushkin to bow toward his woman and his mother at the same time.

The Hermitage Hotel looks like the Hotel Europa. We have returned to the scene of my amorous crime. Pushkin and I used to stand outside that hotel and watch the women and the men walk by in their furs. Some of the women looked like Tanya. They looked so warm. Pushkin and I, we were always cold in the St. Petersburg winter. We called it Leningrad then. Leningrad sounds and feels colder than St. Petersburg. We were always cold and we were half hungry, not because food was expensive—it wasn't—but because the food in St. Petersburg in the eighties wasn't very good. More than once we went into the Hotel Europa and sat in the bar and I fed you blini. I watched you stuff your sweet chocolate face with small and thin, beige and scorched black buckwheat pancakes made with a batter raised with yeast, slathered with caviar. I watched you eat while I drank vodka shots. We both sniffed in the scent of the Russian ladies in their Russian furs.

This is what is most important about the Hotel Europa. I am wondering how much of this Pushkin remembers. Soon I will know.

I remember being glamorous and poor. We were a part of the expatriate community, a part of the café society of the place and period, such as it was, two in a long if slight trail of dark pilgrims who traveled from America to Russia to see, to know, to be something radically different.

Love felt different in Russian. There is more room in the language for light and shadow. The two of us survived on a fellowship meant to support one. You went everywhere with me, because life does in fact go on. That which does not kill you does in fact make you stronger. At twenty-two I was old enough never to let you go again. After the three years we had been separated, it was years and years before I wanted to be apart.

I believe I am paying for that now. Perhaps in those years that came after Leningrad I held you too close to me. I held you so close because I didn't want you to get a good look at me. I didn't want you to see me, and I didn't want me to see myself reflected in your eyes. I had learned to be afraid of mirrors on my mother's knee.

I arrive at the bar, find a corner table in the back, take out a pack of cigarettes, and begin smoking. I have not smoked since Russia. When you come back from your honeymoon, I hope I will give you pieces of this document. I know you will have the poem. I close my hands, breathe in deeply, and try to figure out if I can feel Minnesota Fats at the table. I'm wondering if he can provide me any aid.

Pushkin walks into the room. I want to stand, but I don't. I want to throw myself into his arms, but I don't. I am thinking of those boys outside Mrs. Perkins's house, aligning their little fingers to the laces on the football without really knowing what they were doing. Those boys sending the slightly elongated leather lemon into the air. He looks so good I am almost glad I left him there. I want to smile, and I do.

"Hey."

"Hi."

Pushkin puts his arms around me and lifts me from my chair. It's a tackle. I am sacked. I'm gonna tell and he knows I'm gonna tell. When he gets his arms around you, you can't shake him off. This time I don't run off the field. The sideline is the last defender, but I won't play it this time. If I go down, I'm going down on the field. You can't get into the end zone running the wrong side of the white line.

"We want you at the wedding."

"Yeah?"

"Yeah!"

"I brought your present."

"Yeah?"

"Yeah."

"Yeah?"

"I'm afraid of saying more than a syllable."

"Yep?"

"Yep."

"Will we like it?"

"I hope."

I open up my big Longchamps bag and pull out a sheath of paper wrapped in leather cord—laced like a football. I hand it to Pushkin. He raises his eyebrows, but he doesn't grab the pages. Maybe he senses these pages, the page I'm writing here, the pages I have left back at the house. Maybe he senses the pistol too. I am holding my gift out to him.

"What is it?"

"A story."

"What story?"

"Actually it's a rap-song poem."

"What?"

"The Pushkin."

"The Pushkin?"

"'The Negro of Peter the Great.' Written by your namesake."

"Fuck that."

"What?"

"He was bugging."

"Bugging?"

"I hated that story."

"You won't hate it now."

"I hit you in the head throwing that whatchucallit? Modern Library Giant with that story in it across the room."

"I can still feel the scar in my scalp."

"I caught you in the head with the corner."

"I shouldn't have dodged."

"You hadn't moved I wouldn't a hit you."

"I know that."

Pushkin reaches into my hair as if it is something he has done recently. He reaches naturally and quickly. I shudder. It's been a very long time. The tips of his fingers are rough.

"Let me get this straight. You giving me, your black son, about to marry a very nice white Russian lady, a story about a black Russian obsessed by how good he doesn't look to white women and the white women who are disgusted by his thick lips and kinky hair?"

"Yes."

"Exactly how is this an appropriate present?"

"It didn't have an ending . . ."

"The son-o-bitch . . ."

"Which son of a bitch might that be?"

"Pushkin. Pushkin wrote his nigger-hating nigger-self into a fucking corner—that's why the story is incomplete. I understood that when I was thirteen years old. I couldn't a read another page of that shit, and he couldn't a written another page."

"I fixed the story."

"Fixed the story?"

"It has an ending now."

"The bride stabs her groom to death and then herself?"

"The bride falls in love with the groom when she touches his thick lips and kinky hair."

"You fixed the story."

"Yes."

"You rewrote Pushkin?"

"Yes."

"You an audacious bitch, to be sure."

"I would rewrite God if it would make you feel better."

I take out another cigarette. I'm wondering if Minnesota Fats could teach me a trick shot from the other side of the grave.

"There's something else you want to know."

"Yeah, there is."

"Something has happened to your father."

"My father?"

"Yes."

"Is he alive?"

"Not anymore."

"How many days did I miss him by?"

"Not many."

"You goddamned bitch."

"Precisely put. I am, I was, a goddamned . . . well, nothing quite as blessed as a female dog, as your Tanya or my Tanya for that matter."

"Shit. I wanted to see the motherfucker once before I died."

"I was your daddy. Your daddy and your mommy."

"I think you got an early version of Alzheimer's. Who was he?"

"Sven Andersson."

"Mr. Andersson? The whitest man in America?" Pushkin sat straight, unblinking, unmoving. "I'm gonna kill that son of a bitch."

"Spady beat you to it."

Why I go and say that. I said that, I said, "Spady beat you to it," and then I heard a sound. There's a George Jones song that stings me. It's a song about a man who claims he has heard the sound of his dear old mama crying, sounds of war, of desperation and desolation. None of these, he says, is as bad as the sound of the closing of the door, the sound of his woman leaving.

I said, "Spady beat you to it," and Pushkin sobbed. It is the saddest sound I've ever heard. A sob breaks through his throat and I almost, almost die. I did not think it possible for this man to cry. He never had. A tear brighter than a diamond rolls down his face. He shakes his head and flings it off.

"I didn't figure this."

"What did you figure?"

"That you'd been date-raped at college."

"You can't count."

"Sometimes babies come early."

"Not as big as my darling."

"That's why."

"That's why what?"

He shakes his head and something—a tear, spit, sweat—flies from his face to mine.

"Pushkin?"

"Why I'm out on the football field."

"Why?"

"I figured you'd been raped."

"I was born to carry you."

"I want to carry you."

"You do, you carry me in your heart."

"When somebody weighing three-something plows into me, it's like I'm erasing some old pain of yours. There's something I celebrate every time I spill my blood."

"Pushkin?"

"I knew somebody hurt you bad. That's what I liked about getting hurt. Saying back to your pain, 'Ain't no big thang!'"

I am thinking of the ballroom; I am thinking of dancing with Pushkin in this ballroom tomorrow. I am thinking of telling him no more than he needs to know. I am thinking of standing in his arms and moving to the music with his hand supporting me at the base of my spine, with his hand in mine.

And I am thinking of something else altogether. This is what the man who was the boy I bore needs to know: Othello did not believe that Desdemona loved him. The Moor of Venice did not believe that his white wife could love him faithfully. Othello was deceived, not by trysting and cuckolding, not by a white man in his bed, but by a black woman in his memory. Othello was deceived by twisted vanity, vanity tainted; he was deceived by looking into the marred mirror, the distorted glass foxed with mold, waved with time. The marred mirror lies and the best physic is a mother's loving eyes.

What did Othello's mother's eyes reflect? Why could he see a handkerchief and accept it as a token of infidelity and not see the reality that Desdemona loved him above rubies? We only know he made himself crazy, then he made himself sad. He made himself foolish. He was deceived because he did not perceive his own beauty. A sense of the beauty of the baby is the pleasure of the mother to conceive, the pleasure and the duty.

And then there was Pushkin, Pushkin who knew his Othello and should have been better informed. Pushkin, whose mother was dark and whose father was light. This Pushkin did not believe his woman was faithful. Perhaps he didn't believe because he was unfaithful himself. Perhaps he didn't believe because he had discovered the joys of erotica at too early an age in his father's library and had a more than libertine knowledge of the hunger in the heart of woman and man. Perhaps all these things—and they are all a part of it, but the biggest part is this: Pushkin felt the doubt in his mother's kiss. He saw her tan loveliness caress the white-and-pink skin of his father, saw her hand search the surface of his hair with her fingertips, saw those same fingertips burrow into the curls of his father's wig, saw all of this. Pushkin saw his mother longing for the white kiss and doubted any woman could value his body. He felt her dark and doubting kiss, felt her own doubt in her own beauty, her own awkward sense of her own awkward beauty. Like so many sons, he felt eclipsed—except on paper, where, page after page, it is the black marks that are significant, page after page of whiteness looking for blackness, page after page of Tanya looking for you.

I have written page after page pursuing you, only to discover I am chasing the courage to see myself as Leo's daughter. It is Leo's daughter who loves large enough to embrace you and whoever you love.

I have done for you what I would not do for myself—claim the earthy strains and strangeness of blackness as well as the rare stars of pure African genius, claim the low and the high and let them be wed. I have done for you what I would not do for myself—refuse to be frightened.

Peculiarly, it was not Leo or Martha Rachel who inspired me most. It was Lena. Because Lena was such a bad mother, I determined to be a good one. Ultimately it is a simple matter of inversion: I will be who you need me to be—a woman sufficiently aware of her past to step around it into her future, because you need me to. Because Lena was not.

I believe Tanya loves you because I know I love you. I believe that she thinks you are the best-looking man who ever lived because I believed you were the prettiest boy God ever set on earth. I believe that she wants to lie down beneath you because I remember wanting to lie down to birth you, spreading my legs to let your magnificence proceed from my womb into the room, exploding every reality that came before your birth into lesser truths and new possibilities. We arrange the fragments of life and memory, with mirrors of love and yearning and need, into things of beauty. Love and need and yearning are the mirrors in the kaleidoscope. Life itself is the tube. You look down it and twist, and beauty takes shape and changes. Colors over and over again. You believe that she loves you because you know that I love you. You knew that I loved you.

For once Lena wasn't lying. "Your mother told me."

"What?"

"She wanted me to hate you like she hated you."

"She told you Andersson raped me?"

"She told me you slept with him for money."

"She said that?"

"Not in those words."

"What words did she say?"

"I don't remember."

"You believed her."

"No."

"Why?"

"There's no whore in you, and I knew Leo's Red would never flip for a vanilla farmer-geek. I don't care what the fuck he invented, he did not know how to swing his dick—"

"Pushkin!"

"Princess Mommy."

It's my turn to choke back the sob.

"Aunt Diana said it was your very first time and he almost broke your mind, but she didn't tell me who it was."

"Not almost. He did not almost break my mind. Leo's love would not let me go to crazy."

"When I walk out on the field and I see some motherfucker who wants to hurt me and I remember the motherfucker who wanted to hurt you, that motherfucker across the line is mine. The dance is on and I already won, 'cause it's never about him after that. It's always about you, and you and me is a good thing. I walk off the field, straight and tall, just like my moms."

"I'm not tall."

Pushkin sinks down into the club chair as if it still has spades and diamonds and clubs and hearts needlepointed all over it. He hangs his head like a boy and stretches one of his long arms across the table.

"When I was four-foot-five, you were five-foot-four."

I push my bundle of words toward him, all tied up in leather laces. His hand falls to my shoulder; I flinch. His knuckles bump-brush over the cashmere covering my breast. His hand falls in a fist upon my words on paper. He is seizing my transformation of poison into antidote. His eyes are open. He is ready to drink it down.

For Pushkin, my son, I have sacrificed, syllable and sound, everything.

TWENTY-TWO

The Negro of Peter the Great

Pushkin's mama's daddy's daddy
Was the dark Abraham
Was the brilliant stolen man

One of many but the favorite
Of the czar of czars
The star among stars
Was the stolen black man
Was the dark Abraham
Pushkin's mama's daddy's daddy
Pushkin's great-grandpappy
In the genealogy of you, in the genealogy of me
Preeminent will be the eminent Russky
Pushkin the O.G.

More than Shakespeare, Milton, or Proust
More than Ibsen, Chekhov, or Faust on the loose
Beyond Marx and Freud
In the outersphere atmosphere of genius and void
Shimmers the man who invented the modern Russian
    language
If you hang with me here, I'm sure I can arrange this
For you to understand
Black bright bliss
A literary kiss

One of the many sent overseas
Students, not emissaries
Sent beyond the borders
On czar's orders—

Peter the Great needed to know more than he knew
Knew Russia needed to know it too
So he sent our boy Abraham to Paris
To military school back when war was cool
Lickety-split Abraham jumped quick
Became captain of the artillery
He was dressed to kill with lead and frillery

Abraham played his part in the Spanish War
Showed he knew just what fighting was for
He was a warrior's warrior
Enemies begged to see no more of him
Of the stolen black man
The brilliant Abraham
Who shot back to Paris
To start courting ladies on a terrace
At the Bois de Boulogne
Wearing a flowery French cologne
He was never, ever alone

Across the globe
Far away and cold
The czar kept a-czaring deep in Russia
Bought himself a life or two from the king of Prussia
But the czar was not too busy to ask after his Abraham
The brilliant black man
And he liked what he heard when he asked
That his adopted son, his anointed one, was equal to the
    task
He heard, "Your stolen man has a valiant hand
He carries himself well; he's moving right along."
Peter wanted him back
Needed to know what he knew
Abraham said dis, then Abraham said dat
Abra'm said skinny, then Abra'm said phat
He said he was recovering from a wound

He said he would come on soon—as he found the money
He said he needed more education
But he was pondering fornication

Peter said, Take care of yo'self
Peter said, Keep after your books
Peter usually held his green tight but he opened his hand
    on Abraham
Poured over his stolen black man
With his purse and his power
Hour after hour
Washing over Abraham with advice, money, and caution
Paris was the place—then
LouisLouisLouisLouisLouisLouisLouisLouisLouis
    LouisLouisLouisLouisLouis
Fourteen Louises were dead now
Who called themselves the king of France
Was it like that?
It was Louis the XIV was dead and buried
With him the churchiness and the p's and q's of his
    people
Without a nary nothing left

The Duke of Orleans
smart and nasty
Didn't hide nothing
Never been a faster fast he
At the Palais Royal there was an orgy every night
And the whole town knew it

John Law came to town
Sized it up, sized it down
And hunger after gold joined hunger after booty
And every kind of person was after every kind of looty

Open house every day in Paris society
Everybody wanted to be amused without propriety
Everybody wanted to get confused in their entirety
Everybody wanted what everybody wants
And everybody flaunted what everybody flaunts

And women rose up as queens
In these baroque and brocade scenes

And the queens ruled
Princes were strict-schooled
Tyrant queen you could loll upon and taste
All the sweet, sweet time a man could waste

Into this world strode Abraham
The stolen black man, he turned heads
Well made, well played, he turned heads
He got the women looking
They wanted to see *le nègre du czar*
They enveloped him in invitations
To their halls and to their beds
He was a prize to be won

The big man himself—of Paris at the time—
Asked him to hop on by
And he made all the other parties too
Day parties and night parties,
Call-ins, call-outs, call-ups
He was in it deep
And it was deep in him
And the thought of extracting himself from Paris
Was wherefore, wherenot, whereas
And another thing kept him there
He loved—somebody

They call her the Countess D
And she was not young but she still had some beauty
    about her
A virgin behind a wall with the nuns and the priests
Till a man came and got her
An aging man with true wealth sought her
Put a ring on her finger but no love in hands
Then he took her innocence
Giving neither pleasure subtle nor pleasure intense
Time to come, she made him pay in pain
She took a man, then another to her bed,
She made that old count pay in his head
So folk thought she was creeping out with Merville
And Merville let it be thought
And Merville brought Abraham to the Countess D
He wanted Abraham his good fortune to see

Now the countess she was chillin'
Didn't have much to say to this most delicious of Ham's
    own children
And strange to say, that touched him deep
'Cause he was so used to being the exotic interest, so to
    speak
He was flattered she thought him just ordinary
She made him feel like a real he
Abraham, he did not like to hear sweet words
They brought him pain, brought the fear of sarcastic
    shame
Every compliment falling from a woman's lips
Sounded to him like "exotic beastie," sounded like "space
    creature"
Sounded like someone too different

Now Abraham did not aspire to learn
What it was, what it is, to love and be loved in return
So he talked straight to the Countess D
No kind of mack, no kind of perfidity
The countess was enchanted without intentionality

Step by step
She fell into liking the looks of him
Syllable by sound, she fell into loving the note of him
His dark-haired head among the white powdered wigs
The Countess D digs
Abra'm wore a bandage, a mark of his battle
How can a wig eclipse a bandage?
You know it can't
And he was twenty-seven years young
(a dark-eyed handsome man)
(ways just like a baby child)
And he was tall and slim
More than one honey glanced up at him
And a few bad bees too
But he glanced at nobody till
The Countess D into his eyes looks, sees
And his caution quit
Quick as that, zap zip
Abraham wanted to know and be known
Oo oui, baby, love was sown

Now love and be loved is a precious thing
Love and be loved, more than a wedding ring
He tried to happen upon her every day
Coming upon her was heaven at play
And she knew what a woman knew
How a man loves her before he himself do
And the flavor of that love:
A love that asked not a thing from her
A love that sings without expectation of answer
Touched that female place
Touched it more tender than valentine or lace

When in the presence of other young sweeties
The Countess D only Abraham entreaties
And Merville was the first to catch a whiff
Of the changing drift of the impending cliff
Of its very deliciousness

Now Abraham, he be knowing
Through Merville's sadness showing
That he had a chance with the countess
And a chance was all he needed
He started in to loving him some her
But his love felt too hot
And she said, Let's be friends
And he said, Let's not
Then they did it till the break of dawn
Abraham and the countess got it on

The world sees everything
The world saw this
The world saw the countess and the Negro kiss

Some of the ladies said it was fine
Some of the ladies said the countess must be blind
Folks were cruel and folks were kind
For soot, for soothe
They tried to hide the truth
But the truth began to show
As their love began to grow

It was a crisis they could have expected
Love's calamity

Face it with equanimity
Hard sweet bang leads to soft sweet baby
More often than may be
Love's calamity
a baby baby baby
People were talking and talking and talking
Except the count
He knew nothing, said nothing, the gossip he was
    ducking
Would the baby be black, would the baby be white?
Would their way be dark, would their way be light?
The countess was scared to death
She counted every cloud breath
And day by day, come what may, her Abraham by her side
Her strength began to slide
She was busted of brain
When the labor pains came
They tricked the count out of the house
He was glad to leave and slow to perceive
The count Abraham prepared to deceive
The doctor came and he was in on it too
There's some desperate things desperate folk will do
And in the end desperate folk need desperate friends

Now Abraham walked his paces in the next room
Wondering if his woman's womb would be his baby's
    tomb
He heard all the screams as if in a dream
Then one that woke his heart
He heard his baby cry
Hi, Hi, Hi, Hi, Hi,
Rushing from where he was supposed to be to where his
    lady was
He saw a little black baby and lots of blood
His son had been born without a hitch
But he was black as pitch so they made the switch
With a small pink burden a poor pale girl brought

But not before Abraham lifted his dusky hand
And blessed his boy
And the countess, feeling joy,

Reached out for the once stolen dark man
But the doctor pulled him away
Saying too much excitement for a single day

They put the black baby in a basket, it almost as well a
   been a casket
They vanished him from the air, carrying him down a
   secret stair
Abraham watched as they put the pink baby in the silk
   crib
In the room where his woman and baby oughta lived
It was time for Abraham to go and he did
It was time for the count to come home
Abraham left the house so very alone
Abandoned, abandoning, and unatoned.

Mama's little baby, Daddy's little maybe
'Tis 'tis 'tis his, his, his,
Said the Count D, said it royally
He said it was and left nothing to say
Just left the countess and Abraham a hard hand to play
Back in the day
A silence reigned

II

Time marched on like a soldier
Maybe Peter the czar was calling
But Abe wouldn't leave the woman
Who responded with reciprocation to the fact of his love
His love inside her
His love in the baby
His love in her eyes
She responded with reciprocation to the act of his love
But what of the little seed far away?
Would he grow to see a brighter day?

Then it came
As if from nowhere but midair Russia
A letter from the czar, would he cuss ya?
Maybe he was a friend of the Count D's
Couldn't expect he would be pleased

But the czar wrote a strong-hearted letter
He knew what was up and hoped it got better
Knew why Abraham was still there
Told his boy to take good care
Peter the Great also wrote to the count, he said,
"He's my boy no matter what he do,
And what in the fuck business is it to you?"
Abraham remembered Peter's love
And he made up his mind like a true man does
Nobody has a life to burn
Everybody got a living to earn

Abe knew what he had to do and he was going to do it
Get back to Russia, nothing to it
Then and there he decided to return
His friends in Paris said, Don't and Won't
Looked at his black skin, said,
You don't belong to white Russia
Looked at his wound and said,
For France you were almost dead
For France you have shed your blood
In la belle France you will always be loved

But Abraham heard in Peter's words on paper
That Peter wasn't looking at nothing
Peter was color-blinded by love
Abraham heard the duke call Russia
"half savage" and Abraham knew
The duke thought Abraham was half savage too
Almost as clearly as he knew
That neither Russia nor he was half savage

The duke let him go
Wrote a note to the czar
Paris didn't know
But Abraham finna go

Abe was soul-sick
But our boy got ready quick
Spent his last Paris night
Seeking the sweet and tight
Chez la contesse D

He chez she, but
She did not know he was out the do'
It was their usual night
She was her usual bright
She was herself, rolling straight
She kept on having to ask him
Where you at, baby
He never said
He kept his eyes lead

After the other guests had gone
With night hanging on
The countess, the count, and Abraham
The woman, the elder, and the man
Braided like a plait running down a brown girl's back
Sitting in front of the fire
Needing time to conspire
Abraham wishing the count would go anywhere else
But he stayed tight by the fire bright
And finally the countess, thinking of the next night and
   the next night
Thinking to get her beauty rest
She said, *"Bonne nuit"*
Abraham went cold
Abraham got chilled to the bone
"Bonne nuit," said the countess again
He said nothing
He did nothing
He thought so many words unspoken
Sought love unawoken
He got up and went
Almost spent
Returning to his rooms, he wrote a letter

He addressed the mother of his child by her first name
Leonora, he wrote
He said many things
But the cut of it was this:
One day you gonna stop loving me
He said, How it is said to be and how it is be different
He said, Folk are watching

You ain't comfortable
Remember the birth of our boy?
My refuge, pride and joy
Remember our abandoned toy?
When will I be your abandoned boy?
Bye, my love
Then Abraham threw that letter away

He wrote,
I am a miserable creature
How could I link your
Gentle beauty to African me?
But I did when we conceived our son
Bye, bye, baby
I pull away. I turn away,
As if from rolling in your arms
Remember, recall and recall
Dark me, your once everything, and all

Before the missive could be pensived by his pretty
He was rolling across Europe
Rolling toward Petersburg
On tracks greased
And rolling with ease
His mind was rolling back
Rolling toward Paris
And rolling with pain

In seventeen days they crossed the border
It was fall, the roads were rough
Like his mind, muddy and tough
The horses needed changing
His soul needed rearranging

It was like that night in Bethlehem
Travelers in the road
It was a roadhouse
And they stopped and Abe poked his head in
There was a tall man in a lime caftan
A smoke cloud rising like a wreath
A clay pipe in his teeth
He was reading a German newspaper
An article about a learned fakir

The man looked up and exclaimed
"Godson!"
Abraham wanted to run to him
But he remembered he was a subject
And waited for the czar to advance
And take him in an embrace
The czar had loved this man
When he was a stolen boy
The czar's own bouncing brilliant pride and joy
The czar had been waiting for the slave
For two days

Peter told Abraham
(the godson the chosen one)
To have his carriage follow behind
He had a place for Abraham
By his royal side in his royal carriage
They arrived in Petersburg in imperial time

The infant city crawled before Abraham
Spawned by the man beside him
A hunger in Peter transformed
Into this place
As if Peter had impregnated his soil
Abraham gawked at Petersburg
As the women of Paris had gawked at Abraham
Unfinished dams, unfinished canals
Told the win-win of human ambition
Over nature, but at that moment
There was only one magnificent thing in the city
God's own river, the Neva
Now there were two:
The Neva and the Negro
Peter the Great, he grow
More in love with his river and his man every day
The czar's carriage stops at the palace
Stops at the czarina's garden
A full-grown woman
Maybe thirty-five, good-looking, sharp-dressed
Reminding Abraham of the Paris he and she had left
    behind
She was dressed in Paris

Peter kissed her on the lips as he reached for Abraham's
  hand
They were braided like the plait down a different brown
  girl's back

It was Catherine, called Katinka
Peter told her to treat Abraham as she treated him
And Catherine's dark eyes took Abe in
And her young daughter's took him in as well

Peter took Abraham to table
They spoke of the world
The politics in prose
Then the czar rose to rest
Leaving the czarina and the grand duchesses with the
  guest

Much later with greater weighter
Peter said to Abraham
Take up a slate and follow me
Abraham did as he was bid
Followed his czar
And his czar continued to amaze him
The czar invited him to stay the night

Alone that first dark in the palace
In the infant city of Petersburg
Abraham Hannibal remembered his younger self
He remembered knowing Peter
When he did not yet know what Peter was
Or how it signified
In Russia or the world
Now he recognized the heft of the invitation to return
The possibility of being yoked to Peter
His spirits lifted
He was czarly gifted
He was bizarrely lifted
And Paris felt far away
And close as the czarina's gown
Abraham felt ambition rise in him
For the very first time
Felt what it was to be in Russia and

Godson of the czar
Even as he lay himself down on a cot
Prepared in haste
A cot in a palace
And filaments of fantasies of the light in the night
Rolled his mind back to Paris
His dark soul embarrassed

III

Next day
Peter made our boy Abraham
Captain-lieutenant of his artillery
Decked him out in martial imperial frillery
The mighty Menshikov, cold and cool
Bumped chests with him
Sheremetyev shouted out to his friends in Paris
Golowin invited him to his crib for a bite
Everybody else wanted him too
He could eat out for a month

He was in it
And it went round and round
They, the czar and the captain-lieutenant,
Carried the weight
And it was heavy as Abraham was coming to know
And the czar was stronger than Abraham knew
And Abraham he was coming stronger too

It was Russia
A monster of a factory
And everybody had his place
At his little bench to work
And Abraham had his
Sitting at the bench of state
Discovering that hard steady work is hard steady work

He started thinking on the Countess D
And maybe their little baby
He imagined her crying—for him
And then the other idea came, the dark twin
Or was it light, which creates betraying sight?

He saw her not weeping
But opening her mouth for another tongue
Desire and rage banged in his head
He could almost wish the French bitch was dead

Back to his bench
Hard at his papers
He heard a knick-knock
Of a Young Friend newly arrived from Paris
Now he's gonna know
Which one was it
The tears or the tongue?

The Young Friend had greetings from all the friends in
    Paris
And he had a letter from the countess
Abraham started to tremble to think of her caress
But Young Friend was babbling, searching for a new
    good time
What's up? Where you buy your threads? Who's playing
    tonight?
Abraham replied, "The big boss is down the hall."
And Young Friend laughed, handing Abe the letter
Hoping Abraham might touch what might make him
    better

The letter was what he would have wanted it to be
She complained so tenderly, did she,
"You say my peace is dear to you,
So why you do what you do?"

Now Young Friend returned
A little by the czar burned
Czar wouldn't even let him bow
Made him stand on some strange contraption somehow
Got him off his game
Young Friend felt mad, insane
For a moment
But he was pleased to see
The czar was struck by his finery
And the czar had read his report
And knew he was a returning visitor of import
So Young Friend to the palace was invited

But he wanted his friend Abe to go and get excited
Young Friend no longer knew how it was done here
Abraham said, I'll come, have no fear

Then Abe got down to his own question:
What about the Countess D, how true is it she misses
    me?
Now the Young Friend, fool that he was, told it quick
Said first the countess was heart-broke sick
Then she took up with a fine marquis
And consolated she seemed to be
Young Friend was quick of mind, if not of heart
He noticed Abraham's eyes
He was perplexed. "Don't you know women don't grieve
    long,
A woman's a woman and a woman will move on."
And assuming a man will move along quicker,
Young Friend started riffing on parties and liquor

Alone at his bench
Abraham read the perfidious letter
He cried a few tears and he felt a bit better
He would have preferred staying in his crib
But the czar's a czar, and he did as he was bid

He called on Young Friend
The fool wasn't ready
They tore out on the street. Abraham appeared rather
    steady
As Young Friend fool peppered him with questions
He wanted the whole 411
How this and that, how everything was done
They rolled up
And the crowd parted like the sea
Every other mouth murmuring
"My man, Abraham. Abraham, the dark man"
They passed the red-carpet riffraff
Went into the hall
Biff, baff

Smoke was thick
Candles were burning
Shiny women with their diamonds

Shiny men with their medals
Old women remembering old times living in the new

The czarina and the grand duchesses made their way into
    the scene
Talking here and there
Their man Peter the Great was in the next room with the
    foreign men
Young Friend wanted to get in there
They quit the refined air
To be in a smokier smoky place
With chessboards on the tables
And winy punch, pitchers of beer
But Peter, Peter, Peter the Great was near
All the men were smoking and drinking from thick mugs
Peter was playing dice with a sailor
Petersburg is a watery place
Where sailors are significant
A buffoon entered the room
Announcing that the dances had begun
Young Friend was fixin' for some fun

The first two or three were nothing like he needed them
    to be
Bow, curtsy, strangeness over and over
When they announced a minuet
Young Friend pronounced, "You ain't seen nothing yet!"
Among the women was a girl of sixteen or seventeen
Expensively but elegantly dressed
Sitting beside an old man
Young Friend jumped to her
But someone intervened
Said you do not understand this scene
She gets to ask you
You don't ask
And even if you do, where are your bows one, three, and
    two?
It's punishment for you!

The guests gathered round Young Friend in a circle
His face was turning purple
Peter himself jumped into the ring

He was into this punishment malmsey thing
They gave Young Friend a great big flask
Said, Drink it all, that is your task
And after he did it, Peter stayed hard
Said, "I don't wear breeches of velvet
You're an arrogant poppet and can't help it."
Young Friend began to stagger and fall
The crowd was amused by it all
And the girl he had chosen
Impelled by her father
Chose Abraham
She chose the czar's chosen one
She cast down her blue eyes and gave Abe her white hand
They danced the minuet
And when it was over Abraham found Young Friend
And took him home
Young Friend was cursing all the way
Until all he could remember was the bowing and the
    scraping
And the cigar smoking

IV

Now Gavrila Afanasyevich Rzhevsky
Was an old-style Russky
His daddy's daddy's daddy
And all his daddy's daddy's daddies
Belonged to the nobility
He had beaucoup acres
And beaucoup ducats
He liked to have folks to his table
He was rich and he was able
He had all the valets and mammies and cooks you could
    want
And he had a beautiful daughter of seventeen
A girl who had lost her mother when she was still a petite
    queen
An untouched child brought up in the old style
She could stitch in gold, Natasha was seventeen years old
But she was illiterate
Could not read or write

Couldn't do a thing for herself
A maid dressed her, a maid cleaned her
She learned the German dances
From a Scandinavian officer living in the house
I believe he was from Sweden
An older gent wounded in an earlier war
His right foot had a hole in it, but his left worked fine
The right could but maybe shuffle
The left could step the steps
Dance the minuets, almost leapt
The daughter learned from his left foot
Natasha Gavrilovna was the girl who could dance
All Petersburg knew this
Especially after Young Friend she dissed

It was a day for visiting
It was a holiday
Friends and family were in her father's dining room
Natasha took around a silver tray with golden goblets
The men wished the drink was still served with a kiss
The way it was in the old days
They were longing for the old ways
The men sat on one side of the table
The women sat on the other
Each side according to rank
At the end of the table sat the woman-dwarf, the
    housekeeper
Beside her was the Swedish dancing teacher

The old foods were served
The guests were near silent
Till the host called for the fool
Now this old female was dripping jewels
Was powdered and rouged
Tarted up and tinseled down
Looked like she had been around
Sagging titties in a low-cut gown
And the host's sister said
Word: sometimes the fool needs to be heard

And it seemed by the way the fool dressed
The Russian noblemen were impressed

By the ridiculousness of the
Hair too tall to walk in a door
Oh boor, Oh boor
Waist too small to breathe
Man deceive, man deceive
A woman ain't nothing but a lie
Oh my, oh my

Then a man
From a big plantation spoke
Had too many acres and serfs to choke
Had a young wife and a peculiarly lucky life
Though there seemed a little chisel in it
And he said, My wife can wear what she wants
As long as my wealth she does not flaunt
Used to be the grandmother's dress
Went to the granddaughter in a dowry
Now it's thrown away
So much bling, bling
Is no Russian aristocratic thing

And Gavrila Afanasyevich
Filled up his glass with Hennessey
Let me tell you, let me let you see
We to blame, they do what they do
And we go insane.

Kirila Petrovich
Disagreed
He said, I would shut my woman up in her room
Before I let her spend my money
I get the honey, she don't get much money
But when the czar calls and invites gals to his party
At their beauty they throw our money and their arty
His wife said, What's wrong with answering the call?
He said, Everything and all
Women too busy about their clothes to keep house fo'
    sho'
Women dancing and talking to men they don't know

Someone said, I have a word for your ear, but the wolf is
    prowling near
Everything happens here

Some young buck wants to fuck your daughter
(Who gets drunk and pulled into a slaughter?)
And somehow someone started imitating Young Friend
Put a dish on his shoulder, pretended it was a hat
And everybody laughed at the pretensions of that
And somebody else said,
He is not the first
Won't be the last
To come back from Paris acting an ass
Only Abraham is an exception to this
Of all the Russians sent to France
In search of education, finding romance
Abraham with stolen black hands
Most, praise God, resembles a man
And who is this about to arrive
Some of the guests ducked, some of the guests dived
And some of them jumped into a hedge
Just as we saw the czar's own sledge!

Now some of the servants had gotten lazy
But at the czar's arrival they all went crazy
For Peter's eyes were old but they were not hazy
He called to the daughter of the house
She stepped forward quiet as a mouse
He looked directly at her, but why it's hard to infer
Would there be bliss in her bower
Why did he say, "You grow lovelier by the hour"
And when he kissed her on the head
She didn't know she'd wish she was dead
Not yet, not yet, not in time for the heart to protect

Now the host he snatched up a tray
It was a way to beg Peter to stay
He served the czar with both his hands
Even though he was a noble man
And everybody sat back to the table
At least everyone who was able
The dwarf and the dancer stayed away
The highness of the czar not to betray
Then the czar's own man
Took out a strange spoon

It had a green handle made from an animal's bone
Czar brought his own implements when eating from
   home
And the guest also returned to eat
And the host just marveled at his joy complete
And the czar tried to talk to the fool
But the fool talked sweet and cool
At last Peter came to what he came for
He asked Gavrila to speak with him behind a closed door.

V

Half an hour later the door opened
Peter walked out, bowed to who was there
Peter had unburdened himself of care
The host handed him his red coat
And thanked him unprovoked
Peter rode off
Gavrila Afanasyevich stayed back
But his mood was now black
Bing bang bong something was wrong
Let his face fall with gloom
Sent his daughter to her room
Change is in the air and
Change don't care

Gavrila called his wife's father
He called his sister too
They needed to powwow
See what they would do
The O.G. laid his head on the oak bed
The woman sat in an old chair
Change was in the air
And change sho' nuff don't care
Gavy locked the door
Then sat at the prince's feet on his own floor

You may be wondering
Why would we do that thing
You may be wondering
Why the czar and his golden rings

Were here today
You don't say
He was here today
And now—
He wants you to be ambassador
To be a rich gray-eyed boor
He was here today
And now—
Natasha is in play
He was here today
And it's about her wedding day
Hooray! Hooray!
As the matchmaker is, the bridegroom must be
With whom does the czar Natasha see?
Whom, whom, that is the question on which I loom
Whom, whom, all this gloom and Natasha's doom
That's whom
What, not what, but
But what?
Is it Dolgoruky?
Too in love with hisself.
Shein? Troyekurov?
Too many Benjamins, too little sense.
Yeletzky? Lvov. Raguzinsky.
Who?
For the brilliant black man
For the stolen Abraham
For the stolen Abraham
That's his plan, that's the czar's man, the stolen Abraham
Don't let our girl succumb to the touch of the black devil
Maybe so, maybe no, the czar has many favors to bestow
Hide her high, hide her low, don't let her love a bought
    Negro
Bought bought boughtboughtbought bought
Hide her high, hide her low, don't let her touch a bought
    Negro
It could be a house of mirth, this Negro is not of
    common birth
His is not a simple suntan, his father was a Negro sultan
The Musselman took him prisoner and sold him in
    Constantinople

But his family tried to ransom him with diamonds and
    opals
Our ambassador bought him and gave him as a present to
    the czar
That little black gift raised him far
We have heard all this!
Abraham we still dis and dismiss
Hide her high, hide her low, don't let her marry a bought
    Negro
By the way, what did you say, by the way?
I said, Come what may
The czar's word is word
And he heard what he heard
And now it's mine to make it word
We must love, honor, and obey
The words our czar say
A cry, so high, so loud, so long, it was girl's song
A cry, a door opened, and Natasha lay close to death
    gone
On a blood-spattered floor
Her hope was splattered more

They carried Natasha up to bed
Dreams and nonsense filling her head
They carried Natasha to bed
They carried her body, they carried her dread
They carried a frightened little girl
Who cried "Valeryan!" at every little whirl
Save me, save me, save me
She sighed
She should have cried
Brave me, brave me!

Now somebody heard, her father they disturbed
With news of the name she called aloud
A name that left her daddy appalled, not proud
Valeryan, son of a poor man with a poor gun
Son of a dead man, on life's run.
Valeryan, he had given a home, and his daughter with
    this name stoned
It was settled then and there
Change was in the air and change don't care

Natasha would wed Abraham
It was Natasha and the brilliant black man
Not Natasha and the frozen orphan
They sent for the doctor
No one knew what for
They sent for the doctor
And her daddy locked his sober door

Across town Abraham didn't know the news
Abraham at his bench with his old Paris blues
Till the czar said, Abraham, I the man have a plan
Did you like the girl with whom you danced?
Would you give her a second glance?
She was sweet, she was demure
A second glance for sure, maybe,
Is she pure, that lovely lady?
Would you take her to be wed?
Would you take her to your bed?
Wed, bed, what is it you said?
My czar, I wonder if she rather she was dead,
Who knows what's in a woman's head
I want to know what you want
Would you take her to be wed?
Would you take her in your bed?
I would not take her eyes as my mirror
If I looked in those eyes I might learn to fear her
What's up with that?
You good-looking man and that's a fact
A girl goes where her daddy say so
And I'll give him reasons not to say no
I've taken a woman to my bed,
Could I take a girl to be wed?
Why not? Why not. Why not?
Make race a blot, get love besot
Why not, why not
Can one believe in love?
Can one if everyone else does,
Can one trust love?
Besot, why not?

The duty of man is to love a woman
I will not shirk my duty

I want my taste of beauty
I will not ask for her love
I will not ask her to fit me to a T
Just for her fidelity
I will make her my friend, by tenderness day and night
    without end
I will make her my friend.

Abraham left his bench
Contemplating the noble Russian wench

He was walking by the Neva
He was feeling love's own fever
And then Peter came round the bend
Peter with his love without end
Peter said what was in Peter's head
He said, You are more than my godson
You are my good son
I have chosen your loving one
It's gonna be all right
Your bride will be wearing white

VI

It was time for prayers
Change was in the air
And change don't care

A girl was sick with dread
A girl was sick in her head

A candle burned
Her stomach churned
She was staring at the icon
Thinking I can—
But not the black man
I can let a man touch me with his hand
But not the black man
That I cannot stand—
A servant maid sat at a spinning wheel
It was like a fairy tale, not like real
How long have I been this way?
How many, many days?

The little maid just didn't know what to say
A sound was heard
A loud sound without words
Natasha with memory piqued
Remembered her dusky destiny
She shrieked

The gentlemen had finished their dinner
Soon they would come see how much thinner
This illness had tricked Natasha into being
Let us let the doctor be tricked into seeing
You are better
We need a note that says so
They took the note down to her father
Who announced to his honored guest
She's getting rest at my bequest.
But see this letter
She's getting better

Abraham wore his uniform
He listened to obscure talk, talk obscure as cuneiform
They talked of their bloodlines
Abraham thought this was a good sign
As if they knew his black blood was blue
But Young Friend saw it another way
He asked, Why waste your time this way?
He said, Women will trick you,
You know how they do, he said
I have cuckolded men I don't look any better than
And mirror to mirror, sometimes they the better man
But a woman will want what she ain't got
And women will love you, then love you not
All kinds of things happen in this world
And worse ones when you tangle yourself to girls
And you
With your suspicious mind
Right on time with rage
And you
With your flat nose, how do you suppose
Not to doubt, and how 'bout
Your thick lips, will her eyes close when you she sips?

Will her tininess survive your thick lips?
What's up? Shut up. Motherfuck.

It not your duty
To tickle another man's baby's booty
I could say the same to you
Make sure the baby's booty ain't blue

In another room
Hung low with brocade and doom
The old lady, the aunt, had this to say:
Make her marry him and she will pass away
He scorches her eyes, his love she will despise
Her daddy did not listen to this
He knew what was what and had to insist
Abraham comes to this house as a bridegroom
We best let him see his pretty bride soon
For the czar in all his might and power
Can bring the world down on us in an hour
And the Negro Abraham is his chosen one
Abraham is his more than a son!

At last the aunt knew where it stood
To protest any longer would do no good
If she must know, I must go, and make it so
It be a blow from a friend or from foe
But it be better if we let her know, bit by bit, that this is it
So the aunt went to do her duty, up in the girl's room
And the dad, he went looking for the bridegroom

Abraham was thrilled, he was chiller than chilled
That his bride-to-be was no longer sicker than he
It was cause for a celebration, it was a time of unspoken
    reparation
Young Friend, who had done the sin of loving his boy's
    woman
He made haste out of the house, before cat turned on the
    mouse

Up in the house, after vanished the mouse, Natasha's
    getting ready
Her heart nor her head was steady

Her daddy looked stern; she wished for a lover she could
    prefer
And the disaster was getting closer and closer
Abraham the color of sin? Abraham himself walked in
And her head fell to the pillow
Her head fell from high to low
Her heart went beat beat beat beat
She had to sleep sleep sleep sleep
The men up and left the room, up and left her to her
    gloomy doom
Guarded only by a great big maid sitting at an ancient
    loom
Or was it at the spinning wheel? Whatever, her fate was
    sealed

Natasha, she opened up her eyes, saw no one to despise,
    no reason for lies
Every soul except this big maid had vanished; she got her
    present wish
For the time being, for the time seeing, her tiny friend
    was not there
Change was in the air and change didn't care
Natasha said to the maid bewitched and beware, Take
    care
Bring the shortest of the shorties to me, bring her here
    and let us be
Now this small woman was a sight to see
She had a kind of mad and endless energy
She had her finger in it all, she knew just who to call
She wasn't very tall but she was in no sense small
Except she was good to the strong and brutal to the
    weak
She took the lambs to the slaughter and the axes to the
    sheep
Natasha should know better than to trust her
But Natasha hoped she wouldn't bust her

Natasha's world was up in flames, Natasha thought she
    go insane
Thought, My daddy may be a hero, but he's trying to
    marry me to a Negro zero

256

Will not anyone speak out for me, who am I and what I
    must be?
The world shouted back:
It's not you changing station, it's the black man's
    elevation
Each and every heart in the house, from emperor to the
    dormouse
Bends at the knee to your husband-to-be
But girl, it's not as bad as all that, these ain't the old
    times, that's a fact
Back in the day, well, if you marry the Negro now you'll
    have your own way
Men used to keep wives under lock and key, but that is
    not how this will be
Negro or no, the man got dough, and that the ray me
    will gild your world to be
And when the cat's away little mousies get to play
Valeryan, is all the bride-to-be had to say, Valeryan
And why she go and say that
It sealed her doom and that be a fact
Why she have to go and say that
Raving about the orphan got her daddy angry
And being angry caused him to agree
Now there's a wedding
Soon you'll see
This is it, babe, submit or be overcome, the night is
    young
But the night ain't done
And this gave her hope sweet as true dope
I might die before I wake
I pray for that for true love's sake
Not to be the last one breathing
To be the one with love deceiving.

VII

Later that night the time was ripe
Valeryan came to the dancing instructor
Asking, Sir, do you remember me, do you not see
The scrapeface I used to be

257

I see what you were, you still are
A little soldier, a little star

VIII

Standing tall, standing all
It may be news but there are no pews
In a Russian Orthodox church
Abraham and Natasha erect at attention
Bodies declaring an intention
Not to lurch
To engage now, engage somehow
With God
Standing in one circle
Waiting on two or five or six different miracles
In the center of a round and sacred room
Await a white bride and a black bridegroom

Natasha is praying
As the priest is saying
Something Natasha doesn't hear
Her pink ears deaf with fear and loathing
Deaf with disdain for the man she betrothing
She don't hear nothing
She just see
How dark her future be
A blue-black man
With giant hands
Now she's
Praying praying praying
As the priest is saying saying saying
Something she can't hear, muffled in fear
Praying that Abraham drops dead
Praying to replace him with the man in her head
Praying that she be delivered from evil
From the clutches of this bridegroom devil
Her fingers spasm as she contemplates the chasm
Wedding flowers fall
Petals bashed and appalled
Her bouquet lies on the floor
Peter's guards stand by the door

Abraham shifts the Easter cold in his bones
Stomping one foot, then another, African cold and alone
His eyes rest on Natasha's hands dangling by her sides,
    helpless
She looks kind of pretty but dull and feckless
As he remembers a girl from long ago
Who loved him and would not let him go
He remembers her hands cupped and powerful
Blasting through the surf as she swallowed water by the
    mouthful
He was sailing on a ship from Africa's shore
As that girl screamed never again no more
Screamed as she swam, waves high above her head
Swimming far from land knowing soon she would be
    dead
But she would not have her brother stolen from Africa's
    shore
Without a powerful beauty screaming, "Adore!"
Nothing would stop that girl from screaming her love
But life moves on, it always does
But the memory of powerful beauty
The memory of desire without duty
The memory of Africa and France
Chilled through the bones this Russian romance

Abraham looking straight into Natasha's eyes
Her lids hang low, low as she sighs
A petal on her toe
The growth of love is slow
He's thinking about the baby he left in France
Of that baby's mother and if he has a chance
With this Russian girl, in this Russian world
In the nights so white, in the cold so bright
In the slit so tight, in the nights so white
He has been stolen and now he has abandoned
Are acts of evil ever random?

Once Peter accepted a nine-year-old boy for a gift
Then decided the fate of this child to lift
Yes, Peter the Great chose Abraham's mate
Yeah, Peter the Great chose Abraham's fate

Elevation into the aristocracy
Power for the mad world to see
Peter thinks the girl is pretty enough
Peter hopes Abraham won't be rough
Peter the emperor of all the Russias
Peter loves Abraham as much as
No more than, his born son
Alexander the half a man
In the palm of his hand he holds
A handkerchief of velvet and in its folds
Hard liquid light
Diamonds shining cold and bright
A ruby as big as a ripe cherry
A dark red ruby bright as a berry
Hard liquid light
A ruby sharp and bright

Natasha's nurse, to mitigate the curse
Meditating on a prayer, wishing she was anywhere but
    there
The tiny old girl stands in a curve
Stands in shadow, losing her nerve
She lets her brain turn back to the day lil Natalia was born
What was the road to this day
That finds her charge so forlorn
Peter turns to see
What the fuss must be
A mouse scurries near the dwarf's feet
The dwarf gives the emperor a smile sweet
Peter ignores this and turns away
Entranced by his favorite's wedding day

The priest prattles on and on
Natasha scans the faces of the other men
As the priest is calling for the renunciation of sin
Peter looks firm
Her daddy looks stern
The priest keeps prattling on

The crowns are placed upon their heads
One for the girl, one for the man

Natasha's pale fingers placed in Abraham's black hand
And the crown that rides above her brow

Bring back the blood memory of Jesus
Hanging on the cross
Jesus, the day his life was lost
So we were saved
A crown of thorns on his head
Unloved Natasha thinks of Jesus dead
Tears flowing down her face
A tear or two drips onto the candle she holds
And the light goes out

In the darkness wide
The bride with her groom by her side
Shivers and prays that God delivers
Us from evil and black devils
She feels Valeryan standing in the back
Under this veil Valeryan is black
She feels all the beauties her soon-to-be lacks
Her father stands looking across the crowd to Peter
He'd marry her to this man if he knew the man would
    beat her
For Peter is the czar of all the Russias
And he could make Natasha's daddy ambassador to
    Prussia
Or some other place
Wear some foreign lace
Her aunt accepts what is at hand
For a Negro he's a handsome man
And what does a woman want
Except for freedom from want
And this man comes with coins of gold
And this man is virile, he ain't old
The girl could do worse than this
But God save me the devil kiss

Peter looks at the girl
He hopes she's grateful he's given her the best of his
    world
Peter looks at his godson

The one a princely black brother tried to ransom
And Peter wonders even now why he did not sell
  Abraham back
To those who loved him and shared his skin black
He wonders if love will let you own,
Or was his heart but a stone,
Will love let you own
Another man?

Peter recalls the day of Abraham's baptism
The same priest stands before him now
Twelve years or more stand between them somehow
On that day he gave the boy his own name
The day the priest absolved him of Adam's stain
But Abraham chose for himself Hannibal
Who rode the Alps on an elephant animal
Hannibal the black warrior
Does he recall the Gloria
Of Egypt or someplace darker
When I am dead and gone
Maybe soon, maybe long
My Peter called Abraham
My true-loved dark man
Let his blood bind
With this land of mine
In the womb of the little Natasha
I'll plant his seed in Russia
What's the rush ya?
In the womb of the little Natasha.
Get out your whips and lasha.
If you're a slave they don't ask ya
In the womb of the little Natasha,
Peter would plant his seed in Russia

And when I dead and gone
He'll have allies of his own
His babies will be half grown
Before I'm dead and gone

A wind blows through the cave of a sanctuary
Blowing across souls expectant and wary

Abraham sees this girl so slight
Imagines her thighs white
And the curve of the cleft
Of the hollow between her breasts
So young and so high-born
So very wet, so very warm
Struck like a blow to the chest
The memory of bereaved and bereft
Of a woman not so very young
And his own noble black French son
How can he tell Natasha about that one?

IX

Later that night in the marriage bed
All kind of fear dancing in her head
Body so cold it might as well be dead
Abraham kisses the tip of each finger
Abraham allows his kisses to linger
Kisses up the length of her pale arm
Kisses down her thigh strong and warm
Abraham kisses her sweet nose
Then Abraham kisses all her toes
Natasha's mind is quite confused
Her thoughts with passion are suffused
She is waiting for him to kiss her lips
But he parts her thighs with his fingertips
Then he kisses her sex with his
And she swoons till she sees stars and moons
And she spins as he sends passion coursing through her
And she doesn't know what men do
But she wants him to do her
Her eyes are open wide
Her surprise she does not hide
There is the taste of care on his tongue
The taste of hunger for her flesh so young
And he whispers words of beauty
And it is easy to do her duty

And it is not just that she wants more and more
It's just that she screams, Adore, Adore

X

Sun rises and Abraham is still asleep
In the morning light she searches
The body of this man that rum purchased
Or so said those ignorant fools
That surround French Paris military schools
His lips are rich and abundant
His hair has a kinky curl
And those man thighs that make you want to be a girl
But the warmth of the color of his skin
Darker than honey, softer than night
A velvet black infused with light

XI

The little maid comes into the room
Shivering sadly like entering a tomb
She leads her young lady down the hall
Bathes her with water and ointments her fall
The little maid expects tears and fears
But Abraham's praises are all she hears,
"When he is inside of me
I can taste eternity
How beautiful, beautiful brown babies will be
I will birth them for the world to see
His love is my destiny
As I taste eternity."

TWENTY-THREE

A FISHERMAN RECOGNIZES a fisherman from afar.

Last night after Gabriel and I got erotically reacquainted, I fell asleep and dreamed of making love to him again.

I was down on my knees; he said, "I love you"; I was on my hands and knees; he said, "I love you." I was on my back; he said, "I love you." I was looking down at his face; he said, I love you. I was lying on my side, he spoke soft into my ear: I'm weary of being alone, my horse is tired, let us take this turn home. Later he said, "There is no position you can get into that I won't love you, lady." I pressed my spine into his stomach and cried like a baby.

I cried myself awake the morning of Pushkin's wedding.

Gabriel was taking his rest.

We sleep in an old bed from his family. It has four posts and a canopy we made ourselves from antique matelaisse. I tell him I love him because he fucks like an angel beneath a canopy of roses, but it's really because he restored my canopy. Shelter is a sweet thing.

I have a housekeeper whose skin is brown like mine. I don't ask her to dust my bed. Too many black women have dusted this bed who didn't get to sleep in it for too many years. I want to honor those women. I want to honor the woman who cleans for me now. I will dust like them. And I will sleep for them in the bed. I take my rest for them. But that is all.

When I am awake in the bed, it is not for any berry-brown-them-who-dusted or against the lilylike ladies-who-did-whatever-they-did; it is for me.

• • •

265

Somehow it seemed a sacrifice was required. I have wanted you to make the sacrifice. I have wanted her to be the sacrifice. Just in time—let it not be too late—I have discovered that what is required is not a sacrifice but a gift, a proper token, for my weary traveler.

Not Daddy's presses, not the strange painting, not the first edition of *The Souls of Black Folk*, not a drop of blood . . . I remember Diana saying, "On that bridge called his back I walked across the water." Pushkin, I laid me down low to let you walk across my mind.

Sometime in the middle of last night, I told Gabriel that I had finally answered Pushkin's question. He responded with a question of his own. "You tell the boy a lie, or you tell the man the truth?" I had to laugh—while I beat Gabriel with a pillow. He would have saved me a lot of worrying and wondering if he had reminded me a few months ago that I always had the choice of lying, or at least lying until I told the truth. I could have chosen any dead black man who had been alive in 1977 and didn't leave DNA samples. Who could refute me? At the end of the day, after all we've been through, it is sweet to know I was woman enough to tell it and Pushkin was man enough to hear. We were probably grown enough to tell and hear the truth a month after you were born. I just didn't know it.

I no longer have something I have worked on for a very long time. You have the poem. I don't know if you will like it. I want you to love the poem. I remember the very first poem you ever loved. It was written by Claude McKay. Do you remember McKay? Do you remember the first anthology I ever gave you?

McKay was the poet from the Caribbean who came to live and write in Harlem, then rushed off to Russia. When you were just four you loved a beautiful, colorless poem called "Russian Cathedral." I recall taking you to see a sculpture in Petersburg and teaching your four-year-old self to prattle these lines: "Bow down before the wonder of man's might. / Bow down in worship, humble and alone; / Bow lowly down before the sacred sight / of man's divinity alive in stone."

I intend to give up on statues and start bowing down to the sacred sight of man's dignity alive in love.

I want to come to your wedding.

I have given you a gift of fiction and I have given you a gift of truth. The poem is the fiction and your father's name is the truth. And it is absolutely the other way around as well.

This girl of yours is something. I have seen her reading *The New Negro*. She sat on the deck of the ferry to Lopez reading it. I teased her that all the New Negroes in that book are dead and buried now. She had a comeback for me. She fumbled through her pages.

"Someone called Arnold Rampersad says it is the Bible to the first generation of African American intellectuals."

I told her that I knew Arnold Rampersad. She was impressed.

"Is he cute?"

I like this bold girl. There is a saying in Russian that roughly translates "A fisherman sees another fisherman from afar." I was looking at a girl looking to be rolled into the mystic. I recognized someone I had forgotten in the reflection. Me.

One night on our island off Lopez, I escaped into my bedroom with my cell phone for what I thought would be a long conversation with Gabriel, but a storm moving through cut us off. I was returning to the dining room when I heard them whispering about me.

"I like your mother."

"Why? She doesn't like you."

"Is that why you like me?"

"Not even a little bit."

"She knows that I am clean."

"Yeah, but she thinks you're stupid."

"This is the limits of my language."

"You should talk Russian with her."

"I was a dancer. No one gave me anything to read. My Russian is worse than my English. I am reading in English. All the time." One day her English will be better than my Russian.

Tanya has written some of the wedding service, the service I will be hearing in just a few hours. She has patched pieces of poetry onto and into the Episcopal service. She is a maker of rituals.

A week or two before the strange lunch at Prince's Hot Chicken, where and when I got disinvited to the wedding, I wondered aloud if we couldn't have a moment before the wedding where we prick someone black's finger and she swallows a drop of black blood. Tanya shrugged her shoulders at my suggestion. Bobbed her little white head.

"Why?"

"The one-drop rule." Pushkin connected a dot.

"There used to be a law in some states that one drop of blood made you black." I connected a few more.

"*Show Boat*," Tanya says, connecting the last one. I was pleased and surprised. "It was on AMC."

"Did you hear 'Old Man River'?"

"I hate musicals."

Pushkin dropped his voice into an exaggerated baritone and sang through his own laughter: "I'm tired of living and I'm afraid of dying."

"Does it have to be blood?"

"What?"

"Do any other—"

Pushkin covered her mouth with his immense hand. "A tear, for example—do other bodily fluids count?" Tanya nipped his hand. Pushkin yipped. I bit my tongue to stop from laughing. She is so much like the original bitch I loved. Tanya shrugged again, smiling.

"Why should we validate the old rules?"

Of course she was right; to be sure she is wrong. The old ways are all we have and will be honored. I would wonder what else she's been swallowing except there's no reason to wonder. I was just trying to get my head back into my game.

That day she told me she was going to read one of Countée Cullen's poems to Pushkin during the service. I was frozen by her choice. I was furious with her choice. I didn't know whether she knew the poem she had chosen from *The New Negro* or from *The Negro Anthology of Verse* or from some other source. I didn't care where she had read it first. I had read it before she was born. I'd known the poem for so long I didn't remember not knowing it. I remembered wrapping myself up in the poem as a girl, blanketing myself in the warm simplicity of a poem addressed "To a Brown Boy," which spoke more sweetly to me than the companion poem, "To a Brown Girl." I remember thinking that day a thought that seems absurd now, absurd but real: "She's snatched my boy—now she's coming for my poem."

I was assaulted by the audacity of the thing. It astounded me that Tanya would or could address my son, saying, "That brown girl's swagger gives a twitch / to beauty like a queen; / Lad, never dam your body's itch / when loveliness is seen. / For there is ample room for bliss / in pride in clean, brown limbs, / And lips know better how to kiss / than how to raise white hymns." The poem closes with lines that betray now but that never betrayed before. "And when your body's death gives birth / to soil for spring to crown, / Men will not ask if that rare earth / was white flesh once, or brown."

We have been so out of touch these past weeks, I don't know what the wedding service will be. I do know something. If Tanya gives Pushkin this poem at the wedding, she will not be the first to give it to him. I was the first. The year he was in fourth grade I found a good copy of *The New Negro* for him. These are the words that haunt me now. "Men will not ask if that rare earth was white flesh once, or brown."

If this door swings wide, it should swing in both directions.

Tanya is Pushkin's rare earth. I saw that on the beach near Lopez. However long it's taken me to acknowledge it, that is what I saw. If she does not have a brown girl's swagger, which gives a twitch to beauty like a queen, her loveliness is seen. Visible to Pushkin, and visible to me. No less visible because it is noticed by many, and no less visible because it is noticed by some who would refuse to see Pushkin's beauty or mine.

Tanya is not one of these. She believes in the beauty of a brown girl's swagger. She appraised me like I appraise strong competition.

Tanya sees Pushkin's beauty. I don't think I can lie about it.

TWENTY-FOUR

SPEAK NOW, or forever hold your peace.

The time has come to end our talk of Othello. The time has come for me to say I will not play the Iago in the piece. The time has come for my son to stand with his bride before the priest and be wed. The time has come for Pushkin to lay Tanya down in her marriage bed.

I have seen myself in the eyes of my son; I am prepared to be generous.

Tonight you will fly away. Fly away far, out into the Pacific, to Samoa, where nobody, but nobody, cares about any of this.

The time has come for the gun and the pen to be put away, the gun for good. I threw my Pushkin pistol into the Cumberland River—along with Leo's watch. It was time. I don't need the watch to help me remember. I have Tanya.

I will make copies of pieces and parts of this manuscript to give to my newlyweds. You can read it as a long footnote to the rap song I began writing the night of the first day Tanya and I spoke of Pushkin.

I look at you now, Tanya, and I am starting to see what he sees: a woman who looks like the girl I used to be. He remembers me young and shuffling. He remembers the graduate student with a kid on her hip, piles of unpaid bills, spilled coffee on her desk, and pages and pages of scribble and type. I was twenty-two years old when he was four. You are twenty-two years old now. It is not so very young, and it is no coincidence.

You have the skin of an angel. It is hard for me to tell you that. It would be impossible for me to tell a white girl that, but you are no longer white. If you have read these pages, if you have sucked in these words, sucked in these words like a bee sucks in clear nectar and turns it into golden-brown honey, if you have sucked in these words, they have blackened your mind. You are no more white than Queen Elizabeth is black.

I saw a woodpecker this morning, tapping a ring of holes around the trunk of a tree. I saw his comb of flaming red atop his head. I am waiting to see the sap flow—that is the future. The past is a little girl on her father's hip, a little beige girl in starched cotton up on her father's silk-suited hip, waving her brown-sugar finger and saying, "Look at all the little peck-a-woods, Daddy." Can you forgive me for that day in the Saunders ice cream parlor? Will it make it harder or easier for you to forgive me if I forgive myself? I remember all the pink faces, the blue eyes, the green eyes, the gray eyes, and the hazel. I remember the brown eyes too. There were not so very many of those. I remember the shades of blond hair, from ash to maize to amber, and I remember the redheads. I remember that my father was, until he died, a green-eyed black man with red-hued hair. He spit the word *peckerwood* into my ear because someone had spit it at his brow. I don't remember this. I figured that out later. I figured something else out later too.

Daddy was wrong. That day, hiked up on his hip, parroting his prattle, I was wrong too. I have been proud of that moment, proud that any dark child in any year of the sixties would dare to speak those words out loud. Prouder still that before Woodstock, before Selma, before the riots in Detroit or Watts or Washington, before anyone said it loud, "I'm black and I'm proud," before Eldridge Cleaver and Bobby Seale, before that beautiful brown professor with the big 'fro on the West Coast, before Angela Davis, a black man raised a child so sure she was safe to speak.

I remember that moment on my father's hip and I try to fathom what it might have meant to him.

Proust had his madeleine. I have baked my madeleines. I did not dip them in citrus-scented tea and remember a lifetime. I baked them twelve in a Teflon mold and twelve in thin tin. I called the darker ones, baked in Teflon, Pushkins, and the light ones, baked in tin, Natalias. I served them with blackberries in martini glasses splashed over with blackberry liqueur. If I bake them again, when I bake them again, I will call them Pushkins and Tanyas. I will call them Tanyas in honor of you and in honor of a little white poodle I used to know. I cannot do you much more honor than allow you to share that little dog's name.

I will call them Tanyas because Tanya provoked my memory.

I will go to sleep, rest, and be thankful.

These are the stories I have told you, the stories of unheralded beauties, mothers and gangsters, who wrested poetry from existence. These are the stories of my people. They are the stories of folk who squeezed love from madness. I leave it to you to judge whether or not some of their doings were heroic.

This is not a thing to be forgotten. Those of us who remember are black.

Again I recall being up on my father's hip. So safe I didn't contemplate danger. It was maybe 1963 when this happened. It would not be so many years later nor so many miles away, at the Algiers Motel, that white policemen would take a group of black men hostage and slaughter them in a matter of short hours. Maybe one of those policemen and his kids were sitting in Saunders that day. Maybe my pointing finger and my spitting words are what he was thinking about when the deal started going south. And if he wasn't thinking about me, maybe he was thinking about some other "mischief" Malcolm X had inspired. Maybe he was thinking about that.

Of course, no one was listening at all. People were lost in their own conversations. There was not a person in that room except my daddy who could possibly imagine that a little black girl would have anything of significance to say. And if they had been listening, they would not have believed their ears.

I remember my words and I can barely believe those sounds. Following the wedding ceremony, I will walk into the ballroom of the Hermitage Hotel, the Russian walnut paneling will be shining bright, and I will put my arm around your waist, Tanya. If you point your little finger onto the dance floor and lean your head toward my ear and say, "Look at all the little peck-a-woods, Mommy," I will include in your observation all the red heads, black, white, or brown, and I will know that you have heard me. I will know that you are black.

And it is my idea now that it is not a drop of blood that makes you black but the stories you know, the sounds you feel. And so our Pushkin is very black.

And I will be Russian. I am Russian. It seems to me so clear now how it has come that my son chose a Russian woman. I fed my soul bites of Pushkin's poetry and prose. When I supped on syllables of Pushkin, it was a profound communion. When I sipped the syllables of Pushkin, I drank the blood of Mother Russia. In the water and the wine Christ appears. In the water and the wine Christ is present. In the poetry and the prose, in the syllables and the sound, Russia arises from its past, vast and languorous, snow-covered and thawing. When I was small and the world grew too complicated, when I, the daughter of a refugee from Montgomery, Alabama, discovered myself to be exiled from Motown, from Detroit City, discovered myself shipwrecked on the Potomac, when I stopped longing for a home that was lost, destroyed, exploded, when Martha Rachel died and I did not attend her funeral, when I stopped hearing my own heartbeat, I heard Pushkin. I had Pushkin. It was almost all I had.

Perhaps I am more Russian than you.

I take my seat in the first pew of the church on the groom's side. The pew opposite me is empty. Pushkin has told me that you are an orphan. It is a different thing altogether to see the empty pew. I pull down the kneeler and fall on my knees. I bend my head. I hear myself breathing. I do not hear my heartbeat, but I hear each breath.

And then I catch a scent of something—a distant whiff of rotting flesh and rosewater, the faint aroma of ripe blackberries. I open my eyes and expect to see the dead poet Pushkin, expect the full delusion to descend, expect to know that the break with reason has in fact occurred, sanity has snapped like a desiccated twig across an uplifted knee. I open my eyes and all I see is the green of the wall behind the altar. I see that and I feel the ghost of Pushkin, the ghost of Leo, and the ghost of Martha Rachel.

There is a song I fell in love with from the CD you gave me; it helped me with your wedding present. The song is Tupac's "Breathing." I have lived this song. I hear it play in my head above and beyond Pachelbel's *Canon*. "Breathing" captures the desperate optimism of a man in a shootout. With bullets flying everywhere, the narrator is determined to be the last motherfucker breathing. There's a lovely compressed sense of the treasure, the *blang-blang* more than the *bling-bling* inherent in life, conveyed in this song. There is unintentional irony as well. Tupac knew before he died, and we discover in his death, that the *blang-blang* of life can be extinguished with a *bang-bang*. In the room of reality, courage, will to live, and independence are triplets in the same womb. I have listened to that song over and over and felt my heart beat to the sound of young warriors abandoned by their families, abandoned by their compatriots, young warriors who need no one. The sound of my heart has been the sound of a young warrior who wishes to be left alone with death.

Alone with death, you just lean over and dance. Alone with death—death is not frightening, for it is never really death that frightens most; what frightens most is the knowledge that one you love is dead. This savages the heart. I wear the savages visited upon Martha Rachel's heart in my mind. She was not resurrected from the grave with red on her palms. Her skeleton lies buried in a bronze-colored casket in the Elmwood cemetery, in the city called Detroit, in the state called Michigan.

I have wept salt tears over Martha Rachel's grave. I have wept so many tears that flowers will not grow. I hear Tupac singing his song, I hear him cognizant of the men who wake up every morning planning to kill him, about knowing from the womb that life is bitter. I hear him speak of sleeping in vests, as if that is some protection. I remember the days he straddled life and death before taking a last assisted breath, just trying to be the last motherfucker breathing.

But what of the last fucked mother?

The last fucked mother breathing hopes she is pregnant. The last fucked mother breathing has been raped by a line of men. She hopes she carries babies from two different seeds in her belly. The last fucked mother breathing awaits birth. She prays for a son and a daughter, a second Adam, a second Eve, whom she will dress decorously in leaves. They and theirs will populate a world. She hopes her children will populate a world. The last fucked mother breathing expands into the future. She births life.

The last motherfucker breathing dies after killing.

I had thought to kill Tanya. Not with bullets, not with a Glock or other man-manufactured instrument of destruction. I had thought to kill her by associating her with the men of her color who raped the women of our family. This is as absurd and powerful as being chased through the streets by the illusion of a statue come to life until you have a very real heart attack responding to your own delusions of darkness.

I believe that Tanya loves Pushkin because I know Pushkin to be lovable. I believe Tanya desires Pushkin because I know he is beautiful. I believe Tanya will be faithful because I know Pushkin provokes piety.

The poet Pushkin doubted Natalia because he doubted his own beauty. All the ugly words in his unfinished story "The Negro of Peter the Great" stood between me and you. There are phrases that echo in my mind: "The thought, that nature had not created him to enjoy requited love." What do we imagine when we imagine a creature not created to enjoy requited love? Do I imagine my own son? Do I remember my own self and project that onto him? Do I ignore that you love him, desire him? I see your eyes shining from across the altar rail, as hungrily as the Countess D desired Abraham in the front of the story. Do I expect you to notice and appreciate his dark and curly head when I am so conflicted by my own? I like to think of Abraham in the French court with his bandaged head, surrounded by all the men in powdered wigs. The nakedness of his brown brow, the vividness of the coloring, conspire to spark Eros.

You are a motherless child a long way from home. And I am another. Consider your body washed with my salt tears and dried with my curly-head hair. To him this once I give silence. To you I have given words and I take away words.

In the end, words failed Pushkin. How he knew Shakespeare! The way he had studied *Othello* and still allowed himself to be lured into the duel over Natalia suggests the heft of the self-loathing inherited from the generation before his own. Pushkin's mother was dark. We assume she cradled her dark infant gently, but the grandmother, the czar's Negro's white wife—what was her tone when she kissed the heads of her own brown babies?

I wash over you with a surplus of love. Wash over my son's children with a portion. Do what I would not do for so long. Break off a little piece of your love for them.

And when the time comes, I will break off more pages of this manuscript and bind them together for my grandchildren, pages of Motown and pages of Alabama. If my grandchildren's skins are white as the driven snow, their souls will be black as the ace of spades.

What was Pushkin thinking when he conceived the idea of having one of the relations exclaim something to the effect of "Do not ruin your own child, do not deliver poor little Natalia into the clutches of that black devil"? What do I say to the voice in my head that wants to confront Pushkin with racist observations and concerns, the voice that says to me, "Do not ruin your own child, do not deliver poor little Pushkin into the clutches of the white she-devil"?

I say to myself, Self, do not deliver Pushkin into the clutches of insecurity in which Pushkin his namesake lived and suffered, then died before his time. I have pondered on the last days of Pushkin. As he looked into the face and onto the breast of his bride, what was his handkerchief? What token proved her sexual infidelity? What proof sent him not to pick up the pillow but to stride out into the street? Today the audience in that small replica of the Globe Theatre in Washington, Off-Off Broadway, in the high school, in the schoolhouse, wherever *Othello* is performed, find the handkerchief a ridiculously small piece of business to carry such a large point, to carry us to the bloody period, the dagger in the heart, the bullet in the chest. Tupac knew something about the "bloody period," the wound that leads to death. What, though, about the wound that leads to life? I have a handkerchief for Tanya. I have embroidered it with strawberries. I have embroidered it with my own hand. Othello got his from his mother. I believe it was a token of her sex. The soothsayer who gave it to her said that its mere possession would subdue Othello's father to the love of his mother.

I had a handkerchief, but I never wished to subdue Pushkin's father to my love. I never loved Pushkin's father. Pushkin's father never knew me. He was just my mother's boss. I knew him. I opened my eyes and looked into his once, the very moment after a cell of his collided with a cell of mine and a soul burst open in my womb. I opened my eyes to what was, to whatever existed beyond my imagination, whatever was truth, and I embraced reality as a taste of God—bitter or sweet.

You wanted to invite Pushkin's father to the wedding. He wanted me to tell his father's name, and now that man is dead. This is not what I intended, but I am happy for it.

I will be no Brabantio. I can surround myself with women, sisters, bright, brilliant, and brown, who will mourn the loss of another fine black brother to a woman of the white persuasion, but I can't listen to what must now be nonsense. Who remembers Brabantio? Educated ears know Iago, who poured poison into the Moor's ear, but who prepared the ground for doubt? Desdemona's daddy, that's who. Brabantio, when he listened to his so-called friends talking about an "old black ram tupping your white ewe," when he let them rave about having "his daughter covered with a Barbary horse," when he let them describe the possibility of her wallowing in the gross clasps of a lascivious Moor. Brabantio listened and doubted. He assaulted Othello. I believe it is the words of Brabantio, not Iago, that fed the monster jealousy.

When Othello saw the handkerchief, did he remember his black mother with his black father or did he remember Brabantio decrying "the sooty bosom of such a thing as you"?

I will not pollute my boy. In the apartment in which the poet Pushkin lived at the time of his death, I imagine all the little mirrors were broken by his wife, by his Natalia, for she understood that they had betrayed him. In betraying him, the mirrors had betrayed her. She should have put out Pushkin's mother's eyes. What Pushkin had inherited, the token in pigment and curl and bone structure, he could not treasure. How his wife's heart sang with the exotic beauty of his *blang-blang* he did not know. She knew. When he died, she mourned him.

There are dead people walking all over the streets of every city. Puny little souls doing disgraced things with pillows and knives and guns, because they do not know themselves to be exquisite. I have buried too many pieces of myself to see a single piece of my son Pushkin die.

Tanya, if you be white as the snow falling on the rooftops of the blue and gold and yellow buildings of Petersburg, I will love you if you love him. If you reach for him in the deep of his night and claim with the syllables I claimed when I required another language to say every important thing, when I gave up English to honor all the lies that had been told me. When I abandoned the English "I love you," I took up the Russian "Can one trust love?"

One must trust love if one will trust in anything at all.

And sometimes love is a broken-down numbers man braided tight to old loyalties, schooled in the discipline of trying to be the last motherfucker breathing.

And sometimes it's more than that.

The last fucked mother breathing prays for life, surrendering every false propriety, holding fast to the transformations that daily visit the brave and unsqueamish.

The queen of spades is trumped by hearts.

I have poured blackness in your ear. Ain't thinking about nothing but Pushkin 'n' Tanya and all the grands I'm gonna have and how they gonna call me Precious.

TWENTY-FIVE

THEY ARE MARRIED.

We walked from the church to the hotel. The reception, a Russian-creole lunch with plenteous caviar, was at noon. By three o'clock we were all playing touch football in the palm court of the Hermitage Hotel.

Our big rule was, nobody gets hurt. The other rule was, you can't play any position you ever played professionally.

It was a sight to see. Most of the team was there. Diana played with two of her girls clinging to her chiffon skirt and a third zipping round her. The girls were all thrilled to be in on the secret Cousin Tanya whispered to them after the coin toss. They didn't keep it for twenty seconds: "She's really black!"

Unknown to my nieces, she really isn't. Their father provided the drop of blood (knife slashed shallowly across palm) that Tanya licked (she whispered the details to me at halftime) to honor not me or the ancestors, but them—the little brown girls—and history.

This once, Pushkin played quarterback. Tanya played receiver.

I called quarterback before Pushkin, but he got it. Quimby (yes, Quimby, with his purple eyes, was present and accounted for) called that a rank violation—of both rules. Pushkin sided with Quimby. It's a very old habit.

He is blasting me beneath a painted blue ceiling. I'm wearing the beige dress. Pushkin's wearing a sharkskin suit and some brand-new gaiters. They look like Diana's old ones. I need to send Eve a picture.

"Moms, you are stone-pro quarterback. Nothin' but. You made

something happen. Every time it was third and long, you made something happen."

"Tried to."

"That's a wild-assed blue-eyed nigger of a poem."

"Is that a good thing or a bad thing?"

"It's a bastard of two strong things."

"I like that."

"That bad boy could make a few enemies."

"I ain't scared."

After Pushkin throws a rainbow, Tanya scores a touchdown. She leaps into Pushkin's arms to celebrate. I play holder for the field goal. Quimby is the kicker. Potted palms are our uprights. I catch the ball. I turn it. I plant. I get the laces going the way they need to go. I am steady at impact. He kicks a field goal. Motown beats Music City by three.

Making my way back to the ballroom from our palm-court playing field, I stop for another shot of vodka from the ice fountain carved to look just like a huge but still mini Bronze Horseman. Tanya slips an arm around my waist. We are twin towers. I consider asking her if she really walked around the statue with her mother. I don't ask the question. The answer doesn't matter. That was the story she told Pushkin; the things it changed are changed.

The siege of Leningrad lasted nine hundred days; the siege of Windsor lasted seven hundred and two.

Tanya giggles into my ear. "Pushkin is one lucky son of a bitch."

I have to giggle back and agree.

I found my way to Gabriel Michael on the dance floor. I cut in on him and Diana.

On our first anniversary, Gabriel Michael gave me the plans for a house he wanted to build for me. It's an intriguing house, with bridges inside and out, womblike rooms without windows, and rooms with whole-wall windows, a house full of safe spaces waiting to be made sacred, a house built to withstand fire, flood, and the end of the world.

It is something other than Pushkin's McMansion or my prairie house in the city, reflecting my desire to inhabit a house neither of blue leaves nor of the past, echoing .

I want to put our house in the Village up for sale. I too am moving out of my mom's house. I hear you sing America, Walt. I hear you too, Langston. Yep, and now I hear Tupac.

Rip-rapping along with Tupac as the DJ spins, invisible in the heat and history, I am tip-tapping away, tip-tapping to Gabriel and Happy Home. I finally moved out my mom's house.

"Red, baby, move out of your mom's house. Before it burns down over your head." Yeah, Martha Rachel is talking to me from heaven. Somebody is squeezing a butt cheek, cueing someone to hit a cymbal to bring the curtain down. She-bang!

Acknowledgments

My crew: brave, true-hearted, and bold:

David, Mimi, Jun, Kimiko, Anton, Ann, David, and Kirk, it is not that I would walk to hell and back with you, it is that I have. And it is far more than that. Thank you for making joyful life and creation possible. Thank you for being my perfect husband, best friend, godfather, sister, editor, co-mother, friend-boy, and story-listener.

Konstantine, Courtney, Melissa, and Lucius, experts respectively on Russian literature, football, Detroit, and Afro-American studies, I thank you for your intelligence.

Florence, God-mommy Lea, Grandma Bontemps, Edith, Jane, Mary Jane, Kate, Vivian, Caroline C., Sonia, and Joan, thank you for being Mommy forces.

Leslie, Marc, Jed, thank you for being my first friends.

Rex, Brad, David W., Gordon, Lamar, Tony, Ken, Mike, Siobhan, Cliff, Steve, Allen, and Forrest, thank you for your chivalry.

Wes, Walter, Debbie, Laura, Charles, thank you for teaching.

Amanda, Daphane, Beverly, Kerry, Elizabeth, Jennifer, thank you for reading. Liz, thank you for copy editing.

Harvard University, thank you for the shelter.

Jenifer, Jerre, Joe, Miles, Swain (the Kilpatrick-Stockton crew), Wendy, and Zick, thank you for getting my first book published.

John Seigenthaler, thank you for being.

Harper Lee, thank you for writing to me in your own hand. It changed my life. Toni Morrison, thank you for giving up an Easter Sunday to write to the court on my behalf. Pat Conroy, thank you for telling what you knew.

I call in my heart the name of every author who stood with me when publication of my first book was blocked. I am in your debt.

Richard Albert Ewing IV is my new nephew; I thank Sandy and Rick for him.

Kazuma, Takuma, Charlie, Moses, Lucas, and Cynara, wild-eyed adventurers all, are my dearly beloved godchildren.

As always, I must acknowledge Caroline, bright and beautiful, who inspires me to commit to words on paper the language and lives of people like us. I love Caroline more than the moon loves the sun—you are my everything.